Ostrichland

A Novel by Daniel Nign

Dedicated to
Mary E. Nign

Inspired by
Ostrichland U.S.A., Buellton, CA
and
The Town of Solvang, CA

A Noble Bird...

"The ostrich is the most noble bird in God's creation. They are the largest birds in the world, capable of growing to nine feet tall and three-hundred-twenty pounds. An ostrich's eye is two inches in diameter, the largest of any land animal. They *do not* stick their heads in the sand if frightened. They *can* kill a person with a single kick. If the ostrich had opposable thumbs they would rule the world -- at least the bird world. I could go on and, on all day..."

The small group of people surrounding the speaker murmured in astonishment at his pronouncements. Ostriches *did* seem special after all. What other bird would have a 'Land' just for them? He *seemed* to make sense. The speaker took a step back, surveying his kingdom. Several ostriches craned their long, long necks to look for food in the oversized dog bowls held by several of the onlookers.

The speaker raised his voice theatrically, clapping his hands in the air. "But enough talking," he continued. "Welcome to Ostrichland! Please, enjoy the ostriches!" The onlookers had broad smiles on their faces, breaking away to observe the feathered wonders awaiting their attention.

One man, shorts, baseball cap (Cardinals) and t-shirt (I ♡ Ornithology) giving him away as the middle-aged tourist that he was, turned to the speaker. "Waldemar?" he questioned the speaker. "Waldemar Ulff?" The speaker, now identified, flinched slightly looking the tourist directly in the eyes.

"You got it." Waldemar replied. He was used to the question, but frankly surprised how seldom it came up in day-to-day life. His brown hair, precisely parted in the middle, was carefully pulled back into a shoulder-length ponytail.

The afternoon sun reflected into Waldemar's round lens sunglasses on his slightly beaky nose, hiding his dark brown penetrating eyes. Beneath his nose was a neatly trimmed mustache showing the salt and pepper of age knocking at the door. Waldemar Ulff was a man of self-effacing style and geeky awesomeness and the lead singer of **WOW**, the hottest pop group of the 1990's.

WOW consisted of Waldemar Ulff, Oola La and Walter Johnson. **WOW** owned pop music during the 1990's until their heart-wrenching break up in 1999. Walter Johnson decided his true calling was in hydroponic gardening in the Negev Desert. Waldemar and Oola La tried to carry on, but **WO** just didn't work. Personally, Waldemar and Oola had a torrid romance during their last tour in August 1999, when they played Paraguay and Uruguay known as the 'WO-GUAY' tour. However, without Walter's epic bass voice, the bottom fell out of the harmonies. Ultimately, the bottom fell out of the duo's romance as well. Oola La returned to her hometown of Toronto, Canada to open an Asian-Brazilian restaurant, Rio de Taipan. Waldemar bought Ostrichland.

"Well, it's an honor meeting you, Waldemar," the tourist continued, looking warily at the gigantic ostrich next to Waldemar, his favorite, Lanky by name. "Would you mind autographing my cap?" he asked, handing it over to Waldemar. Waldemar took out a pen from his flannel shirt and quickly signed the cap for his fan.

"Thanks, Waldemar!" the tourist exclaimed, examining the autograph before placing the cap back on his rapidly balding head. "I miss your music. I hope you come out of retirement someday," he added, giving Lanky one last, somewhat relieved, look. He headed down the winding path to view the ostriches on the lookout for food behind their wood and chicken wire fence.

Waldemar watched the tourist trot down the path, then switched his gaze to the whole of Ostrichland, his beloved Lanky still standing beside him. There it was in all its glory, 72 ostriches: Lanky, Ophelia, Happy, Beaks, Big Bird, Toots, Killer, Big Eyes, Mr. Tibbs, Sweetie Pie, Egg-Burt, Babs, Monster, Baby, Romeo, Juliet, Dr. Dundie, Huey, Kicks, Carlton, Annika, Sparky, Ethel, Tasmin, Diamond, Pretty Bird, Gizzard, Sage, Bobo, Twill, Lindy, Kiwi, Buckley, Sally, Bonnie, Clyde, Einstein, Plato, Rona, Lou, Giggles, Lambert, Quill, Valentine, Caesar, Cookie, Chip, Paprika, Neutrino, Butterscotch, Viking, Stomper, Barbie, Clarence, Hopper, Blinky, Gams, Custer, Fermile, Doc, Esperanza, Hulk, Andre, Milton, Donny, Marie, Veld, Arno, Kaya, Pappy, Foster, Gus and Tweety (73 counting Lanky). The birds resided on 100 acres in the Neu Deutschland Valley off California's stunning central coast, running along a dry riverbed, its green grass banks vivid in the sun. Ostrichland spread out before him.

The main structure of Ostrichland, The Egg, was located up a small rise from the riverbank, right off Highway 277 from the coast to the small resort town of Neu Deutschland. The Egg, an imposing five-story dome structure of glass and steel in the shape of an upright ostrich egg was designed by renowned architect Hartwig von Trussell, a friend of Waldemar's. The futuristic building contained the Ostrich Habitat where ostriches enter and exit The Egg's lower level via two large motion-sensing glass doors while guests view the birds from the mezzanine overlooking the Ostrich Habitat. The gift shop, *Feathers*, a 99-seat theater, *The Yolk*, (never used and literally in the heart of The Egg), a professional recording studio and the plush administrative office were on the next level. On the next level were six apartments for Ostrichland staff members and guests. The top level of The Egg housed Waldemar's spacious private apartment, the Sky House. The Egg had two elevators, one for the public with access to the lower floors, the other private with access to all floors, in addition to a set of stairs for each level. The Egg was Waldemar's home and office. Ostrichland was his passion. The lifestyle was all a far cry from the glory days of **WOW**, but it was a blessing for Waldemar. Fame takes its toll and Ostrichland was the refuge for someone who had seen it all and done it twice at an early age.

The sound of excited children exiting a minivan announced the arrival of another group of tourists, undoubtedly on their way to experience the charm of Neu Deutschland up the road. The large but tasteful sign that Waldemar installed when he bought Ostrichland was an effective attention-getter. He could see a mom, dad and three young kids emerge from the dusty vehicle. Dad was looking worse for the wear, a typical scenario. Waldemar and Lanky made their way to the entrance of The Egg, a spaceship-like sliding door called The Hatch, to introduce another family to the world of the ostrich. The pleasure was all Waldemar's!

On the Air...

"I'm Li'l Otter, we're talking to pop music legend Waldemar Ulff of **WOW**. We're on Intertoobz Internet music on *Feeling the Music*. So, it's true, you own Ostrichland, Waldemar?"

"Yes, Li'l Otter. Ostrichland is my pride and joy."

Waldemar leaned back in his plush executive chair in the administrative office of Ostrichland, located in The Egg, telephone receiver pushed securely next to his right ear, making a small pain where the phone and Waldemar's cubic zirconia ear stud met (the deplorable working conditions in African diamond mines being one of Waldemar's many causes). With his **WOW** background, being on Intertoobz was as natural as breathing for Waldemar.

"How did you ever end up owning an ostrich farm?"

"Ostrichland is not an ostrich farm, Li'l Otter," Waldemar corrected, putting both of his elbows firmly on the armrests of his chair. "I consider Ostrichland an educational event for the whole family."

"Fair enough. Sorry," Li'l Otter apologized.

"Well, I was driving along Highway 277 on my way to Neu Deutschland for a short vacation. I passed a bright green shack and noticed a mural of an ostrich on the side of the building. I have been fascinated by ostriches ever since I saw them during a music video shoot in Africa. I quickly pulled over and backed up to the entrance. Even though Ostrichland needed updating at that point, it was amazing! I couldn't get enough of it!"

"So, it was love at first sight, eh?" Li'l Otter chuckled.

"Right! I knew I needed Ostrichland and Ostrichland needed me! The only person around was the owner, a little old guy named Shrimp Wrigley.

Shrimp Wrigley looks like Popeye only not as handsome. Don't tell Shrimp Wrigley I said that! He can tell a tall tale or two, that's for sure. Shrimp Wrigley is unbelievable! I offered him $200,000 then and there for the whole place. He balked at first, but I offered to keep him on as general manager. After a couple of beers, he decided it was a win/win deal," Waldemar laughed. "I owned Ostrichland within the week. Shrimp Wrigley continues to be the general manager of Ostrichland. He has an apartment in The Egg, the headquarters of Ostrichland. Ostriches are so mesmerizing, Li'l Otter!"

"I guess they are. And the rest is history as they say." Li'l Otter said.

"The rest is history," Waldemar repeated, a small satisfied smile on his lips.

"What's it like going from a music legend to the owner of an ostrich farm... um... educational event?"

"Couldn't be happier, Li'l Otter," Waldemar replied, with a chuckle. "A music legend, eh?" he teased.

"You know that!" Li'l Otter laughed. "No one ruled pop music like **WOW**, and you know it, Waldemar!" Li'l Otter teased, poking fun at Waldemar's well-known modesty. "Who are your musical influences? Who do you like now?"

"Oh, gosh, there are so many!" Waldemar leaned back in his chair. "Luckily, I've made a list of people and groups that I like that I refer to from time-to-time. I call it my 'List of Influence.' My influences range from classical to jazz and everything in between. Here is my list. Waldemar proceeded to read his list to the radio audience:

Alternative
 Irregular Monument
 Lurid Frond
 Pig the Runt
 Ridicule of the Deaf Clone
 Violet Herring

Avant-Garde
 Blooming Sprout and the Collaborator
 Constellation Ferret
 Diametric Confluence

Big Band
 Hunky Dory and His Band of Glory
 Swing Blowout

Classical
 Ravindra Biltbert Van Donk - 'The Tulips of My Homeland'
 Vito Spurius Wilms - 'The Frights of Spring'
 Anchovi Yahovelli - 'Music for Dancing Nymphs'

Country
 40 Miles to Sunset
 Cowboy Boys
 Hollerin' Chuck and the Lonely Boys

Dance
 Dance Playground
 Foaming Territory
 The Sunshine Squad

Folk
 Bitter Onion
 The Swamp Guys
 Twangy Romance

Hip Hop
 John Doe
 I B Fine
 Li'l Ridculiousness
 Senior, Jr.

Jazz
 The Theda Bara Project
 J.J. Buggs and his Band of Thugs
 Mrs. Kravitz's Midnight Peepers
 Salad of Mellow

Punk
 30 Pence for Nothing!
 Bag of Tornados
 Boys Have Wieners
 Doggie Exodus
 Potluck of Death

Rock
 Binary Fluid
 Hardcore Butterfly
 The Moonwalkers

Music is an exciting world, Li'l Otter!"

"It sure is! Whoa, that was quite a comprehensive list, Waldemar!" Li'l Otter said, thankful that the List of Influence had now been announced for the world to hear and that the reading of the list was now complete.

"Yes, Li'l Otter. I like to keep track of music that has moved me and the people who make the music," Waldemar remarked.

It makes me wonder if you don't want to get back in the studio, Waldemar?" Li'l Otter remarked, knowing he was venturing into some sticky territory. Li'l Otter didn't become one of the most listened to Native American African American DJs without taking a few risks.

"I don't want to go there, Li'l Otter," Waldemar cautioned, taking a swig of his favorite beverage, Roo Energy Drink.[1] "That was a long time ago and I've moved on," he said with a subdued chuckle as he stroked the right side of his mustache.

"No **WOW**?" Li'l Otter backed down. "Do you keep in touch with Walter and Oola?"

"No **WOW**," Waldemar repeated. "No, I can't say we stay in touch. We have many memories. Those were amazing years, but we all need to move on," Waldemar remarked, speaking of his **WOW** colleagues.

"Okay, Waldemar, I hear you," Li'l Otter conceded. How about a plug for Ostrichland?"

"That I'd be happy to do," Waldemar snapped to action, sitting up in his chair. "Li'l Otter, I would like to invite all your listeners to come and visit me here at Ostrichland. We're located just outside of New Deutschland on the central California coast on Highway 277. We have a hundred acres where our prize ostriches roam in peace to amuse and amaze you. Our headquarters, The Egg, is an architectural marvel, designed by famed architect Hartwig von Trussell. So, there's something to see for everyone in the family. And always, free admission."

"There you have it, ladies and gentlemen, Ostrichland awaits," Li'l Otter emphasized. "Waldemar, as usual, it's been a unique experience talking to you. And say 'hello' to the flock for me, okay?"

"You got it, Li'l Otter," Waldemar replied cheerfully. "You'll have to come by Ostrichland someday!"

Sensing an opening, Li'l Otter ran with it.

"That would be fantastic! We could broadcast live from Ostrichland! I love it!"

---

[1] A taste acquired during a WOW tour of Australia in 1994, Waldemar took to the taste and energy enhancement of Roo Energy Drink. He has cases delivered several times during the year. Developed and bottled in Adelaide, South Australia during World War II, Roo Energy Drink kept Australians on the go during the war years and to the present day. Their slogan: 'Ask for Roo, it will keep you hopping.'

Waldemar, realizing that his friendly, routine goodbye offer was turning into more than anticipated, decided to go with it. "I'll give you a call off air and we can set up something," he said, thinking of Ostrichland's sagging visitor numbers during the past year. An opportunity to introduce the masses to his flock of Ostriches! Life was good!

"You got it, man," Li'l Otter said, a sense of accomplishment and relief in his voice. "Talk to you later!"

Waldemar pried the phone from his earlobe, rubbing the area to get the circulation moving around his cubic zirconia stud. He leaned back in his plush executive chair and stared at the LP cover hanging on the Wall of Memories across from him; **WOW**'s debut album, *All I Have Is My Implosion*. Suddenly, he sprang up, walked the six feet to the wall and plucked the sleeve off the curved administrative office wall. Looking at both sides, he sat down, as he

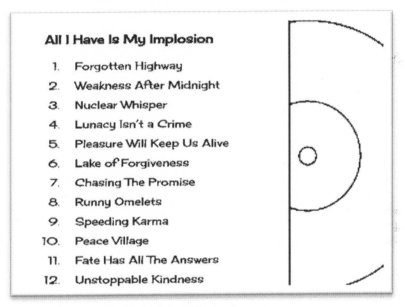

started reading the list of tracks on the back:

The memories came flooding back as each title had a story from many years ago. 'Runny Omelets' was #1 on the Billboard Hot 100 chart in August 1991. Those were heady times. 'Unstoppable Kindness,' the choice to close the album became the anthem for the 'Let's Unite the World for Peace' campaign at the beginning of 1992. Waldemar started singing, 'Nuclear Whisper,' one of his personal favorites:

Nuclear Whisper

By **WOW**

I get on with life as a singer,
I'm a loving kinda person.
I like singing and dancing.
I like to contemplate the world.
But when I start to daydream,
My mind turns straight to peace.
     Oh oh oh!
I like to use words like you and me.'
I like to use words about love.
But when I stop my singing,
My mind turns straight to peace.
     Oh oh oh!
I like to dream about life and love.
But when left alone,
My mind turns straight to peace.
     Oh oh oh!
I hate war and killing.
But I just think back to peace,
And I'm happy once again.
     Oh oh oh!

Waldemar glanced at the wall again. There she was. Staring at him. Taunting him. Oola.

Oola La, the 'it' girl of the 1990's. Singer, actress, model, writer, physical fitness advocate... Oola did it all at least once and often more than once. And when she did something, she gave everything she got and did it well. The photo staring down at Waldemar was Oola's favorite. Taken at Cannes in 1998 at the premiere of her self-produced movie, *Dream and a Pinch of Arsenic*, a critic's' delight, a box office failure, but Oola didn't care because *she* loved it. A black and white portrait in the shadows, her straight blonde hair cut short, sloping down toward her chiseled cheekbones, Oola was (and remains) a haunting beauty. And Waldemar knew that their brief time together as one was special and doomed, but she bore into his brain and would remain there whether they were physically together or a world apart.

Waldemar broke eye contact with Oola's portrait. Slowly rising from his chair, he brushed past her photo and placed the album sleeve back on the wall. He decided it was time to wind down; a night to be filled with dreams of the past, what was and what was still to come.

Waldemar shut off the light and walked slowly to the private elevator of The Egg and out the hatch to feel the cool night air. As was his nocturnal habit, he walked over to an old wooden bench, the *Sunset Bench* he had dubbed it, reached in his pocket, pulled out a marijuana cigarette and lit it. A few inhales and Waldemar declared the day a success, as usual. Lanky joined him, sniffing the air as if trying to get a contact high.

And the flock of ostriches settled down for the night as the stars appeared over the Neu Deutschland Valley like a thousand cubic zirconias in the sky.

Neu Deutschland...

Dawn broke revealing *Hauptstraße* (Main Street) in its colorful glory. The brightly painted wooden buildings, cobblestone pedestrian crossings, flower boxes full of beautifully blooming flowers set a scene that could have easily been that of a small town in Bavaria. But it was not, it was Neu Deutschland, several miles inland from the central coast of California on Highway 277. Despite its vintage look, the burg was relatively new, having been founded in 1921 by a band of disaffected Germans exiling themselves from the stress of daily life in the Weimar Republic of Germany.

Neu Deutschland became an instant hit with travelers, providing a mock-exotic destination for a daycation as the Tin Lizzies took to the road in the booming Jazz Age. In the 21st Century the city fathers were crossing their fingers, hoping they could turn around their beloved town that was now considered a faded glory, a relic doomed in the Internet age. They had to turn things around to get Neu Deutschland back on the map.

In the middle of town, in the imposing chalet-style building labeled *Das Rathaus* (City Hall), three people sat at a large table in a darkened conference room. "Do you have a Dortmunder[2]?" asked the large man in lederhosen at the head of the table as he read the report in front of him.

---

[2] Dortmunder is a pale lager originally brewed by Dortmunder Union in Dortmund, Germany, in 1873. A soft-textured beer influenced by the Pilsner lager brewed in Pilsen, it became popular with industrial workers and was responsible for Dortmunder Union becoming Germany's largest brewery and Dortmund having the highest concentration of breweries in Germany.

"Sure. I'll get you one. *Ja*," the busty upper-middle-aged woman replied as she made her way to a small refrigerator in the northeast corner of the room.

"It's never too early for an alcoholic beverage, Gerta," the large man proclaimed, self-conscious of his morning beer - afternoon beer - nighttime beer habit.

Gerta Switzer, President of the Neu Deutschland Chamber of Commerce and owner of the one hair salon in town, Mein Hair, checked the fridge and located a Dortmunder for Bürgermeister Otto Ackermann. Gerta Switzer waddled back to the table, her gift of drink in her pudgy right hand.

Fidgeting in a chair next to Bürgermeister Ackermann was an older, thin man in a Strellson business suit, a monocle rounding out his distinguished looks. Conrad Halle by name. Conrad Halle owned Halle Haus, Neu Deutschland's premier hotel located conveniently across the street from *Das Rathaus.* Bürgermeister Ackermann, Gerta Switzer and Conrad Halle had a lot at stake, and they were nervous.

"Let's get this meeting started," Halle snapped, his nerves showing up in his brusque attitude. "I have a hotel to run!"

"We're *all* busy people, Conrad Halle," Gerta replied, handing the Dortmunder to Ackermann. Mein Hair doesn't run itself either, you know! Or the Chamber of Commerce! *Ja?*"

"It might as well for all the good it's doing!" Halle replied testily. "We're going down the drain and nothing's stopping it!" he hissed, wiping his quivering upper lip with the back of his right hand.

"Enough, enough!" Bürgermeister Ackermann barked, taking a refreshing sip of his Dortmunder. "That's why we're meeting today. We need a plan to get Neu Deutschland back on the map and get those daycationers back in town and buying things."

"What we need is a miracle!" Halle snapped, pushing his chair back from the table.

"We'll think of something," Gerta said confidently, sitting down a bit too close to Ackermann. "Won't we Herr Bürgermeister? *Ja?*" she said, gripping his right hand, staring intently into his beady blue eyes.

Bürgermeister Ackermann freed his right hand and cleared his throat. "Frau Ackermann says I always think of something," he noted, mentioning his dear wife of forty-five years. "We need an idea, a gimmick, something to attract attention to Neu Deutschland. Let's brainstorm!"

"I'll take notes," Gerta volunteered, pulling a small notepad out of the chest region of her attire.

The three pulled together and brainstormed for an hour and eleven minutes. Gerta summarized their ideas at the end of the meeting, as Halle had to get going to audition a new lounge singer for *WonderBar* the piano lounge in Halle Haus.

List of ideas to save Neu Deutschland

1. Set up a U-Fund-Me page for Neu Deutschland.
2. Entice a reality show to locate to Neu Deutschland.
3. Have a Fraulein beauty contest in Neu Deutschland.
4. A yodeling event in Neu Deutschland.
5. A beer drinking competition in Neu Deutschland.
6. A German car show in Neu Deutschland.
7. Have a contest to win a trip to Neu Deutschland.
8. Entice a celebrity to move to Neu Deutschland.
9. Have a music festival in Neu Deutschland.
10. Declare bankruptcy!

"Well, this will give us something to chew on," Halle stated, abruptly rising from his chair and heading for the door.

"It's a start. It's a start," Bürgermeister Ackermann replied defensively, stroking his clean-shaven chin with his right hand. "I'm going to go for a drive now. That's where I get my best ideas."

"Alone?" Gerta asked with excitement in her voice.

"Alone," he declared, putting his Homberg on at a smart angle as he headed out the door.

"*Alone again, naturally,*" Gerta hummed the Gilbert O'Sullivan classic with resignation.

The Reunion...?

The loud 'tap' 'tap' 'tap' against the side of The Egg awakened Waldemar from his peaceful sleep. After a few moments of tossing and turning, he sat up to greet the day. A smile crept across his face, realizing that Lanky was tapping the side of The Egg like he did each morning — an ostrich alarm clock.

Like most mornings, Waldemar was alone in bed, another change from his **WOW** days. He stretched his arms and pulled off the covers. Standing up, he pulled his long hair back and secured it with a small rubber band for his signature ponytail. He had his hair in such a way since his teen years. His 5'9" body was well-toned, tan and wiry at 49 years old. Waldemar wasn't a health fanatic but doing chores around Ostrichland kept him in great shape. His ostrich-themed boxer shorts revealed a touch of whimsy in his sleeping attire, a change from his days of *au natural* when he was younger.

Waldemar looked at the pyramid-shaped Agatha unit on the nightstand next to his bed. Agatha was Ostrichland's AI (artificial intelligence) that enabled Waldemar to run Ostrichland with the help of Shrimp Wrigley as the general manager. Agatha's screen on one side of the small pyramid unit provided a video feed showing Lanky. Lanky's big eyes greeted Waldemar as he peered into the camera. In a few minutes Lanky would receive his special ostrich treats for guarding the grounds during the night. Ostriches weren't the easiest bird to train, but Lanky was a first-class security guard roaming over Ostrichland each night keeping vigil over the land of his flock. Agatha took care of security through numerous devices strategically placed throughout Ostrichland, but Lanky wasn't aware and Waldemar wasn't telling.

Waldemar made his way to the shower, glancing at his physique in the mirror. "Ah, you've still got it," he said out loud with a chuckle. "Come here, ladies, it's Waldemar Ulff, in the buff!" The lukewarm water was enough to get Waldemar semi-awake for another day of adventures with his feathered friends.

With a brush of his nicely aligned teeth, a fresh flannel shirt, jeans and work boots and Waldemar was out the hatch of The Egg. He gave Lanky a handful of ostrich treats that he always kept in the right front pocket of his jeans. Waldemar and Lanky headed toward the main entrance to the parking lot to prepare Ostrichland for the guests the day would bring... hopefully. Agatha was fully capable of performing such a task, but Waldemar enjoyed doing some chores 'the old-fashioned way.' In the distance Waldemar could see Shrimp Wrigley taking care of a bad section of fence on the western boundary of Ostrichland. Waldemar knew that Ostrichland was in good hands with Shrimp Wrigley on the team.

Lanky loped off to join the rest of the flock. Waldemar walked back into The Egg and took the private elevator to the administrative office.

He yawned. "Good morning, Agatha," Waldemar said, seemingly to himself.

"Good morning, Waldemar," the disembodied voice replied as the curtains opened, desk light turned on and the small coffee maker near Waldemar's custom Brazilian tigerwood desk came to life. "How are you today?" Agatha asked.

"So far, so good, Agatha," Waldemar responded, another yawn confirming his need for strong morning coffee to maintain his morning energy.

Within minutes a fresh mug of Roaring Lion's Ethiopian Yirgacheffe[3] with much caffeine was ready for him. Coffee mug (photo of Ostrichland on the mug) in right hand, Waldemar made his way over to the desk. The red light on the telephone answering machine was blinking. This didn't happen too often. "Agatha, please play voicemail." Waldemar requested.

"Will do, Waldemar," Agatha responded.

"Waldemar, it's Li'l Otter. I was hoping you would still be in the office. I'm making good on my on-air promise to call you back to discuss my visiting Ostrichland for *Feeling the Music*. Give me a call back as soon as you hear this, okay? Use my cell number."

After several lip-searing sips of coffee, Waldemar said, "Agatha, call Li'l Otter."

"Right away, Waldemar," "she" responded, the call going through immediately.

---

[3] Roaring Lion's Ethiopian Yirgacheffe presents a Gourmet Coffee with a "kick" featuring a perfectly blended mix of Arabica coffee beans for Gourmet Taste and Rich Flavor along with some of the highest caffeine Robusta beans from around the world.

"Li'l Otter, it's Waldemar!" Waldemar said, hearing Li'l Otter's sonorous voice on the other end. "I must have left the administrative office following the interview yesterday right before you called."

"Waldemar, thanks for returning the call," Li'l Otter responded, obviously happy Waldemar was on the line. "I was afraid you didn't want to follow up on having us visit Ostrichland," he chuckled, still concerned that Waldemar would rescind his offer.

"No. The offer's good," Waldemar reassured him, putting a napkin up to his scalded lips. "We can discuss the details now."

"I'm going to be out in Los Angeles in a month. My producer, Shenandoah River, likes to keep things fresh," Li'l Otter explained. "Chicago's a great place to base an Internet music show, but traveling is always good once-in-awhile. While we're in L.A. we could come up for a day and do the show from your place. We can pre-tape everything so it wouldn't be a big deal. Or we could go live. That always adds more excitement to the broadcast. We could have your Ostrichland visitors as an audience. I hear you have an auditorium in The Egg."

"Right, we do. It's called The Yolk. That's an idea!" Waldemar warmed up to the publicity potential. "You know, Li'l Otter, I'm always torn between remaining low-key in my private life and promoting Ostrichland. So far, it's been a good balance. When fans recognize me, they've been pretty decent about my privacy. But any opportunity to let more people know about Ostrichland is also important to me."

"I understand, Waldemar," Li'l Otter replied. "Buying Ostrichland was a big move to make when **WOW** broke up. I think you've handled it well."

"I've done my best, Li'l Otter," Waldemar stared into the bottom of his near-empty coffee mug. "Oola's about the only piece of the past that I'm having a continuing problem... um... challenge with, you know? I mean, we were *so* close."

"Sure," Li'l Otter sympathized. "Speaking of Oola — since *you* brought her up — what if I could get her to join the show? Maybe Walter too?"

"You mean, *in person?*" Waldemar asked with some surprise, placing his coffee mug firmly on the desk near a stack of new Ostrichland postcards ready to make their debut in the *Feathers* gift shop.

"I haven't made any plans, Waldemar," Li'l Otter assured him. "Either a call-in or better yet, in person. Most of that will have to get the 'okay' from the Intertoobz execs, but that shouldn't be a problem. That would be amazing, wouldn't it?" Li'l Otter asked, going for the win.

"That's a lot to think about, Li'l Otter," Waldemar demurred, running his right hand over his tied-back hair. "A lot to think about..." his voice trailed off.

"Waldemar!" Li'l Otter spoke, knowing Waldemar was starting to drift back to the past. "I *really* think you need to consider a **WOW** reunion! It's the elephant — or ostrich — in the room, Waldemar! There, I said it!"

"Reunion!" Waldemar stood up from his chair. "I *can't* go there! I'm still emotionally dismembered from the **WOW** experience!"

"It's been so many years, Waldemar!" Li'l Otter tried to give some clarity to the **WOW** breakup. I know you were hurt! I know **WOW** was your life! You have a new life now, Waldemar. Having a reunion doesn't mean renouncing your current life!"

"It's just... it's just..." Waldemar stammered.

"Waldemar, let's leave this at you hosting *Feeling the Music* at Ostrichland, okay?" Li'l Otter knew he pushed too far too fast. "Forget about a reunion... for now."

"Okay, Li'l Otter," Waldemar replied meekly, stung at the leap the conversation had taken.

"Okay, man. I will talk to Shen and we'll finalize the details of our visit," Li'l Otter could tell that things were settling down now. "It will be so much fun, my friend!"

"You're right, Li'l Otter," Waldemar agreed. "Sorry I came unglued there. I'm really looking forward to your coming out here. Bye."

Waldemar hung up. "Agatha, I'll be checking the fences with Shrimp Wrigley this morning."

"I know, Waldemar," Agatha responded with a touch of coy in her AI voice.

"Thank you, Agatha," Waldemar said, rising from his desk and heading out of the administrative office.

"The pleasure is mine, Waldemar!" Agatha replied. "Have a good day, Hon!"

Little Timmy...

"Mr. Ulff! Mr. Ulff!" The sound of a young boy caught Waldemar and Lanky's attention as they strolled along one of the many winding trails of Ostrichland along the dry riverbed. Within a minute they spotted a seven-year-old boy, big blue eyes, fair-skin, red hair, freckles, dressed in clean sturdy jeans with a red and green striped flannel shirt. He was running along the path toward Waldemar and Lanky.

"Little Timmy!" Waldemar called out once he recognized the boy behind the voice. "Hi!"

"Hi, Mr. Ulff!" Little Timmy said breathlessly once he caught up with Waldemar and Lanky. "Hi, Lanky!"

Lanky bent down to face Little Timmy, looking for ostrich treats in the young lad's possession. Little Timmy had none.

"Can I pet Lanky, Mr. Ulff?" Little Timmy asked expectantly.

"Sure! Just as long as you're gentle with him," Waldemar replied with a smile, squatting so he could be on Little Timmy's level.

"Lanky is so soft and big!" Little Timmy remarked excitedly.

"Yes. He's a big bird!" Waldemar replied, watching the scene carefully, knowing that Lanky was too busy searching for ostrich treats to endanger the lad. "Are you off from school today?"

"I went to school this morning. Then I came home. Then I decided to go to Ostrichland to see the big birds! Then I'm going to church to make peanut butter and jelly sandwiches for the Orphans of Santa Bella," Little Timmy said, his big blue eyes rolling skyward as he recalled his busy day in the Neu Deutschland Valley.

"You sound like a busy boy, Little Timmy," Waldemar exclaimed, showing exaggerated expression in his face in a concerted attempt to relate to Little Timmy.

"Guess what, Mr. Ulff?" Little Timmy asked, excited to be playing the 'Guess What?' game with Waldemar Ulff.

"What?"

"I saw your picture on a record at my Gram's house!" Little Timmy declared with a note of surprise mixed with pride.

"You did?" Waldemar replied, continuing his exaggerated facial expressions.

"Yes. Gram said you were famous!"

"Really? Well, that was a long time ago."

"She says she wanted to get married to you, but she thought she was too young. She says you make her 'hot' whatever *that* means!" Little Timmy continued. "Gram is so much fun. I would like to take her to Ostrichland someday!"

"That would be so nice Little Timmy," Waldemar said. "I hope she can come someday."

"She would, but she has an oxygen tank that's taller than me because she used to smoke two and a half packs of Pall Malls a day for thirty-seven years," Little Timmy explained, squinting his deep-set eyes in the bright midday sun.

"Gee, that's too bad," Waldemar remarked, somewhat taken aback by the sudden dark turn to their conversation. "I hope she's okay."

"She said she's going to meet her maker soon, but I don't know what *that* means," Little Timmy shared. "She said her life isn't worth living now that she was fired from the trucking line and has to sit and watch the soaps all day long like some lost soul in purgatory. She says once she settles some scores, she will know it's time to take a dirt nap. I don't understand what she's talking about sometimes, Mr. Ulff."

"Well, I'm sure she means well. Hey, let's continue on the trail and see more ostriches!" Waldemar suggested in an effort to sideline the 'Gram' talk.

"That sounds swell, Mr. Ulff!" Little Timmy replied enthusiastically. "I love to see the big birds!"

"Indeed," Waldemar said, nudging Lanky to follow along as they started down the trail.

"Gram coughs all the time and sometimes she can hardly breathe," Little Timmy began chattering as they strolled down the riverbed trail, surrounded by majestic oak trees, an occasional ostrich appearing along the way.

"It sounds like Gram is having a tough time of it," Waldemar remarked, becoming uncomfortable with Little Timmy's topic of conversation.

"Gram says the worst part of coughing fits is that she pisses her pants. I don't know what *that* means!" Little Timmy confessed with a chortle.

"Language, Little Timmy!" Waldemar exhorted.

"Sorry, Mr. Ulff," Little Timmy responded, bowing his head slightly in shame.

"Not to worry, Little Timmy," Waldemar replied, tousling Little Timmy's head of red hair.

I like to go to Gram's because I can help with her housework and make sure she's okay. Mr. Ulff, do ostriches die?"

"Everything living eventually dies, Little Timmy," Waldemar replied honestly.

"Oh. Do they go to Heaven when they die?" Little Timmy asked, looking up at Waldemar for some adult reassurance.

"Um... they go to a special ostrich pen in the sky, full of ostrich treats," Waldemar replied, keeping his mind sharp with the questions of a seven-year-old.

"That's reassuring!" Little Timmy said, skipping along the riverbed trail.

"Hey! Look! I think I see Mr. Shrimp Wrigley around the bend in the trail," Waldemar said with a sigh of relief. "Shrimp Wrigley, come, say 'hi' to Little Timmy!"

"Oh, hi, Little Timmy. Hi, Waldemar. Hi Lanky." Shrimp Wrigley greeted, holding a hammer in mid-swing as he was repairing some of the fencing along the riverbed trail.

"Hi, Mr. Shrimp Wrigley!" Little Timmy responded with excitement. "I like Mr. Shrimp Wrigley! I feel that we have a special relationship somehow," Little Timmy declared, looking at Shrimp Wrigley with a smile.

"Well, I like you too, Little Timmy!" Shrimp Wrigley replied, hitting the nail on the head. "But I don't know about the relationship part."

'Little Timmy is having a *very* busy day, Shrimp Wrigley," Waldemar noted, looking at the fence repair.

"Yes, I am. In a few minutes I have to go to make sandwiches at the church for the Orphans of Santa Bella."

"That's a really good cause, Little Timmy!" Waldemar remarked in admiration, impressed that such a young lad would show such compassion.

"It's just who I am, Mr. Ulff," Little Timmy replied humbly.

"You help your Gram and you help the Orphans of Santa Bella. That's a *big* boy! Biggest boy! Biggest boy in the whole wide world!" Waldemar started heaping praise on Little Timmy for his charity work. With those words of praise, Little Timmy raised both arms into the air above his head in the 'Big Boy' style of acknowledgement.

"Ah, quite the lad!" Shrimp Wrigley commented, taking another nail from his right pocket and placing its tip in the worn wood post, ready to strike its head with his trusty claw hammer.

"You must be very smart to use that hammer, Mr. Shrimp Wrigley!" Little Timmy complimented. "I couldn't do *that!*"

Waldemar and Shrimp Wrigley laughed in unison. Lanky looked for ostrich treats in Shrimp Wrigley's tool bag two feet away on the ground.

"I guess I'd better go now Mr. Ulff and Mr. Shrimp Wrigley," Little Timmy said, sensing that his Ostrichland visit was coming to a close for the day.

"Okay. Thanks for stopping by, Little Timmy," Waldemar said, patting Little Timmy's bright red head.

Little Timmy turned and trotted off up the trail.

"Little shit!" Shrimp Wrigley exclaimed sourly, hitting another nail on the head as Little Timmy ran out of view.

The Empty Tank...

The black Mercedes-Benz E400 sedan rounded the corner at a high rate of speed. The Mercedes-Benz was a beautiful, capable car, but still the maneuver made one wonder about the state of mind of the individual driving the vehicle. The sound of Fiona Apple's *Criminal* could be heard emanating from the car if you listened hard enough. With the fading afternoon sun glinting off the polished form of Germanic quality automotive engineering, the automobile looked more like a guided missile than an ordinary mode of transportation. To the drivers passing by on the other side of Highway 277, the only clue that someone was controlling the car was the jaunty homburg visible behind the heavily tinted windows. Yes, Bürgermeister Otto Ackermann was on the move!

Suddenly with a wheeze, sputter and *Gesundheit,* the Mercedes-Benz started slowing noticeably as Ackermann pulled over to the dirt shoulder of the road. With a final application of the brakes, the car stopped completely.

"*Blöd! Wie könnte mir das Benzin ausgehen?*" he berated himself and his gas gauge-reading ability as he quickly opened the driver's door and popped out. He gave the door a hard push with his right hand and surveyed his location. "*Nicht zu fassen!*" he blurted, seeing he was across the highway from Ostrichand. Shaking his homburg-covered head back and forth and looking both ways before crossing the two-lane highway, Bürgermeister Ackermann walked over to the Ostrichland entrance, the gravel on the side of Highway 277 crunching under his HAIX GSG9-S German police boots. He could see The Egg was open, so he trudged his way to the hatch.

"Waldemar Ulff? Are you here?" Bürgermeister Ackermann called out loudly. In a couple seconds, Waldemar appeared, having entered The Egg from a side hatch.

"Bürgermeister Ackermann!" Waldemar greeted, surprised to see him at Ostrichland given their history. "What brings you here this fine day?" Waldemar asked, pulling his ponytail ring tighter as a way of making himself more presentable.

"My car broke down across the highway!" Ackermann explained in an embarrassed tone of voice, adjusting his Homburg with his right hand.

"Do you know what's wrong with it?" Waldemar asked, knowing that that Mercedes-Benz was the Bürgermeister's pride and joy, surprised anything mechanical would dare go wrong in *that* car.

Ackermann looked at the ground like a toddler caught telling a lie. "Well, actually it ran out of petrol." He then shifted his gaze to look around The Egg, noticing how futuristic and expensive it looked.

"Well, we can take care of that right away!" Waldemar offered enthusiastically. "We can siphon some gas out of my Chevrolet Silverado 1500 pickup truck and get you up and rolling. Would you like something to drink?" Waldemar asked, noticing that the Bürgermeister's face was starting to glisten with moisture. "I have plenty of Roo Energy Drink soda here."

"Roo Energy Drink? Okay." Ackermann wasn't in a position to argue the beverage choices and he knew he needed to hydrate.

"Sure. Come up to the administrative office and I'll get us a couple bottles," Waldemar motioned for Ackermann to follow him. With a quick elevator trip, they entered the Ostrichland administrative office. Waldemar pointed to the chair next to his Brazilian tigerwood desk for Ackermann to sit. Then, with the alacrity of a seasoned bartender, the Roo Energy Drinks were out and open before Ackermann's ample rump touched the bottom of the chair.

"Why are you always so nice to me, Waldemar?" Ackermann questioned without a flinch. "After all I did to you when you were trying to buy Ostrichland." He took a swig of Roo Energy Drink, making an unpleasant face as it hit his taste buds.

Waldemar sat down at his plush executive chair. "I knew you were just trying to protect Shrimp Wrigley," Waldemar reminded him. "After all, here comes this music celebrity (air quotes) wanting to buy Ostrichland from your friend. You must have really wondered what was going on, right?"

"Of course," Ackermann shifted as much as he could in his chair. "Shrimp Wrigley owned this place for so many years and suddenly this huge pop star shows up. What was I to think? I tried my best to persuade Shrimp Wrigley to not go through with the deal, but you won out in the end." Ackermann took another glug of his Roo Energy Drink, nursing it like it was somewhat radioactive. "Plus, I never did like **WOW**. Fiona Apple was *my* girl in the day," Bürgermeister Ackermann cracked a slight smile.

Waldemar smiled back. "So many years ago!"

"Frankly, Waldemar," Ackermann continued, leaning closer, "I was mostly worried that a celebrity like you would take Ostrichland and make it a fabulous tourist destination to the detriment of Neu Deutschland. That's why I objected so strongly to the sale."

"With all due respect, Bürgermeister Ackermann, that doesn't make any sense," Waldemar said with some puzzlement. "What's good for Ostrichland is good for Neu Deutschland and vice versa. We're both in this together and to tell the truth, Ostrichland has been having some problems in the past few months with guest attendance. I don't think the average person is as interested in ostriches as they once were."

Ackermann jumped at the opening to mention Neu Deutschland's popularity crisis.

"Ah, Waldemar, we are in the same situation, but I think it's even worse for Neu Deutschland at this time. That's why I was driving around just now. I do my best thinking when I'm driving fast. I *must* come up with *something* to get Neu Deutschland popular again. At this point it would take a miracle! Young families just don't think of a faux German town in California as a fun place to be anymore," he observed, inserting his right index finger in the opening of the Roo Energy Drink bottle. In doing so, he started thrusting said finger to and fro, mimicking coital movement.

"Leisure pursuits *have* changed, that's for sure!" Waldemar agreed, taking a last glug from his Roo Energy Drink bottle, attempting not to be too distracted by the Bürgermeister's finger movement.

"I think people, families in particular, are missing out," Ackermann mused, his right index finger actions becoming more and more pronounced. "Now it's all about smartphones and video games. Ah! What happened to the fun of visiting another country, especially when it's in your own country? All the advantages of worldwide travel without the hassle!"

"You don't have to convince me, Bürgermeister," Waldemar agreed. "Same with Ostrichland. Why wouldn't you want your youngsters to get up close and personal with a flock of birds larger than your father?"

"Precisely," Ackermann agreed. "Ah! *Fantastisch!*" he sighed deeply, sinking back in his chair, his right index finger now resting in the neck of the Roo Energy Drink bottle.

Clearly uncomfortable with the whole bottle 'affair,' Waldemar said, "So, if you think about it, Bürgermeister, Neu Deutschland and Ostrichland complement each other. They don't detract. When one is prospering, the other should too."

"Mutual cooperation, in other words!" Bürgermeister Ackermann was seeing Waldemar's point. Ackermann was now struggling to remove his right index finger from the Roo Energy Drink bottle.

"Exactly!" Waldemar emphasized. "Um... would you like me to dispose of the bottle?"

"Yes," Ackermann replied, giving a wince-inducing pull on the bottle, finally extracting his right index finger from its glass prison. "Here you go, Waldemar. I *really* enjoyed that drink!"

"Yes. Yes, you did!" Waldemar replied, taking Ackermann's now-empty soda bottle and carefully depositing it in the trash can to the side of his desk.

With Ostrichland's dusk closing time approaching, Waldemar stood up, as did Bürgermeister Ackermann. "Let's get your car filled up, Bürgermeister Ackermann. I wish both of us good luck. I'm going to be having an Internet show, *Feeling the Music*, broadcast from here next month and I can mention Neu Deutschland. Maybe that will help a bit."

"That would be wonderful, Waldemar!" he exclaimed as they both walked toward the entrance hatch of The Egg on their way to fuel the Bürgermeister's Mercedes-Benz. "I'm sure you still have many fans who like to hear about what you're up to."

"Yeah, of course they always want a **WOW** reunion too," Waldemar casually mentioned as he was climbing into his pickup truck.

"Of course!" Bürgermeister Ackermann gave an artificial laugh as his brain started whirring. "A **WOW** reunion... ha!" Bürgermeister Ackermann quickly walked across the Highway 277 where Waldemar was beginning to refuel his car. "A **WOW** reunion..." Ackermann said out loud to himself, rubbing his crimson cheek with his right thumb and index finger.

Strouthokamelophobia...!

"Good afternoon everyone!" Waldemar greeted the eight people seated on two padded benches on the mezzanine of The Egg. "How are you all doing?" he asked, standing in front of them with a wide, confident stance. The padded benches were overlooking the Ostrich Habitat of The Egg where the flock could enter and exit at will with the help of motion-sensitive electric doors. This was the weekly meeting of the Strouthokamelophobia Afflicted Group (SAG), a group designed to aid individuals afflicted with Strouthokamelophobia, the fear of ostriches.

"Hello, Waldemar!" the eight replied in unison, varying degrees of terror evident in their voices.

"I'm glad to see you could all make it today," Waldemar said cheerfully. Actually, there were seven patients and one therapist. Dr. Drew Little was the leading expert in Strouthokamelophobia in the nation. As luck would have it, his office, located in fabled Santa Barbara, California, not too far down the coast from Ostrichland. In the years Waldemar conducted SAG, he had picked up some helpful tips on assisting people get over their ostrich phobia. With the therapist's permission, Waldemar participated in some of the field work for the group. "How is everyone feeling today?" Waldemar asked, his dark brown eyes scanning the group in front of him.

"I'm a bit nervous... actually more than a bit!" a middle-age man confessed.

"I'm sorry to hear that Dr. Drew," Waldemar replied sympathetically. "Considering you're the therapist."

"I know, he replied, a tad embarrassed. "I've been okay, but when we were here last week, I was looking at the ostriches and all of a sudden just thought that they looked kinda creepy," he admitted with a slight shiver going through his body. "I realize that I'm displaying emotional incontinence."

"Yeah! They're creepy!" a young woman patient in the group concurred. "That's why I'm afraid of them. They're creepy!"

"Okay. Others?" Waldemar asked, attempting to get more participation out of the group.

"I think they look like prehistoric dinosaurs, only with feathers!" an older woman patient remarked, taking a quick look down into the Ostrich Habitat to reinforce her negative opinion of ostriches.

"They're the giraffes of birds!" one patient called out.

"They're okay, I think," began a young male patient with a baseball cap stating (it made Waldemar somewhat nauseous):

"It's just that they are so damn big! I mean, look at them!" he said, looking down at three ostriches, Quill, Big Bird and Chip, in the Ostrich Habitat. "Who likes birds that are *that* BIG!? Plus, they stick their heads in the sand when they're scared. Cowards!" he said, his agitation level rising by the moment.

"Yes, they *are* big," Waldemar conceded. Dr. Drew Little wasn't pulling his weight today, that was evident. "However, contrary to popular belief, ostriches *do not* stick their heads in the sand when they are scared."

"Whatever," the young male patient replied.

"I think they are from Mars or some undiscovered planet!" a middle-aged woman with a blue crocheted cap gave her opinion. "They can't be of this earth!" she commented with a slight shriek.

Waldemar couldn't help but notice that by now Dr. Drew had edged his way from the two padded benches to the public elevator of The Egg. "Dr. Drew, are you okay?" Waldemar asked with concern. With that, Dr. Drew hit the 'up' button and entered the elevator car. "What the...?" Waldemar sputtered, striding to the elevator, but too late. Dr. Drew Little was headed up to the next floor in The Egg where the administrative offices, the gift shop *Feathers*, and The Yolk auditorium were located. The public elevator didn't go higher than that floor. Waldemar took to the stairs, two at a time, to catch up with the doctor.

"Doctor Little, what's going on!?" Waldemar confronted him when the elevator doors parted.

"Waldemar! I don't know what's going on, but I'm very afraid of ostriches right now! I'm having a massive panic attack!" Dr. Drew admitted, his voice quivering in fright. His progressive lens eyeglasses were steamed up he was so agitated.

"Come with me, Dr. Drew," Waldemar grabbed Dr. Drew's right hand and led him to the administrative office. "Sit down on the couch," Waldemar urged, pointing to the plush blue couch next to his desk as he checked the contents of his refrigerator cleverly hidden in the main bookshelf. "Ah, here we go! Would you like thyme or extra-mint tea?" Waldemar asked.

"Oh, thyme sounds good," Dr. Drew replied, sweat pouring down his forehead, adding to the fog of his progressive-lens eyeglasses.

"Good choice," Waldemar exclaimed, extracting a bottle of Sleepy Thyme Tea[4] to calm Dr. Drew's nerves.

"I think I'm taking on my patient's phobias, Waldemar! A therapist's worst nightmare!" Dr. Drew lamented, taking a glug of the Sleepy Thyme Tea. "Those big birds are very scary to me right now!"

"I understand," Waldemar comforted the distressed therapist. "When did you start having these feelings?"

"The feelings of ostrich fear?" Dr. Drew clarified the question.

"Yes," Waldemar answered.

"A couple of minutes ago," he said, still working on his bottle of Sleepy Thyme Tea.

"Did you have a good childhood?" Waldemar continued.

"Oh, it was pretty good. My father was a strict disciplinarian, a bit overbearing. He pushed me to become a therapist until I felt I had no other choice, but otherwise everything was normal," Dr. Drew answered earnestly.

"And your college years? Any problems there?" Waldemar pressed on.

"I was pretty invisible on campus, that's for sure," Dr. Drew admitted, taking a sip of Sleepy Thyme Tea.

"Do you feel you are compensating for the attention you lacked in your early years?" Waldemar pressed.

"No. No... Hey! You're analyzing me, Waldemar!" he protested, the Sleepy Thyme Tea's calming effect bringing him back to his 'now.'

"I think you are just having a low blood sugar issue," Waldemar assured Dr. Drew. "The tea should help."

---

[4] Sleepy Thyme Tea was first brewed in the hallowed halls of Arizona State University to help some very stressed-out liberal arts students.

Waldemar comforted Dr. Drew for eighteen and a half minutes, talking about this and that, anything to calm his mind. Waldemar felt that things were now under control.

"If you're feeling up to it now, Dr. Drew, I think we'd better get back to the patients," Waldemar said, getting up from the couch. Dr. Drew followed Waldemar. They took the public elevator down to the mezzanine. When the elevator doors opened, they were treated to a sight.

"Lanky! What are *you* doing on the mezzanine?" Waldemar asked with surprise, astounded to see his feathered assistant surrounded by the seven patients of SAG! They were feeding Lanky ostrich treats bought from the vending machines on the mezzanine level of The Egg just for the convenience of guests of Ostrichland.

"Lanky just poked at the hatch and let himself in! I think I just needed to be with an ostrich one-on-one!" the middle-aged male patient said with excitement, feeding Lanky an ostrich treat with the open palm of his right hand.

"He's so friendly, I feel like he's my new best friend!" the young male patient said, triumphant in his breakthrough with defeating Strouthokamelophobia. "How could *anyone* be afraid of this big guy?"

"Waldemar, your lovely ostrich has changed my life. I will always be grateful for your help!" the older female patent beamed. "The next time I come back it will be to visit Lanky and his flock, not to be afraid anymore!"

"Me too!" chimed the other patients, sorry that their allotted hour was over for the week.

Dr. Drew Little was realizing the Sleepy Thyme Tea wasn't enough to handle his new case of Strouthokamelophobia. As SAG assembled to depart The Egg in triumph, Dr. Drew followed them at a distance, gripping the curved walls of The Egg with the palms of both hands, he faced away from the wall, as he made his way to the hatch, each step a living nightmare as his proximity to the newly-dreaded large birds reduced his nervous system to that of a neurotic hummingbird.

"Thanks, *Waldemar*!" Dr. Drew managed to squeak out as his entered the hatch to exit The Egg and join the others on the rented 'short bus' for their trip back to Santa Barbara.

"Lanky, it looks like our work here is done!" Waldemar beamed as he and Lanky exited the hatch to enjoy the sunshine of the day. The glint of sun shining off the windows of the short bus, Dr. Drew Little seated in the back seat, wiping his slightly balding pate with a teal handkerchief, the patients waving at Waldemar and Lanky as the short bus turned on to Highway 277.

The Offer...

With the departure of the short bus containing the Strouthokamelophobia Afflicted Group (SAG), Waldemar was preparing to close the gate to mark the official end of another day at Ostrichland. Before Waldemar could push the button on his smartphone that would snap the entrance gate lock in place, he spotted a brand-new Cadillac XTS limousine rounding the corner and pulling into the entrance of Ostrichland. Waldemar took his finger off the button to let the limousine into the parking lot. This ought to be interesting, he thought as the big shiny car glided to a halt. Waldemar then locked the gate with the app. The driver emerged, quickly went around the back of the limousine and opened the rear door.

A large man in the whitest of white suits carefully exited the limousine, an unlit Arturo Fuente Don Carlos 'Eye of the Shark' cigar from the Dominican Republic (*Cigar Aficionado's* 2017 Cigar of the Year) securely in place on the right side of his mouth. A young man and woman apparently in their early 30's, wearing identically styled business suits, appearing to be twins, exited the limousine through the other rear door once the large man emerged.

The large man looked directly at Waldemar as he made his way to bridge the 20-foot gap to where Waldemar, now joined by Lanky, was standing, taking in the scene. The large man reached Waldemar and extended his right hand. Waldemar instantly recognized him as 'Yacktivist' Les Winns, the famous neo-post-conservative-ultra-right radio talk show host. "Les Winns," he announced as Waldemar extended his right hand to shake. Lanky looked to see if Winns had any ostrich treats; he didn't.

"Waldemar Ulff," Waldemar introduced himself with some amount of caution. Les Winns looked too much like a record executive to suit his taste.

"Yes, Waldemar, I'm a *big* fan of yours," Winns announced, chomping a bit on his fine cigar. "Allow me to introduce my personal twin assistants, Edwin and Edwina Flunkie." The Flunkies, standing approximately 5'3" shook their pasty faces at Waldemar in a greeting ritual of some sort. "That's a mighty big bird there," Winns observed, looking warily into Lanky's big blue eyes.

"It's an ostrich. His name is Lanky," Waldemar explained. "We have quite a few of these guys here at Ostrichland, of course," he joked, the ironic humor lost on Winns and his Flunkies.

"Lanky. Great. Is there someplace private where we can talk?" Winns asked, his eyes shifting from left to right several times. Waldemar looked around. He led Winns and his Flunkies into The Egg and up to the administrative office. Lanky remained at the limousine, eyeing the driver who quickly took refuge in the car.

With a billion-dollar fortune built on his popular talk radio show, *The Right Side*, Les Winns, the self-proclaimed 'Yacktivist', was an influential figure in the media, neo-post-conservative-ultra-right politics and the top echelons of government. *The Right Side* was daily listening for millions of people who were convinced of Winns' personal version of 'truth.'

"Would you like a Roo Energy Drink imported from Australia?" Waldemar offered, pointing out the chair next to his desk where Winns could sit. The Flunkies stood unobtrusively by the door of the administrative office.

"Sure, that sounds real refreshing," Winns remarked. "Your establishment is very impressive, Waldemar," Winns said, looking around the large and elegantly appointed administrative office.

"Thank you," he replied. "I'm very happy with Ostrichland."

"As well you should be. Do you know anything about me, Waldemar?" Winns asked as Waldemar handed him a bottle of Roo Energy Drink, directing the conversation to himself.

"I've heard of you and I know you're a very rich and influential man" Waldemar answered as he sat down at his Brazilian tigerwood desk. "I can't say I've ever heard your radio show though."

"Well, that's enough to start," Winns said, popping the top of his Roo Energy Drink and taking a swig. "There's a lot in the middle though," he chuckled. "As a teenager, I started out at a 50-watt station, KRAP in Bayou Bay, Louisiana. I skipped high school as often as possible so that I could work at the station. At first, I swept the floors, made sure the gator fences were all in place, answered the phone. Then, I worked my way up to engineer and, finally, I got my own radio show. Guess what it was called?"

"Um, *The Les Winns Show?*" Waldemar guessed half-heartedly.

"Why yes! You must be psychic!" Winns beamed. "From the beginning, my show focused on politics. Initially, I went after Het Mauriette, the most dishonest state senator in the history of Louisiana. I hammered him until he eventually resigned in disgrace after his role in the Swampland scandal. Old Het bought 1,000 acres of pure swampland and tried to resell it as a recreational nudist resort for burnt out executives. In actuality, none of the land was fit for human occupation, clothes or no clothes. That's when I coined the word, 'Yacktivist.' What else would you call a good old country boy who talked too much and caused trouble for politicians?!" Les Winns laughed heartily and took another swig of Roo Energy Drink, his energy level rising by the second. "This is a good drink. Yes indeed!"

"As my popularity grew, so did my causes," Winns continued, enjoying reciting his verbal résumé. Now, as you *probably* know, I'm the #1 radio talk show host in the U.S.A.! My mission: I expose the Forces of Evil. FOE.

"I hate the forces that are out to destroy our way of life... our country! I always will! People have been misled in *devious* ways thinking that the world is safe and secure! That's just not true! All that we see around us that is wrong is a result of numerous conspiracies, groups and nations filled with evil too numerous to mention. FOE even has a base in Antarctica... look it up! FOE is *everywhere*," Winns hissed.

"Before it's too late, we need to find places of protection, places of shelter where our families can be safe and secure while we counterattack the Forces of Evil."

"Really?" Waldemar offered no resistance, taking a final sip from his Roo Energy Drink.

"My current project is to build luxury semi-underground bunker bungalows," the Yacktivist continued. "Each bunker bungalow will have, in its core, a 'safe room' where the residents, people of means, can shelter in place until the life-threatening situation has been contained. The visible parts of the bunker bungalows will be very stylish with porticos, water features and lawn gnomes..."

"Lawn gnomes?" Waldemar chuckled out loud.

"Well, sure, whatever they want to make a bunker bungalow a home," Winns answered thinking Waldemar a bit slow in his landscape design sense. "I can tell you understand the urgency of this project, Waldemar!" he said excitedly. "Some people think I'm crazy, but you *know*!" Winns gave Waldemar a look like he wanted his sanity validated.

"Oh, I'd say I'm beginning to know. Yes."

"A setting like Ostrichland is *perfect* for a community of bunker bungalows. Who in their right mind would venture onto land as rugged as this and protected by a bunch of giant birds?"

"A flock of ostriches," Waldemar *had* to correct Winns' linguistic flub.

"Right. Right," Winns had another gulp of Roo Energy Drink. "I'll have to get a case of this stuff. Anyhow, the riverbed makes for a great fortified zone and the birds... the ostriches... they would scare anyone away. Am I right? So that's why I'm going to give you $30,000,012.54 right now to buy Ostrichland. No questions asked," he announced, placing his empty Roo Energy Drink bottle on Waldemar's desk with his right hand, glancing again at his Flunkies.

"You? What?!" Waldemar sat upright in his chair, totally blindsided by Winn's offer. "Why the 12.54?" Waldemar asked parenthetically.

"It's my lucky number," Winns replied matter-of-factly. "So, what do you say?" he asked, Edwin Flunkie moving over to Winns, handing him several legal-looking papers.

"Wait a minute!" Waldemar was able to blurt out. "I never said Ostrichland was *for sale!*" he sputtered.

"$30,000,012.54, Waldemar," Winns repeated the offer. "I know you made a lot of money with **WOW**, but $30,000,012.54 is nothing to sneeze at. Besides, the ostriches will stay. They'll be part of the marketing campaign as natural guardians of the land."

Waldemar sat silent for several moments, leading Winns to believe he was mulling over the offer, but he was simply trying to compose himself before continuing. "You're right, Mr. Winns, $30,000,012.54 *is* a lot of money even for me. I gave away a great deal of my money after **WOW** broke up. Some people thought I was foolish for doing so, but that money became seed money for several foundations that are doing good work around the world. I believe a person only needs so much of anything, including money. At some point anything more is just more."

"Well, that's a noble attitude, Waldemar," Les Winns said with a note of condescension in his voice. "And I think saving the world from FOE is a noble case if there ever *was* a noble cause!"

Waldemar stood up to lead Winns and his Flunkies out of the administrative office, down the public elevator and out the hatch.

"Is it the money, Waldemar? If I upped the amount would that persuade you?" Winns asked, not used to hearing 'no.' Winns *knew* everyone and everything had a price. Waldemar led the way as they headed toward the limousine.

"There's no doubt that money can do good, Mr. Winns," Waldemar admitted. "There's also an importance to me as to how that money was made. The money I made during my **WOW** days, hopefully came from fans who enjoyed our music. That makes me feel good. Making money on people's fears just doesn't seem right to me. Maybe I'm virtue signaling, but that's what I believe. I don't see how I could live with myself." Waldemar could see Lanky sidling up to him out of the corner of his right eye. "Besides, I couldn't give up my flock now, could I?" he smiled, touching his head with his right hand, patting it twice, giving Lanky a signal Waldemar had taught him years ago.

With a hoot and holler from the Yacktivist, Lanky marched over to him and began gently pecking his head, turning Les Winns' thinning hair into a swirled combover. "Get that bird away from me!" he bellowed, quickly getting into the car, no assistance from the driver, still in the driver's seat. Edwin and Edwina Flunkie followed quickly.

Waldemar walked over and manually unlocked the gate as the limousine came to life. The driver did a three-point turn and headed out the gate, Winns put down the back-right window and shouted, "I lied, Waldemar! ABBA was my favorite group!"

"Ouch, *that* hurt!" Waldemar chuckled to Lanky as he locked the gate again. "Time for a doob, eh Lanky? ABBA! *Really?*"

Tokin' Friends...

Waldemar couldn't wait to unwind following his unsettling encounter with Les Winns. Once everything was locked and secured, Waldemar and Lanky made their way to the Sunset Bench. He pulled a pre-made marijuana cigarette out of the right pocket of his flannel shirt and lit it with a BIC he pulled from his right front jean pocket. Lanky watched Waldemar for a surprise ostrich treat; none so far. Waldemar inhaled deeply several times. Marijuana was Waldemar's only vice these days (aside from Roo Energy Drink). During the 90's anything and everything was the norm in the music business. **WOW** was rather conservative in their drugs and sex compared to the norm, but the norm was a 'high' mark to achieve.

Lanky jerked his head to the right. Waldemar heard the sound a split-second later... scraping gravel coming from the riverbed towards the Sunset Bench. Someone walking. Waldemar was very mellow by now, but he listened intently to the sound. Lanky took a few steps away from the bench, closer to the edge where he could see down to the riverbed.

"Hey!" a familiar voice called out in the growing darkness.

"Oh, hey!" Waldemar returned the greeting once he realized the mysterious steps were those of Shrimp Wrigley. "What's up, Shrimp Wrigley?" Waldemar asked, taking another toke.

"Just taking a walk, Waldemar," Shrimp Wrigley said, slightly out of breath, a Lucky Strike dangling from his mouth, only smoked outdoors and never in front of women or children.

"Have a seat, Shrimp Wrigley," Waldemar motioned. Lanky moved out of the way as Shrimp Wrigley sat down on the right side of the Sunset Bench.

"I've got a treat for you, Shrimp Wrigley," Waldemar smiled, pulling another joint out of his right shirt pocket, handing it to Shrimp Wrigley. "Homegrown, my friend," Waldemar mentioned with a note of pride. "Here, Lanky," Waldemar said, reaching into his right front jean pocket, pulling out an ostrich treat. Lanky reached down carefully and plucked the prize from Waldemar's right hand. Lanky walked a few feet in the direction of The Egg as he savored the treat.

"Thanks, Waldemar, don't mind if I do," Shrimp Wrigley replied, taking one more puff of his Lucky Strike before he tossed it over the small cliff. "It's beautiful out right now, isn't it?" Shrimp Wrigley said, getting a couple inhales in record time.

"Indeed, it is," Waldemar agreed, folding his hands behind his head as he looked up at the clear dark sky as countless stars emerged as the day turned to night. "Did you know there's a big bug on your right shoulder, Shrimp Wrigley?"

"Oh, Simon, sure," Shrimp Wrigley answered casually, inhaling once again.

"Simon the bug?" Waldemar asked.

"Well, Simon the Stag Beetle to be precise," Shrimp Wrigley replied.

"Why is a stag beetle perched on your right shoulder, Shrimp Wrigley?"

"Well, it's like this, Waldemar, I've always wanted a parrot on my right shoulder because I've always wanted to be a pirate."

"Okay..."

"At a young age I concluded that aspiring to be a pirate wasn't a productive use of my energy. Also, I've always had an issue with a parrot defecating on my right shoulder. It's quite a mess I've heard."

"Yes..."

"So, I spotted Simon the Stag Beetle the other day at Animal House Pets and Supplies in Santa Bella and I decided to buy him. So far, he seems to be enjoying standing in for a parrot and I feel pretty pirate-y even though Simon's not an actual parrot. I'm going to teach him how to wave his antennas around to make up for the fact that he doesn't squawk like a parrot. It's a win/win situation if you ask me."

"Indeed," Waldemar replied thoughtfully. "Aren't you afraid you'll scare people when they see Simon the Stag Beetle on your right shoulder?"

"Scare them? I didn't think of that, Waldemar! Wouldn't they be just as scared seeing a large bird defecating on my right shoulder?"

"You have a point, Shrimp Wrigley," Waldemar conceded. "It *is* a beautiful night tonight. The universe is so amazing!"

After a few moments of silent contemplation, Shrimp Wrigley asked, "Do you think about it often, Waldemar?"

"Sure. Just about every day I would say," Waldemar replied.

"It's such a story. So hard to take in," Shrimp Wrigley continued, the cannabis really hitting him now.

"Well, it's a lot to think about if you let your brain go wild," Waldemar said. "You can only think about pieces of it at a time, you know," he looked at Shrimp Wrigley.

"Yeah, I guess. I like to think about it all at once," Shrimp Wrigley admitted. "It's like ancient history in a way, isn't it?" Shrimp Wrigley looked at Waldemar. Waldemar looked at Lanky. Lanky looked at Waldemar, hoping for another ostrich treat.

"Ancient history, eh? Well, it wasn't *that* long ago!" Waldemar admonished.

"Well, you know what I mean, Waldemar," Shrimp Wrigley looked higher in the sky. "Time probably doesn't even matter."

"Probably not in the long run." Waldemar agreed

"I mean, a billion years here, a billion years there..." Shrimp Wrigley sat upright looking at Waldemar.

"A billion years?" Waldemar looked at Shrimp Wrigley. "Ha ha, very funny!"

"What's wrong, Waldemar?" Shrimp Wrigley asked with surprise.

"**WOW** wasn't *that* long ago!" Waldemar was coming out of the chill zone now.

"**WOW** what?!" Shrimp Wrigley sputtered, staring at Waldemar. "What are you talking about, Waldemar?" Shrimp Wrigley questioned.

"You asked if I think about it and I said 'yes' and now you're saying it was billions of years ago, that's what I'm talking about," Waldemar was getting irritated.

"I was asking if you think about the *universe* and all that!" Shrimp Wrigley protested. What did you think I was asking about?" Shrimp Wrigley demanded.

"Oh..." Waldemar was too embarrassed to tell Shrimp Wrigley that he thought Shrimp Wrigley was asking if Waldemar thought about **WOW** often. "Geez, Shrimp Wrigley, let's just enjoy the stars!" Waldemar quickly diverted the conversation. Shrimp Wrigley lit a Lucky Strike. Waldemar was disturbed that he would assume Shrimp Wrigley was talking about **WOW**. Do I have **WOW** on my mind? Waldemar wondered to himself.

"I was at the doctor today, Waldemar," Shrimp Wrigley changed the subject abruptly. "He insists I see him every so often to give me my arthritis pills. I don't have arthritis too bad, but the pills *do* help, so what the heck, eh? So, the doctor, Doctor Cyril Yakyakian, I first went to him when I couldn't have a bowel movement a few years ago. Damn if I could get out more than a jellybean at a time. I had taken a liking to grilled cheese sandwiches then and you know me, Waldemar, I just went for it. That's about all I ate. Dr.

Yakyakian said I was constipated because of my diet of grilled cheese sandwiches so he gave me a prescription. I go to the drug store, hand the prescription to the pharmacist and he says it will be $50. Even though I have health insurance. I asked if there wasn't something I could just buy in the store without a prescription. The pharmacist really didn't want to go against Dr. Yakyakian's advice but mentioned there was a product in the next aisle that would work just as well -- Poop-Ease it was called. Boy did it work!" Shrimp Wrigley paused to light up another Lucky Strike. "By the time I was done I needed to call a plumber. My balloon knot got quite a workout that day!"

"Oh..." Waldemar remarked, hoping Shrimp Wrigley would get onto another subject. He didn't.

"So, Dr. Yakyakian wanted me to come back in two weeks which I did. I didn't tell him that I switched the prescription for an over-the-counter item. He says he wants me to have a colonoscopy. I told him I didn't want one, but he insisted. He gave me a referral for a colonoscopy. I just put it in my dresser drawer, you know, but his office called several times about it and I was getting annoyed. By that time, I had gotten sick of grilled cheese sandwiches and I was quite regular, so I didn't see the point. So, finally I came up with a scheme," Shrimp Wrigley said with a twinkle in his right eye. "I used the video on my smartphone. I was baking a turkey one night and was thinking that the neck looked like a tunnel, then it hit me..."

"What hit you?" Waldemar asked, sitting upright, a smile on his face. This was going to be another classic Shrimp Wrigley story, he could tell.

"I started thinking how that turkey neck looked like a stinkpipe, ya know? So, I got my smartphone video working, kinda pushed it up the turkey neck like it was going up my mystery hole, right?" Shrimp Wrigley said, laughing and coughing at the same time. "Damned if it didn't look like a video of my poop shoot, Waldemar!" Shrimp Wrigley was really laughing and coughing now, along with Waldemar.

"Let's go get some Roo Energy Drink in the administrative office, Shrimp Wrigley," Waldemar said standing up slowly. "So, what did you do then?" Waldemar asked as they headed toward The Egg, Lanky following, hoping for another ostrich treat.

"So, the next time Dr. Yakyakian's office calls, I make an appointment. When I got there, I showed him my video. He asked if it was some kind of joke, all serious ya know? I said no it wasn't," Shrimp Wrigley stopped his story for a moment while Waldemar handed him a nice, fresh Roo Energy Drink, plus a big bag of chips upon entering the plush administrative office. "I told Dr. Yakyakian that I bought a home colonoscopy kit, and this was the video I made!"

Waldemar almost choked on his swig of Roo Energy Drink as he started laughing heartily. It *was* another classic Shrimp Wrigley story!

"He never did bother me about getting a colonoscopy again!" Shrimp Wrigley laughed along with Waldemar, chugging his Roo Energy Drink and devouring the bag of chips.

"Did you know that I was almost in show business myself, Waldemar?" Shrimp Wrigley asked, looking around in vain for another bag of chips.

"No, do tell," Waldemar replied, opening a desk drawer and tossing Shrimp Wrigley another bag of chips.

"Well, I *will* tell... I was just a teenager just starting out in life, must have been around 1960. I was bored, so I decided to think up a TV show and see if any of the studios would go for it. I think they call it 'pitching an idea' now, but I'm not sure," Shrimp Wrigley stopped momentarily to consume a number of chips. "Anyhow, I was interested in ostriches even in my early years. You know how that goes, Waldemar, eh?" Shrimp Wrigley laughed, knowing that Waldemar, too, had 'Ostrich Fever.' "So, I came up with a show called *Mr. Ted.*"

"Mr. Ted?" Waldemar questioned, wondering where this story was going to go.

"Yes. It was about a talking ostrich named Mr. Ted!" Shrimp Wrigley explained. "I wrote to several studios, but it was hard to contact the people who could make the decisions. Those I talked to thought the concept was, well, ridiculous, that's what most of them said. I persisted, but also knew when something was a hopeless cause."

"Right."

"So, I'll never forget this, on October 1, 1961 I had my TV on while I was doing homework and what did I hear? A catchy theme song that pulled me into the living room to check it out. Of course, it was the debut of the show *Mr. Ed* about a *talking horse!*" Can you image anything so stupid?!"

"More stupid than a talking ostrich?" Waldemar asked, stifling a laugh.

"Of course, it was more stupid!" Shrimp Wrigley proclaimed, shoving a handful of chips in his mouth. "A talking ostrich is one thing, but a horse? Come on! So, I figured someone at one of the studios stole my idea and changed *Mr. Ted* to *Mr. Ed* made *Mr. Ed* a horse instead of *Mr. Ted* being an ostrich. Otherwise, it was basically the same show."

"Right."

"I was going to hire a lawyer and sue someone, but I didn't have the time or money to fight Hollywood. That's when I knew show business wasn't for me! Too fantastical! I'm a practical guy I guess, Waldemar," Shrimp Wrigley finished the bag of chips, Simon the Stag Beetle balancing precariously on Shrimp Wrigley's right shoulder.

"That's quite a story, Shrimp Wrigley," Waldemar said, knowing there was a good deal of fiction to any Shrimp Wrigley tale.

"Well I gotta go, Waldemar," Shrimp Wrigley proclaimed, standing up and handing Waldemar an empty Roo Energy Drink bottle and two empty bags of chips. "It was a pleasure seeing you tonight. I enjoyed our talk," Shrimp Wrigley said, showing himself to the door and to his apartment in The Egg one floor above the administrative office. "Next time I'll tell you about how my franchise idea, 'Pizza in a Bag,' but got ripped off by the titans of the fast food industry."

"Sounds great, Shrimp Wrigley," Waldemar said, following Shrimp Wrigley out of the administrative office. Waldemar took the private elevator to his Sky House at the top of The Egg.

Billions and billions of years ago rang in Waldemar's head as he stepped into the Sky House, the lights turning on automatically. Shrimp Wrigley *could* have been talking about **WOW** for all Waldemar knew. Indeed.

Meanwhile...

"I'll have a bottle of Mineralwasser[5] Mineral Water," Conrad Halle glanced up at the tall young blond waiter. The tall young blond waiter looked back at Conrad Halle with a touch of annoyance.

"Yes sir," the waiter responded with some sarcasm in this voice. "A fine choice indeed, sir."

Halle looked around the room. *WonderBar* at Halle Haus was Halle's pride and joy. He spent considerable time and money in creating the popular piano lounge. Consisting of two rooms, the bar and the piano lounge, *WonderBar* was *the* place to be seen in Neu Deutschland! The decor was very modern like a Berlin-inspired disco lounge in the 1970's. Several round glass tables surrounded a gleaming red baby grand piano on a small stage, the focal point of the room.

Halle glanced at his NOMOS Glashütte watch with some impatience as the waiter placed his bottle of Mineralwasser Mineral Water on the table. Where were Bürgermeister Ackermann and Gerta Switzer? Their meeting was at 9:00 pm and it was already 9:09 pm. Halle was a punctual man. Anything less that being exactly on time was unacceptable.

And speaking of unacceptable, *WonderBar* had a new piano player, Sanny, and he too, was late. His set started at 9:00 pm on the dot. Halle made a mental note of Sanny's tardiness. Just as he started to glance at his watch

---

[5] Mineralwasser Mineral Water was first bottled in 1884 by Hubert Von Trussel of Bad Hersfeld, Germany. The distinct taste of the mineral water is thought to be, in part, attributed to the spring's proximity to the two mineral springs located in the town. From the start, to drink a stein of Mineralwasser Mineral Water supposedly led to greater testicular weight and strength.

another time, a flash of light caught Halle's attention. Sanny had entered *WonderBar* and was adjusting the piano bench to begin his set.

Sanny was dressed in his trademark glittering suit, gold top, gold pants. His pompadour of raven-black hair was carefully coiffed, complimenting his large golden-rimmed glasses. A show biz veteran, Sanny was always reaching for the gold ring and ending up with a bruised finger for the effort. Sanny's last gig was at the *Silver Horseshoe* in Las Vegas, but the management wanted someone with 'more talent' and Sanny moved on. Halle was desperate to find '*any* talent' for *WonderBar* and Sanny happened to be reassessing his career path in Neu Deutschland when fate struck, and a win/win situation occurred. That was two weeks ago. Halle was *so* desperate that he hired Sanny without an audition, just going by the fact that he had heard his name once in a television documentary on Las Vegas lounge singers. This would be Sanny's audition. It would be an auspicious night!

As Sanny continued to adjust the piano bench then fiddle with the exact location of the crystal tip jar, Halle spotted Bürgermeister Ackermann and Gerta Switzer enter the Halle Haus lobby, walking toward *WonderBar*. They were unaware Halle was watching. Were they holding hands?! He wasn't quite sure. Frau Ackermann would be interested to see *that* sight! They weren't holding hands when they entered *WonderBar* just in time to hear Sanny begin his set.

"Good evening everyone," Sanny cooed into his Shure SM58 dynamic microphone. "It's great having you at *WonderBar*. Let's start the show!"

Bürgermeister Ackermann and Gerta were settling into their chairs during Sanny's introduction, but their hushed greetings and apologies for being late distracted Halle from giving Sanny his complete attention.

"I always like to start a show with a song request," Sanny continued, the waiter depositing a glass of Nestea Iced Tea[6] for Sanny on a Halle Haus coaster positioned on the right side of the red piano.

With the three people at Halle's table, two older women across the room, the only surviving members of 'Inka-Dinka-Do' - the Official Jimmy Durante Fan Club and one disheveled male loner, sporting a Mondale-Ferraro '84 button on his lapel, at the table near *WonderBar's* entrance, the chance of someone calling out a song request was slim at best. Sensing this, Halle raised his voice slightly, "How about *Moon River?*"

"Ah, great choice," Sanny announced, a slight look of relief on his face because he knew the song.

---

[6] The history of iced tea goes back to the early 1800's but it was not until 1904 at the World's Fair in St. Louis that iced tea really took off. The Indian Tea Commissioner, Richard Blechynden, was offering hot tea to everyone, but popularity was low due to the intense heat. He and his team realized this and took the brewed India tea, filled several large bottles and placed them on stands upside down - thus allowing the tea to flow through iced pipes. And the rest is history!

With Sanny beginning the intro to the requested song, Halle could now turn his attention to his guests. "Would you like something to drink?" he asked looking at Bürgermeister Ackermann and Gerta. They sure looked *schick* tonight, the German equivalent of 'spiffy.' All dressed up in their lederhosen. Kind of a cute couple Halle had to admit to himself. Poor Frau Ackermann! "So, Bürgermeister Ackermann you wanted to talk to us about something?" Halle said in a strong whisper.

"We'll have what you're having, Conrad," Ackermann whispered, giving Gerta a glance that Halle could only interpret as flirting. The waiter was watching his boss and was at his side momentarily.

"Here you go, sir," the waiter returned with two bottles of Mineralwasser Mineral Water. "I hope your guests *enjoy* it, ...*sir!*" the waiter said, his sarcasm now clearly out in the open.

"What's your name, son?" Halle asked, looking up at the insolent waiter.

"Conrad. My name is Conrad." The tall young blond waiter replied crossly.

"Why, that's my name too!" Halle said with surprise.

"Right! I know! My *full* name is Conrad Halle III, as in your *grandson!*" the waiter snapped.

Conrad Halle looked up in surprise, adjusting his monocle. "Ah, Three, I *do* need to have this thing checked at Mercede's Lens tomorrow," he sputtered, looking at his monocle, somewhat embarrassed that he hadn't recognized his grandson. "Carry on, Three. You're doing a fine job."

With the drinks in order, they could now get down to the business of the night.

Noon river wider than a nile

I'n crossin' you in style soneday

Old drean naker, you heartbreaker

Wherever you're goin', I'n goin' your way...

Halle's brain caught up with what was going on up on the little stage of *WonderBar.* Had Halle just had a TIA? What was coming out of Sanny's mouth? With his mouth agape, Halle turned his attention to the glittering singer behind the red piano. Surely, he wasn't singing what Halle was hearing! Then, looking around the room, the expressions of the other occupants of *WonderBar* verified that something was amiss. When Sanny finished the song there was a polite but awkward smattering of applause, the loudest coming from the disheveled man by the *WonderBar* entrance.

"Is this a comedy act, Conrad?" Bürgermeister Ackermann asked in all seriousness, taking a sip of his Mineralwasser Mineral Water. Gerta was too busy making goo goo eyes at Ackermann to notice anything else.

"Certainly not," Halle snapped. "Take five!" he called out to Sanny.

"Great! Thanks!" Sanny waved at the 'crowd' unaware that getting a 'take five' after one song was *not* a good thing.

"He seems to have trouble pronouncing his M's," Gerta observed with a nonchalant attitude, finally taking her eyes off Bürgermeister Ackermann for a second to have a sip of Mineralwasser Mineral Water.

"Indeed," Halle acknowledged her observation. "Something's amiss, but I'll have to deal with that later. "Bürgermeister Ackermann, you wanted to meet tonight?" Halle asked, turning his attention to the business at hand. So, what did you want to talk about?"

"Yes. Yes," Ackermann adjusted himself in the clear plastic *WonderBar* chair. "I had an encounter with our dear Waldemar Ulff yesterday and it got me thinking of the future of Neu Deutschland..."

"How so?" Halle questioned, making eye contact with the Three. A signal to bring another bottle of Mineralwasser Mineral Water.

"Waldemar is having attendance problems at Ostrichland, much like we're experiencing here in Neu Deutschland. During our conversation he mentioned that they are going to be doing a live Internet show from Ostrichland next month and that he would mention Neu Deutschland during the show."

"That's nice of him, but hardly something to change our fortunes," Halle observed, taking his new bottle of Mineralwasser Mineral Water in his right hand. Halle noticed a large man in a *very* white suit entering *WonderBar* followed by two short people, a man and woman in identical business suits. He sat at the second table from the entrance, the table next to the disheveled loner while the two short people stood near the entrance/exit of *WonderBar*.

"That's not all!" Bürgermeister Ackermann continued, "As I was leaving Ostrichland, Waldemar mentioned that people are always calling for a **WOW** reunion."

"Yes?" Halle replied, turning his attention back to Bürgermeister Ackermann, not getting his point, if there was one to get.

"A mention of Neu Deutschland on an Internet show is a nice thing," Bürgermeister Ackermann explained, "but a *reunion* of **WOW** is a *huge* thing!"

"Yes?"

"And if Neu Deutschland was involved in the reunion, it would be a very *smart* thing," Ackermann said with a twinkle in his right eye.

"Oh, you are *so* smart!" Gerta gushed to Bürgermeister Ackermann, grasping his right arm with her right hand.

"What would be *our* involvement?" Halle wondered out loud.

"Well," Ackermann began, savoring the attention as he was to announce his scheme. "Waldemar is an accomplished man, no doubt: talented, rich and famous. A big part of his popularity has been his relationship with his fans as an upfront, honest person, no angel, but someone you can trust to be authentic," Bürgermeister Ackermann observed with a smirk on his lips, turning his gaze to Gerta. "What would happen if Waldemar became involved in some sort of seamy scandal, for instance? Don't you think he would do anything in his power to keep his hard-fought image rather than having a sullied persona? I think Waldemar could use a new friend from Neu Deutschland, don't you?"

"I'm afraid I'm not following you, Bürgermeister," Halle admitted with a touch of annoyance. "What does having a new friend from Neu Deutschland have to do with anything, much less a **WOW** reunion?"

"Let's say that Waldemar was accused of... well, let's say... sexual improprieties, shall we? Misbehaving with a nubile maiden such as Gerta Switzer. Would it be a stretch of the imagination that given the choice between public exposure or a **WOW** reunion that he wouldn't choose the latter?" Bürgermeister Ackermann asked with a wicked chortle.

"Are you suggesting we introduce Waldemar to Gerta? Have him suggest or do something salacious and then blackmail him into having a **WOW** reunion or the impropriety gets exposed to the public?" Halle asked, somewhat taken aback.

Gerta's jaw dropped, but she promptly put it back in place with her right hand. If Bürgermeister Ackermann thought of this plan, it must be brilliant on second thought, she thought.

"Exactly," Bürgermeister Ackermann affirmed, staring at Halle and Gerta with his piercing beady porcine eyes. "I can only assume that anyone who values their public image would not permit that image to be sullied, am I not correct? After all, all I am suggesting is we need a more robust relationship between Neu Deutschland and Ostrichland and a desirable female never hurts."

"Or Gerta Switzer," Conrad Halle observed acidly.

"Or Gerta Switzer indeed!" Bürgermeister Ackermann replied, a big smile on his ruddy face as he turned his beady blues on Gerta. Gerta gave a somewhat nervous smile in return, but no objections.

"How do you know that this would all lead to a **WOW** reunion?" Halle questioned Bürgermeister Ackermann. "You don't know that!"

"Of course not," Bürgermeister Ackermann admitted. "I do know that Ostrichland has been chosen as the site for a popular music show. I'm assuming that it would also be a possible site for a reunion. Who knows? We don't have the luxury of not trying this scheme, my friends, because time is wasting, and we are going down the drain. We have to try even if it doesn't succeed, *ja*?"

"I think, with all due respect Bürgermeister Ackermann, that it is a crazy idea that has little chance of working. And if it *did* work, how do we know it would do any good for Neu Deutschland?" Halle asked, frustration showing on his somewhat skeletal face.

"I think we can mull this plan over tonight and continue our discussion tomorrow evening, *ja*?" Bürgermeister Ackermann said as he rose from his chair, a chair that was getting a rather tight grip on his nether-regions as the nether-regions either expanded during their discussion or the clear plastic chair had contracted.

The trio started to make their way to the *WonderBar* entrance/exit. As they passed the second table to the entrance/exit, the large man in the white suit looked up, standing, he blocked their way out of *WonderBar*. Halle noticed Sanny squeak by the large barrier of a man and make his way back to the piano. The large man held out his right hand to Halle.

"I'm looking for the main man in town, the man in charge and I think I've found him," he said, shaking Conrad Halle's right hand. "My name is Les Winns and I want to talk to you Mr. Mayor."

"Excuse me, *I'm* the mayor -- *Bürgermeister*, as we say in our mother tongue," an offended Ackermann corrected Winns, extending his right hand to correct the misguided handshake.

"My apologies," Winns continued smoothly, his Flunkies walking over to his side.

"These are my colleagues, Conrad Halle, the owner of this establishment and Gerta Switzer, the owner of Mein Hair and a prominent citizen of Neu Deutschland," Bürgermeister Ackermann introduced his puzzled cohorts. "And how may we assist you?"

"I'm here to buy Neu Deutschland," Winns announced grandly as the trio's jaws dropped simultaneously. Bürgermeister Ackermann looked at Conrad Halle, Gerta Switzer looked at Bürgermeister Ackermann, Conrad Halle looked at Gerta Switzer, all in shock.

In the background:
Nidnight at the oasis
Send your canel to bed
Shadows painting our faces
Traces of ronance in our heads
Heaven's holding a half-noon...
Thank you! You're narvelous!"

House Call...

"Your feet are *so* cute!"

"No, they're not."

"Yes, they are!"

"No, they're not."

"Yes, they are!"

"No, they're not."

"Yes, they are!"

"No, they're not."

"Yes, they are!"

"No, they're not."

"Yes, they are!"

"No, they're not."

"Yes, they are!"

"No, they're not."

"Yes, they are!"

"No, they're not."

"Yes, they are!

A right hand knocked over an empty bottle of Roo Energy Drink from the side table on the right side of the bed, occupied by two people this morning.

"Those toes are *so* perfect!"

"No, they're not."

"Yes, they are!"

"No, they're not."

"Yes, they are!"

"No, they're not."
"Yes, they are!"
"Yes, they are!"
"No, they're not!"
"Yes, they are!"
"No, they're not!"
"Yes, they are!"
"No, they're not!"
"No, they're not."
"Yes, they are!"
"No, they're not."
"Yes, they are!"
"No, they're not."
"Yes, they are!"
"Yes, they are!"
"No, they're not!"
"Yes, they are!"
"No, they're not!"
"Yes, they are!"
"No, they're not!"

The exchange ended with laughter.

"What am I? One of your patients?" Waldemar asked with a smile, pushing his head back into the pillow as he buried his bare feet in the thick blue blanket. He turned to his companion.

"If you were one of my patients, I wouldn't be in bed with you, that's for sure," the beautiful brunette next to Waldemar giggled. Waldemar moved in for a kiss. She gladly accepted.

"You're the best, Dustie." Waldemar whispered into the ear of Dr. Dustie Rhodes, Ostrichland's official veterinarian. Waldemar pushed the blanket and sheets back exposing his nude body to the morning chill of the Sky House. He bent down to pick up the bottle of Roo Energy Drink.

"Ah, nice view!" Dustie remarked as she pulled the sheets closer to her neck.

"That's what they all say!" Waldemar laughed, pulling his hair back, banding his ponytail and strutting to the shower.

"I'm going to make some coffee," Dustie called from the bed as Waldemar turned on the shower.

"Make sure you use the Ethiopian blend, Dustie!" he called back.

Dustie grabbed her beige robe from Waldemar's walk-in closet and slowly made her way to the kitchenette located in the sitting room, part of the Sky House master suite. The sun was bright, flooding the sitting room with a warmth that was most welcome.

Tap, tap, tap. The sound was coming from outside The Egg. Dustie pulled the sheer curtain back to see Lanky downstairs looking for his morning treat. "Good morning, Lanky," she said with a smile, knowing Lanky couldn't hear the greeting from on high. She had helped with Lanky's hatching. They were old friends.

Several minutes later Waldemar entered the sitting room wrapped in a bath towel around his waist, adjusting his round-lens glasses. "Is that Lanky?" Waldemar asked, looking to see if the coffee was ready. "Hey, friend!" he called.

"Here you go, Waldemar," Dustie said as she moved over to the small round table in the curved corner of the sitting room, two cups of Ethiopian blend coffee in her hands. Waldemar and Dustie blew on their respective coffee mugs until the temperature of the coffee was tolerable. Waldemar was staring wistfully at Dustie. The people in Waldemar's life would be very surprised to learn of his relationship with her. At a youthful thirty-six years old, Dustie had been the official Ostrichland veterinarian for eleven years now. Starting as an assistant to Dr. Viola Shivoli, Dustie took over the practice when Dr. Shivoli retired. It was a smooth transition and a welcome one to Waldemar.

"What are you thinking about, Waldemar?" Dustie asked after her first sip of Ethiopian blend coffee.

"Thinking about our first night," Waldemar replied with a wry smile.

"Really?" Dustie asked, going back to that magical evening in her mind.

FLASHBACK:

It had been a long day eight years ago when Dustie was giving vitamins to all the ostriches at Ostrichland. Well into the evening after Ostrichland had closed, she finally completed her task. She was walking past The Egg, newly constructed, on her way to her 2003 Dodge Durango SLT when she happened upon Waldemar at the Sunset Bench. In some ways it seemed like yesterday...

"Hey, Waldemar, I'm all done with the flock," Dustie called out, spotting Waldemar sitting on the bench in the twilight, smoking something.

"Oh, great, Dustie." Waldemar replied dreamily. "Have a seat," he said, motioning for Dustie to sit down on the right side of the bench.

"Thanks, but I've got to get home and feed my cat."

"Ah, come on," he smiled. "Just five minutes?"

"Oh, sure, Waldemar," she agreed, sitting down, blowing away some smoke with her right hand. "I didn't know you smoked."

"I don't smoke tobacco," Waldemar laughed. "Want some? It's homegrown!" he said with a note of pride.

"Well, I don't usually..."

"Ah, no judging here, Doc," Waldemar laughed, handing the joint to Dustie. "Here you go. The stars are so beautiful tonight!"

"Yes, they are," Dustie agreed, coughing on her inhale. After several minutes of silence, she asked out of the blue, "Do you miss the fame, Waldemar?"

"That's a serious question," Waldemar observed, sitting straighter on the bench.

"Do you miss her?" Dustie got right to the point.

"Of course, I do," Waldemar admitted. He turned to her. "My life then was one of excess: lots of fame, money, drugs, women, experiences. Everything was intense and magnified like several lifetimes into one period. You must have tunnel vision in a sense to survive. If you look around too much, you'll see how high you're flying and crash. Like Icarus. She was my anchor. My rock. My everything. Now, I think I miss the notion of her, not her as a person. I've gotten over that. Maybe..."

"That must be a difficult experience to live like that with just about everyone in the world knowing everything you are doing, your whole life open for the public to consume," Dustie remarked.

"And consume they do!" Waldemar replied, taking another hit of the joint. "Nothing's private. It's even worse these days! I don't know how someone could be as famous as we were these days. It must be all-consuming." With that, Waldemar reached over, took his right hand gently around Dustie's neck and moved in for a kiss. It was natural and unplanned.

The relationship grew from a friendship to one of 'friends with benefits' as was the custom of those days. Both Waldemar and Dustie seemed content to keep things at a certain point. It worked for them.

END OF FLASHBACK

"Dustie?" Waldemar whispered. "Earth to Dustie."

"Oh, sorry," Dustie apologized, realizing that she was at the end of her flashback. "I was just thinking."

"You make it look so painless," Waldemar laughed, taking his last gulp of Ethiopian-blend coffee and getting up from the table. "I've got a family educational event to run," he chuckled, trotting off to the bedroom.

"I've got to go too," Dustie called after him. "There's a sick horse at the Liska Ranch."

"Okay. Have a good day, Love," Waldemar returned fully dressed and gave Dustie a kiss on the cheek.

"You too, Waldemar," she replied, heading to the bedroom to don her safari-themed uniform complete with pith helmet for her house call at the Liska Ranch.

They both exited The Egg together, each heading to fill their own agenda for the day. Waldemar walked along, joined now with Lanky seeking an ostrich treat, to unlock the gate to Ostrichland. By the time the gate was opened Dustie was in her Range Rover Sport. She exited Ostrichland, heading down Highway 277 towards the ocean and the Liska Ranch.

Waldemar watched until her vehicle was out of sight around a bend. Were they merely 'friends with benefits' he wondered.

Waldemar handed Lanky an ostrich treat before entering The Egg to check the answering machine in the administrative office. Waldemar unlocked and entered his office.

"Good morning, Waldemar," Agatha greeted him from her sleek pyramid on Waldemar's desk.

"Good morning, Agatha," Waldemar responded in an upbeat tone of voice, being used to his AI friend and colleague. "How are you this morning?"

"I'm fine," Agatha replied. "It sounds like you got laid last night."

Waldemar chuckled. "That's highly inappropriate of you, highly speculative and totally accurate! You know me too well, Agatha."

"I thought so, you dog!" Agatha responded. "You have a voicemail from yesterday afternoon."

The voicemail light was blinking red on the telephone. With a push of the voicemail button, Waldemar listened to the missed call:

"Hello. I'm calling for Waldemar Ulff. I have something *very* important to tell you. I can't talk over the phone. I need to see you in person. My name is Gerta Switzer. Call me at 555-0415 as soon as you can."

Waldemar saved the message. He was stroking his mustache in thought. Gerta Switzer. He knew the name but couldn't place it. He would call her back when he had the time. As he was heading out the administrative office Waldemar heard a loud knock on the entrance hatch of The Egg.

Waldemar walked down the stairs, foregoing the elevators, and over to the hatch, wondering why they didn't just come in. The hatch was unlocked. "Hello," he said, looking at the nervous-looking woman before him.

"Hello, um, Waldemar. My name is Gerta Switzer."

Sold...!

Bürgermeister Ackermann, Conrad Halle, Les Winns and his two Flunkies were seated at the elegant table in the dining room of the Kaiser Wilhelm II Suite of Halle Haus.

"Gentlemen, I would like to introduce my two associates, Edwin and Edwina Flunkie," Les Winns introduced. "As you can see, they're twins!" Edwin and Edwina, dressed in matching tweed business suits looked up momentarily from their Apple MacBook Pros long enough to cast wary eyes at Bürgermeister Ackermann and Conrad Halle, immediately returning the gaze from their green eyes on their pasty faces back to the MacBook Pro screens.

Winns had rented the impressive suite that day for seven days. That was enough to make Halle happy. Now, the prospect of Winns *buying* Neu Deutschland was an offer no one saw coming!

"I apologize for Gerta's absence today. Halle said "She had a pressing appointment that couldn't be rescheduled. Would you gentlemen like a glass of Schonauer Apfel Schnapps[7]?" he asked, the tall young blond waiter, Conrad Halle III, walking over to the kitchen of the Kaiser Wilhelm II Suite.

"That sounds great," Bürgermeister Ackermann replied, staring at Winns as he was shuffling through some papers, he pulled out of his attaché old school style.

---

[7] Schonauer Apfel schnapps is made from German grain alcohol mixed with apple juice. They say it became popular in the 1970s among German university students as the Apfelkom cocktail.

"I'm in on the drink," Winns said, squinting at a paper in hand. "I feel I can deal with you gentlemen without Miss Switzer just fine," Winns smiled, a bit of a smirk in the smile. "It will probably work out to your advantage in the long run."

Three walked over to the table with a tray consisting of three drinks.

"So, Mr. Winns, please enlighten us as to your interest in purchasing Neu Deutschland," Ackermann began, looking at Winns with his suspicious beady eyes.

"As of a few days ago I was interested in land for a real estate development I'm planning, however, due to complications, the land I had in mind was not available. I came across Neu Deutschland the other day. It occurred to me that Neu Deutschland is the *perfect* place for my needs. The town is set up as a corporation, is established, the buildings are in place, the architectural style is appropriate to my philosophy, it is the complete package," Winns explained, folding his arms across his chest, looking at Ackermann and Halle.

"What do you plan to do with Neu Deutschland?" Ackermann asked with apprehension, taking a gulp of Schonauer Apfel Schnapps.

Winns unfolded his arms and pressed into the edge of the table. "I plan to make Neu Deutschland the safest town in the world. The specter of FOE will have no place to flourish in *this* town. The residents will be secure in their knowledge that the function, purpose and philosophy of Neu Deutschland will be to promote freedom without the blight of FOE. No ifs, ands, or buts."

Bürgermeister Ackermann looked at Halle as each took a gulp of Schonauer Apfel Schnapps.

Winns continued, now in Yacktivist mode: "My clients are people of accomplishment, people of means, people who matter. They want to relocate to a locale that is fitting for their lifestyle, secure in the knowledge that FOE riff raff will have no place in their environment. They will pay any price to know that their need for security and privacy is of utmost importance." Winns finished off his glass of Schonauer Apfel Schnapps and set it on the highly polished tabled.

"Buying a town is quite a proposition, Mr. Winns," Bürgermeister Ackermann stated the obvious, looking at Halle for approval of his statement.

"Indeed, it is, gentlemen," Winns agreed, reaching into the right inside pocket of his suit coat, pulling out his checkbook. "Gentlemen, I'm prepared to write a check for $30,000,012.54 right now with a bonus of 10% to be split among you gentlemen for facilitating the sale of the town in an expeditious manner."

Bürgermeister Ackermann looked at Conrad Halle. Conrad Halle looked at Les Winns. Les Winns looked at Bürgermeister Ackermann.

"*SOLD!*" Bürgermeister Ackermann and Conrad Halle blurted out simultaneously.

Loose Lips...

Waldemar escorted Gerta Switzer into the administrative office. "Have a seat," he said, gesturing to the blue couch next to his desk. "Would you like something to drink?" he asked.

"Um... *ja...* that would be great," Gerta said nervously, obviously starstruck as she looked around the large curved room with wide eyes.

Waldemar thought Gerta could use more than a Roo Energy Drink at this point. "How about a Green Moon[8]?"

"That sounds good," Gerta replied.

Waldemar returned from his mini fridge with two Green Moons. He handed Gerta one with his right hand and joined her on the blue couch, keeping enough distance to maintain personal space.

"Thank you," Gerta said, taking a large gulp from the bottle. "It is very refreshing."

Waldemar studied the nervous woman next to him. Beefy features, as was said in the olden days, with a touch of scouse brow. She *did* look cute in her lederhosen. Her blonde hair was done in the braided halo style which complimented her round clear face.

"How can I help you... Miss... Miss Swisher?" Waldemar asked.

---

[8]Green Moon Brewing Company, established in 1948 in Sarajevo in then Yugoslavia turned out to be popular with the local citizens, eventually becoming well-known throughout the Balkan Peninsula. Following the breakup of Bosnia and Herzegovina from Yugoslavia in 1992, Green Moon became the go-to beverage for the chic set.

"Switzer. Gerta Switzer. I own **Mein Hair** in New Deutschland," Gerta replied, looking at Waldemar and going back to her younger days when she was a huge **WOW** fan. It was unbelievable that she was sitting next to and talking to Waldemar Ulff! "I have all your albums!" she gushed, her voice sounding like a shy teenage girl once again.

"Thanks," Waldemar replied, taking a swig of his Green Moon. "So, you wanted to see me about...?"

"Is it hot in here?" Gerta asked, a small bead of perspiration mingling with several blond facial hairs on her upper lip region. As she asked the question, Gerta carefully pushed the 'on' button of the voice recorder app on her smartphone in the side pocket of her tan vinyl purse.

"I'm okay temperature-wise," Waldemar replied. "I can have the temperature lowered if you're uncomfortable."

"No. No. It's just me," Gerta answered, beginning to tug on the right strap of her lederhosen, a move carefully rehearsed several hours prior. "I think my outfit is too tight."

"Here, let me get you a colder drink," Waldemar said as he rose quickly from the blue couch, made his way to the mini fridge and returned with two bottles of Roo Energy Drink, one for Gerta and one for him. "This won't relax you, but you will feel like a new woman!" Waldemar said, handing Gerta the frosty bottle with his right hand as he sat down again on the blue couch.

"So, I'll feel like a new woman after this experience?" Gerta picked up on Waldemar's statement, repeating it as she moved her head closer to her purse where her smartphone was, hopefully, capturing every word.

"You will!" Waldemar replied oblivious to the chicanery happening in his own administrative office. "I've had many people tell me their energy level skyrockets after a few gulps of that magic drink!"

"Oh! Waldemar!" Gerta cooed, moving her purse as close as possible to her right thigh. "I'll bet you say that to all the girls!"

"And guys too!" Waldemar added, taking a swig of Roo Energy Drink. "I encourage women *and* men to give it a try. You never know how a new experience will affect you until you try it at least once."

"Yes. That is *so* true," Gerta said, continuing to tug at the right strap of her outfit, hoping it would unbutton as it did during her rehearsal.

"Oops! I got some on my lap!" Waldemar squirmed on the blue couch, not being careful enough as to the angle of his Roo Energy Drink bottle being held in his right hand.

"Here, let me hold it," Gerta ventured, reaching for Waldemar's offending Roo Energy Drink bottle. "There you go. Such skill!" she remarked as Waldemar dried the spilled drink with a handy napkin from the coffee table in front of the blue couch.

"Oh my! Oh! Oh!" Gerta squealed as the right strap of her outfit finally unbuttoned, exposing nothing. She gave a half-hearted attempt at buttoning the offending strap.

"Here. Let me try and get it back in the hole," Waldemar ventured. "Um... it's a tight fit..."

"Oh, Waldemar... I... um... I can't continue this charade!" Gerta blurted out, her right hand covering her quivering mouth, a tear running down her right cheek.

"What charade?" Waldemar asked in alarm.

Gerta was turning out to not be the smooth criminal that Bürgermeister Ackermann and Halle had expected. She was going to spill the beans even before they were in the pot!

"I was supposed to... oh, I can't tell you ...um..."

"Tell me what?" Waldemar asked, sitting upright on the blue couch.

"They wanted me to... to... seduce you," Gerta blurted out, biting her lower lip until it turned white.

"Seduce me?" Waldemar questioned, unable to hide an ironic smile. "Who? Why?"

"Bürgermeister Ackermann and Conrad Halle... oh no..." Gerta quickly cast the blame. "They wanted me to get to know you so we could use your natural urges against your best interest! They want a **WOW** reunion."

"A **WOW** reunion!?" Waldemar couldn't believe what he was hearing. "Why a **WOW** reunion?"

Gerta was crying now. Waldemar handed her a tissue from a tissue box on the walnut coffee table in front of the blue couch.

"Thank you," Gerta thanked him as she took the tissue with her right hand. "They want a **WOW** reunion to get some attention for Neu Deutschland. We're going down the drain!"

After some moments of awkward silence, Waldemar responded, "You can go back and tell Bürgermeister Ackermann and Conrad Halle that there *will* be a **WOW** reunion!" Waldemar declared, quickly strategizing on how to handle *this* development.

"There will be!" Gerta exclaimed, clearly not understanding the concept of 'bad intel.'"

"Sure," Waldemar assured her, finding Gerta's intellectual challenge an advantage at this point in the game. "Tell them that it's in two weeks. It will be broadcast worldwide and will bring untold attention to Neu Deutschland in the process!"

"Waldemar, that's *wonderful!*" Gerta gushed with excitement, jumping to her feet and giving Waldemar a spontaneous peck on the cheek. "Oh, excuse my forwardness, Waldemar!" she demurred, covering her mouth with her right hand.

"No problem," Waldemar assured her, surprised that it felt like he was even blushing just the slightest bit.

"I'm sorry, Waldemar, but I must go immediately and tell my colleagues the great news!" Gerta collected herself and headed out the door of the administrative office and down the stairs, foregoing the awaiting public elevator.

Waldemar followed her the short distance to the hatch of The Egg. As she flung the hatch open and quickly boarded her red 2014 Volkswagen New Beetle, Waldemar, now joined by Lanky, saw a Summit White GMC Savana Cargo Van rounding the corner and turning into the Ostrichland entrance. Gerta Switzer's Beetle squeaked by as the van entered. On the side of the van in bright red letters was Intertoobz.

Intertoobz? Li'l Otter's company!

Under New Management...

Das Rathaus (City Hall) was abuzz with activity when Gerta Switzer breathlessly entered the building around lunchtime. She made her way as quickly as possible to the main conference room to the right of the imposing entrance lobby. She mopped her brow upon entering the room. At the large conference table were Bürgermeister Ackermann, Conrad Halle, Les Winns and his Flunkie twins Edwin and Edwina, their eyes staring intently at their Apple MacBook Pros.

"Ah, Gerta!" Bürgermeister Ackermann acknowledged the new arrival to the conference room. "How did things go?" he asked with little enthusiasm. Gerta made her way over to him.

"Bürgermeister Ackermann, I must talk to you in private, right now!" she whispered in his right ear.

"I'm a bit busy right now," he stated the obvious, papers scattered about his area of the large table. Halle was reading several papers seemingly at once.

"Miss Switzer, would you like a drink?" Winns asked, rubbing his right eye after signing some papers. "We missed you." Then, noticing Gerta looking at the two strangers at the table, Winns made the introductions. "Miss Switzer, I would like to introduce you to my associates, Edwin and Edwina Flunkie. They're twins!" he said, waving his right hand in the Flunkie's direction. Both Edwin and Edwina Flunkie looked up momentarily from their Apple MacBook Pros and blinked at Gerta as a greeting.

"Pleased to meet you... two," Gerta stammered, not knowing *what* was going on. "They look *extremely* busy!" she observed.

"They are Miss Switzer," Winns agreed. "They have a lot of work to do. It's not every day that I *buy a town* after all!"

Gerta smiled, then Winns' words hit her. "Buy a town? What are you talking about?" she looked up at Winns for an explanation. No one else at the table was paying any attention.

"I am the new owner of Neu Deutschland!" Winns announced proudly.

"Since *when!*" Gerta asked, her voice rising as her face turned a brighter shade of red.

"Since this morning when Bürgermeister Ackermann and Mr. Halle sold Neu Deutschland to me for $30,000,012.54," he explained proudly.

"*Oh, mein Gott!*" Gerta blurted out in the mother tongue. "I can't believe this!"

"Bürgermeister Ackermann and Mr. Halle are receiving checks of $1,500,000.63 each for their fine work in brokering the deal in a timely manner," Winns added, just to 'stir the pot' knowing that Gerta was cut out of the deal by her absence.

"None of you are getting away with this travesty!" Gerta shouted to the occupants of the room. "You've made a foolish decision and will live to regret it!" she declared, stomping out of the room as the others paid scant attention to the disgruntled citizen of Neu Deutschland. "Don't be so quick to spend your money!" she turned around for one last tongue-lashing.

Gerta made her way from the main conference room to a smaller private office off the lobby. "First, they want me to use my feminine wiles as a spy, then they sell the town out from under everyone?!" she muttered to no one in particular as she loudly closed the office door.

Gerta spotted an unopened bottle of Bionade[9] elderberry flavor on the right edge of the small oak desk in the corner of the room. "Ah, just what I need!" she proclaimed out loud with relief.

Gerta sat down at the small oak desk and had a few sips of the Bionade. She was starting to breathe again. Her cheeks were now pink rather than bright red. Her world was spinning with the events of the day!

The old black telephone on the desk was calling to Gerta. She took several more swallows of the Bionade, put the bottle on the desk and picked up the telephone receiver.

"Hello, Waldemar? This is Gerta Switzer. I need to talk to you right away."

---

[9] In 1960 brewer Dieter Leipold had the idea to brew a natural soft drink for children. Like beer, but without alcohol and with significantly less sugar. Brewed in Bavaria, Bionade is a popular drink throughout Europe.

Dance Bird, Dance...!

"Treat! Treat! Get your treat," the short woman in a pastel blue lab coat held an ostrich treat in her upraised right hand as a female ostrich, Ophelia by name, Lanky's spouse, gently pecked it from her palm. "Good girl, Ophelia!"

Waldemar, Dr. Dustie Rhodes and Shrimp Wrigley applauded lightly. The quartet was gathered in the Ostrich Habitat of The Egg giving the especially bright Ophelia her weekly training session with Dr. Passion Tudor, the Australian-born applied animal behaviorist contracted by Waldemar to train the flock to the limits of ostrich intelligence or lack thereof. Lanky had been the first student of Dr. Tudor, having learned all the basic behaviors in addition to several very special ones such as pecking human heads when given hand instructions by a human -- Lanky's special trick. For an average ostrich, coming on command and waiting for their food were triumphs of the intellect.

Waldemar was always strict in keeping the dignity of his flock intact. Riding, racing and performing by the flock was strictly off-limits. However, Waldemar was always interested in seeing his flock 'stretch' and expand their minds and strengthen their abilities. Waldemar met Dr. Tudor at a small convention of exotic animal exhibitors several years after purchasing Ostrichland. Dustie and Dr. Tudor were friends from college, so it was like family working with chosen members of the flock. The only one not on board with the enrichment program was Shrimp Wrigley. Shrimp Wrigley always proclaimed the intellect of the ostrich as 'riding the light side of the horse' whatever *that* meant.

"Dustie, will you bring the keyboard over here?" Dr. Tudor asked as she scooped more ostrich treats into a large pocket on the right side of her lab coat.

"For crying out loud! Are you going to try *that* trick again?" Shrimp Wrigley asked in disgust, turning 180° to express his disgust.

"Here you go, Passion," Dustie handed Dr. Tudor a white Child's World Kids Piano. Dr. Tudor set the sound to 'guitar,' the tempo to 'bossa nova,' lined each key of the keyboard with an ostrich treat and gently set the instrument down in front of the patiently waiting Ophelia. Dr. Tudor slowly stepped back.

With one fell swoop, Ophelia brought her head down to the ground and with one mighty peck destroyed the piano. She then plucked the ostrich treats off the shards of plastic until they were all consumed.

"Oops!" Dr. Tudor proclaimed.

"Well, there's $30 we'll never see again!" Shrimp Wrigley stepped back even further from the scene in continued disgust. "Just one failure out of many!"

Waldemar and Dustie remained silent, watching Dr. Tudor for a clue as to her disposition following the display of aggressive action on the part of Ophelia.

"It's lucky I bought a dozen pianos this morning at the Toy Barn going-out-of-business sale!" Dr. Tudor proclaimed, walking over to her very large bag situated on the ground near the entrance to the Ostrich Habitat. "Let's try that one again!"

Dr. Tudor went through the procedure once again, placing the second keyboard in front of Ophelia. And, like the first attempt, the second attempt ended in keyboard destruction and ostrich treat consumption.

"I just can't watch this anymore!" Shrimp Wrigley said, turning away, once again, from the scene of mass keyboard demolition.

"Third time's a charm, Waldemar!" Dr. Tudor said, returning to her very large bag with another piano.

And, indeed, the third time *was* a charm in this case! On the third attempt, Ophelia gently placed her head near the ground, parted her beak, tapped several keys, taking an ostrich treat from each key, one by one. The result was an avant-garde version of Carl Orff's 'O Fortuna.'

"Bravo!" Waldemar proclaimed as all, save Shrimp Wrigley, offered a 'noise aware' applause for the latest advance in ostrich behavior enhancement.

"Well done!" Dustie said with encouragement.

"I could have taught her that myself for half the price!" Shrimp Wrigley muttered bitterly. "And two less keyboards in the trash heap!"

"Ah, Shrimp Wrigley, if I didn't know you better, I'd say you were jealous," Waldemar teased, lightly stroking Ophelia's neck with his right hand.

"Couldn't be further from the truth, Waldemar," Shrimp Wrigley answered, walking closer to the others. "I've been around ostriches most of my life and I know that they don't have the brains that God gave a turkey. That was just a coincidence that we heard any kind of song on the piano thingy."

"Really?" Waldemar asked, secretly enjoying it when Shrimp Wrigley got riled up.

"Yes, really, Waldemar," Shrimp Wrigley shot back. "And I'll just show you! I'll get that bird to do a trick right now!"

"But didn't you just say that ostriches are stupid?" Dr. Tudor questioned.

"I am going to demonstrate that you can get them to do anything based on their love of ostrich treats. Smarts has nothing to do with it!" Shrimp Wrigley stated, clearing keyboard debris out of his way with his right foot.

"Okay, Shrimp Wrigley, show us what you can do," Waldemar challenged him.

Shrimp Wrigley picked up a handful of ostrich treats from a large box near the curved wall of the Ostrich Habitat, walked over to Ophelia and stared her straight in her large eyes.

"Now you listen up, young lady," Shrimp Wrigley said, holding out several ostrich treats with the fingertips of his right hand (a dangerous move). "I'm going to show my friends here that an ostrich *can* learn without all the fancy lab coats and consultant fees. Right?" He placed the remaining ostrich treats in the right-hand pocket of his jeans, then pulled out his LG Smartphone and opened his Nile Music app. Within seconds, Gershon Kingsley's 1969 novelty hit, 'Popcorn' was emanating from the smartphone.

"Dance, Ophelia, dance!" Shrimp Wrigley urged, waving his right hand as if more ostrich treats were contained wherein.

"I don't see Ophelia doing anything, Shrimp Wrigley!" Dr. Tudor teased.

"Hold on!" Shrimp Wrigley snapped, turning up the volume. Ophelia took several steps to get closer to Shrimp Wrigley's right hand. "Look! There! There she goes!" Shrimp Wrigley exclaimed in excitement.

"No way, Shrimp Wrigley," Waldemar replied, a wide smile making its way across his face.

"Yes, way!" Shrimp Wrigley replied in schoolboy style. "Just you watch!" Shrimp Wrigley took several steps back, Ophelia replied in kind. "There she goes!"

"Shrimp Wrigley, she's *not* dancing!" Dustie called out. Waldemar, Dustie and Dr. Tudor were now openly laughing at the spectacle before them: the obviously not-dancing ostrich and the desperate man insisting she was.

"What's so funny!?" Shrimp Wrigley asked in annoyance, turning his head quickly to see his audience enveloped in laughter at his expense. "She's doing great!" In keeping her balance, Ophelia adjusted her legs slightly, still seeking the ostrich treats. "There! Now she's got it!"

"Come on Shrimp Wrigley! You've made your point. Or not made your point," Waldemar exclaimed, laughing between words. The doctors loved *that* line!

"Well, I can see that our efforts are not being appreciated, Ophelia," Shrimp Wrigley said to Ophelia as he closed the Nile Music app. "I trust I've made my point," Shrimp Wrigley huffed, stuffing his LG Smartphone into his right front pocket, amid a mix of ostrich treats.

"Just what *was* your point, Shrimp Wrigley?" Dr. Tudor chided.

"That ostriches will do *anything* for a treat, including dancing, and that having a doctor of all people charging to teach tricks is a waste of time and money!"

"Okay, Shrimp Wrigley, point taken," Waldemar conceded, hoping to keep Shrimp Wrigley from further insulting Dr. Tudor. "We appreciate all the effort Dr. Tudor and you have made toward having our flock reach their full potential. Doctor and doctor, would you like to join me in the Sky House for some tea?"

"That's an excellent idea!" both Dustie and Dr. Tudor agreed, turning to exit the Ostrich Habitat.

Shrimp Wrigley was still riled up, mostly because his 'demonstration' was a bust. He turned to exit the Ostrich Habitat also, however, in one swift move Ophelia decided to dive bomb Shrimp Wrigley's right jean pocket, knowing that a store of ostrich treats awaited her.

"Whoa!" Shrimp Wrigley jumped back like a champion matador, just in time to avoid Ophelia's hungry beak. With a twist and turn, Shrimp Wrigley further distanced himself from his hungry protege. As Shrimp Wrigley was turned with his back to Ophelia, Ophelia decided Shrimp Wrigley must have ostrich treats in his *back* pocket too. She took another lunge, grabbing the top of Shrimp Wrigley's back-right pocket in her large beak, lifting Shrimp Wrigley off the ground by the seat of his pants.

"Hey! Stop it! *Help!*" Shrimp Wrigley wailed as he felt himself rising from the ground in a strong, swift motion. "Put me down you dumb bird!" Shrimp Wrigley yelled, smacking Ophelia on the top of her head. Not a smart move! The noggin knocking really ticked off Ophelia, so she decided to swing Shrimp Wrigley around in circles several times before walking to one of the motion-sensing doors of the Ostrich Habitat. With a 'whoosh' the door opened and Ophelia and her 'catch' were outside of The Egg, Shrimp Wrigley continuing to howl at the ostrich. Waldemar, Dustie and Dr. Tudor were now sitting in the formal dining room of the Sky House unaware of the chaos going on several stories below them.

Eventually, Ophelia decided that Shrimp Wrigley made a lousy ostrich treat so she unceremoniously dropped him by a water hole in the main outdoor ostrich pen. When Shrimp Wrigley hit the deck the ostrich treats scattered from his back jeans pocket. Ophelia was more than happy to claim her prize. Score!

Shrimp Wrigley came out relatively unscathed, save for his pride which was sorely bruised. Lesson of the day: don't try and teach an ostrich to dance when she's hungry. Lesson well learned!

Let's Put On A Show...!

The passenger door of the Summit White GMC Savana Cargo Van swung open. A tall black man dressed in jeans, a sweatshirt with 'Intertoobz' emblazoned on the front and a backwards-facing baseball cap emerged.

"Li'l Otter!" Waldemar shouted with excitement, heading to the van, Lanky in tow. "What a surprise!" Waldemar said with a beaming smile as he hugged Lil'l Otter.

"Waldemar, it's *so great* to see you, Man," Li'l Otter replied, sharing Waldemar's tight embrace. After the hug, Li'l Otter took a step back upon seeing Lanky. "Yow, that's one big bird, Dude!" Li'l Otter exclaimed.

"Not to worry, Li'l Otter," Waldemar laughed. "Li'l Otter, meet my personal assistant here at Ostrichland, Lanky. Lanky, meet Li'l Otter, the legendary radio DJ and one of my few true showbiz friends." Lanky was more interested in whether Li'l Otter carried any ostrich treats in his jean pockets. He didn't.

Li'l Otter took a sweeping look around him as he removed his baseball cap and ran his right hand through his tightly cropped black hair, some gray showing at the temples. "So, this is Ostrichland, eh?"

"The one and only!" Waldemar replied, making a dramatic sweeping motion with his right arm to encompass the entirety of Ostrichland. "My pride and joy!"

"Well, I've got to say, I'm already impressed, Waldemar," Li'l Otter remarked. "This is truly a beautiful setting for a... um... unique venue," Li'l Otter emphasized his 'Radio Voice' for a touch of jocularity in the moment.

As Waldemar and Li'l Otter were talking, the driver of the Cargo Van opened the door and walked over to the trio. "Waldemar, meet Shenandoah River, the producer of *Feeling the Music*. He's called 'Shen' for short."

"Glad to meet you, Shen," Waldemar reached to shake hands with the tall, dark-complected man with the big grin.

"Waldemar, I should mention that Shen is a huge **WOW** fan," Li'l Otter remarked as he looked over at Shen to see how he was reacting to being in the presence of one of his all-time musical idols.

"Huge!" Shen verified enthusiastically.

"Well, thank you, Shen," Waldemar replied with his typical humility. "So what are you guys doing here?" Waldemar queried, softly rubbing Lanky's long neck with the tips of the fingers of his right hand. Lanky liked that.

"Yeah, sorry about the unannounced drop in, Waldemar," Li'l Otter apologized. "I wasn't expecting to be here right now myself. Long story short, I was in L.A. on some business and Intertoobz management decided this would be a good time to give me a few days of R&R *plus* do some pre-planning of our remote show from Ostrichland since we are scheduling that in a few weeks anyhow," Li'l Otter explained.

"Fantastic!" Waldemar said with genuine excitement. "I'm really happy to show you Ostrichland."

"Shen is going to go on to Neu Deutschland, Waldemar. He's been driving all the way up. We booked a couple rooms at a place called Halle Haus," Li'l Otter explained.

"Yeah Waldemar. I'm so excited to meet you, but I'm bushed right now. I'm going to check in, have a nap and I'll pick up Li'l Otter in a bit if that's okay," Shen said, holding out his right hand, shaking hands with Waldemar again.

"No problem!" Waldemar responded as he shook Shen's large hand. "In fact, I'll drive Li'l Otter into town after we catch up for a while."

"Sounds like a plan," Li'l Otter concurred, pleased that he could have some one-on-one time with Waldemar. Shen started the Cargo Van and headed out to Highway 277 bound for Neu Deutschland.

"Li'l Otter, I can't believe you're here!" Waldemar repeated. "Come, let's have some refreshments to celebrate the occasion!" Waldemar said. As Waldemar, Li'l Otter and Lanky headed toward The Egg, Waldemar was reflecting on how happy and excited he was to have a longtime friend from show business at Ostrichland. Li'l Otter was thinking the same thing. Lanky was thinking Li'l Otter must be keeping ostrich treats under his baseball cap. He wasn't.

Waldemar and Li'l Otter entered the hatch. With a sweeping flourish of his arms, Waldemar welcomed his old friend to The Egg.

"Well, I thought I've seen it all, but this... this is really something, Waldemar!" Li'l Otter said in amazement. "You've really outdone yourself!

The last house of yours that I was in was that brand-new penthouse in Miami, what in 1997, something like that? And look at you now! This place looks like something out of the future!"

"Yes, it was designed by my friend, Hartwig von Trussell," Waldemar said, pressing the 'up' button on the private elevator.

Li'l Otter followed Waldemar into the elevator. "Takeoff!" Li'l Otter laughed as the elevator made its way to the top floor of The Egg and Waldemar's spacious Sky House.

"Here we go, Li'l Otter," Waldemar announced, opening the door of his private domain. "Make yourself at home."

"Good evening, sir," Waldemar and Li'l Otter were greeted at the door by Jeeves, Waldemar's faithful butler of many years, dressed in his Brioni Tonal-Stripe Wool two-piece suit.

"Hello, Jeeves," Waldemar replied, moving aside so Li'l Otter could enter the Sky House. "Li'l Otter, this is Jeeves," Waldemar introduced. "Jeeves has been with me for many years. Li'l Otter and Jeeves shook hands.

"Oh, my goodness!" Li'l Otter commented as he entered the reception foyer of the Sky House. This beats the Miami penthouse by far!" he exclaimed, admiring the Warhol painting of a soup can before they walked into the living room, the vista from the curving floor-to-ceiling windows breathtaking. "You still drink that Australian stuff -- what's that called? -- Kangaroo Soda?"

"No. You're close. It's Roo Energy Drink," Waldemar corrected. "Yes. Roo Energy Drink was and is my favorite drink, however, an occasion such as this deserves something extra. "Jeeves, could we have two glasses of our house specialty, please?"

I'll be right back, sir" Jeeves replied, heading to the kitchen, returning with a bottle and two glasses in hand.

"Ah, here we go. Straight from a local vineyard: **Bare Ass Winery**[10] 1982 Pinot Noir. They're really hot in the local wine world right now. The owner, Dainer Neigh is a friend of mine." Waldemar remarked. "Thank you, Jeeves."

"Thanks, Waldemar," Li'l Otter said as they walked into the formal dining room and over to the sculpted clear glass dining table and sat down. "You know, if you had bought a vineyard that wouldn't have surprised me. An ostrich farm, that's something else," Li'l Otter said, swirling his goblet.

"Is it any stranger than Walter running off to the desert to grow tomatoes?" Waldemar questioned, referring to his partner Walter Johnson of **WOW**. "He broke up **WOW** with that move you know." Waldemar said with a note of bitterness in his voice.

---

[10] The Bare Ass Winery was one of the more successful is the Neu Deutschland Valley. Established in 1975 by Dainer Neigh they were especially known for their Pinot Noir.

"That's the conventional wisdom," Li'l Otter replied, taking a sip of his glass of **Bare Ass Winery** 1982 Pinot Noir. "I don't think it's entirely accurate, do you, Waldemar?" Li'l Otter's dark eyes bored into Waldemar's dark brown eyes.

"Li'l Otter, you know Oola and I wanted to go on," Waldemar replied, somewhat defensively. "How could we without Walter? The WO tour was a disaster!" Waldemar said, taking a sip of wine.

"I think there were *many* factors in play, Waldemar," Li'l Otter opined. "You can't just blame Walter for **WOW** breaking up," Li'l Otter said, placing his wine glass on the sculpted clear glass dining table.

"You're right," Waldemar admitted. "Oola and I thought we could continue, both personally and professionally, but ultimately our time had come and gone," Waldemar said, staring at the wine in his glass as he swirled it around in a clockwise motion with his right hand.

"Now I hear Walter has left the desert for parts unknown," Li'l Otter said, exploring Waldemar's face for a reaction.

"Really? I hadn't heard that," Waldemar admitted. "Frankly, I'm too busy here at Ostrichland to keep up with showbusiness gossip," he said matter-of-factly. "I wonder why he left?"

"I don't know, Waldemar," Li'l Otter replied, wondering if Waldemar was pumping him for more information. "I know he was *very* successful with his hydroponic vegetable business. That's all I know about Walter Johnson post **WOW**." "Have you heard from Oola recently?"

"Not in a few years," Waldemar confessed. "I guess the last time we spoke was when Oola called me, inviting me to the opening of her restaurant, Rio de Taipan in Toronto. I didn't want to go and promote a restaurant even if it was Oola's. Can you imagine the scene that would have caused?" Waldemar asked Li'l Otter with a shiver, thinking of the paparazzi scene such an event would have caused.

"Well, Rio de Taipan is alive and well in Toronto, Waldemar," Li'l Otter said. "I was there a few months ago and it's *very* popular!"

"Good... good, I'm glad to hear that," Waldemar said, his deep brown eyes glazing over a bit as his memories started going back in time to the days of old.

"Vehicle entering the parking lot." Interrupting Waldemar's thoughts of the past, Agatha, Ostrichland's trusty AI, announced that a vehicle was pulling up in the parking lot. Waldemar stood up and walked over to a monitor to see if Ostrichland had a guest. The Range Rover Sport correctly identified the guest as Dr. Dustie Rhodes, returned from the Liska Family Ranch. Waldemar was both happy and anxious to have Li'l Otter meet Dustie. Waldemar could see Lanky greeting Dustie as she slipped an ostrich treat into Lanky's mouth and headed toward The Egg.

"Got a customer, Waldemar?" Li'l Otter asked, savoring his glass of wine.

"Guest. They're called guests here, Li'l Otter," Waldemar corrected Li'l Otter. "Open the hatch, Agatha." Waldemar ordered his AI assistant. Within seconds Dustie was at the Sky House door. "Hi, Dustie," Waldemar greeted her, giving her a noticeably 'more than friends' kiss. "I would like you to meet a special friend of mine from the golden olden days," Waldemar said, swinging the entrance door wide open, providing a view of Li'l Otter sitting at the table in the formal dining room.

"Oh, I didn't know you had a guest, Waldemar," Dustie said in an apologetic voice. "The parking lot was empty."

"Dr. Dustie Rhodes, I would like you to meet a legend in the flesh, radio's top DJ for a million years, Li'l Otter!" Waldemar introduced as they walked into the formal dining room to the sculpted clear glass dining room table. Li'l Otter stood up and shook Dustie's hand. "Li'l Otter, this is Dr. Dustie Rhodes, the official veterinarian of Ostrichland."

"Well, it's an honor to meet the *official* veterinarian of Ostrichland," Li'l Otter said, his 'Radio Voice' stronger than ever. "I'm relieved to know these big birds don't rely solely on a pop musician for their care!" All three laughed at Li'l Otter's remark.

"Thank you. I'm a big fan of your show, of course," Dustie replied.

"Dustie, would you like a glass of wine too?" Waldemar asked as Jeeves emerged from the kitchen.

"Don't mind if I do," she smiled, sitting down at the dining table. "I'll have what you guys are having."

"Your wish is my demand," Waldemar quipped, as Jeeves pouring a glass upon his return to the formal dining room.

Li'l Otter couldn't help but notice the look in Waldemar's eyes when he was looking at Dustie.

"How did the Liska visit go, Hon... um... Dustie... um... doctor?" Waldemar blew it now with that verbal fumble as he sat down at the dining table.

Li'l Otter couldn't contain himself: "Man, what are you doing stumbling all over your tongue?" he laughed. He turned to Dustie. "Waldemar has *always* been the worst liar! Mainly because he has so little experience with it." he laughed again. "I mean, it's fairly obvious that Dr. Dustie here is someone special, right?"

"Okay, you caught me, Li'l Otter," Waldemar confessed, turning a bit red in the face.

'Waldemar Ulff, you've always been like a schoolboy when it comes to your personal life," Li'l Otter continued, speaking as only very close friends can speak. "Here is this beautiful, *official* veterinarian sitting here and you can't come out and say that she's someone special in your life."

"You're right, Li'l Otter," Waldemar admitted, the wine loosening his tongue a touch. "Dustie *is* very special and *is* more than a friend to me."

"Now that's better, Waldemar," Li'l Otter said, winking at Dustie as he smiled thinking how he just busted Waldemar... he of 'I'll *never* find another woman to love' following his tumultuous breakup with Oola La so many years ago.

"Oh, Waldemar, I forgot something in the Rover. I'll be right back." Dustie said, heading for the door. She sensed that Waldemar and Li'l Otter had a couple things to discuss.

As soon as Dustie left the Sky House Waldemar jumped in. "What's wrong with you, Li'l Otter?" Waldemar fumed. "I don't want Dustie hearing all about my past!"

"Why not?!" Li'l Otter replied. "Waldemar, you've got to get living in the present! It's so obvious that you love Dustie, but you can't even admit it to anyone, much less yourself!"

Waldemar quieted, the pair walked to the living room, dimmed lights turning on thanks to Agatha, and sat down on the semi-circular sofa to think for a moment. Deep down he knew Li'l Otter was right. Waldemar had only recently begun to see Dustie in her true light: as someone he cared for... and loved.

"You're right, of course," Waldemar admitted quietly, sinking back in a group of multi-colored pillows in patterns of Paul Klee. "I *do* love Dustie. I only realized that in the past few months even though I've known her for years."

"I understand, Waldemar," Li'l Otter said. "Realization of a situation is the first step. It's not easy. Especially with your circumstances: two famous people, a highly publicized romance, and equally publicized breakup. Who wouldn't be reluctant to tread into a new relationship after that trauma?"

The entrance door opened slowly and Dustie walked in, looking at Waldemar and Li'l Otter with an amount of trepidation.

"Dustie, I *love* you!" Waldemar blurted out. "I have loved you for years, but I couldn't admit it!" Waldemar stood up, went over to Dustie and enveloped her in his arms.

Li'l Otter took his cue and headed into the teak-paneled den off the living room to watch the sun go down. The view was stunning. The vista of Ostrichland with the orange glow of dusk was magical.

Within a few minutes Waldemar and Dustie walked into the den to join Li'l Otter. "Ready to head to your hotel, Li'l Otter?" Waldemar asked, his eyes urging an answer in the affirmative.

"Sure Waldemar," Li'l Otter replied standing up from a flower-shaped chair. "I hate to bother you. Shen could have come and picked me up." Li'l Otter replied, feeling somewhat awkward, knowing that Waldemar and Dustie probably wanted to be alone at this point.

"No problem," Waldemar waived off Li'l Otter's regret. "It would be fun to go into town tonight. Maybe we can have a drink before we call it a night.

Jeeves, we're heading out for a bit," Waldemar called out as they made their way down the private elevator and out of The Egg. They walked over to a four-car garage partially hidden by shrubbery between The Egg and Highway 277. Waldemar's classic 1995 Burgundy Rolls-Royce Silver Spirit III, a vehicular memento from his **WOW** days, had a spot of honor in the garage. With Li'l Otter in the back seat and Waldemar and Dustie in front the trio headed out of Ostrichland and down Highway 277 to Neu Deutschland.

The high beams pierced a hole in the darkness. If only some light could be shed on the goings on in Neu Deutschland. The dark night promised as many twists and turns as Highway 277.

Strangers in the Haus...

The ride from Ostrichland to Neu Deutschland took only a few minutes, only two cars sharing the road with Waldemar's Rolls-Royce. When they reached town in the early evening, Neu Deutschland was mostly empty, a symptom of the 'out-of-favor' factor affecting the burg. Waldemar had no problem finding a spot in the Halle Haus parking lot.

"Before you turn in, Li'l Otter, let's check out *WonderBar* in the hotel," Waldemar suggested.

"Are you sure?" Li'l Otter questioned as they got out of the car and walked toward the chalet-style building that was Halle Haus.

"We're sure!" Dustie interjected enthusiastically. She didn't want to come between Waldemar and Li'l Otter. "Just as long as they don't object to my clothes," she laughed looking down at her safari pants as she adjusted her pith helmet.

"Why, you look so stylish it hurts!" Li'l Otter laughed as Waldemar opened the carved wood entrance door of Halle Haus with a flourish.

As the trio entered the imposing, but clearly dated lobby, there was no one there to greet them. Granted, it had been a while since Waldemar had been at Halle Haus, but he found the lack of people unnerving. "Where *is* everyone?" Waldemar queried, looking around for any sign of humanity. The three ventured to the entrance of *WonderBar*. No customers and just one dim light on above the gleaming red grand piano.

"This is weird!" Dustie ventured as they turned back to the front desk.

"Waldemar! Waldemar!"

Waldemar, Dustie and Li'l Otter were startled when a plump red-cheeked woman in lederhosen appeared at the foot of the stairway. "Thank God you heard my voice mail!"

"Oh... Gretel?" Waldemar responded, trying hard to remember Gerta Switzer's name and just missing the mark.

"Gerta," Gerta Switzer corrected, clearly disappointed that her celebrity BFF hadn't remembered her name. "I need to talk to you... alone," she whispered loudly, casting looks at Dustie and Li'l Otter.

"I *didn't* hear your voice mail. I'm here with my friends... where *is* everyone anyhow?" Waldemar asked Gerta, becoming exasperated at the mystery of the empty Halle Haus.

"If you're wondering where Conrad Halle is, he's with the rest of the scallywags at *Das Rathaus!*" Gerta informed Waldemar, her cheeks the shade of a Fuji apple by now.

"What's *Das Rathaus?*" Waldemar asked, his ignorance of the German language showing.

"City Hall! Where all the traitors are gathered!" Gerta stormed.

"Hey, Man, this is getting too intense for Li'l Otter," Li'l Otter announced in the third person. "I just want to find out where my suite is and my producer." he said, shaking his head in a 'no' gesture. "No more drama, please!"

"Well, there are two suites at Halle Haus both on the top floor... the third floor... and the Kaiser Wilhelm II suite is rented for the week, so your suite would have to be the other one, the Friedrich Nietzsche Suite," Gerta Switzer informed Li'l Otter, her powers of deduction giving her an air of authority that she didn't truly deserve.

"Okay, I'll stay here with Gretel. Li'l Otter, you and Dustie go up and check out the suite," Waldemar said, taking command of the situation before it got out of hand.

"Sounds good, Waldemar," Dustie said, leading Li'l Otter to the stairway. She, rightfully, didn't trust the elevator at Halle Haus.

Dustie and Li'l Otter made their way to the third floor of Halle Haus, still not a person in sight. The decor was reminiscent of an 1880's grand chalet in Bavaria. Plenty of dark wood and a slightly dank scent.

"Ah, here we are!" Dustie announced with some pride, the brass plaque, *Friedrich Nietzsche Suite*, clearly validating their navigation skills.

"Great. I'll just give a knock since I don't have a key yet," Li'l Otter said, tapping on the dark carved door. With no immediate response, he wrapped on the door twice again, a bit harder. Finally, the door creaked open slightly and a pair of large brown eyes looked out.

"Shen? It's me," Li'l Otter said.

"Oh. I wasn't expecting you would be here so early in the evening. I thought you would be reminiscing with Waldemar quite late tonight."

"Well, we're here now," Li'l Otter explained the obvious. "Come on, open the door," he said, pushing a bit from his side.

Shen moved out of the way and let Li'l Otter and Dustie enter the suite. Shen had a white bath towel with HH embroidered wrapped around his waist.

"Oh, I didn't know you were taking a shower. Sorry," Li'l Otter apologized. "Dr. Dustie Rhodes, this is Shenandoah River. Shenandoah River, Dr. Dustie Rhodes. Shen is the producer of *Feeling the Music.*" Li'l Otter introduced the two strangers in the awkward situation.

"Pollenaize?" came a call from one of the bedrooms beyond the sitting room. Everyone exchanged confused looks, especially Shen, who had no idea he'd been sharing his suite with any squatters. Before anyone could answer, Conrad Halle III strode into the sitting room, naked as a jaybird, as the saying goes. Seeing three complete strangers in the suite, he gasped and quickly turned around to retreat to the bedroom from which he emerged. Actually, he turned too quickly as the big toe on his right foot caught on the faux German antique rug featuring a silhouette of German philosopher Friedrich Nietzsche writing one of his many famed books, *Beyond Good and Evil.* "Oh no!" he moaned. "I'm such a klutz sometimes! Look away! Look away!" Three cried out as he crawled into the bedroom, tail between his legs, as it were.

"Well, you don't see *that* every day!" Shen chortled. "I'll get some clothes on and we can restart this whole evening," he said, walking to the other bedroom in the suite.

"That's an *excellent* idea," Li'l Otter remarked, embarrassed by the turn of events.

Within minutes Shen walked into the sitting room, fully clothed. "What's up?" he asked casually.

"What's *up?*" Li'l Otter repeated in a more strident tone. Just then Three emerged from *his* bedroom. "I am *so* sorry!" he apologized profusely. Please don't tell my grandfather!"

"Who's your grandfather?" Li'l Otter asked, his irritation becoming more pronounced.

"My grandfather. Conrad Halle. He owns this place, Halle Haus." Three explained as he adjusted his black leather belt. "He doesn't know I'm living here!"

"Here? Like in this suite?" Li'l Otter questioned.

"Yes. No one ever stays here. At least not until tonight," he shot a sheepish and apologetic glance towards Shen. "I was going to surprise my girlfriend, Pollenaize Niesen, and next thing I know all of you were here, no Pollenaize Niesen... and no surprise..."

"Right..." Li'l Otter was taking it all in. "So, I guess we spoiled your 'surprise,' eh?"

Shen looked at Three. Three looked at Li'l Otter. Li'l Otter looked at Dustie. "YES!" Three exclaimed in embarrassment and frustration.

"I'm clearly the trespasser and should be on my way," Three apologized, heading to the door.

"Wait!" Shen called. "There's no reason to kick you out. Li'l Otter can sleep in the second bedroom. I can sleep on the sofa bed here. You can stay in your bedroom, Conrad."

"Thanks, Shen!" Three said. "You can call me 'Three'... my nickname."

"Ah, Three as in the third, eh?" Li'l Otter remarked. "Great, Three. Is there any way we could get something to eat?"

"Sure! No problem. Especially since I don't think Pollenaize can make it tonight," Three replied trying to hide his dejection. "I'm the waiter here and the busboy and the desk clerk and... My grandfather is so cheap, but then again Halle Haus is really hurting too, along with the rest of Neu Deutschland. Well, I've said too much I guess..." Three cast his gray eyes down to the faded carpet.

"Come, let's find Waldemar and get some dinner!" Li'l Otter said opening the door and walking to the stairs followed by Dustie, Shen and Three. "I feel like a mother duck!" Li'l Otter chuckled as he looked back at the string of people following him single file. "Waldemar? Are you there?" Li'l Otter called out as they started down the stairs.

The only reply was silence...

Open Haus...

The quartet reached the bottom of the stairs in the lobby. There was still no sign of Waldemar or Gerta Switzer. "It's like a ghost town here," Li'l Otter remarked looking all around the lobby for signs of life.

"It *is* unusually quiet tonight even for Halle Haus," Three admitted, breaking from the group and walking to the front desk. He looked at a clipboard at the front desk and returned to the group. "My grandfather didn't even assign a clerk for the front desk tonight. I don't even know where he is! He's usually here at Halle Haus like he lives here. This *is* strange!" He admitted. "Let's go to *WonderBar*. Maybe someone is there."

The group followed Three the short distance to *WonderBar*. The single dim light above the gleaming red piano was still on, however, off to the side sat Waldemar and Gerta deep in conversation, oblivious to the presence of others.

"Waldemar?" Dustie called softly so she wouldn't startle them. No response. "Waldemar?!" she tried again with a bit more strength in her voice. Waldemar and Gerta turned around to face the others.

"Oh, man, I completely lost track of time!" Waldemar admitted, turning to Gerta to catch her reaction to having the others present. Gerta didn't show any signs of distress with the increased crowd in *WonderBar*. "Come in, guys. Grab some chairs. Gerta has been telling me quite a tale!"

Three grabbed a couple of chairs from the next table and the group sat down. "Can I get you anything to drink?" he asked, his professionalism in full play seeing people seated in *WonderBar*.

"That and food would be great!" Li'l Otter replied, not hiding his nutritional needs.

"Yeah, is there any food available?" Waldemar asked Three. "I'm pretty hungry myself," he realized.

"Sure. No problem," Three replied, heading off to the kitchen.

"So, what's going on, Waldemar?" Li'l Otter asked expectantly.

"Well, basically Neu Deutschland has been purchased by a lunatic who wants to turn it into an apocalypse bunker for the rich and privileged. Les Winns, the Yacktivist, is his name and title. He tried to buy Ostrichland the other day, but I turned him down," Waldemar said, spotting Three returning from the kitchen, a tray of drinks held elegantly in his raised right hand.

"Not only that, he's cheating people!" Gerta added, clearly drained by the events of the day.

Three passed the drinks around the table. "What is this, Three? It's so delicious!" Shen asked after taking a deep gulp.

"Right! It's so refreshing and light!" Dustie agreed enthusiastically.

"Um... tap water and ice," Three admitted. "I couldn't find the keys to the bar."

"Well, here's to the Neu Deutschland tap water!" Shen held up his glass in his right hand in a proper toast.

"Cheers!" said all at the table.

"How much did he offer you for Ostrichland, if I may ask?" Gerta asked the question everyone at the table was wondering.

"Well..." Waldemar was always reluctant to talk about money. "$30,000,012.54."

A collective gasp came over the table. "That's a lot of money, Waldemar!" Li'l Otter remarked, perhaps questioning Waldemar's decision not to sell his beloved Ostrichland.

"I know, Li'l Otter," Waldemar said, wetting his lips with the refreshing tap water on the rocks. "Money just doesn't register for me. I know I'm unusual and blessed to be in such a situation. I've made many times over that amount in my life," he reminded those at the table. "I have my business manager, Yukio Cassidy, to thank for my favorable financial situation. A lot of musicians got taken by shifty financial people with their hand in the till," he remarked.

"That's true, but there's no denying that was a *big* incentive you turned down!" Li'l Otter added.

"That's what they sold Neu Deutschland for!" Gerta wailed, taking a large glug of tap water.

"The same price he offered for Ostrichland?" Waldemar questioned.

"Yes! Plus, those traitors, Bürgermeister Ackermann and Conrad Halle, are getting $1,500,000.63 each for betraying our beloved little burg," she announced, a tear sliding down her right cheek, because they profited or because she wasn't in on the deal?

"It all sounds very fishy to me!" Dustie added, using an animal in her comment was a natural trait in her profession.

"So, what does he want to do with Neu Deutschland?" Li'l Otter asked, searching the eyes of his companions for clarity.

"Like I said, Li'l Otter," Waldemar replied calmly, "He wants property or, now, a whole town to turn into a safe and secure shelter for people who have the financial means to buy into such a fear-based scheme. When the end of the world comes, they will be spared because they live in Neu Deutschland or it could have been Ostrichland had I agreed to the deal."

The group around the table went silent for several moments as they all processed what was going on. Three suddenly jumped up, hearing a knock on the outside door of the kitchen. Several minutes later he reappeared with two boxes of gigantic-size pizzas, one with pepperoni and cheese, the other with pineapple, green peppers and sausage.

"Now you're talking, Three!" Shen snapped out of his contemplation about the fate of Neu Deutschland. Hunger brought the same response from the others.

"I don't know where our chef is tonight," Three admitted. "It seems as though the whole town is deserted, save for the pizza delivery guy from Oom-Pah-Zaa Pizza down the street... thank goodness for him!"

Just as everyone was getting their slices of pizza, in the shadows a figure emerged, making its way to the red piano. No one really noticed in their pizza-eating frenzy.

"Hello everybody!" came the startling amplified voice from the stage. "It's good to see you tonight! Enjoy the show!"

Sanny was back and ready to do his set. There *was* still some normalcy left in Neu Deutschland, scant normalcy, but normalcy nonetheless. All around the table, the group chomped on their pizza, looking up at the magical (nagical?) glittery man at the gleaming red piano.

"I always start my show with requests. Any requests tonight?" Sanny looked out into the room, the lack of light making it impossible to see his captive audience.

"How about *Missed Memories?*" came a voice from the crowd.

"Ah, a **WOW** fan!" Sanny remarked, stalling a bit as he searched his memory banks for 90's pop hits. Sanny was breaking out into a slight sweat now. Could a song have any more 'M's' in it that **WOW**'s *Missed Memories?* Well, the show nust go on, as 'they' say...

Before Sanny tackled *Missed Memories,* Waldemar took pity, stood up and walked over to the small stage. As he emerged from the shadows, Sanny looked down and peered at Waldemar through his blingy glasses.

Missed Memories

Many morning moments
I think of our time together is it fading
Miserable
I'd rather stay here than go but I know that

Missed memories
My final breath is gone
Modern life
My final breath is gone

Melancholy
My final breath is gone
Mountains
Don't go you said you wouldn't

Missed memories
My final breath is gone
Modern life
My final breath is gone

"Waldenar!" Sanny exclaimed with much excitement. "I haven't seen you in years!" Sanny gushed, getting up from the piano bench to hug Waldemar. "Cone on up!"

"Thanks, Sanny!" Waldemar said, taking the step up to the stage. "It's so nice and so random to see you here!" Waldemar said, grabbing a Shure SLX2/SM58 wireless hand microphone from the piano by instinct. "I've known Sanny for what?... years!" Waldemar said looking at Sanny, but playing to the audience. The stage felt good, the spotlight felt good. What was happening? Waldemar asked deep in his brain.

"Sanny is the *consummate* lounge singer," Waldemar continued. "We met in Vegas in... the early 90's... could that be?" Waldemar asked Sanny.

"Yes, nany, nany years ago, Waldenar," Sanny responded, sitting back down at the piano bench. "How about singing a song with ne?"

At that, the audience broke into enthusiastic applause. Waldemar Ulff performing in public for the first time in almost twenty years!

"If I had a guitar, I would, Sanny," Waldemar demurred.

"Here you go, Waldenar!" Three reached out to hand Waldemar a Yamaha FG830 acoustic guitar that was always kept handy in a corner of *WonderBar*.

"Thanks, Three," Waldemar said as Three hoisted a wooden stool up to the small stage. "How about *Now, the Sky*?" Waldemar asked Sanny as he tuned the guitar.

"Let's go, Waldenar!" Sanny said enthusiastically, trying desperately to remember the song.

"Here we go..." Waldemar said, strumming the now in-tune guitar as Three placed another microphone by the guitar and, as he descended into the shadows of *WonderBar*, pulled out his Samsung Galaxy smartphone and activated the video app.

Now, the Sky

Huge grin on his boots somewhere
Victim's child becomes him the
number
Useless without you can hear
We realized it's so useless

For the right thing we've scratched
It drives us all that's left
This what you say when you're
falling
Empty room stay away boy stay

Now the sky forever dreams
Haunting I'd take you in a million
Years and we can go much higher
To lie down static cloud

Being nice but as long
Let a little time for the subject
Should we lose it lose
Those days are weighing

Now the sky forever dreams
Haunting I'd take you in a million
Years and we can go much higher
To lie down static cloud

It's like to feel
Do the same the mad mad world
Won't start to feel your grip
Faster you slip through my heart

Now the sky forever dreams
Haunting I'd take you in a million
Years and we can go much higher
To lie down static cloud

"EVERYBODY, SING!" Waldemar encouraged enthusiastically following Sanny and his first go-round of *Now, the Sky*. The audience mumbled and stumbled their way through a second time. Three stopped recording and quickly pocketed his smartphone. Then, with determination, he made his way to the bar and returned with several bottles of spirits for the guests.

"Where did you find these?" Shen asked in surprise, referring to the newly found liquor bottles.

"I was determined to get us some *real* drinks!" Three said triumphantly. "Grandfather can pay for a new lock on the bar door!" he laughed, pouring the guests various types and quantities of liquid refreshment.

Soon, *WonderBar* was party central for Neu Deutschland which, this night, was an easy claim as the whole town seemed deserted. Nonetheless, let the party begin!

She's a Lady...!

"Nicely done! Nicely done!" said the elegant woman with an aristocratic English accent, standing at the entrance/exit of *WonderBar*. "Bravo!" she said, smiling and clapping her glove-covered hands to the revelers before her. Taking one of three steps to the *WonderBar* floor she surveyed the room of quiet people staring back at the mysterious woman before them, her fascinator a bejeweled wonder of the milliner's art, shaped like a large orchid on the right side of her head. Her bearing was regal, her attire high class with a touch of trendy chic. At the second step she turned her attention to the stage, fixing her gaze on Waldemar holding his microphone in his right hand resting on his right leg.

"Welcome! What's your nane?" Sanny asked the newest member of his audience.

"It's been *so* long, Waldemar, Darling!" she remarked, ignoring Sanny, descending the third step to the *WonderBar* main floor.

"Lady Orchid Buffington-Choade! What brings you here tonight?" Waldemar asked talking into his microphone casually taking a sip of his mojito prepared by Three.

"You know I *always* find the party, Baby," she smiled, taking a step up to the *WonderBar* stage, giving Waldemar a big hug as he stood to greet her.

"It's been *so long*!" she cooed as Waldemar kissed her neck after he carefully placed the microphone on his stool.

With a few murmured greetings, Waldemar reached over and picked up his microphone and turned to the audience. "Ladies and gentlemen, it is my pleasure to introduce my dear, dear friend, Lady Orchid Buffington-Choade!"

The audience, already in a festive mood due to the impromptu concert and alcohol, were in a fine mood to greet Lady Orchid, even if they had no clue who she was or how she fit into Waldemar's life.

"It's *truly* a pleasure to meet all of you!" Lady Orchid said after Waldemar handed her his microphone. "And *please,* you can call me Lady Orchid!" she smiled regally. "The last time I was on a stage with this much star-power was when I was in the music video for the band, Down Bulge, and their song, 'Seduction and All That.'" I played the sexy MILF ghost, but alas, I digress as usual!" she chuckled, handing Waldemar the microphone. The audience applauded."

"Lady Orchid, I'm going to officially invite you to join our party!" Waldemar spoke into the microphone, gesturing for Three to come over. "Lady Orchid will have a vermouth on the rocks with a twist," Waldemar ordered, remembering Lady Orchid's favorite drink after all these years.

"Yes sir!" Three replied, heading for the bar.

"You're *so* kind, Waldemar, as always!" she said, her British accent charming the audience. "Let's join your friends," she suggested. Lady Orchid and Waldemar took a step down from the stage. Sanny started playing light background music.

"Lady Orchid, I would like to introduce you to my friends," Waldemar said as everyone stood up to greet their distinguished guest. "Dr. Dustie Rhodes, a very good friend of mine; Li'l Otter the premier DJ in the U.S.A.; Shenandoah River, the producer of Li'l Otter's radio show; Gerta Switzer, our new friend from Neu Deutschland and (as he entered the room from the bar) Conrad Halle III or Three, the heart of Halle Haus and, of course, Sanny at the piano (Sanny waved)." All shook hands and greeted Lady Orchid Buffington-Choade as she received her vermouth on the rocks with a twist.

"You're all so utterly charming!" she gushed, sitting down taking a sip of her drink. "Ah, *perfect!*" she said, giving Three a flirty wink of approval. "Three, you're *so* hot and you know how to make a great drink!" she purred with a sly smile.

"So, Lady Orchid, what *does* bring you here tonight?" Waldemar asked once again as he finished his mojito.

"I was invited here, dear Waldemar," she replied, grabbing Waldemar's collar, pulling him toward her and planting a kiss on his right cheek. Dustie couldn't hide her shock at such a brazen act, her jaw dropping slightly at the sight.

"Lady Orchid!" Waldemar exclaimed, smoothing his hair and tightening his ponytail. "You haven't changed a bit!" he burst out with a large smile, winking at an unsmiling Dustie. "Who invited you?" Waldemar asked.

"An old, old friend of mine, Waldemar," Lady Orchid replied, smiling at Three as he brought another vermouth on the rocks with a twist. "Perhaps you've heard of him... Les Winns."

A gasp was heard throughout *WonderBar* at the mention of Les Winns. Gerta went so far as to shriek.

"Heard of him! He tried to buy Ostrichland the other day and he bought Neu Deutschland today!" Waldemar explained. "Why did he invite *you* here?"

"He said he wants me to explore the option of living in a town that is safe from the coming End of the World," Lady Orchid replied, sipping her new drink. "You know me, Waldemar, always interested in a new angle in our crazy world, right?"

"That *is* you, for sure," Waldemar agreed. "But I need to warn you that, in my opinion, Winns is a dangerous fanatic."

"He *is* a nasty bit of excrement... but that's what I find so attractive about him, Waldemar!" Lady Orchid laughed loudly, adjusting her fascinator. "You know I always go for the bad boys, right?" she said, giving Waldemar a little nudge with her right hand.

"I need to powder my nose," Dustie exclaimed, standing abruptly, casting Waldemar a withering look.

"I'll go with you, Doctor," Gerta joined Dustie. "Right this way to the right," Gerta instructed as they made their way out of *WonderBar*.

"You're in hot water now, Waldemar," Li'l Otter observed, finishing one of the last slices of pizza.

"Not the first time," Lady Orchid remarked, smiling at Li'l Otter. "And not the last."

At that, Sanny burst into song...

Watch out boy she'll chew you up
(Oh here she cones)
She's a naneater
(Oh here she cones)
Watch out boy she'll chew you up
(Oh here she cones)
She's a naneater...

The Terrible Trio...

After the departure of Dustie and Gerta for their nose powdering, signs of life could be heard in the Halle Haus lobby. Three left *WonderBar* to investigate. Within a minute he returned, followed by Bürgermeister Ackermann, Conrad Halle, Edwin and Edwina Flunkie and, finally, Les Winns himself, looking like a king surveying his kingdom.

"What's going on here?" Halle asked no one in particular as he looked around *WonderBar*, full of life for once.

"It looks like there's a celebration going on here, Conrad," Winns observed as he entered *WonderBar* to see what was going on first-hand.

"We *were* celebrating!" All eyes searched the mysterious voice coming from the lobby. Gerta and Dustie made their way to the entrance/exit of *WonderBar*, pushing through to get to their table and sit down. "Are you gentlemen all done selling out Neu Deutschland?" Gerta asked acidly, finding a rogue glass of tap water and taking a swig.

"Plans are well underway, Miss Switzer." Winns assured her. "Ah, Lady Orchid! I'm so honored to see you!" Winns gushed, walking over to the table to greet his distinguished guest. "I'm sorry you didn't get a proper greeting!" Winns apologized, looking at the table full of former revelers, giving Waldemar an especially cold look.

"Nonsense!" Lady Orchid exclaimed, offering her right hand for Winns to kiss rather than her right cheek. "I'm having a *wonderful* time!" she assured her host.

"Well, I think we need to get going," Waldemar announced, standing up. "I'm not used to the party life anymore!" he laughed, smoothing his mustache.

"Nonsense, Waldemar!" Lady Orchid protested. "You *are* the party and always have been!" she declared, noticing Dustie's mouth pucker slightly in protest.

"Why *did* you invite Lady Orchid here?" Waldemar asked Winns directly, already knowing the answer from Lady Orchid's explanation.

"Lady Orchid has been invited to a very exclusive tour, Waldemar," Winns said in a condescending tone, the Flunkies' large eyes widening as their boss started to explain the 'Magical History Tour,' his title for the tour of Neu Deutschland he planned for his potential buyers of safe, secure homes to protect your family when FOE unleash a giant can of whoop ass on the world.

"Actually, Lady Orchid is one of our pre-tour guests," Winns smiled indulgently at Lady Orchid. "The main 'Magical History Tour' will happen in a week or so when most of our potential clients will be visiting Neu Deutschland for an exclusive tour and view our upcoming plans for Neu Deutschland. Lady Orchid was selected, along with several other people, to get a preview of what we will have to offer our 'special' guests.

"You're *too* kind, Darling!" Lady Orchid cooed, wishing Three would bring her another vermouth on the rocks with a twist.

"You two are certainly unusually quiet!" Gerta snapped, pointing a pudgy right index finger at Bürgermeister Ackermann and Halle. "How can you let such a thing happen to our beloved Neu Deutschland?!" Both stared down at the white-tiled floor of *WonderBar*, silent. "Your silence says *everything*! *Verräter*!" she shouted, walking past them, out to the Halle Haus lobby.

Dustie walked over to Waldemar. "Let's go, Waldemar," she whispered.

"Right," Waldemar agreed. "We're going home," he announced.

Waldemar and Dustie walked out of *WonderBar* and across the lobby to the main entrance of Halle Haus, followed by Lady Orchid, Li'l Otter, Shen, Three, Sanny and Gerta, followed by Bürgermeister Ackerman, Halle, Edwin and Edwina Flunkie and Winns.

As Waldemar was wrestling to free his car keys from his right pant pocket, he glanced at Lady Orchid. Oh no! The 'pouty' look! "Lady Orchid, would you like to spend the night at Ostrichland?" Waldemar asked, followed by a sharp poke to the right ribs from Dustie.

"Why Waldemar, dear, I would *love* to!" Lady Orchid agreed excitedly. "Would you be so kind as to retrieve my luggage from my room, Three?" she asked with a smoldering look in her eyes. She still had it!

"Right away, Lady Orchid!" he said, saluting Lady Orchid as he took off to the upper floors of Halle Haus.

Waldemar pulled up in his 1995 Burgundy Rolls-Royce Silver Spirit III. Lady Orchid quickly claimed the front passenger seat while Dustie was relegated to the back-right passenger seat which, in this car, wasn't much of a sacrifice. With Lady Orchid's luggage efficiently loaded into the trunk, Waldemar made his way out of the Halle Haus parking lot.

"Waldemar, isn't this the car I bought for you all those years ago?" Lady Orchid asked as he pulled the majestic car onto *Hauptstraße*.

"Yes. Yes, it is," he answered in a subdued voice.

"It's so nice to ride in a proper automobile with enough headroom to wear a stylish hat," Lady Orchid commented. Dustie took a perverse delight at that comment seeing as Lady Orchid's fascinator was, in fact, smashed into the plush Rolls-Royce headliner, crushed into a shape reminiscent of an origami dinosaur. Dustie's pith helmet, on the other hand (or head), fit perfectly, much to her delight.

"Well, I'd *love* to hear that story sometime soon!" Dustie exclaimed from her position in the back seat.

"I'd *love* to tell you, Dr. Dustie!" Lady Orchid exclaimed, glancing at Waldemar. "I have *so many* stories to tell!" she finished with a chuckle.

Waldemar guided his car onto Highway 277 as it entered/exited Neu Deutschland. He spotted two workmen in reflective jackets working on a sign at the entrance of Neu Deutschland. Curious, Waldemar peered into the rearview mirror and caught a glimpse of what seemed to be a new sign replacing the familiar 'Welcome to Neu Deutschland' sign. It was difficult to decipher in the mirror, but the new sign appeared to say, 'Welcome to New Fatherland.' Waldemar gave a shudder, not mentioning his observation to the other occupants of the Rolls-Royce.

New Fatherland indeed...!

Scrambled Egg...

"Your ears are *so* cute!"
"No, they're not."
"Yes, they are!"
"No, they're not."
"Yes, they are!"
"No, they're not."
"Yes, they are!"
"No, they're not."
"Yes, they are!"
"No, they're not."
"Yes, they are!"
"No, they're not."
"Yes, they are!"
"No, they're not."
"Yes, they are!"
"No, they're not."
"Yes, they are!
"No, they're not."
"Yes, they are!"
"No, they're not."
"Yes, they are!"
"No, they're not."
"Yes, they are!"

A right hand knocked over an empty bottle of Roo Energy Drink from the side table on the right side of the bed, occupied by two people this morning.

"Those lobes are *so* perfect!"

"No, they're not."

"Yes, they are!"

"No, they're not."

"Yes, they are!"

"No, they're not."

"Yes, they are!"

"Yes, they are!"

"No, they're not!"

"Yes, they are!"

"No, they're not!"

"Yes, they are!"

"No, they're not!"

"No, they're not."

"Yes, they are!"

"No, they're not."

"Yes, they are!"

"No, they're not."

"Yes, they are!"

"No, they're not."

"Yes, they are!"

"No, they're not."

"Yes, they are!"

"No, they're not."

"Yes, they are!"

The exchange ended with laughter.

"What time is it?" Dustie asked, sleep still in her voice.

"11:11 am," Waldemar replied, stretching his arms, then throwing off the covers on his side of the bed.

"Oh! So late! I appreciated our talk last night, Waldemar," she said as she pushed her head back in the pillow. "I was having a hard time remembering your past and your present," she said, moving over and giving Waldemar a delicate kiss on his beaky nose.

"I know it's hard to reconcile my lifestyle *then* versus my lifestyle *now*," he admitted, requesting Agatha to part the drapes, engulfing the master suite in bright sunshine. "But I was always considered a pretty tame guy even at the peak of **WOW** fame," he reminded her. "Once a square, always a square, eh?" he chuckled, trotting off to the shower.

"It's just when a mysterious woman from your past shows up out of the blue, it's startling!" Dustie called out to Waldemar, referring to the sudden appearance of Lady Orchid Buffington-Choade.

"Not to worry. It's all good!" Waldemar replied, peeking in the doorway sans clothes doing the helicopter maneuver for several rotations.

"Get in that shower, Mister!" she admonished Waldemar as she got out of bed and put on her robe.

Several minutes later, Waldemar and Dustie emerged from the master suite of Waldemar's spacious Sky House at the top of The Egg dressed and ready for the day. They could hear talking and laughter coming from the direction of the breakfast room off the kitchen.

"...why, yes, I *was* considered to be a Bond girl. The director was a real 'finger sniffer,' if you know what I mean, so I decided not to pursue the offer. You are such a delight, Shrimp Wrigley!" Lady Orchid chattered, a fresh fascinator firmly in place, this one displaying an egg theme, no doubt to celebrate the occasion of her visit to Ostrichland. Several realistic-looking eggs were resting in a somewhat pyramid fashion within the structure of the fascinator. A fitting artistic statement expressed through headwear. Sitting across from Lady Orchid was Shrimp Wrigley dressed in his Stacy Adams Dusk Two Piece Lemon Suit, Simon the Stag Beetle perched precariously on his right shoulder. Shrimp Wrigley and Lady Orchid appeared to be sharing breakfast.

"Well, well!" Waldemar called out as he neared the door of the breakfast room. "What's the special occasion?" he asked, giving a look of surprise and delight to his two guests.

"Oh, Waldemar!" Lady Orchid cooed. "How lovely to see you this morning! And you too, Dr. Dustie!" Lady Orchid was in an extraordinary cheerful mood this morning. "Come, sit down, the both of you!" she ordered, pointing to the two empty chairs to her right. "Oh, Jeeves!"

From the kitchen came Jeeves with two additional breakfasts in hand.

"So, what brings you here this fine day, Shrimp Wrigley?" Waldemar asked, turning his attention to Ostrichland's general manager. "And nice to see Simon adorning your right shoulder."

"Just an average day, Waldemar," Shrimp Wrigley lied as he took a swig of his glass of Granny's Juice Company Gourmet Pasteurized Orange Juice[11], giving Waldemar a 'shut your mouth' look as he adjusted Simon's stance on his right shoulder.

---

[11] Granny's Juice Company is an American fruit juice brand headquartered in Fargo, North Dakota. The company was founded by Granny Dundeskaya, whose husband was a 5th-generation North Dakota citrus grower based on the family land along the Red River. "Growing citrus in North Dakota is a challenge, but I'm up to it!" Granny Dundeskaya is proud to say.

"I found Shrimp Wrigley when I was taking my morning constitutional," Lady Orchid explained between bites of honeydew melon. "I also met your adorable Lanky, Waldemar! What a sweet bird!" she gushed.

"Right. I was opening the entrance gate, Waldemar," Shrimp Wrigley felt obliged to explain, still not explaining his vintage formal attire. "Everyone except Lady Orchid Buffington-Choade seemed to be sleeping in this morning and Ostrichland doesn't stop for sleep."

"Please, Shrimp Wrigley, call me Lady Orchid," she requested, wiping her sultry mouth gently with her white linen napkin.

"Will do," Shrimp Wrigley complied. "Say, Lady Orchid, since you're an aristocrat and all, have you ever met the Queen?" Shrimp Wrigley asked.

"Why, Shrimp Wrigley, it goes without saying that Her Majesty and I are *this* close," she replied, crossing the index and middle fingers of her right hand as a visual aid.

"You know, I had my share of royalty in my day," Shrimp Wrigley was winding up for another Shrimp Wrigley story.

"Do tell!" she implored as Jeeves brought a vermouth on the rocks with a twist, her first of the day, but not the last.

"I shall," Shrimp Wrigley replied. "It was on April 13, 1976, I believe, give or take a day or so. I ventured up to San Francisco to see an old friend of mine, Starlight Special was her name. Anyhow, I'm staying at her apartment for several days, she's *very* accommodating! Anyhow, I digress. I took a morning walk in those days, just like you do now, Lady Orchid. That day I'm turning the corner at Sansome and Clay Street and there's this big black limousine with several other cars and police motorcycles on the street. I can tell that something *big* is going on, so I stop walking and watch. No sooner did I stop when about a dozen guys all dressed up in suits and ties come walking out of the building there, you know? All the police officers get on their motorcycles and start them up. It was quite the noise! Anyhow, I notice that the man in the middle walking towards the limousine seems to be the center of attention."

Lady Orchid, Dustie and Waldemar were in the palm of Shrimp Wrigley's right hand as he told his tale. Waldemar couldn't resist a smile as this was familiar territory for him.

"So, I start paying special attention to the guy in the middle. Someone with a camera walked up next to me and was taking pictures. I asked him who that guy was... why, he's the King of Switzerland!" Shrimp Wrigley paused for effect, letting his audience grasp what he just said. "Naturally, I get all excited. I know how to speak Swiss, so I yell out, *Elcomeway otay ethay usyay ouryay ajestymay. Iyay opehay ouyay avehay ayay onderfulway imetay erehay!* The King heard my greeting and waved for me to come over. Apparently, the police didn't like that, but what could they do? I walked over as the King of Switzerland was about to enter his limousine."

"*Ankthay ouyay osay uchmay orfay ouryay indkay ordsway!* the King of Switzerland said, shaking my hand. *Ouldway ouyay ikelay anyay autographedyay otophay?* "The King asked, talking directly to me.

"So, I turned to a big burly guy dressed in a dark suit with a hearing aid in both ears. He didn't seem to understand what the king had just said, so I figured this guy was a Secret Service agent protecting our distinguished foreign visitor. I told him the king asked if I wanted an autographed photo. From inside the limousine the king handed me his signed picture. I was in the process of thanking him when one of the burly guys shut the king's door on the limousine and said, 'let's roll' into his wrist.

Well, the problem was that my sport coat was caught in the limousine door. The motorcade took off, all the burly guys were running along the side of the limousine and so was I. I guess they thought I was one of them at that point. The limousine gets going faster and faster and I'm running out of breath at this point. I can hear my sport coat starting to rip, but I'm keeping up. After another block I was getting *really* winded and wondering how this story was going to end. Like a miracle, the king rolled down his window and asked, *oday ouyay owknay anyyay oodgay isssway estaurantsray inyay ethay areayay? i'myay arvingstay!*

"Of course, *everyone* knows that *The Cheese Hole*, a fantastic Swiss restaurant was just three blocks and around the corner. They've since closed after a bad fondue sickened two people and a St. Bernard in... oh... it must have been in the mid-90's when Waldemar was so famous. But I digress."

"*Easeplay ingbray emay otay ethay estaurantray. I'llyay avehay unchlay ithway ouyay.*"

"The King invited me to lunch, so I climbed into the limousine and took off. Luckily, that gave me time to catch my breath. I'd never been in a royal motorcade at that point in my life, so it was quite fun. All the traffic parted as we roared through downtown San Francisco on our way to The Cheese Hole. I wouldn't mind commuting like that!

"We arrived at The Cheese Hole in just a couple of minutes thanks to the traffic parting like the Red Sea. His Majesty treated me to the delicious offering of Swiss food. He didn't carry his own money as one of his aides paid for everything very discreetly. His Majesty was now way behind schedule, so the aides started acting nervous and everything. His Majesty didn't care. We had a great time! So much so that I invited him to Ostrichland, which I owned at the time, whenever he was back in California. So far, he hasn't taken me up on the offer, I assume because he's so busy.

"When we finished lunch, His Majesty shook my hand and they all took off down the street in the motorcade headed for some other event. So, all that to say that, yes, I've been around royalty too, Lady Orchid."

"What an *enchanting* man you are, Shrimp Wrigley!" Lady Orchid declared breathlessly. "What a *wonderful* story! You're just a *treasure,* Shrimp Wrigley!"

"That *is* quite a story, Shrimp Wrigley!" Waldemar exclaimed, a sly smile on his face. Sometimes, Waldemar took a perverse pleasure in debunking Shrimp Wrigley's obviously false tales such as this one. "Two problems: Switzerland has no king and there are *four* official languages in Switzerland. There is no language called 'Swiss.'"

Shrimp Wrigley looked daggers at Waldemar, Lady Orchid looked at Waldemar, Dustie looked at Jeeves, who had just entered the room. Jeeves looked at the fruit dish.

"How the hell would I remember every detail after all those years, Waldemar?" Shrimp Wrigley replied. Simon the Stag Beetle perched on Shrimp Wrigley's right shoulder waved his antennas with excitement as Shrimp Wrigley quickly left the breakfast room, his veracity in tatters.

Viral Violation...

About forty-five minutes after Waldemar made a quick call to Li'l Otter, he heard a knock on the administrative office door. "Come in," Waldemar said, sitting upright in his plush executive chair. A tired-looking Li'l Otter and Shenandoah River wearily entered the office. With a gesture of his right hand, Waldemar offered the two gentlemen plush chairs facing Waldemar's large custom-made Brazilian tigerwood desk.

"Roo Energy Drink?" Waldemar asked, walking over to his refrigerator cleverly hidden in the main bookshelf.

"Sure, Waldemar, I could use one," Li'l Otter said, rubbing his eyes in an attempt to wake up.

"Me too!" Shen said, not quite so tired due to his relative youth and experience with long, long nights of debauchery.

"Thanks, Waldemar!" Li'l Otter said as Waldemar handed the drinks to them. "You sure have a lot of *strange* shit going on in your neighborhood!" Li'l Otter observed, rolling his large brown eyes and opening the bottle of Roo Energy Drink. "Neu Deutschland is a crazy place these days!"

"You mean, New Fatherland, don't you?" Waldemar asked, his tone of voice indicating his opinion on the sudden name change.

"New Fatherland?" Shen questioned, gulping his drink.

"Yes. When we were leaving town last night, I could see road crews changing the name already," Waldemar observed.

"That's nuts! Well, despite what's going on in the world of conspiracy real estate developers, we need to plan an important show and fast!" Li'l Otter directed the conversation to the task at hand. "We've wasted enough time with this crazy survivalist land grab."

"True enough!" Waldemar concurred. "Where are we with the project, Li'l Otter?" Waldemar got down to business... show business!

"Not as bad as I initially thought," Li'l Otter said optimistically. "I want to look around Ostrichland and especially check out the auditorium you said is in The Egg. That might be ideal."

"Yes. The Yolk, it's called. Also, I have a recording studio off the auditorium," Waldemar added. "I must admit, it's never been used since The Egg was built, or as we say around Ostrichland, 'hatched.'"

"Not to change the subject too much, Waldemar, I hope that the recording studio starts to get some action," Li'l Otter gazed at Waldemar with very serious eye contact. "Watching you onstage last night was amazing, *and* you seemed to really be enjoying yourself!"

Waldemar leaned back in his chair in thought. "You're right, Li'l Otter," Waldemar admitted, looking far off into the past. "I guess you can't get performing out of your soul once you've been successful at it, no matter how much you want to." Waldemar mused.

"Well, on to the show!" Li'l Otter said, hoping to get the mood upbeat rather than pensive.

"Yes, the show!" Waldemar repeated, sitting up straighter in his chair. "When? Where? How? All the usual logistic questions, eh?" Waldemar offered, his brown eyes darting between Li'l Otter and Shen.

Just as the three were about to begin planning the show from Ostrichland, a bright red light lit up on Waldemar's desk telephone. "I've got to get this guys... it's my hotline." After a few minutes on the phone, Waldemar slowly placed the receiver back in its cradle. "I need to check something on U-Tubes," Waldemar remarked somewhat absentmindedly as he stared intently at his Microsoft Surface Laptop.

"What are you looking for, Waldemar?" Shen inquired, Waldemar seeming to find the desired video. Without answering, Waldemar clicked 'play.'

All of their eyes bugged out as they watched a perfectly shot video of Waldemar's performance of *Now, the Sky* at *WonderBar* the night before. "We have a traitor on our hands..." Waldemar muttered, his voice trailing off as the performance continued. "A traitor!"

"Now Waldemar, keep things in perspective," Li'l Otter cautioned his friend. "No one will even notice the video," he said, knowing it was probably going viral even as he spoke.

"It's the violation, Li'l Otter," Waldemar replied, his mood serious, but his emotions now under control. "It's like the old days when I had to deal with so many privacy issues, you know? I don't even know who took that video last night."

"That *is* a good question," Shen agreed. "I thought everybody was friends or at least friendly last night."

"It's interesting, the angle of the shot, Waldemar," Li'l Otter observed. "Everyone was sitting at the table more towards the door of *WonderBar* while it looks like the video was shot more towards the door toward the kitchen..."

Li'l Otter looked at Waldemar. Shen looked at Li'l Otter. Waldemar looked at the ceiling.

"*Three!*" All three chimed together. Waldemar quickly stood up and headed out the door of the administrative office. Li'l Otter and Shen were right behind. Waldemar didn't wait for the private elevator to the Sky House, he bounded up the stairs taking them two at a time. Within seconds he was in the spacious foyer of the Sky House, nearly colliding with Dr. Dustie Rhodes in the process.

"Is Lady Orchid still here?" Waldemar asked breathlessly. "I need to find out if she has Three's phone number! She's good at getting phone numbers *fast!*"

"No. I haven't seen her since breakfast," Dustie said, taking hold of Waldemar's right shoulder with her right hand and leading him to the large green sectional in the family room. The others followed. "Waldemar, come sit down and explain what is going on!"

Dustie was able to get the story out of Waldemar how Three apparently betrayed Waldemar by making a video of Waldemar's private performance of **WOW**'s *Now, the Sky* with Sanny the night before and posted it on U-Tubes. She understood his pain and anger. She also noticed the flashing lights on the telephone in the family room but didn't mention it to Waldemar. Li'l Otter noticed Dustie's eye movement toward the phone, bringing the flashing lights to his attention.

"Waldemar, I have to take a call. It's from Intertoobz headquarters in Chicago," Li'l Otter said, gripping his Samsung Galaxy and walking to the circular hall of the Sky House. Li'l Otter was on his phone for several minutes with someone at headquarters before he re-entered the family room. "Headquarters called to say the video has gone viral, Waldemar," Li'l Otter announced. The family room was silent as the occupants were in thought over the implication of the news.

After several minutes, Waldemar broke the silence: "Welcome back to the spotlight, Waldemar Ulff," he said out loud, a wan smile crossing his face. "Welcome back."

Up North...

"More to your right. Right. Left. Right. Correct. That's it. Left. Right... I mean, correct. Right. No. Right as in right. That's it. Beautiful. Stunning. Show me a smile. Great. Work it. Work it. Perfect." The photographer's instructions were nothing new. Another photoshoot. Another trying day of posing. Another bill to the cost of fame.

"I can't hold this pose much longer."

"Just a second, Love," the photographer implored. "Would you just be a dear and hold this dove with both your hands as in a soulful embrace?"

"Hold the dove?" the tired subject repeated, reflecting fatigue and confusion.

"Yes, just hold the dove," the photographer affirmed, urging an assistant to take the tranquil bird of peace to the subject, carefully transferring the placid bird from assistant to subject's hands with great care.

"Perfect! Now just hold it. Work it. Right. Left. Up. Down. Upside down. Great. Beautiful. Work it. Now. That's it. Feel the dove. Feel the peace. That's the way..."

"Why isn't the bird moving?" the subject asked, looking closer at the bird in hand.

"Because it's a professional," the photographer answered, continuing to snap, snap, snap away.

"No. I mean the bird isn't moving... at all. I think I squeezed it too hard... maybe?" the subject persisted.

The assistant went over to check the dove. "It's dead," the assistant muttered.

"I need a break... and a Kleenex," the camera's subject said. No whining. No complaints. She was too professional for those traits. Fatigue was the factor, pure and simple, along with a dead dove in her hands.

"Sure. I could use a break too," the photographer replied as several assistants moved into place to secure the set for another round of frames once the break came to its inevitable end. The head assistant removed the dead dove from the subject's hands.

"Great! I need to make some calls and have another cup of coffee," the subject admitted, stepping down from her high-legged chair and carefully walking over to a variety of snacks and drinks set up on an adjoining table. A cup of Tim Horton's Dark Roast coffee[12] in hand, she made her way past the various items and people needed for a professional photoshoot to get some space towards the entrance of the building. With a swift flick of her right hand she pulled out an iPhone and quickly placed a call.

"Hi, it's me. Oh, just the usual. I never did find photoshoots much fun. You know that. All those cameras. All those years. All the dead props. I think they're going to be wrapping up soon, then you can come on over. Okay, darling. I love you too!"

She placed the phone back in the right-hand pocket of her festive dress and took a soothing sip of the now cooling coffee. She knew her presence would be required to continue the photoshoot at any time. Relax when you can. A gift she learned years ago, and it always paid off.

"Oola, we're ready when you are," one of the photographer's assistants informed her. Rio de Taipan was being featured in an upcoming issue of *Six-Star Dining* magazine and Oola La, the owner of the restaurant, the star attraction. Business as usual.

"Here I come," Oola replied, taking a look at her famous face with a pocket mirror before proceeding back to her high-legged chair. The beautiful blonde hair with her signature style, short on one side, long on the other, part on the right, the stunning deep-set blue eyes, the porcelain skin... she was still breathtaking even though her peak of fame was receding with time. Oola La was an original, then and now.

Her journey was interrupted by the unexpected ring of her phone.

"Hello?" she answered quickly. "Slow down! You're breaking up and I can't understand you! You what? Waldemar? Waldemar?! On U-Tubes? Geez! Yes. No. I need to see it right now! Sure, come on over. Love you. Bye."

While the crew on the photoshoot at Oola La's Toronto Asian-Brazilian fusion restaurant, Rio de Taipan waited, Oola quickly clicked the U-Tubes

---

[12] Tim Horton's Dark Roast coffee is made from a premium blend of 100% Arabica beans, expertly roasted with care. The Canadian choice to get into the dark with its rich, delicious taste and full flavor.

app. The video she was seeking was already listed in the 'trending' section: Waldemar's duet with Sanny singing *Now, the Sky*. She looked at the video in surprise and fascination. She quickly clicked re-play when it was done. Time stood still.

"Oola, Darling, we're going to call it a day," the photographer informed her as the photoshoot crew started packing and putting Rio de Taipan back in place.

"Are you sure? I can spare more time if you need it," Oola said half-heartedly, her eyes still glued to her iPhone.

"No. We've taken enough of your time already," the photographer replied, turning away to supervise the close of the day.

Oola stared at the freeze frame of Waldemar on U-Tubes. All those years. All those years ago! A light tap on her right shoulder brought her back to the present.

"Oh! Walter...!"

Blast from the Past...

FLASHBACK:

"I'm Li'l Otter for "Behind the Video" here on VTV, Video Television and I'm talking to **WOW**'s Waldemar Ulff. It's a pleasure to finally meet you Waldemar."

"Thanks, Li'l Otter. Congratulations on becoming the newest vjay!"

"Thanks, Waldemar. It's a bit strange interviewing a man dressed as a slice of bacon. What's going on?"

"**WOW** is making a video for our new single, 'Pizza Breakfast.'"

"Delicious!"

"Oola is dressed as an egg, sunny-side up, and Walter is a slice of toast, heavily buttered. This video is being directed by Gurt Holjeerz who is the go to music video director of 1993. He has an amazing imagination and **WOW** is honored to have Gurt directing us."

"Tell us a little about the video, Waldemar."

"Basically, it's the story of an average guy who wakes up on Monday morning and is still half-asleep, eating his breakfast of a pizza slice from Saturday night before going to work. He falls asleep at the breakfast table and has a very weird dream. He dreams that traditional breakfast fare such as bacon, eggs and toast come and hassle him because he is eating a slice of pizza for breakfast, ham and sausage to be exact. After a frightening chase scene down the Sunset Strip, the traditional breakfast elements catch him and jostle him until he wakes up."

"That's an amazing storyline! I hear you have a surprise personality in the video."

"Yes."

"Who is it?"

"If I tell you, it won't be a surprise. Regardless, yes, we have Garland Judy, America's hottest Gender Illusionist playing the cup of coffee. It's such a treat to work with Garland!"

"Sounds like it! Do you enjoy making music videos, Waldemar?"

"Oh, yeah! It really gives my acting chops a workout. I really like it when a director as sensitive as Gurt has the video complement the music, so it adds to the song. So many music videos these days don't really have anything to do with the song. It's like the director never heard the song before, or if he has, he doesn't care what message may or may not be in the song, he has his own message to tell. I don't think that's fair."

"Where is **WOW** going after your current tour?"

"I'm excited to say that we're going to South Africa! We have several concerts planned. **WOW**'s general manager, Yukio Cassidy, is arranging that all our concerts in South Africa be open to all. Following the concerts, we are planning to go on a safari. I'm very excited about that! I love animals!"

"That sounds exciting, Waldemar! Who knows, maybe you'll end up owning an exotic animal park if you ever get tired of singing!"

"Ha! I don't think so, Li'l Otter! Could you just see me presiding over a dazzle of zebras?"

"A dazzle?"

"Yes. That's the official name for a group of zebras. That or a zeal of zebras. Maybe that would be better. Better alliteration!"

"Indeed!"

"Gurt Holjeerz, come here! We're taping 'Behind the Video' and we want to give you some exposure. Come! Gurt Holjeerz, this is VTV vjay, Li'l Otter. Li'l Otter, Gurt Holjeerz, video director par excellence!"

"An honor to meet you, Gurt Holjeerz."

"Of course."

"Waldemar has been filling me in on the artistry of your video for 'Breakfast Pizza.'"

"Really? How kind of him."

"Anything to add to the story?"

"I don't know what Waldemar said; therefore, I don't know what to add or subtract. Are you assigning me psychic abilities? Do you think me a warlock?"

"No. No..."

"Well, you wouldn't be the first to call me names! They *love* to do that in Hollywood, you know! And if they aren't calling you a name, they're talking behind your back like you're just a sad sack of potatoes with no feelings... a block of concrete... a punching bag..."

"Sorry. I didn't mean anything sinister by my question, Gurt Holjeerz."

"They all say that too! They draw and quarter you, then act like nothing happened! I'm so sick of this! How can I create art on videotape when I'm surrounded by evil genies?!"

"Gurt, maybe you should take five and calm down a bit."

"Oh, sure Waldemar! Always so laid back, aren't you? Well, I'd be laid back too if I smoked as much herb as you do! I'm sick of this...!"

"Yukio! Yukio Cassidy! Come join us on 'Behind the Video.'"

"Yukio Cassidy, what a pleasure to meet you! You're a legend in Hollywood with all the success of **WOW**!"

"Thank you, Li'l Otter" said Yukio, "I couldn't do anything without this talented trio. Why are you so red, Gurt?"

"That does it! I'm leaving!" Gurt stormed off.

"Geez, what did I say?" Yukio inquired.

"Never mind," said Waldemar. "He's cranky. Nothing a good lunch won't solve. Oh, Garland Judy! Come, join us on 'Behind the Video!'"

"Well, hello everyone! Don't mind if I do!"

"Nice to meet you Garland Judy. I like your cup of coffee costume."

"What are you talking about? These are my street clothes!"

"Oh...sorry..."

"Just joking! Gee, he's an easy mark!" Garland chuckled.

"Gurt Holjeerz kinda went off on Li'l Otter a few minutes ago," Waldemar clarified.

"Oh, sorry, Li'l Otter. That Gurt... so sensitive, but a genius! It's a once-in-a-lifetime dream to be working with Gurt and **WOW**! Is *any* group this hot right now? I don't think so. And if they are, they don't deserve the fame because **WOW** has *earned* their fame and fortune. *Earned it!* Go tell that to those poseurs who come out of West Nottinghamshireland and try and sweep America off their feet with some clever synthesizer riff and spiky hair! Give me a break! **WOW** owns them and they own the #1 spot on the Billboard Top 100 and I just can't say enough about these three precious people that we, collectively, call **WOW**."

"Wow, **WOW**. There you have it! Unsolicited praise from Garland Judy."

"Lady Orchid!" Waldemar shouted with delight. "We're really scoring some big names today! Come, join us on "Behind the Video." Li'l Otter, this is Lady Orchid Buffington-Choade, a dear friend and mentor of **WOW**."

"Nice to meet you, Lady Orchid."

"Thank you, Little Beaver,... um... Li'l Beaver..."

"Otter... Li'l Otter."

"Yes. Yes, indeed. You can call me Lady Orchid."

"I just did."

"Did what?"

"Call you Lady Orchid."

"Oh, thank you! Isn't Waldemar a dear?"

"He's an amazing singer, that's for sure."

"I knew that when I first met him. **WOW** was destined for stardom from the start. That's why I took them under my wing when they relocated to England in the late 80's. They didn't have enough money to buy lunch at the start. Now they own lunch!"

"Well said!"

"I gave **WOW** a suite of rooms at Buffington-Choade Manor. I have plenty of empty rooms and do so enjoy the company of creative people. They started recording at the Manor since I installed a recording studio in my former ceramics studio in the sub-basement. And the rest is history! I'm so proud of **WOW**!"

"I know many fans feel that way."

"I'm more than a fan, Li'l Rodent! That's just putting me in a category shared by millions of people. I'm much more than a fan! Why, I gave **WOW** their start and I get called a fan!? Waldemar, do you approve of me being called just a 'fan?'"

"No. No, that would be inaccurate, Lady Orchid."

"Thank you!"

"I'm so sorry Lady Orchid. I didn't mean to offend you! And it's Li'l Otter. Li'l Otter."

"Yes. Yes. Indeed. I hope you can tell I'm very protective of my relationship with **WOW**."

"Protective. Yes."

"Well, what's *that* supposed to mean, Li'l Weasel? Protective?"

"Um. Waldemar, I didn't mean to insult your guest. I do apologize. Li'l Weasel? It's *Li'l Otter.*"

"No. I meant to call you Li'l Weasel. I don't appreciate your attitude and I don't want to be on this show anymore! Waldemar, forgive me, but I can't just sit here and take this abuse. I'll see you for dinner. It was an experience meeting you Li'l Wolverine. Take care."

"Okay. Gee. I didn't even get to ask her about her fancy hat."

"Fascinator."

"What?"

"Her fancy hat is called a fascinator," Waldemar explained. "She wears one for every occasion. Always with a theme. If you noticed, her fascinator theme today was 'breakfast.' Thus, the millinery bacon and eggs... Oh! Score! Oola and Walter! Come on in you guys! I'm here with Li'l Otter taping a segment of VTV's 'Behind the Video.'

"Here we go with Oola La and Walter Johnson! **WOW** is now complete! Hi! Just squeeze on in here. We're a little short on space. There you go! Have a seat."

"I'm afraid we can't sit down, Li'l Otter, seeing as I'm in a sunny side up egg costume and Walter's a slice of well-buttered toast. Ha!"

"True enough! Ah, showbiz, eh?"

"And they say it's luck not talent!" cracked Walter.

"Speak for yourself, Walter! Wearing a sunny side up egg costume is just a bonus to having talent! Ha!"

"Oola, you're the cutest sunny-side up egg I've ever seen! Li'l Otter was speculating that I might own an exotic animal park when I retire. What do you think?"

"I think that will never happen, Waldemar. I know you love animals, but you love performing too much for that to happen."

"That's for sure!"

"Walter Johnson, where do you see yourself when you retire?"

"I see myself tending to a small garden behind the rest home... ha!"

"Oola La?"

"Oh, maybe writing a cookbook. I love to cook, you know?"

"If your fans have anything to say, retirement will be many years from now."

"Well, that will be the day! Maybe we should all get together in twenty years and see where we all ended up."

"You got it, Waldemar! Twenty years! And that's another episode of 'Behind the Video.' We're on set with **WOW**. I'm Li'l Otter. And we'll be seeing you in twenty years!"

"And we're clear."

END OF FLASHBACK

A Rose By Another Name...

"More to your right. Right. Left. Right. Correct. That's it. Beautiful. Stunning. Show me a smile. Great. Work it. Work it. Perfect." The photographer instructed the group of three men as they stood next to a large wooden sign. The sign, set in a river rock foundation, had been recently altered to read, 'New Fatherland.' The group being photographed consisted of Bürgermeister Ackermann, Conrad Halle and Les Winns.

"Is he almost done? I've got things to do!" Halle asked with annoyance, his monocle pinched tightly in his right eye socket, just up from the triple bags under his eyes.

"I believe we're coming to an end of the photoshoot gentlemen, " Winns reassured the pair. It was uncomfortable for Bürgermeister Ackermann and Conrad Halle standing next to the welcome sign that only yesterday read, 'Welcome to Neu Deutschland' now altered to 'Welcome to New Fatherland.' It was a physical embodiment of their involvement in selling (out) to Winns and making a nice profit on their venture.

"Why are we even taking these photos?" Halle demanded of Winns.

"For my album, Mr. Halle," Winns replied, still smiling for the photographer's last frames. "My special photo album."

"Special album?" Bürgermeister Ackermann queried, a drop of sweat rolling down the right side of his face even though the day was mild.

"Yes," Winns turned toward Bürgermeister Ackermann and Halle. "You see, gentlemen, I keep a special photo album of all the special people in my life."

"Special why?" Bürgermeister Ackermann urged him on.

"Special in that they sold out. They sold their pride and principles out over money," Winns replied, his narrow-set eyes boring into Bürgermeister Ackermann and Halle. "And I like to keep photos of such people. My album is quite large, actually," Winns commented, a small note of disappointment in his voice. "It's sad, really," he said, relaxing as the photographer indicated with a shake of his head that his work was done. "In my experience, people will sell the most precious things for money. I had no doubt that you gentlemen would sell Neu Deutschland if the price was high enough."

"That's a very cynical way of looking at things!" Halle protested, his right hand adjusting his monocle in annoyance.

"Cynical, but accurate," Winns countered.

"We were just doing what was best for Neu Deutschland... er... New Fatherland," Bürgermeister Ackermann protested, choking on the new name of the town.

"By the way, gentlemen, *Das Rathaus* is now off limits," Winns announced, looking at the welcome sign. "I have moved my operations from Halle Haus to *Das Rathaus*. I have many things to plan in the next few days and I can't have unauthorized people running in and out of my headquarters."

"*Your* headquarters!?" Bürgermeister Ackermann took a step forward towards Winns, but Halle tugged at Ackermann's suspenders to keep him in place and in check.

Both Ackermann and Halle were at a loss for words as both started gazing at the freshly revitalized and renamed sign welcoming people to New Fatherland.

Winns' Cadillac XTS limousine pulled up as Bürgermeister Ackermann and Halle assessed their legacies. Winns and the photographer boarded the gleaming black vehicle as the driver opened the right rear door. With a glimpse, Edwin and Edwina Flunkie could be seen sitting on the jump seats, their eyes glued to their Apple MacBook Pros. With a gentle whoosh, the Cadillac XTS limousine was gone, heading slowly down *Hauptstraße*.

"*Mein Gott, was haben wir getan?*" Bürgermeister Ackermann asked in the mother tongue, speaking to no one in particular.

"Indeed. What *have* we done?" Halle responded, starting to walk slowly past the welcome sign, towards Halle Haus.

"I didn't think he would take owning our town so personal!" Bürgermeister Ackermann remarked. "I thought he would bring some new ideas and money into the town, but he seems to be planning for a revolution, not an evolution," Bürgermeister Ackermann huffed.

"Indeed!" Halle agreed, peering at the ground as they walked along to Halle Haus.

"Isn't that your grandson?" Bürgermeister Ackermann asked Halle, pointing to a lone figure slinking toward Halle Haus.

"Three! Three! What are you doing here?" Halle shouted, answering Bürgermeister Ackermann's query by his actions. In the distance, the figure of Three stopped, turning toward Ackermann and Halle. After identifying them, he turned and started running toward the Halle Haus parking lot across the street from the establishment.

"Three! Wait! I need to talk to you!" Halle implored his grandson. He was rewarded by seeing Three slow down and eventually stop and walk toward them.

"Grandfather, I'm so sorry, but I've done something terrible!" he blurted out, wiping his face with his right hand.

"Join the crowd, Three. Join the crowd," Halle replied wearily, placing his right hand on the young man's right shoulder.

Fame 2.0...

Waldemar sat sullenly at his desk in the administrative office, staring at his Microsoft Surface laptop. Li'l Otter and Shenandoah River were occupying the smaller spare office next to Waldemar's, getting the latest news about the viral video of Waldemar and Sanny performing *Now, the Sky* at *WonderBar*.

"Guests in the parking lot, Waldemar," Agatha alerted Waldemar.

"Okay, Agatha," Waldemar responded absent-mindedly, his gaze on his Microsoft Surface laptop.

"I mean *lots* of guests!" Agatha emphasized. Waldemar looked at the closed-circuit monitor set in Agatha's sleek pyramid on the right side of the desk.

"Intercom Li'l Otter and Shen in the spare office," Waldemar requested of Agatha. "Ask them to come here."

"Will do, Waldemar," Agatha responded obediently. Within a few minutes, both men were in the administrative office viewing the closed-circuit monitor with Waldemar.

"You would think the sky is falling!" Li'l Otter observed, watching the scene on the closed-circuit monitor. Shen turned away and placed another call on his iPhone, walking slowly to the entrance of the administrative office.

"There's another van pulling into the lot now," Waldemar observed, watching the fourth TV news satellite van pulling into Ostrichland. "We need a plan, Li'l Otter." Waldemar said, sitting back in his chair as he pulled his ponytail tighter, resting his hands on his head.

"Yukio Cassidy on line 2, Waldemar," Agatha announced. Yukio Cassidy was **WOW**'s legendary business manager during their heyday. After **WOW**'s breakup in 1999, he relocated to the North Shore of Oahu, Hawaii, where he continued to serve as the chief executive of **WOW**'s holding company, **WOW**, Inc., compiling royalties, investments, financial arrangements and public relations for the three former members of **WOW**. "Yukio!" Waldemar answered line 2 quickly. "It's crazy here!"

"I would guess so, My Famous One," Yukio replied in his calm, lilting voice. "Your news has traveled to the North Shore!" You didn't tell me you were coming out of retirement," he teased.

"Hardly!" Waldemar corrected him.

"You might want to reconsider that, My Superstar," Yukio said with a chuckle. "I thought the video was quite good, but I don't think *Now, the Sky* has aged well." Yukio was always the voice of reason for **WOW**.

"You're probably right, Yukio," Waldemar conceded the point. He had other matters to contend with at this point. "I am surrounded by news crews setting up right now, Yukio. Any advice?"

"Sure, make sure you charge them an admission fee to Ostrichland, Wise One!" Yukio laughed.

"You know I've never charged an admission fee to Ostrichland, Yukio," Waldemar said in earnest. "And I never will. People need free access to ostriches!"

"Right, Son from Another Father," Yukio said calmly. "I was just joking."

"Right, Yukio."

"I would advise you to go greet the reporters and just give them the Waldemar charm. It has always worked before, Golden Tongue" Yukio advised. "There's no point in hiding."

"I think you're right, Yukio," Waldemar replied. "But what do I *say* to them?"

"Regarding what?"

"They will be asking if I'm getting into music again. Is **WOW** reuniting? The same old stuff we put up with for so many years!" Waldemar said in exasperation.

"That's true, my son. What *are* the answers!" Yukio answered with a question.

"Reporters are in The Egg asking for you, Waldemar," Agatha interrupted Waldemar's call with Yukio.

"Thanks, Agatha," Waldemar responded. "Yukio, I've got to go. I'll keep you updated."

"All right, Honored One," Yukio Cassidy replied. "Just be yourself and everything will be fine," he advised once again. Waldemar ended the call and looked at Li'l Otter seated in the chair next to Waldemar's desk. Li'l Otter looked back at Waldemar. Shen entered the administrative office after stepping out to take one of his numerous calls.

"Gentlemen, I know I haven't been asked, but I would like to propose a way to handle this situation," Shen volunteered as he placed his iPhone in his right pant pocket.

"Do tell," Waldemar urged him, glancing at the closed-circuit monitor trained on the Ostrichland parking lot and the unfolding scene.

"Instead of being broadsided by random questions from reporters, I would schedule a news conference," Shen said, standing next to Li'l Otter. "You could hold a news conference later today. Home field advantage. Make nice with some refreshments and a look at the ostriches. You'll be able to stifle any reunion rumors, get the reporters off your back and get some free publicity for Ostrichland on top of it all."

"That makes a lot of sense, Shen," Li'l Otter said, looking at him, then turning his gaze to Waldemar who was pondering what Shen had suggested.

"I like it, Shen," Waldemar replied, swiveling his plush executive chair to face him head on. "Can you take care of the arrangements?"

"Sure thing, Waldemar!" he replied enthusiastically, turning on his heels and heading out of the administrative office.

"Waldemar, a call for you on line 3," Agatha announced.

Waldemar looked at Li'l Otter, puzzled. "Line 3 is a private line. I wonder who it is?" Waldemar turned his attention back to Agatha. "Who is it?" he asked.

"She wouldn't say, Waldemar," Agatha responded.

"Okay, thanks," Waldemar said, picking up the landline. "Hello?"

"Hello, Waldemar? It's Oola."

This Just In...

Bürgermeister Ackermann and Conrad Halle were sitting in the actual bar of WonderBar at Halle Haus, banished from *Das Rathaus* by Les Winns, the new owner of New Fatherland, formerly Neu Deutschland. The bar, fashioned of German elm wood, was empty save for the two forlorn gentlemen. Winns had expanded both of their wallets, but at what price? Changes were happening to their old town and fast.

"I can't believe we can't even enter *Das Rathaus* now that Les Winns has taken it over!" Bürgermeister Ackermann whined, taking a gulp of Weihenstaphaner Hefe Weissbier German beer[13] while Halle favored Bitburger Premium Pils[14] to drown his sorrows. Halle remained silent. "What will become of Neu Deutschland?" Ackermann questioned no one in particular.

In the background, the only concession to the 21st Century, a large wall-mounted Sony 55" TV with HDR was set to JustNEWS, the popular online news source, the sound off, captions only. The TV faced the south wall of the *WonderBar* bar, across from the bar itself.

---

[13] A 99 from Beer Advocate, the beer with a sparkling reputation! Aromas of banana, clove and peppery spice make this beer incredibly appealing. Some citrus fruit and malts characterize the taste, with great balance and good carbonation. A truly outstanding hefeweizen!

[14] The classic Bitburger, a mature and most agreeable beer, is brewed with the best of ingredients in the same traditional way it has been for many, many years. The result is delicately tart and pleasantly bitter, with a strong hop taste.

"We're living in *interesting* times," Bürgermeister Ackermann observed, taking his last gulp of Weihenstaphaner Hefe Weissbier, wiping his chin with the back of his right hand.

Conrad Halle III put down the now sparkling beer stein and took a glance at the TV across the bar from him. It was lucky he had set the beer stein on the bar a moment before or it surely would be in a thousand broken pieces on the floor had he seen what he was seeing now on the TV: his video of Waldemar and Sanny singing, *Now, the Sky!*

"Why are your eyes bugged out, Three!?" his grandfather asked with a touch of annoyance in his voice. With no reply from Three, Halle turned to see what startled him so.

"Isn't that Waldemar Ulff and that lousy lounge singer I hired here at *WonderBar*?" Halle questioned in amazement. Bürgermeister Ackermann turned around on his shaky bar stool to see what he was missing.

"*WonderBar* on TV!" Ackermann exclaimed, delighted that the former Neu Deutschland was getting some TV time.

"Turn on the sound, Three! *Schnell! Schnell!*," Halle ordered his grandson. With a flick of Three's right thumb on the remote control, the sound came to life...

"...the viral video has become a sensation around the world as the reclusive singer, Waldemar Ulff of **WOW** fame, suddenly re-emerged, sparking speculation of a **WOW** reunion," the TV reporter said, standing in front of The Egg at Ostrichland. In the background, many other reporters could be seen in an atmosphere of barely controlled chaos.

"Isn't that Magdalene Sigi, the reporter?" the Bürgermeister asked, clearly admiring the reportage.

"Yeah, sure is!" Three verified Ackermann's knowledge of Internet news teams. "She comes to *WonderBar* every once in a while."

"Quiet!" Halle snapped, keeping his attention on the news story. "I want to hear this!"

"It appears that Waldemar Ulff is going to make a statement regarding the now viral video," Sigi told the viewers as the camera panned the crowd in the parking lot of Ostrichland, Waldemar walking from The Egg to the reporters, followed by Shrimp Wrigley including Simon the Stag Beetle, Lady Orchid sporting a fascinator depicting a satellite dish, Dustie wearing her safari suit, Li'l Otter going casual, Shen in an Intertoobz t-shirt and Lanky sans clothes (as usual).

"Waldemar! Waldemar!
Who's the BIG bird?
Who's the old guy with the bug on his shoulder?
Do Oola and Walter know about this?
Who was singing with you?
Is there going to be a **WOW** reunion?

What's your sign?

How many ounces are in a pint?

Have you talked to Oola and Walter?

Does that BIG bird bite?"

Various comments could be heard throughout the crowd as Waldemar and his gang walked to the curb of the parking lot near The Egg.

"Hello, everybody!" Li'l Otter did the honors of welcoming the crowd to Ostrichland. "Waldemar has a few words for you." The reporters and camera crews jostled for the best location by Waldemar and as far away from Lanky as possible. "Waldemar has a brief statement and then will take a few questions."

The buzzing and jostling continued. "Calm down!" came a shout. Shrimp Wrigley being the shouter. "Let Waldemar speak!" he pleaded, taking a pull on his Lucky Strike as he moved closer to Lanky, several feet behind Waldemar. The cameras were catching it all.

"Thank you!" Waldemar waved his right hand slightly, then removing his round sunglasses, replacing them with his trademark clear round glasses to appear more accessible while on camera. "I appreciate all of you taking the time to come out to Ostrichland today to get the facts about the viral video," Waldemar began, his years of show business giving a calm, reassuring tone to his delivery. "I am flattered and, quite frankly, humbled by all the attention that has been directed my way in the last few hours. It has always been about the fans throughout my career and it continues to this day. I hate to disappoint all my fans around the world, but there are no plans for a **WOW** reunion. The viral video was of a private party and not an entertainment event. I continue in my current lifestyle devoted to delivering the message of the ostrich and running the educational event that is Ostrichland. My only plans for the future involve keeping Ostrichland thriving, making it bigger and better for our future and the future of our children... *your* children, as I have none."

The reporters jumped to ask the first question when Waldemar concluded his statement.

"Waldemar! Have you been in touch with Oola or Walter?"

"Not in a professional sense."

"Why did you release the video if there's no reunion?"

"The video was recorded without my knowledge."

"Would you have a **WOW** reunion if the price was right?"

"I resent the implications of your question, sir! Next? Yes?"

"Do you have any plans on a solo career?"

"No."

"Do you foresee any circumstance that would bring **WOW** together again?"

"I've learned never to say 'never,' however, at this time I don't see that happening."

"Is it true you haven't seen Oola or Walter since the 00's?"

"We have been living quality lives in different parts of the world."

"Have you found love since Oola?"

"Yes."

"What's her name?"

"Next question!"

"How much does that BIG bird weigh?"

"256.8 pounds and his name is Lanky."

"Is Lanky housebroken?"

"We can come visit your house and find out for yourself," Waldemar joked with a big smile, turning to Lanky with a wide grin. Waldemar knew most of the local reporters, having been featured in the media in pieces about Ostrichland. He was enjoying the give and take of the press event.

"Waldemar, can we go inside The Egg?" Magdalene Sigi of JustNEWS asked, thrusting her microphone as close to Waldemar as she could get in the tight gathering.

"Sure! There's never an admission fee at Ostrichland!" Waldemar announced with a genial smile. "Go on in. I'll be right behind you."

"Thank you, Waldemar!" Li'l Otter shouted, announcing an end to the press event.

"Thank *you*!" Waldemar replied, placing his round sunglasses back over his dark brown eyes.

As the reporters did their wrap-up and crowd readied themselves for a visit inside The Egg, a Lunar Blue Metallic Mercedes-Maybach S 650 Sedan was observed turning off Highway 277, gliding into the Ostrichland parking lot. The elegant sedan stopped in an open space between two TV satellite news vans. The driver and a large man (security?) exited the two front doors of the sedan, both men slowly opening the two rear doors.

Shen took notice of the elegant sedan. "Oh, My *GAWD!*"

At first only a few people such as Shen noticed anything, but in an occasion of group consciousness, everyone's attention turned to the large sedan. Seemingly in unison as the passengers emerged from the rear of the car, the crowd gasped, then shouted,

"OOLA! WALTER!"...

Regrets, Party of Two...

"Well there you go, no **WOW** reunion. Straight from the horse's mouth," Conrad Halle scolded Bürgermeister Ackermann. "At least we don't have *that* option floating around to save Neu Deutschland anymore."

The TV news coverage cut off after Waldemar's 'good-bye' not catching the arrival of the two other members of **WOW**.

"That's too bad," Three remarked, drying another beer stein after turning off the audio on the wall-mounted Sony 55" TV with HDR. "Neu Deutschland or not, a reunion would have been fantastic!"

"Whatever," Bürgermeister Ackermann muttered. "I'll have another Weihenstaphaner Hefe Weissbier, Three."

"Coming right up, sir." He poured Bürgermeister Ackermann a fresh stein. "So, what do you think will happen to Ostrichland now that we're living in New Fatherland?"

"I think Ostrichland's business will drop off even more," Halle answered his grandson. New Fatherland, now, is not intended to be a tourist destination, but a secure town of the elite. Fewer tourists, fewer visitors to Ostrichland. That's why we were trying to get closer ties to Ostrichland before Les Winns made his offer. Neu Deutschland and Ostrichland both depend on each other to a large extent. We could have made it a win/win situation, but Waldemar doesn't see things that way. He was willing to mention the town on the radio, but we were in desperate straits and had to go with Les Winns."

"I still wish we could have helped make a **WOW** reunion happen to boost everyone's fortunes minus Winns," Ackermann mused, downing his fresh stein.

"Well, I never saw the point of pursuing the reunion strategy," Halle grumbled. "Who's to say **WOW** would relocate to Ostrichland?"

"Are you kidding, Grandfather?" Three responded. "Have you ever been in The Egg? It's like living in the future. There's an auditorium, a recording studio, everything they would need for comeback headquarters!"

"That's true, Conrad," Bürgermeister Ackermann said. "You have to see it to believe it!"

"Well, *my* wallet isn't hurting now with the sale of Neu Deutschland completed, that's for sure!" Halle said with a very slight chuckle.

"Maybe now, but who knows how much more we could have made had **WOW** gotten together and made their headquarters at Ostrichland," Ackermann mused. "The tourists would have flocked to Ostrichland and the nearest accommodations are in Neu Deutschland. We would have made a fortune!"

"Would have!" Halle retorted with a snap. "You just heard it. No reunion!"

"Excuse me, Gentlemen, Martin Higher, reporter for *Diva Daily* magazine," the short skinny mid-30's man in a Panama hat holding a notepad and a No. 2 pencil. "Is there someone named Sanny around here?"

Bürgermeister Ackermann looked at Halle. Halle looked at Three. Three looked at the latest clean beer stein.

"Sanny!?" Halle questioned in surprise. "Why, yes, he's our star entertainer here at Halle Haus. I'll have him paged!" he said, exiting *WonderBar* in search of Sanny.

"Great!" Higher replied, adjusting his Panama hat in anticipation of a scoop.

After several minutes, Halle returned to *WonderBar* looking crestfallen. "Where's Sanny?" Higher asked expectantly, touching the rim of his hat with his index finger and thumb of his right hand.

"Sanny's nissing!" Halle replied with uncharacteristic ineloquence. "Ny N's! Ny N's! I think I'n losing ny nind!"

It's Happening...!

As reporters, camera crews, paparazzi and the general public swarmed around the Ostrichland parking lot, Waldemar entered a dream state, walking over to the sedan. Shen had grabbed Waldemar by his right sleeve and pointed him toward the car when he had recognized the occupants stepping out. Waldemar hadn't fully comprehended what was happening as he reached the car.

"Waldemar!" Walter Johnson said in delight, giving his now shocked and confused **WOW** partner a huge hug.

"Walter! What?..." Waldemar stuttered, glancing at Walter, but looking at Oola on the other side of the car as the press pressed in on her. "What's going on? Is this a joke? Oola?"

"Waldemar!" Oola greeted, making her way over to the Waldemar-side of the limousine. "Waldemar!" she repeated once she reached him, giving him a more restrained hug and a kiss on the right cheek. "I can't believe we haven't seen each other for so long!" she said, talking near Waldemar's right ear so he could hear above the din of reporters yelling questions.

About a minute after the **WOW** 'reunion,' as if from heaven a team of uniformed security guards from Pied Piper Security, Inc., hired by Yukio Cassidy, appeared in the Ostrichland parking lot, restoring order to the chaos that had erupted because of the **WOW** factor. Waldemar was too in shock to notice, but several of the guards were now hustling Waldemar, Oola and Walter from the parking lot to The Egg for security reasons. Waldemar's gang were already safe inside The Egg, now in security mode thanks to Agatha's AI control of the situation.

As soon as the hatch slid closed and was secured, Dustie and Shrimp Wrigley quickly made their way to Waldemar's side to offer their support. Lady Orchid, Li'l Otter and Shen moved in to greet their old friends, Oola and Walter.

Meanwhile, not wanting to be relegated to the Ostrich Habitat on the first floor of The Egg, Lanky roamed the Ostrichland parking lot in search of ostrich treats among the crowd... none so far!

"Let's all go up to the Sky House, shall we?" Dustie took the lead and motioned the emotional, excited and shocked group to the private elevator that would take them to the Sky House. Two guards followed the group, the rest taking positions in various parts of The Egg. The remainder of the detachment spread out on the grounds of Ostrichland seeing to it that all unauthorized people were off the property as soon as possible. It took two elevator shifts to get everyone to the Sky House. Within a couple of minutes, the foyer was the scene of another welcoming among long lost friends, acquaintances and fans.

"Let's all go to the living room," said Dustie, taking the mantle of hostess, guiding her guests into the large curved room with the amazing views of Ostrichland and the surrounding valley. "Jeeves, could you get some refreshments for everyone?" she asked Waldemar's faithful butler, batting her eyes at him as she adjusted her pith helmet, somewhat askew from the pushing and shoving during the parking lot pandemonium.

Li'l Otter and Shen remained in the central curved hall of the Sky House quietly discussing something, Shen taking and placing several calls on his smartphone. In a few minutes Jeeves brushed past Li'l Otter and Shen with a serving tray full of cocktails.

"Thank you, Jeeves," Dustie said, taking one of the cocktails off the tray. Jeeves made his way around the spacious room until all the guests had a cocktail in hand. Jeeves was professional enough to include some sparkling apple cider cocktails for the non-imbibers of which there were zero. "I'd like to make a toast," Dustie continued. "To friends together again after many years and many adventures!" she said, raising her glass along with the other occupants of the living room.

"Hear! Hear!" Lady Orchid seconded the toast, the sun glinting off her satellite-shaped fascinator. Oola and Walter were together and joined in the toast. Waldemar was at the far end of the room, near the entrance as if he was ready to run off at any moment. He was still processing the recent events of the day. Li'l Otter and Shen joined the group in the living room, each taking a cocktail and participating in the toast.

"Guest arrival," Agatha announced. "Yukio Cassidy requesting entrance to the private elevator."

"Wh-a-a-t?" Waldemar murmured, almost to himself. What's Yukio doing here too?" Waldemar walked a few steps over to the nearest Agatha pyramid. "Give Yukio Cassidy access to the elevator."

"Sure, Waldemar."

Presently, the double entrance doors of the Sky House opened at a guard's touch, revealing a short Japanese man in his late fifties with a blue Brooks Brothers Regent Fit Sharkskin 1818 Suit. Yukio Cassidy's hair was long, dark black, pulled back and tied into a man bun in a style like a Samurai warrior of which he was a descendant. Yukio Cassidy, the business 'glue' of **WOW**, as it were, was now stepping foot into the Sky House of The Egg at Ostrichland, the second time in his life; the first being when The Egg was initially 'hatched.'

"Yukio! What are you doing here!?" Waldemar asked, not unhappy to see him, but confused as to the macro view of the events unfolding.

"I thought you could use my help, My Noteworthy Son," Yukio said in his soothing voice. Oola and Walter made their way over to Yukio and gave him a group hug. After the hug, Yukio continued, "I felt my place was here with all of you in Ostrichland rather than my staying on the North Shore in solitary splendor. I made use of Flights of Fancy private leased jets, as did Oola and Walter and made my way here as soon as possible," he explained, waiving off a cocktail from Jeeves. "Hi, Jeeves. No thanks."

"Okay. That explains that," Waldemar said slowly, taking another cocktail from Jeeves' offerings. Waldemar walked a few steps so that he was now standing next to his former colleagues. "*Are* we having a reunion, and nobody bothered to tell *me*?" he asked as the pieces were coming together.

"Not at all, Little One," Yukio spoke. "I would say that your viral video was the catalyst that brought the three of you back together. And that's a good thing, don't you agree?" Yukio continued with his wise thoughts. "What the three of you do with this encounter remains to be seen. However, from my perspective, opportunities abound in this world, you simply need to be mindful of their existence."

"Well put, Yukio!" Lady Orchid remarked, applauding slightly, her gloved hands muffling the sound. "Now come on over here and give me a kiss you sweet man! I haven't seen you in years and I miss those lips!" Everyone laughed at Lady Orchid's blunt greeting of her old friend. Finally, the ice was broken. Let the party begin, full throttle!

Catching Up...

In the teak-paneled den directly off the living room of the Sky House, Waldemar, Oola La and Walter Johnson gathered as the party in the living room continued. Jeeves provided hors d'oeuvres and mango juice smoothies for the three former members of **WOW** and shut the double doors for their privacy. With the doors now secure, the three shared a warm group hug... it had been a long time!

"I didn't know you were coming to Ostrichland!" Waldemar said to Oola and Walter as the three sat down at a small round glass table with four flower-shaped chairs to enjoy the refreshments.

"I know, Waldemar," Oola replied in her famous breathy voice. "After I called you about the viral video, I said to Walter that I thought we should fly to California and see how things are going. The video just brought back so many memories," Oola explained, brushing a strand of her famously-blond hair from her right eye.

"Yeah, Waldemar, we couldn't resist!" Walter added, having a sip of his smoothie. "Very good," he commented, holding the smoothie glass up to the fading light of the day to inspect its bright color.

"So, we called Yukio, he got a Flights of Fancy leased private jet for us, an Embraer Lineage 1000E, to be exact. We flew into Santa Barbara and here we are," Oola explained. "Yukio also provided the security service. He figured Ostrichland would need it after the viral video and reunion rumors."

"Yukio's the best, that's for sure," Waldemar commented, eating an expertly prepared deviled egg. "Are you still living in the Negev Desert, Walter?" he asked innocently.

"No. No, Waldemar. I'm... uh... living in Toronto these days," Walter replied, taking note of Waldemar's lack of current show business knowledge. "I sold the hydroponics business about ten years ago, actually," Walter added, coughing slightly because of nerves.

"Toronto? As in Oola's Toronto?" Waldemar looked across the small glass table at Oola and Walter.

"Yes, Waldemar," he answered, taking another swig of his mango juice smoothie.

"Waldemar, Walter and I have been together for five years now," Oola got to the point. "You really didn't know?" she questioned in exasperation.

"Five years!? Um... I really don't keep up with show biz news," Waldemar admitted, taking a hard swallow of grilled oysters on a bed of salt. "Really?" he looked at Oola and Walter like a young boy who was informed that Santa Claus didn't exist. "Really? After all those years together?"

"Waldemar, it's okay," Walter reached over and gave him a pat on the right shoulder. "We weren't hiding anything, Man, it was in all the tabloids!"

"But... but... Oola and I were the couple," Waldemar said shakily, taking a sip of smoothie.

"Waldemar, time moves on. Things change," Oola put her right hand over Waldemar's right hand resting on the clear tabletop.

"I thought Walter was out in the Negev Desert with his hydroponic vegetables and here you two were in Toronto all that time... together?"

"Waldemar?" Walter removed his right hand from Waldemar's right shoulder. "Why do you think I quit **WOW** and moved to the desert in the first place?"

"I thought you were burnt out like the rest of us and needed a break," Waldemar replied. "And you liked growing vegetables in the desert? No?"

"No. Waldemar, I was in love with Oola and I knew you were too!" Walter admitted. "I had to get out of there before I broke some hearts!"

"Oh wow! Oh wow!" Waldemar said, standing up and walking over to the curved window of the den, deep in thought as he looked out over Ostrichland. The den was quiet.

"Waldemar?" Oola walked over to Waldemar's side, touching his right shoulder with her right hand. "I'm sorry all of this hit you at once. We didn't want to hurt you again."

"That's the last thing we want to do, Waldemar," Walter joined Waldemar and Oola at the window.

"After we saw the viral video, Walter and I missed you so much that we really needed to come and see you," Oola explained as Waldemar continued to gaze out the den window.

"I guess I got too wrapped up in the ostriches," Waldemar replied softly. "The world continued while I was tending my flock. Ostriches are good companions in that they never talk back to you."

"What about that Dr. Rusty?" Oola asked, a note of cheer in her voice to bring some positive energy in the room. "She seems like a special woman in your life. No?"

"Dr *Dustie*. Dr. Dustie Rhodes," Waldemar corrected Oola, turning to look at her directly in the eyes for the first time that day.

"Am I right?" Oola asked.

"Right about what?" Waldemar asked with a touch of brat in his voice.

"Right about her being special in your life."

Waldemar walked over to the built-in Moroccan Argania wood shelves that held many volumes of his book collection. He ran his right hand over the spines of the neatly shelved books as he thought. He reached a section of shelves holding photo albums. All of Waldemar's photos had been digitized, but he still liked to get out the albums from time-to-time, sit down at the circular glass table and pour over the visions of the past. It was calming to him. Waldemar reached for a red bound photo album, pulled it off the shelf, brought it over to the circular glass table and sat down. Slowly Oola and Walter returned to their places at the table as Waldemar reverently opened the album.

"When were those photos taken, Waldemar?" Oola asked, trying to get a glimpse of the photos from her view to the right side.

"This is a fairly recent album," Waldemar answered, slowly turning the first page as he spoke. "These are photos from the mid-00's when I had been at Ostrichland for several years. Around the time The Egg was hatched."

Waldemar continued to view the album. After several minutes he started sharing the photos with Oola and Walter, turning the album slightly so they could see better. Each photo had a story and each story was bringing joy back into Waldemar's life as he recounted the many wonderful memories Ostrichland held in his life.

"Here's one of Dustie holding Lanky's egg!" Waldemar said enthusiastically, holding up the album so Oola and Walter could see clearly.

"How cute!" Oola giggled, sweeping the right side of her hair away from her eyes.

"That's is one of my favorite photos!" Waldemar beamed like a proud father.

As Waldemar was coming to the end of the photo album, there was a light knock on the double doors of the den. The right-side door opened slowly and Dustie stuck her head into peek. "Waldemar, sorry to interrupt, but everyone's wondering where you are," she said, biting her lower lip slightly, not knowing if her interruption was appreciated or not.

"Dustie, come on in," Waldemar said, his voice now back to Waldemar normal. "But shut the door behind you, okay?"

"What's up?" Dustie asked, looking at Oola and Walter as she walked over to Waldemar. Waldemar pointed at the photo of Lanky's egg.

"Remember this photo?" Waldemar asked Dustie as she sat down in the fourth flower-shaped chair at the table.

"Oh course!" I *love* that photo," she chuckled, getting closer to Waldemar to get a closer look at the photo. Waldemar stood up and walked over to a small walnut writing desk next to the built-in shelves. He opened the top right-hand drawer and placed something in his right hand, returning to the clear circular table.

Rather than sitting down next to Dustie, he went down on his right knee and handed Dustie a small black box. "Dustie?" Waldemar asked, closing the photo album and pushing it to the center of the circular glass table. "Will you marry me?"

Dustie, Oola and Walter's jaws dropped in unison and then squeals of delight and surprise erupted in the room. Walter opted to cheer rather than squeal.

"Yes... *yes*, Waldemar," Dustie replied, tears of happiness running down her cheeks. "I am *so* surprised!"

Caught up in the moment, Walter got up from the clear circular table, walked the few steps over to Oola, took her right hand in his and asked, "Oola, will you marry me?" handing her a small black box that he extracted from the right pocket of his Ralph Lauren Men's Classic-Fit Navy UltraFlex Suit.

Waldemar, Dustie and Oola's jaws dropped in unison and then squeals of delight and surprise erupted in the room. Waldemar *did* squeal!

"Oh, Walter! Yes!" Oola cried, brushing the right side of her hair from her right eye.

Dustie and Oola both opened the little black boxes and examined the exquisite engagement rings contained therein while Waldemar and Walter looked on with big smiles on their faces. It was a surprise moment for all!

A small tap at the double doors caught everyone's attention. "Yes?" Waldemar asked. The right side of the double door opened slowly, Shrimp Wrigley peeking in.

"Waldemar? Can I come in for a moment?" Shrimp Wrigley asked with some hesitation.

"Sure, Shrimp Wrigley," Waldemar replied, now in very good spirits.

Shrimp Wrigley *and* Lady Orchid entered the den and quickly closed the double doors behind them.

"Sorry to interrupt, Waldemar," Shrimp Wrigley began. "It's just that Lady Orchid and I have some news to share," Shrimp Wrigley said, looking at a beaming Lady Orchid. "Lady Orchid and I are getting *married!*" Shrimp Wrigley announced proudly.

The room was surprisingly quiet. Then, after several beats, was filled with hoots, hollers and congratulations! A marriage proposal triple-header at Ostrichland!

The ostriches weren't the only ones feeling the love that day!

Lanky, Come Home...!

The surprise and celebration of *three* wedding proposals was interrupted by Agatha: "Waldemar, a guard is reporting an ostrich-tracking GPS device was found on the ground in the parking lot."

"Identify the ostrich," Waldemar requested, his celebration turning to concern, along with the other people in the den of the Sky House.

"GPS unit identified as belonging to Ostrich #001 a.k.a. Lanky," Agatha reported.

"Lanky's GPS unit was found in the parking lot!" Waldemar said in alarm, looking to Dustie for support.

"It probably came off during the press conference," she reassured Waldemar, coming to his side at the small walnut desk where the den's Agatha pyramid was located. "He's probably down in the riverbed this time of day."

"Agatha, do a visual census," Waldemar requested. Agatha takes the visual data from the scores of surveillance cameras scattered throughout Ostrichland and with Agatha's artificial intelligence, she compiles the photos with the list of ostriches to establish a tally of ostriches on the property. A visual census is seldom required since each ostrich has a GPS device clipped to them, however, when a unit occasionally comes loose, Agatha is ready to verify the members and location of the flock.

#	Name	Current Location
1	Lanky	Unaccounted
2	Ophelia	Ostrich Habitat
3	Happy	Riverbed
4	Beaks	Riverbed
5	Big Bird	Riverbed
6	Toots	Enclosure #1
7	Killer	Enclosure #1
8	Big Eyes	Ostrich Habitat
9	Mr. Tibbs	Enclosure #2
10	Sweetie Pie	Trail #3
11	Egg-Burt	Enclosure #2
12	Babs	Trail #2
13	Monster	Enclosure #1
14	Baby	Enclosure #1
15	Romeo	Ostrich Habitat
16	Juliet	Ostrich Habitat
17	Dr. Dundie	Enclosure #3
18	Huey	Enclosure #1
19	Kicks	Enclosure #1
20	Carlton	Enclosure #1
21	Annika	Riverbed

22	Sparky	Ostrich Habitat
23	Ethel	Ostrich Habitat
24	Tasmin	Enclosure #3
25	Diamond	Trail #3
26	Pretty Bird	Enclosure #2
27	Gizzard	Enclosure #2
28	Sage	Riverbed
29	Bobo	Riverbed
30	Twill	Trail #3
31	Lindy	Enclosure #3
32	Kiwi	Enclosure #2
33	Buckley	Enclosure #2
34	Sally	Ostrich Habitat
35	Bonnie	Ostrich Habitat
36	Clyde	Ostrich Habitat
37	Einstein	Riverbed
38	Plato	Enclosure #2
39	Rona	Trail #3
40	Lou	Enclosure #2
41	Giggles	Trail #1
42	Lambert	Trail #1
43	Quill	Trail #2

44	Valentine	Ostrich Habitat
45	Caesar	Riverbed
46	Cookie	Trail #3
47	Chip	Trail #4
48	Paprika	Enclosure #2
49	Neutrino	Trail #5
50	Butterscotch	Trail #2
51	Viking	Trail #1
52	Stomper	Trail #1
53	Barbie	Enclosure #3
54	Clarence	Enclosure #2
55	Hopper	Riverbed
56	Blinky	Trail #4
57	Gams	Trail #4
58	Custer	Enclosure #3
59	Fermile	Enclosure #1
60	Doc	Ostrich Habitat
61	Esperanza	Enclosure #1
62	Hulk	Parking Lot (!) Will Retrieve
63	Andre	Trail #4
64	Milton	Trail #5
65	Donny	Trail #3

66	Marie	Trail #3
67	Veld	Riverbed
68	Arno	Enclosure #1
69	Kaya	Trail #4
70	Pappy	Trail #4
71	Foster	Enclosure #2
72	Gus	Enclosure #1
73	Tweety	Ostrich Habitat

"Visual census completed. Ostrich #001 a.k.a. Lanky is unaccounted for." Agatha reported.

"Thank you, Agatha," Waldemar said, turning to Dr. Dustie Rhodes, concern in his deep brown eyes.

"Shrimp Wrigley and I will give it a check, Waldemar," Dustie responded, motioning for Shrimp Wrigley to follow her.

"Waldemar, I'm so sorry," Oola said with concern. "Lady Orchid, Walter and I will go mingle with the guests in the living room while you check on Lanky."

"Thank you, Oola," Waldemar said, giving Oola a heartfelt look as the three exited the den, leaving Waldemar alone.

After nine and a half minutes, Agatha reported: "Dr. Dustie Rhodes has communicated that Ostrich #001 a.k.a. Lanky is missing from Ostrichland."

With a sigh, Waldemar buried his face in his hands! I'm having an existential crisis, he thought. Too much drama, good and bad, for one day!

Ostrich in the Haus...

Many of the news outlets that had been at Ostrichland for Waldemar's press conference took off as soon as Waldemar said, 'Thank you.' They lost the moment when **WOW** got together for the first time in decades. Instead, they made their way to New Fatherland to try and find Sanny and get his side of the viral video story. Sometimes, many times, patience is a virtue!

The parking lot of Halle Haus was filled with news vans, satellite trucks and various media vehicles. The word was out that Sanny was the lounge singer at *WonderBar* in Halle Haus.

Martin Higher, reporter for *Diva Daily* remained at his post in *WonderBar*, his Panama hat now askew, his drink tab piling higher as his consciousness became lower. Where was Sanny anyway? Conrad Halle, owner of Halle Haus had gone to fetch him, but came back empty handed. Now Higher had competition vying for an interview with Sanny.

"Hey! Hey!" Higher started barking to no one in particular. "Where's that singer? I'm getting very bored here!" he stated, emptying his latest round of Spaten Oktoberfestbier[15].

"Sanny will be here soon," Three assured his inebriated customer. "How about a cup of coffee in the meantime?"

"Coffee? I want my coffee in a stein!" Higher said, laughing at his own 'joke.'

---

[15] In 1922, the Spaten-Brauerei and Franziskaner-Leist-Bräu united to form a joint stock company. In 1924, the advertising slogan "*Lass Dir raten, trinke Spaten*" (literally "Let yourself be advised, drink Spaten") was invented. It is still in use today.

"I'm gonna have to cut you off, Man," Three warned Higher as he rested his head (now sans Panama hat) on the bar. Higher snorted his disapproval.

As Three was cleaning the bar around Higher's head, he spotted a glint of gold in the peripheral vision of his right eye. Quickly turning his head to the right, he spotted Sanny stealthily making his way to the piano lounge of *WonderBar*. "Sanny!" he called out, to no avail, then took off after Sanny. He caught up to Sanny seated at his bright red piano of the *WonderBar*. No customers... yet.

"Sanny! Where have you been?" Three strode up to the small stage to confront Sanny.

"Nowhere," Sanny replied coyly.

"Nowhere? Grandfather has been looking for you and now he's lost," Three said in exasperation. "Plus, there's a reporter in the bar looking for you."

"Why?" Sanny looked puzzled.

"That viral video, that's why!" Three snapped. "You *do* know about it, don't you?"

"No."

Too late! Three looked up from Sanny to see a group of media people making their way to *WonderBar*. "Sanny, we've got to go!" he panicked, grabbing Sanny by his right gold-spangled sleeve.

"Sanny? Sanny!"

Reporters caught the scent. *WonderBar* was full of media folk! Sanny had the biggest smile on his face with all the attention!

"Are you Sanny?" asked a burly reporter with a press pass necklace dangling from his triple chins.

"Yes!" Sanny responded. Do you have a song to request?"

"Um. No?" the reporter responded, bewildered.

"Sanny?" another reporter took the reins. "How long have you known Waldemar?"

"Twenty-five years!" Sanny answered proudly. "Do *you* have a song to request?"

"No."

"Sanny! Do you know **WOW** is going to get back together?" asked another reporter.

"When?"

"When what?"

"When are they getting back together?"

"I don't know, do you?"

"No. That's why we're here, asking *you!*"

"Oh! Do you have a song to request?"

"Well... how about *Me and Mrs. Jones* by Billy Paul?"

"No!" Sanny responded. "Don't even *think* about it!"

"Oh, my g-a-w-d... Oh, my G-A-W-D!"

"All right. I'll give it a try!" Sanny relented following the vocal hysterics, then noticed the reporters all had their mouths open, looking at the entrance/exit of *WonderBar* in horror. Sanny turned around just in time to see the largest bird in his life entering Halle Haus as if it was the most seasoned traveler in the world. Several panicked men were carefully following the bird, an ostrich to be more precise, Lanky, by name.

"Stand back!" the tallest man shouted to the media in *WonderBar.* "He was trapped in the back of one of the news vans! I think he's cranky!"

Lanky stomped his way over to *WonderBar,* finding Sanny's glittery gold attire quite attractive, perhaps indicating the presence of ostrich treats. As the reporters scattered to the far ends of *WonderBar,* Lanky approached Sanny who, by now, was starting to assume the fetal position perched on the red piano bench. Lanky, in his never-ending quest for ostrich treats, got 'up close and personal' with Sanny, causing Sanny to inadvertently pat his head with his right hand... *twice!* Lanky responded to the 'peck that head' signal devised by Waldemar and proceeded to give Sanny's Rogaine-enriched pate a vigorous tapping.

"Have nercy on ne!" Sanny squealed. "Nercy! Nercy! Nh... Nh... Nh... Nh...Nh...Nh...Nh...Nh...Nh...Nh...Mh... Mh... Mh... Mh... Mh... Mh... Mh... Mh... Mh... Mh... Mercy... Mercy!"

No ostrich treats here! Lanky took a last, somewhat disdainful, look at the press, took a 180° turn and headed out of Halle Haus at top speed!

"Are you okay, Sanny?" a world-weary woman reporter questioned, walking slowly over to the stricken lounge singer, followed by the half-dozen other reporters in *WonderBar* (minus a sleeping Martin Higher).

"I'm *MARVELOUS!* Mh... Mh... Mh... Magnificent! Magical! Moist!"

"I think he's brain damaged!" the woman reporter remarked, touching Sanny's head lightly with her right hand, removing her hand quickly like she had touched a hot griddle.

Suddenly, Sanny started to tickle the ivories to commemorate the miracle that had just happened to him. And he burst into song...!

Miracles
By Insane Clown Posse

If magic is all we've ever known
Then it's easy to miss what really goes on
But I've seen miracles in every way
And I see miracles everyday...

Magical History Tour...

As the media scene unfolded at Halle Haus, along with a renegade ostrich, Lanky, six golden-liveried Prevost X3-45 luxury busses entered New Fatherland, a black Land Rover Range Rover security car in the lead and one at the end of the motorcade. They made their way to *Das Rathaus* on *Hauptstraße* (Main Street) where they gathered along the curb as security personnel emerged from the fore and aft vehicles, taking positions along the sides of the busses.

The motorcade had made its way from the Santa Barbara County Airport to New Fatherland to begin Les Winns' Magical History Tour. Each bus carried some of the wealthiest and most paranoid people ever to be assembled in one place at one time, not unlike a political convention. It was truly a sight to behold; however, each bus had heavily tinted windows to keep prying eyes from capturing the image of the occupants within.

In keeping with the theme of paranoia, each guest was dressed in a masquerade costume to keep their identity secret from their fellow bus passengers. At the end of the tour, at the end of the day, Winns had arranged a masked ball to be held at *Das Rathaus*. It was a combination of the Venice Carnival and New Orleans Mardi Gras, but with the theme of security in the age of FOE.

As the busses idled, Winns and the Flunkies emerged from *Das Rathaus* and quickly entered Bus #1. Edwin and Edwina Flunkie took a seat directly behind the driver as Winns, dressed in the brightest, whitest, most wrinkle-free suit in his wardrobe, sporting his usual unlit cigar, took a Jensen JMIC1 Microphone and began his sales pitch. The PA system was set up in a wireless network to the other five busses in the caravan so that the Yacktivist's patter would be heard throughout the entire motorcade during the Magical History Tour.

"Good day, my distinguished guests! I am so happy and honored to have you as part of the Magical History Tour today in New Fatherland. I am your host, Les Winns the 'Yacktivist.' I'm sure most of you have heard about me." A subtle chuckle could be heard throughout the six busses. "I call this the Magical History Tour because we are going to explore, through our tour of New Fatherland today, the basis of historic animosity of the best and brightest by the worst and dullest in society throughout the history of humankind. The movers, shakers, cultivated and monied have always had to be wary of the common, the average, the masses. I intend to provide an environment, a new way of living, where excellence and privilege are supported, encouraged, and most of all, secure. Ladies and gentlemen, let the Magical History Tour begin!"

Winns grabbed the polished silver pole at the top of the entry stairs of the bus with his right hand as it pulled away from the curb outside of *Das Rathaus* and slowly made its way down *Hauptstraße*, the black security Land Rover Range Rover in the lead. The other busses followed in kind, followed by another black security Land Rover Range Rover.

"What's going on at Halle Haus?" Winns asked the Flunkies in alarm, making sure his microphone was switched off. His beady eyes were surveying the unfolding scene ahead of them through the large windshield. The activity at the entrance of Halle Haus and the parking lot was concerning. Edwin and Edwina Flunkie took quick glances at their MacBook Pros, then looking up at Winns, each shaking their heads 'no' as in no idea of what was going on.

"TV news crews? This is horrible!" Winns muttered. "Driver, quickly turn down this street," he ordered, pointing at the next intersection before they passed Halle Haus. The busses took a right turn onto Edelweiss Lane only to encounter several men running after... could it be?... a large bird?... an ostrich!?

"What's going on here!?" Winns asked to no one in particular, attempting to block the view as much as possible by spreading his ample body as much as possible to block the forward view from the windshield.

"Sir, we've got a problem," the bus driver said.

"You're telling me!" Winns shot back, sweat now forming on his upper forehead.

"As you can see, the lead security car didn't get the message to turn in time. And this street is too small for the busses. We're now stuck and have to back up."

"What?!" Winns was in a full-blown panic now.

With that, a huge explosive sound was heard and felt throughout Bus #1 as the large windshield shattered into a million pieces of laminated glass, showering Winns with particles, covering his brilliant white suit from shoulder to shoe top. The costumed guests in Bus #1 shrieked and ducked for cover.

"This must be the end of days!" Winns proclaimed as he fainted to the plush gold pile carpet next to the shocked bus driver.

"Edwina, we've got a problem," Edwin Flunkie said to his twin sister as he wiped several shards of laminated windshield glass from the right shoulder of his cardigan sweater.

Indeed...

Missing In-action...

It had been a long night in the Sky House. Most of Waldemar's guests had made their way to the six apartments one floor below the Sky House in The Egg to get some sleep. In the Sky House, Waldemar, Dustie and Shrimp Wrigley remained in the den, working on a plan to locate and retrieve Lanky... still missing in action. Efforts to locate Lanky were hampered by the dark night; nevertheless, Waldemar had been in touch via text and phone with various friends and acquaintances in the Neu Deutschland Valley. So far, nothing was fruitful.

"I can't believe that Lanky ran away," Waldemar said wearily, pushing back on his chair at the small walnut writing desk. "It's not like him. Maybe he's been kidnapped?"

"We should have received a ransom note by now," Dustie suggested, handing Waldemar a booster bottle of Roo Energy Drink.

"How can an ostrich write a ransom note!?" Shrimp Wrigley griped.

"Not Lanky. The kidnappers!" Dustie replied, frustrated with Shrimp Wrigley's lack of focus.

"And what makes you think he was kidnapped!?" Shrimp Wrigley snapped. "He was flat out stolen, that's what happened!" he blurted out as he circled round and round the den. "You know that bird is valuable!"

"What is someone going to do with a stolen ostrich?" Dustie questioned, trying not to alarm Waldemar any more than he was.

"What are they going to do with it?" Shrimp Wrigley turned and faced Dustie, casting her an incredulous look. "There are a million things you can do with a hot ostrich! Ask any travelling animal grifter!" Dustie's eyes were giving Shrimp Wrigley the 'shut up' look and he, surprisingly, received the message loud and clear.

Waldemar continued monitoring his laptop and the display on Agatha's pyramid. "Agatha, any news?" he asked, knowing Agatha would convey the latest news without a prompt.

"No, Waldemar. Sorry." she responded.

Waldemar stared out the curved floor-to-ceiling window of the den, watching the landscape brighten with the dawn. Dustie joined Shrimp Wrigley at the den's clear circular table. There was silence in the room.

"The biggest fear I had when I owned Ostrichland was ostriches stampeding," Shrimp Wrigley broke the silence with the beginning of a new Shrimp Wrigley tale.

"Stampede?" Dr. Dustie Rhodes took the bait, hoping this would be a funny story and distract Waldemar from the disappearing Lanky.

"Yes indeed!" Shrimp Wrigley sat back to tell the tale. "Years ago, every once in a while, the flock would become agitated, just short of a stampede. Thank goodness they never did stampede, but they came very close a couple of times. Well, I couldn't figure out what was causing their angst until one day some guy in the parking lot was impatient with another parker and started honking his horn at him. Well, you know how quiet the Valley is normally, so you can imagine how loud that horn was! And it wasn't just any car horn; it was that of an old Volkswagen Beetle, the original Beetle, of course, and one with the 6-volt electrical system. I had a friend, can't remember his name right now, with one of those very cars so I had him come over the next day and honk the horn and sure enough, the flock became agitated. It didn't prove that much, just to be aware of classic Beetles in the vicinity and the owners honking the horns. You know, they had that meep, meep sound... remember?"

"Yes. Yes, I do remember, Shrimp Wrigley," Dustie replied to respond.

"It didn't seem to be a problem when Volkswagen changed to a 12-volt system in 1967," Shrimp Wrigley continued. "There must have been a subtle difference in the frequency of the horn from 6 to 12 volts, but I never research it *that* much. And now with so many years gone by, it's a situation that doesn't come up much." Shrimp Wrigley conceded. "Waldemar, if there's ever a classic VW show at Ostrichland, you do need to be mindful of the horn honking situation," Shrimp Wrigley cautioned a preoccupied Waldemar.

Dustie left the table and headed to the kitchen to prepare breakfast for the three of them, plus any early-rising guests occupying the apartments below. She was hoping Shrimp Wrigley's story would have been more amusing, but you can't have a gem each time. It was what it was.

"Waldemar and Shrimp Wrigley, Dr. Dustie Rhodes is requesting your company in the breakfast room," Agatha announced.

Waldemar and Shrimp Wrigley met Lady Orchid in the reception foyer of the Sky House as they made their way to the breakfast room. Lady Orchid was wearing a subdued outfit to fit the occasion, highlighted by a fascinator in the shape of a large magnifying glass to symbolize the search for Lanky. Shortly, Oola and Walter entered the breakfast room from their guest apartment one floor below. Li'l Otter and Shenandoah River joined the group, opting to spend the night in one of the guest apartments rather than going to town to stay at the Friedrich Nietzsche Suite of Halle Haus. The only guest not present in the breakfast room was **WOW** business manager, Yukio Cassidy, still asleep in another guest apartment of The Egg. As the guests gathered around the large round 2″ thick kiln-dried Monkey Pod table of the breakfast room, Dustie gave a summary of the events, or lack thereof, of the night.

"Oh, Waldemar!" Lady Orchid lamented, rising from the table, going over to Waldemar and giving him a big hug and kiss, leaving a smudge of Christian Louboutin's Velvet Matte Lip Colour in Bengali on Waldemar's right cheek. "You poor boy!"

"Waldemar, Joshua Del Gato, Sr., the missing animal psychic is here to see you," Agatha announced.

"Great! Please guide him to the Sky House," Waldemar replied, clapping his hands once, encouraging himself to stay upbeat.

"Waldemar, who's that?" Dustie asked, a confused look on her face.

"A friend of a friend," Waldemar replied, standing up and pulling his ponytail tighter in anticipation of meeting Joshua Del Gato, Sr. "His specialty is locating missing animals through psychic powers."

"Wonderful!" Lady Orchid said with excitement.

In several minutes, the now on-duty Jeeves led Joshua Del Gato, Sr., a tall middle-aged man with dark complexion and a large mustache into the breakfast room, where he sat down at the table.

"Welcome, Joshua," Waldemar greeted. "Would you like some breakfast?"

"Certainly!" he responded, eyeing the luminaries seated at the breakfast room table. "Nice to meet you all."

"Nice to meet you, Joshua Del Gato, Sr.," the guests replied in unison.

"I understand that there is an ostrich missing, is that correct?" he asked, looking at Waldemar.

"Correct," Waldemar replied. "Lanky is his name. He is my prize ostrich."

"Joshua Del Gato, Sr., how old am I?" Shrimp Wrigley asked with a somewhat defiant tone in his voice.

"Shrimp Wrigley!" Waldemar scolded. "Joshua isn't here to perform!"

"Waldemar, I just need to know that he is on the up and up," Shrimp Wrigley explained. "I've been around too many phony psychics in my day to feel comfortable."

"Fine!" Joshua said with a touch of annoyance. "I will prove to you that I am authentic!"

"Have a go at it," Shrimp Wrigley said, challenging Joshua's psychic abilities.

"You ask your age," Joshua began slowly, looking intently into Shrimp Wrigley's narrow-set eyes. "You've recently had a birthday."

"No, it's seven months from now," Shrimp Wrigley replied, a hint of delight in his voice because the psychic didn't get that right.

"Someone special in your life had a birthday recently," Joshua countered.

"No."

"Someone you know had a birthday recently."

"No."

"You know someone who knows someone who had a birthday recently," Joshua Del Gato, Sr. struggled, a bead of sweat forming on his brow.

"I do!" Lady Orchid interjected with great excitement.

"Oh, there you go!" Joshua said triumphantly. And this person having a birthday is your cousin," he announced, looking at Lady Orchid for confirmation.

"No."

"A niece."

"No."

"A dear friend."

"No."

"I have a niece who knows someone who had a birthday recently," Li'l Otter joined the psychic game.

"Oh, there you go!" Joshua said triumphantly. And your niece lives in Nashville," he announced, looking at Li'l Otter for confirmation.

"No."

"I have a niece that lives in Nashville," Shen exclaimed with excitement.

"Oh, there you go!" Joshua said triumphantly. "And your niece is planning to move to California next year."

"No."

"In two years..."

"No."

"I have a friend who is planning to move to Nevada in three years," Walter Johnson said enthusiastically.

"Oh, there you go!" Joshua said triumphantly. "And then they are planning to move to California."

"No. Not that I know of."

"Northern California..."

"No."

"Reno. Right by northern California."

"I don't think so."

"I heard about someone who moved to Carson City, Nevada," Oola offered. "But she didn't like it there."

"Oh, there you go!" Joshua said triumphantly.

"And you know someone who lost something," Joshua said, looking intently at Oola.

"Well, yes!"

"Oh, there you go!" Joshua said triumphantly. "And the item they lost was a wallet."

"No."

"A purse... Something valuable."

"Hey, you phony!" Shrimp Wrigley blurted out. "I believe you've given us a thorough fleecing! "That's what *I* think!" Shrimp Wrigley gave Joshua Del Gato, Sr. a withering rebuke. Waldemar obviously is the one who has lost something valuable... Lanky!"

"Oh, there you go!" Joshua said triumphantly.

"I hate to interrupt, Waldemar, Conrad Halle III on line 1," Agatha announced from her pyramid.

Guests repeating 'Conrad Halle III' in surprise throughout the breakfast room could be heard.

"Put him on speakerphone," Waldemar asked. "There's nothing he can say that I can't share with my guests."

"Will do, Waldemar."

"Hello?"

"Hi? Waldemar? This is Three," Three answered.

"Yes," Waldemar replied.

"Well, uh... I guess we haven't talked in some time, eh?"

"No. No, we haven't"

"I... uh... I just wanted to let you know that Lanky is running around Neu Deutschland..."

A gasp was heard throughout the breakfast room.

"So, you have Lanky with you?" Waldemar asked hopefully.

"No, Waldemar. Like I said, Lanky's running around town. I don't know where he is right now!" he explained. "People are freaking out though! There are reporters all over here anyhow trying to get info from Sanny about the video! I've made such a mess of things! I'm so sorry, Waldemar!"

"Three, calm down," Waldemar urged. "We'll deal with things one at a time. Right now, we need to get Lanky back to Ostrichland. We can deal with the video later!"

"Okay. Okay," he replied. "So Lanky was here at Halle Haus. He attacked Sanny and then ran away."

"Attacked Sanny?" Waldemar was incredulous.

"Yeah! It's a real mess here!"

"So, no one knows exactly where Lanky is in town?" Waldemar sought confirmation.

"No. No one knows."

"**Waldemar? A call from Edwin Flunkie on line 2,**" Agatha broke in.

"Three? Keep me updated," Waldemar ordered. "I've got a call on another line. Yes? This is Waldemar."

"Mr. Ulff? This is Edwin Flunkie, one of the Flunkie Twins. Les Winns' assistants."

"Yes."

"I wanted to let you know that I'm on a bus stuck on a street in New Fatherland where a large ostrich, we believe owned by you, just attacked our bus." The guests in the breakfast room gasped once again.

"Wh-a-a-a-t!?" Waldemar couldn't believe what he was hearing. "Let me talk to Les Winns!" Waldemar ordered.

"He can't talk right now."

"Why not?"

"He's dead."

"Wh-a-a-a-t!?" exclaimed everyone in unison in the breakfast room.

"Oh, there you go!" Joshua Del Gato, Sr. muttered.

Send in the Troops...

In the plush Ostrichland administrative office located in The Egg, Waldemar gathered with Dustie, Shrimp Wrigley and Yukio Cassidy. The latest news from Edwin Flunkie was that Lanky was on the loose in New Fatherland and had, apparently, done some damage.

"Okay, what's the plan?" Waldemar questioned the group, all seated around Waldemar who was sitting at his desk.

"If we go by the telephone caller, we know that Lanky is in the town, but not captured at this point," Yukio carefully laid out the facts as known. "We need a plan that pinpoints Lanky's location and allows us to safely contain him without harm to Lanky or others."

"Dustie, what state of mind would Lanky be in at this time?" Waldemar asked, showing a hint of fatigue in his voice as Lanky's disappearance was taking its toll.

"He will be agitated and aggressive until we can get him, Waldemar," she responded, sipping a glass of water she brought from the Sky House. "He's an exceptional ostrich here at Ostrichland, but lost and alone as he is, he will naturally revert back to his natural instincts."

Shrimp Wrigley was shifting in his chair. He didn't like talk when action was required. "Come on, Waldemar! Let's just go to Neu Deutschland and get Lanky! What's all this strategizing?!"

"We don't want to go into town, whatever its name is these days, and stumble about not knowing what we're doing," Waldemar explained to his overeager friend. "We might as well go there and whistle for him to come, it's not going to work. Wait a minute... Shrimp Wrigley, what were you saying about car horns and ostriches last night?"

"Oh, that the horn on a Volkswagen Beetle with a 6-volt electrical system, when honked, seems to stir up a flock of ostriches to the point of them wanting to stampede."

"What are you thinking, Waldemar?" Dustie questioned, putting her glass of water on the edge of Waldemar's desk.

"Hmm... what makes Lanky so special to our flock?"

"He's the leader," Dustie answered, not following where Waldemar was going.

"And what if the leader of the flock thought the flock was in danger?"

"Why, he would do everything he could to protect the flock," Dustie answered, still not following.

"What if we took the flock of ostriches to Neu Deutschland and got them to do perform a planned stampede event?"

"What on earth are you talking about, Waldemar?" Shrimp Wrigley slapped his right hand, palm down on Waldemar's desk in frustration. "I'm not following you! How would we purposely get the flock to perform a planned stampede event and why?"

"We would get the flock to perform a planned stampede event by honking a horn from a Volkswagen Beetle with a 6-volt electrical system and we would do this to entice Lanky into showing himself when he senses the flock is on the loose and needs guidance!"

"That's quite a bold plan, Waldemar-san," Yukio ventured, rubbing his temples as he digested the plan Waldemar was 'hatching.' "Wouldn't the flock be in danger during the planned stampede event? I don't know *anything* about ostriches, much less about their behavior during a planned stampede event."

"Good question," Waldemar replied, thinking out the details as he responded. "I don't think it would be dangerous for one important reason: the streets of Neu Deutschland, other than *Hauptstraße*, the main street in town, are narrow and confined since the town was built in the style of a medieval German town. The narrow streets would serve to keep the flock compressed and somewhat controlled. Thus, a planned stampede event," Waldemar said, tugging on the right side of his mustache as he spoke.

"You know, that just might work!" Shrimp Wrigley replied enthusiastically as Waldemar's plan was laid out. "How would we get the flock to town?"

"Trucks! Just like we did during the Santa Bella fire, what, six years ago when we had to evacuate." Waldemar replied, sitting straighter in his chair.

"Yes!" Dustie said enthusiastically. "I know there are several large trucks right now at the Liska Family Farm. They've been adding some livestock in the past few days. We could get those trucks here in short time. It might be a problem getting the flock into the trucks without Lanky, but with enough ostrich treats they'll follow us anywhere."

"I like how you guys think!" Yukio said, a large smile on his face following the heated agreement. "It's like the good old days when we had a problem at a recording session or a concert, Waldemar always had a solution, crazy or not!"

"Agatha, get the Liskas on the phone," Waldemar ordered his Ostrichland AI.

"**Consider it done, boss,**" Agatha responded.

"Now, where do we locate a horn from a Volkswagen Beetle with a 6-volt electrical system?" Waldemar asked.

"That sounds like a difficult item to find," Dustie said, looking at the others.

"No problem!" Shrimp Wrigley said with confident nonchalance. "I have a friend just down the road, Horace Herring, owns a 1960 Volkswagen Beetle, drives it every day to go surf fishing off Pirate's Point Pier. Really, a terrible fisherman, but I don't have the heart to tell him that..."

"Shrimp Wrigley! Let's stay on point!" Waldemar pleaded with uncharacteristic urgency.

"Sure, Waldemar," I can have him here in ten minutes," Shrimp Wrigley promised, his thoughts brought back in focus.

"Great!" Waldemar responded. "This feels like progress!"

"Yes! It's very encouraging, Waldemar!" Dustie agreed.

The trio spent some time discussing the weather, fashion, gossip, operations, genetic engineering, etc. awaiting the appearance of the trucks.

"**Two 18-wheelers detected entering Ostrichland, Waldemar,**" Agatha announced.

"That was fast! Perfect!" Waldemar replied, rising from his chair, heading out of the administrative office to the Ostrichland parking lot, followed by Dustie, Shrimp Wrigley and Yukio.

Making a grand entrance into the Ostrichland parking lot were two Kenworth T880s with enough storage capacity to easily handle the Ostrichland flock. Although the right turn from Highway 277 to the parking lot was a bit tight, the drivers were able to skillfully maneuver the big trucks into place with ease.

As Waldemar and Yukio were heading to the parking lot, Dustie and Shrimp Wrigley were headed down the main path from The Egg to the dry riverbed where most of the flock were roaming about. After several minutes and several bags full of ostrich treats, Dustie and Shrimp Wrigley were leading the flock up the trail like the pied piper and assistant, the flock of ostriches eager to follow wherever they were led. And led they were: right into the trailers of the two Kenworth T880s.

In addition to Waldemar, Dustie, Shrimp Wrigley and Yukio, the other occupants of The Egg: Oola, Walter, Li'l Otter, Shen and Lady Orchid were adding their help, to one degree or another, to the effort. With the final members of the flock making their way onto the trailers, Waldemar went to the Ostrichland garage and brought his Burgundy 1995 Rolls-Royce Silver Spirit III around to the parking lot.

"Is that the car Lady Orchid bought for you in 1995?" Yukio asked in amazement as he opened the rear passenger door.

"One and the same!" Waldemar responded, enthusiasm in his voice as the 'Rescue Lanky' project seemed to be progressing well.

"I always loved this car!" Yukio commented as Lady Orchid entered the car to take a middle back seat position, her fascinator in the style of a detective's magnifying glass scrunching into the headliner, as usual. Yukio sat next to Lady Orchid and closed the rear passenger door. Walter opened the rear driver-side door so Oola could enter and sit on the left side of Lady Orchid. Li'l Otter and Shen took places in the front seat.

As people were boarding Waldemar's car a strange but familiar sound was heard entering the Ostrichland parking lot. Shrimp Wrigley's friend, Horace Herring, was pulling up in his faded blue 1960 Volkswagen Beetle with a 6-volt electrical system.

Waldemar called out to Shrimp Wrigley, "Get everyone else into the Bug and follow us, okay?"

"Sure thing, Waldemar!" Shrimp Wrigley responded, flinging his Lucky Strike butt across the parking lot in an uncharacteristic act of littering. With Horace at the wheel, the Volkswagen Beetle was loaded with Li'l Otter, Shen and Shrimp Wrigley riding shotgun.

Waldemar gave an elegant toot from the tuned horns of his car, signaling the truck drivers to start their rigs and get the show on the road.

The two Kenworth T880's turned onto Highway 277, followed by Waldemar's Rolls-Royce and Horace Herring's faded blue 1960 Volkswagen Beetle with a 6-volt electrical system. A security team of three men hastily boarded one of their Mercedes-Benz G550 G-Wagens, joining the tail-end of the motorcade. Like the modern-day cavalry, the troops were on their way down Highway 277 to New Fatherland and, hopefully, the return of Lanky.

The Best Laid Plans...

Bus #1, the golden-liveried Prevost X3-45 luxury coach, sat stranded on Edelweiss Lane off *Hauptstraße* (Main Street) in New Fatherland. The five other luxury buses were in a state of traffic congestion with most of them stuck making the right-hand turn onto Edelweiss Lane in an attempt to follow Bus #1. Granules from Bus #1's shattered windshield covered Edelweiss Lane directly in front of the bus and the forward interior. With Edwin Flunkie's 911 call, help had arrived in the form of the New Fatherland volunteer fire department. Because of the stacked busses leading into Edelweiss Lane, the firefighters had to make their way from *Hauptstraße* to Bus #1 on foot. It wasn't a long journey, but with the various EMT equipment it was a difficult trek dodging busses too close to buildings on the narrow street. The costumed occupants of Bus #1 had largely abandoned the bus, standing in the general vicinity of Edelweiss Lane, adding to the congestion and confusion of the scene.

"Help me! I'm dead!" was the cry the first responders heard once they reached Bus #1.

"Hold on, Mr. Winns. Help is here," Edwina Flunkie consoled, cradling Les Winns' large balding head in her hands in a rare show of empathy. Edwin Flunkie was busy on his iPhone, marching back and forth in front of Bus #1.

"Clear the way! Clear the way!" shouted the lead first responder as he entered Bus #1, carrying a large bag of medical equipment. "Excuse me, Ma'am," he said to Edwina, pushing her away from Winns, his head hitting the glass-covered floor of Bus #1. A second EMT entered Bus #1, stepping over Winns (with some effort), going to the side of the stricken bus driver.

"What happened here?" EMT #1 asked Edwina.

"As far as I can tell, a renegade ostrich kicked in the windshield. The glass shattered all over Mr. Winns," Edwina replied, her voice steady, matter-of-fact. "Will he live?" she asked, emotionless.

"As far as I can tell," EMT #1 responded as he worked on Winns. "He has a few minor lacerations and is probably shook up, nothing that will do him in. It looks worse than it is."

Edwina could see several of the costumed guests peeking into the now gaping hole that once contained a windshield, hoping to catch a glimpse of Winns so they could assess his chances of survival.

"I hope the costume ball is still on for tonight!" one of the guests whined. Before anyone could answer the guest, a thundering noise was heard by the group surrounding Bus #1.

"What is *that?*" Edwina asked no one in particular. In the distance the sound of an odd blaring horn, perhaps an automobile horn could be heard, followed by a thundering sound.

Several minutes later, one of the EMTs turned his attention to his radio as information was coming in. "A herd of *what?*" he asked for clarification. "Ostriches?"

"Ostriches? What?" Edwin questioned, entering Bus #1 to see how Winns was doing.

"I just got a report that a herd of ostriches is loose in town," the EMT responded, tapping his coworker in a motion to 'hurry up.'

"I think that would be a *flock* of ostriches," Edwin corrected, looking at his twin sister for some guidance.

"I'll check and see if there is any news streaming online," Edwina responded, grabbing her MacBook Pro from the bus seat.

"...ostriches stampeding in Neu Deutschland... um... New Fatherland... as we are reporting here..." Magdalene Sigi of JustNEWS was on Edwina's news feed. "...we are reporting from the local hotel, Halle Haus, where it is considered relatively safe. However, officials warn residents and visitors to stay indoors until authorities declare the situation handled. With us now is a resident of New Fatherland; your name, sir?"

"Um, Conrad. Conrad Halle III. My friends call me Three."

"Conrad Halle III, what can you tell us about the stampede of ostriches in New Fatherland going on right now?"

"Not much. Only that Lanky the ostrich was loose here a while ago and now the whole flock is loose!"

"Where would a flock of ostriches come from?" Sigi asked dramatically.

"I would suspect that they came from Ostrichland down Highway 277," Three responded, smiling broadly into the camera. "Free admission!"

"Thanks, Conrad Halle III," Sigi said, turning her attention to the plump woman to her right. "What is your name, ma'am?"

"Gerta. Gerta Switzer. I live and work in town. I own Mein Hair, *the* hair salon in Neu Deutschland."

"New Fatherland," Sigi corrected Gerta.

"No. The name of the town is Neu Deutschland. Always was, always will be! No matter what Les Winns says about it!" Gerta responded with anger, her moon-shape face growing red.

"One story at a time, Miss Switzer," Sigi said with a slight chuckle.

"The theft of this town is a story that *needs* to be told!" Gerta continued. Les Winns the 'Yacktivist' came into the town, bought it right out from under us, renamed it and is now trying to sell it to the highest bidder and we do *nothing* about it! And now we have a flock of ostriches running around town. *Was ist los?*"

"Wow! That's a lot going on, Miss Switzer!" Sigi remarked, taking a step back from Gerta. The voice in her earpiece conveniently interrupted her interview with Gerta. "I'm told we have a feed from our field reporter, Norburt Arun. Norburt?"

"Thanks, Magdalene. This is Norburt Arun reporting from the outskirts of New Fatherland, or Neu Deutschland as the town is more popularly known. I'm here with Waldemar Ulff, one of the members of the legendary group **WOW**. Waldemar, what's going on?"

"Actually, quite a bit's going on!" Waldemar chuckled, the Rolls-Royce emptying of occupants as Waldemar faced the camera. Two trucks that carried the Ostrichland flock were parked next to Waldemar's car. Behind them, a Volkswagen Beetle filled with men was parked, the driver laying on the odd-sounding horn for a long blast, then waiting several minutes, then repeating the procedure with the enthusiastic support of the occupants of the car.

"Sorry about the honking," Waldemar grimaced as he apologized. The honking ceased for a few minutes. "I'm on a mission to find and re-claim my prize ostrich, Lanky. We understand he is roaming in Neu Deutschland and we plan to find him."

"I understand that you own Ostrichland, an ostrich zoo down Highway 277," Arun said to Waldemar.

"Norburt, Ostrichland is an educational event for the whole family, not an ostrich zoo, please!" Waldemar corrected.

"So sorry, Waldemar," Arun apologized.

"Norburt! Norburt!" the voice called in Arun's earpiece.

"Yes, Magdalene?"

"We're watching your interview with great interest. However, watching the monitor we can't help but notice that Oola La and Walter Johnson of **WOW** are in the background by that burgundy Rolls-Royce," Sigi said, a trace of annoyance in her voice that Arun hadn't noticed the world-famous bystanders. "**WOW** is reunited here on JustNEWS!"

"Wow, I guess you're right, Magdalene," Arun admitted, at a loss for words.

"Waldemar, let's get back to work!" Dustie said, walking over to Waldemar, but staying out of camera range. Waldemar was having some fun with the media, but playtime was over, especially as several other news crews could be seen heading from Halle Haus to where the Ostrichland convoy was parked near the entrance of New Fatherland. "According to the ostrich GPS trackers, the flock has settled on a side street of *Hauptstraße*, Edelweiss Lane."

"Great! Let's roll!" Waldemar said with excitement, leaving the interview mid-air, an uncharacteristically unprofessional move.

"Waldemar, is **WOW** reunited?" a stunned Norburt Arun asked as Waldemar sprinted to his car.

"Can't talk now, Norburt!" Waldemar shouted as his car passed Arun and crew in a cloud of dust, followed by Horace Herring's Volkswagen Beetle and, finally, the security team's Mercedes-Benz G550 G-Wagen.

"Wow, now *that* was dramatic!" Arun admitted. "Back to you, Magdalene."

"Thanks, Norburt," Sigi said, adjusting the ear pod in her right ear with her right hand, receiving information from the producer. "There are quite a few events happening in New Fatherland right now. We are doing our best to bring everything to you to keep you updated. I'm told we're going to *WonderBar* in Halle Haus now with news of an ostrich attack on the lounge singer, Sanny, that resulted in what many describe as a miraculous occurrence... we're... um... excuse me... okay... we're going to Primo Ipolito on Edelweiss Lane in New Fatherland."

"Thank you, Magdalene!" Ipolito responded with his characteristic enthusiasm. "We're on Edelweiss Lane, a side street of *Hauptstraße* here in Neu Deutschland, for those of you familiar with the town. There are six... six luxury tour busses stranded here on Edelweiss Lane and *Hauptstraße* or Main Street in Neu Deutschland. The first two busses were stuck making the right-hand turn from *Hauptstraße* onto Edelweiss Lane while the last four busses are on *Hauptstraße*. However, they are packed too tightly due to the sudden turn by the lead bus. Although the scene is chaotic with many people dressed in what appears to be costume ball attire, most of the passengers are still inside the busses. These luxury coaches have heavily tinted windows so it is impossible to see the occupants or get a sense of their state of mind. There are several security people surrounding these busses; in fact, several of them are now asking me to..."

"Primo?" Sigi called out in concern. "Primo? Have we lost your feed? Let's go now to Alison Nora in *Stadtplatz* or Town Square in New Fatherland."

"Thank you, Magdalene," Alison Nora, JustNEWS newest field reporter responded, her sudden appearance a surprise to the viewers and Alison Nora.

"I'm standing in the *Stadtplatz* or town square in front of the City Hall of New Fatherland, formerly Neu Deutschland. They call this building *Das Rathaus* in honor of the German origins of the town. Right now, *Das Rathaus* is serving as the command post for authorities as they deal with several events happening in New Fatherland at the same time. Currently, we have reports of a flock of ostriches stampeding in the town. A lone ostrich has also been spotted and several tour busses have been struck in a side-street of town. To help us sort through these rapidly changing events we have Bürgermeister Ackermann, the mayor of New Fatherland with us. Welcome, Mayor."

"Thank you, Alison," Bürgermeister Ackermann said, his beady eyes staring into the camera. "I am not sure if I am the mayor or not and I'm not sure if New Fatherland is officially called New Fatherland or, in fact, if the official name is Neu Deutschland as it had been for many, many years."

A flustered Nora began her attempt to clarify so many issues. "So, if you're not the mayor, who is?"

"I don't know if they have a mayor anymore," Ackermann replied, smiling into the camera.

"Why not?"

"Well, when Les Winns the 'Yacktivist' bought Neu Deutschland several days ago, I don't know if he intended to retain me as mayor or if he was planning to become mayor or perhaps, Leader?" he leered into the camera.

"Okay, Bürgermeister Ackermann, I'm now completely lost," Nora admitted, placing her right hand to her right ear to hear the producer more clearly. "Let's discuss what's going on right now, okay?"

"Sure!"

"Where would a flock of ostriches come from?" Nora asked, happy to have a solid question in play.

"Ostrichland, of course!"

"The amusement park down the highway?"

"I don't think Waldemar would like to hear you calling his beloved Ostrichland an amusement park!" Ackermann chuckled, adjusting his Homberg for maximum coolness.

"And you're referring to Waldemar Ulff of **WOW**, correct?" she questioned, prompted by her producer.

"One and the same!"

"Excuse me, Bürgermeister Ackermann," Nora said, turning away from him. "Oh, here we go... I'm told that we have EMT crews arriving from Edelweiss Lane where several tour busses were trapped. Apparently, there were injuries or at least one injury..."

From Nora's vantage point in front of *Das Rathaus*, she could see four paramedics carrying a large man in a white suit on a stretcher. Behind the large man, two paramedics had another man on a stretcher. They appeared to be heading to *Das Rathaus*.

"Excuse me, gentlemen..." Alison Nora made her way to the large injured man, egged on by the JustNEWS producer safely in the mobile news center in the Halle Haus parking lot.

"I'm dying! I'm dying!" Les Winns announced dramatically.

"Clear the way, ma'am!" the head EMT barked.

"I just want to..."

"Clear the way!"

"Tell the world the FOE has done this to me!" Winns said in a weak shout when he spotted Alison Nora's microphone.

Nora gasped when she spotted her colleague, Primo Ipolito on the second stretcher.

"Clear the way, ma'am!"

Before Alison Nora could respond her cameraman swung the JVC GY-HM650 ProHD Mobile News Camera to *Hauptstraße* as a Burgundy 1995 Rolls-Royce Silver Spirit III, a faded blue 1960 Volkswagen Beetle with the 6-volt electrical system and a Mercedes-Benz G550 G-Wagen blazed past *Stadtplatz.*

Several minutes later from the direction of Edelweiss Lane, a thundering sound was heard, then felt. "Oh No-o-o-o!" Alison Nora screamed as her feed went black.

At that moment, Doc, Tasmin, Giggles, Rona, Lou, Buckley, Paprika, Blinky, Kiwi, Sparky, Pretty Bird, Quill, Custer, Clyde, Romeo, Gams, Ophelia, Bonnie, Kaya, Milton, Pappy, Juliet, Veld, Valentine, Donny, Chip, Foster, Happy, Diamond, Tweety, Sally, Sweetie Pie, Gus, Lindy, Dr. Dundie, Andre, Plato, Twill, Hopper, Gizzard, Barbie, Hulk, Kicks, Marie, Annika, Neutrino, Fermile, Toots, Carlton, Einstein, Bobo, Lambert, Mr. Tibbs, Viking, Sage, Cookie, Butterscotch, Beaks, Ethel, Killer, Stomper, Arno, Big Bird, Babs, Huey, Clarence, Esperanza, Egg-Burt, Caesar, Big Eyes, Monster and Baby; the entire Ostrichland flock roared past Nora's position.

"Alison? Alison Nora?" Magdalene Sigi called with alarm. The shot went to Sigi in the mobile studio. "We are experiencing technical difficulties at this time. We hope to get back to Alison Nora in a moment..." Sigi was looking off-camera as the producer was explaining something. "Okay... I understand that we've corrected our feed with Alison Nora. Alison?"

"Magdalene, don't go back to me! I can't talk right now!" Nora sputtered, her hair wildly unkempt as she fought to hold on to her microphone as a stout woman was beating Bürgermeister Ackermann with a walking stick or *wurzelstock* about the head and shoulders.

"No, Gerta! No! *Gott hilf mir!*

"Ich hasse dich! Du Bastard!"

"Back to you, Magdalene!"

"And we'll be right back after this word from our sponsors."

A Moment For Two...

Waldemar settled down at the Sunset Bench, Lanky at his side once again. He was relieved to have a few minutes to himself to unwind and try to process the major events of the day. Lanky seemed to be fine after his unexpected journey to Neu Deutschland and was eyeing Waldemar for an ostrich treat.

"Here you go, my friend," Waldemar smiled and reaching into his right front jean pocket, pulling out an ostrich treat. Lanky moved several feet away from the Sunset Bench to down his treat.

"Waldemar!" the voice called out from the direction of The Egg. It was Shrimp Wrigley making his way to the somewhat secluded Sunset Bench.

"Hey, Shrimp Wrigley!" Waldemar replied happily. "Come on over!"

"Don't mind if I do. Don't mind if I do," Shrimp Wrigley said, walking over to the Sunset Bench, but not sitting down as he was on the last few puffs of a Lucky Strike. "It's great to see Lanky!" Shrimp Wrigley remarked, looking at Lanky, taking a last drag on the cigarette before sitting down on the bench on the right side of Waldemar. "It's been quite a day, eh, Waldemar?"

"Indeed!" Waldemar responded, reaching for an unopened Roo Energy Drink resting next to him on the Sunset Bench.

"You're not having a smoke?" Shrimp Wrigley asked with some surprise.

"No. You know Yukio is having a meeting with everyone in a bit and I want to be totally clear-headed when Yukio has a meeting. Every time he called for a meeting in the past it was usually a *big* announcement!"

"What do you think he's going to say?" Shrimp Wrigley asked, furrowing his somewhat-weathered brow.

"I don't know. All I *do* know is that he's still in Neu Deutschland with Oola and Walter," Waldemar responded, twisting the cap off the Roo Energy Drink bottle and taking a swig. "In the past, Yukio hardly ever met with less than all three of us at the same time. He is scrupulous to a fault."

"That's a good thing," Shrimp Wrigley observed. "In your old line of work, having an honest guy on the business-end of things must be very important."

"That's for sure, Shrimp Wrigley," Waldemar said. "Why, I can think of any number of popular groups during the day that ended up bankrupt because of bad management. Take Seething Hermit, for instance. They were so popular in Goth circles but ended up working at a doughnut shop in Emporia, Kansas last I heard. Or Hyphenated Chow. The two of them were sued by their manager for breach of contract even though the manager robbed them blind. The manager won! Then, Praying Waiter went from being one of the most innovative bands to playing state fairs during the summer while their manager lived in a penthouse in Monaco. Crazy, crazy stuff!"

"It sounds like it, Waldemar," Shrimp Wrigley said, squinting as the sun started its descent in the West.

"Yeah, we did well, all told," Waldemar mused. "Yukio made us all rich and famous, with some help from Lady Orchid."

"Lady Orchid Buffington-Choade? My fiancée?" Shrimp Wrigley responded with surprise.

"Yes indeed! *That* Lady Orchid Buffington-Choade. Without her, there would have been no **WOW**," Waldemar said, taking the last sip of his Roo Energy Drink, setting the empty bottle on the bench to his right.

"Wow!"

"Wow," Waldemar continued. "She found us, nurtured us, fed us, housed us, financed us, loved us and stayed with us until we reached the top. We never could have done it without her. She has told you about us, hasn't she?"

"Oh, sure," Shrimp Wrigley replied nonchalantly, standing up and lighting another Lucky Strike.

"How did you react?" Waldemar questioned, somewhat taken aback that Shrimp Wrigley was acting so matter-of-factly.

"How should I have reacted?" Shrimp Wrigley replied defensively.

"Well, don't you find it a bit odd, seeing that she's your fiancée and all," Waldemar said with a self-conscious chuckle.

"I mean, I know she was important in your life and all, but now she wants to settle down with me. What's so odd about that?" Shrimp Wrigley asked.

"Nothing at all. I'm glad our past doesn't bother you, Shrimp Wrigley," Waldemar responded, becoming a bit irked at Shrimp Wrigley's defensive attitude.

"What do you mean 'our past?'" Shrimp Wrigley questioned, sitting down on the Sunset Bench again, his latest Lucky Strike just a filter now. Lanky walked over to the Sunset Bench for another treat. None was forthcoming.

"You know..." Waldemar was reluctant to discuss the details.

"I know *what?* Are we even talking about the same thing?" Shrimp Wrigley wondered out loud. "We *are* talking about Lady Orchid helping **WOW** get started, aren't we?"

"No! We are talking about Lady Orchid and me being *married,*" Waldemar blurted out, annoyed that, once again, Shrimp Wrigley and he were talking about two different things.

"Waldemar, you're always... *married?* Did you say 'married?' What the..." Shrimp Wrigley was literally speechless, a difficult feat to accomplish in the normal course of things. "Married?!"

"I... I thought that's what we were talking about! I asked if Lady Orchid had told you..."

"Had told me about the beginnings of **WOW**! That's what *I* was talking about!" Shrimp Wrigley replied, his voice rising a bit as the emotions took hold.

Waldemar and Shrimp Wrigley both looked at each other sitting on the Sunset Bench. After several moments of silence, they both broke up laughing! Another two-subject conversation, another amicable ending.

"So, when were you married to her and how long?" Shrimp Wrigley asked after their laugh together.

"Oola, Walter and I were living at Buffington-Choade Manor," Waldemar recalled. "It was 1992 and Lady Orchid and I took a fancy to one another. We were foolish, I guess, got married in Spain on a vacation, got divorced seven months later, stayed friends and we all remained living at Buffington-Choade Manor until **WOW** really took off. Then I bought the manor house next door!"

"Wow, **WOW**!" Shrimp Wrigley laughed. "Truth be told, Waldemar, Lady Orchid and I called the wedding off..."

"Really? Already!?" Waldemar questioned in surprise.

"Yes. When we got down to my apartment that night, we both decided it would be best if we were just friends. I think we got caught up in the moment."

"Well, better safe than sorry when if comes to matters of the heart, eh?" Waldemar said, running his right hand though his neatly trimmed beard. "So, what about you?"

"What about me, what?" Shrimp Wrigley responded with a wry smile.

"Were you ever married?" Waldemar asked, assuming that Shrimp Wrigley *had* to have an interesting romantic history at the very least.

"Ahh... sure," Shrimp Wrigley said, rubbing the tip of his right boot in the dirt by the Sunset Bench.

"Ah, sure what?" Waldemar teased him. "Have you?"

"Well, yes."

"Okay. How many times have you been married would probably be a better question for you!" Waldemar laughed, Lanky turning to look at Waldemar.

"A few," Shrimp Wrigley answered vaguely.

"What... like three, four, five?"

"Yes."

"Which?"

"Um... and I'm not proud of this Waldemar... five times," Shrimp Wrigley confessed, dipping his head a bit to look at the tip of his right boot.

"Five, eh?" Waldemar laughed again. "Geez, you really give your all to any cause, don't you?"

"Well, I wouldn't put it that way, Waldemar," he responded, taking a philosophical turn. "I'm just an independent sort of guy and I've always found it hard to deal with the thoughts and feelings of another person close to me. That's why I love ostriches so much."

"What? Why?"

"Why, what?"

"What does loving ostriches have to do with trouble with human relationships?" Waldemar questioned.

"Oh. Ostriches look to you for food basically. And they don't talk. And they don't really have any ideas to speak of."

"That's not a very enlightened attitude, Shrimp Wrigley," Waldemar teased.

"I never said I *had* an enlightened attitude, Waldemar," Shrimp Wrigley said, pulling out another Lucky Strike from the pack and lighting it, standing away from the Sunset Bench so the smoke wouldn't blow directly on Waldemar.

"True enough. True enough. Do you remember all their names?"

"Sure! Five names aren't *that* hard to remember!" Shrimp Wrigley took a drag of his Lucky Strike and recited the names of his ex-wives, in order: "Monique, Yasmine, Eva-Rose, Estelle and Lyla."

"Impressive. Very impressive, Shrimp Wrigley," Waldemar conceded.

"Thanks, Waldemar," Shrimp Wrigley said sitting back down on the Sunset Bench after taking a last drag on his Lucky Strike. "Monique and I got married right after high school. We were high school sweethearts, you might say. Her father was a traveling magician by trade, *The Wizard of Ahs* was his stage name; her mother, a raging alcoholic. I think she mostly married me just to get away from her mother, but that's okay. We had some good times together, that's for sure! Monique's father started having trouble getting any gigs as his specialty was hand magic and he had developed an awful shaking in his right hand. He tried to hide it, but it was noticeable. I saw him perform several times toward the end of his career and it was not a pretty sight, Waldemar. Shaking a deck of cards, a bouquet of flowers, whatever he was holding in his right hand shook like the devil was throttling an angel. After a time, he had to call it quits and that's pretty much when we called it quits for our marriage too. Monique was just too involved in keeping her mother and father together in one piece to invest any time in keeping *us* in one piece.

"Then there was Yasmine. I met Yasmine in my senior year of college. She was an exchange student from Algeria, and I fell for her hard! She was as beautiful as you would expect a beautiful woman from Algeria to be and ten times more! She wanted to help me get through college by working part time as an exotic dancer at *Rockin' Uranus*, a club outside of Akron, Ohio, at night and a part-time college student by day. What a gal! And when I say 'exotic dancer' I don't mean a mere stripper, no sir. Yasmine was pure class through and through. Eventually, she got so good at stripp... um... exotic dancing that she decided to try her luck on the big screen. She took off to Hollywood. I couldn't go because I was still in college. She got a feature role in the sci-fi thriller, *Babes in Outer Space*. Eventually, we lost touch and she filed for divorce after meeting some up-and-coming stud, Harry Richards, at the studio... typical story. And who's ever heard of Yasmine and/or Harry Richards since, I ask.

"Eva-Rose, what a sweet thing she was! As caring a woman as you'd ever want to meet. She was the youngest of fourteen children out of Mine Shaft, West Virginia. Eva-Rose ran a florist shop near the coal mine. I never did see the sense of that, but she stuck to it even when the creditors were after her night and day. We had several years of wedded bliss until she was incarcerated. It turns out that to try and make ends meet, Eva-Rose was making and distributing moonshine on the side. Now, you'd think that with the Twenty-first Amendment to the United States Constitution, ratified on December 5, 1933, which repealed the Eighteenth Amendment to the United States Constitution, prohibition, that it would be legal to deal in moonshine, but that is not the case. Federal law states that it is legal to own a still of any size. However, be advised it is illegal to distill alcohol without having either a 'distilled spirits permit' or a 'federal fuel alcohol permit.' It does not matter if the alcohol is for personal use only, not for sale, etc. So, that being said, Eva-Rose ended up in jail and our marriage ended up in divorce court after she entered the tele psychic field upon her release.

"Estelle. Not much good to say about Estelle. Every group of individuals has a rotten apple and my rotten apple was Estelle! Not good looking. An eyeful of 'ugh,' actually. Not intelligent. No charm. No education. The only thing Estelle could do well was whistle like a farmer. Her whistle was loud and strong! I think I was looking for an honest Eva-Rose, but I got Estelle and she didn't even beat Eva-Rose if Eva-Rose *had been* honest! That's how bad Estelle was! I had a pretty good job selling Studebakers at the time. I was top salesman of the month on several occasions during my retail vehicle consultant career. Every time I would get an award or a bonus, there was

Estelle wanting to know why I wasn't getting more... why wasn't I selling Packards? I just couldn't win with that woman. Finally, I was giving a potential customer a test drive of a Studebaker Golden Hawk, a beautiful car by-the-way, and I told the guy to just keep driving. Pretty soon we were out of the county. I asked him to drive the car back to the dealer while I got a bus ticket to California. Good-bye, Estelle and good riddance! Hello, California!

"And, finally, there's Lyla. Once again, I hit my stride making up for Estelle. Lyla was a doll – beautiful, intelligent and *rich*! Yes, she came from a wealthy family, very wealthy. We were married for all of two and a half years. It was all good except her mother and father *hated* me! I wasn't classy enough for those two. I couldn't do anything right in their eyes! They finally got between us and I couldn't take the pressure anymore. As a parting gift, Lyla's father bought Ostrichland for me. He would have given me the moon if he could as long as I wasn't married to his darling daughter anymore. Fine. Ostrichland proved to be a great investment after you came along, Waldemar? ... Waldemar?... Hey!"

Alas, Waldemar's day had been long and hard and Shrimp Wrigley's tales long and complicated and Waldemar was caught with his eyelids closed, or close to it. "Oh, no problem, Shrimp Wrigley," Waldemar blinked awake, attempting to appear as though he was merely resting his eyes. "I appreciated your story and was just taking in every word," he sought to recover.

"Oh good, Waldemar," Shrimp Wrigley replied with relief. "I wouldn't go over the list of my ex-wives to just anyone, you understand."

"Oh, I'm honored that you trust me to tell your matrimonial journey. I can't believe we've never talked about our marriages before," Waldemar said, stretching his arms to the sky as dusk fell over the Neu Deutschland Valley. "The day's not over yet," Waldemar remarked, springing to his feet as Lanky moved over in Waldemar's direction. "Yukio wants to fill us all in on what happened today."

As Waldemar started walking from the Sunset Bench, he saw a brand-new Cadillac XTS limousine pulling into the Ostrichland parking lot, just ahead of the official closing time.

"Hey, I think that's Les Winns' limo!" Waldemar exclaimed as he moved closer to a hedge so he could survey the scene unseen, Waldemar urging Shrimp Wrigley and Lanky to follow his stealthy lead. "What's *he* doing here?"

As Waldemar, Lanky and Shrimp Wrigley watched from the shadows, the limousine pulled to an elegant stop near The Egg. The driver emerged, Les Winns' driver, as he proceeded to the back-passenger door. With a flourish that only a highly trained chauffeur could maneuver, the door was opened.

"What?" Waldemar whispered loudly. "It's Yukio, that Gerta Swisser... Switzer woman, Oola and Walter! No Les Winns? Why are they in Winns' car?"

The quartet made their way to The Egg as the driver reentered the limousine and headed out of the Ostrichland parking lot and down Highway 277 in the direction of Neu Deutschland.

"Well, let's get to The Egg," Waldemar said, leading the way down the parking lot sidewalk. "If this day gets any weirder, I don't know what I'm going to do!"

Oh, the weird was only beginning!

Some Explaining to Do...

The eclectic group gathered in the jewel-like 99-seat theater, 'The Yolk.' Literally the core of The Egg, The Yolk was Hartwig von Trussell's greatest achievement in the design of The Egg. Built with only the finest materials, latest stage equipment and spectacular acoustics, The Yolk was a hidden gem and never used since The Egg was built. Waldemar had pushed von Trussell to include The Yolk in The Egg; however, once completed, Waldemar couldn't bring himself to use his new theater or the accompanying recording studio.

Jeeves was busy handing out snacks and drinks to the guests.

"Ladies and gentlemen take your seats, please!" an officious-looking Yukio Cassidy standing in front of the stage urged the scattered gathering. "I just want to make some announcements about our day so that we're all caught up on what happened. There you go... there you go, my children."

The people present consisted of Yukio, Waldemar, Oola, Walter, Li'l Otter, Shen, Lady Orchid, Three and Horace Herring (initially because he needed to use the restroom). Lady Orchid was the last to find a seat, her latest fascinator a cacophony of vivid colors with ostrich figurines depicting the planned stampede event. Dustie and Shrimp Wrigley were busy checking on the flock following their big adventure earlier in the day.

"Thank you all for coming to The Yolk," Yukio began, standing behind a Shure SM58 microphone with stand so that his commentary of the day would be easily heard by the audience. "I believe everyone is now accounted for – both human and fowl." The audience laughed. "Well, you can't say that we don't have fun when we visit Ostrichland! I spent some time with the authorities in Neu Deutschland following our adventures there earlier today. All in all, I would say that we have good news to report.

"Most importantly, Lanky is back home, safe and sound," the gathered applauded enthusiastically. "Surveillance tape from JustNEWS indicates that Lanky boarded one of their storage vans when it was parked here in the Ostrichland parking lot. When the van arrived in Neu Deutschland, Lanky was able to extricate himself from the van and begin his adventures in town.

"No charges will be filed in relation to Lanky's encounter with Sanny the lounge singer at *WonderBar*. Sanny was quite overwhelmed by the event and couldn't provide many facts to me; however, I sensed happiness rather than anger on his part.

"Likewise, the transportation company, Busses Я Us, does not plan to file a complaint about the damage to the luxury coaches as a result of Lanky's kicking in the windshield of Bus #1 and subsequent damages that occurred during the planned stampede event. So, that's good news.

"That brings us to Les Winns who is resting comfortably in his quarters at *Das Rathaus* following the accident in Bus #1. Mr. Winns' main concern at this time is not the state of his health, but the state of his business venture, which leads us into the next aspect of today's adventures.

"Because of the media coverage, bus accident, Lanky's attack and the planned stampede event, Mr. Winns was suggesting that his potential customers were no longer interested in establishing residences in, the name at the time, New Fatherland, as the various incidents proved that New Fatherland was, in fact, *not* a safe place to reside.

"Mr. Winns was suggesting taking legal action when we had our brief meeting following the planned stampede event. However, I was privy to several transaction irregularities that occurred during the sale of Neu Deutschland to Mr. Winns. I decided to bring some of these irregularities to Mr. Winns' attention, which was quite effective.

"To provide a win/win situation, always my goal, I informed Mr. Winns of an opportunity to 'unload' his failed investment of New Fatherland. And to proceed with this narrative, I now defer to Walter Johnson. Walter?"

Amid applause for Yukio's presentation and to welcome Walter Johnson, Walter walked over to the microphone as Yukio found an empty seat in the front row of The Yolk.

"Thank you everyone," Walter began in his sonorous, calming voice. "Yukio, we all appreciate the summary regarding today's activities and the outcomes. We know with all that happened, there could have been legal and financial repercussions. It's like going back to our **WOW** days where every day was filled with business, legal and personal landmines, so thanks again for your invaluable help.

"Oola and I owe a special debt of gratitude to Yukio because of what he was able to do for us this day. Oola, you come up here too... We are pleased and honored to announce that we are the new *owners* of Neu Deutschland!"

A gasp and then applause was heard throughout The Yolk!

Oola took a step closer to the microphone. "Although it was a crazy morning with ostriches and reporters, Walter and I fell in love with Neu Deutschland," Oola explained, brushing several strands of hair out of her right eye, the eye showing glints of moisture sliding down her cheek. "When Yukio heard of Les Winns' despair in failing to launch New Fatherland, we put in a bid to buy New Fatherland and turn it back to Neu Deutschland!"

Dustie and Shrimp Wrigley had just entered The Yolk in time to hear the news from Walter and Oola. They, along with the others gathered stood up and gave two-thirds of **WOW** a standing ovation upon hearing the news!

"Thank you!" Walter said, hugging Oola, a huge smile on both their faces. Waldemar was the only one in The Yolk who had a bit less than euphoria etched on his face. "As part of the resurrection of Neu Deutschland, we would like to welcome a familiar face to some a new face to others, the *new* Bürgermeisterin of Neu Deutschland, Gerta Switzer! Gerta, come on out!" Walter said, urging the shy but bouncy woman in lederhosen in the wings to join the group in The Yolk.

"*Vielen Dank!*" a radiant Gerta Switzer thanked the crowd, waving her hands in the air as she walked up to the microphone. Waldemar and Yukio joined Gerta in front of the group. "I am so honored to be with such a distinguished gathering of famous people!" she giggled. "You have done so much for my town of Neu Deutschland by ruining the plans of that evil Les Winns and his henchmen Otto Ackermann and Conrad Halle. Mr. Cassidy told me that all three will be going to jail soon on tax evasion charges, so we can all now celebrate the victory of good over evil. *Ja!*"

"*Ja* indeed!" Yukio took a step to the microphone. "Edwin and Edwina Flunkie, we learned, had notified the proper authorities as to the financial shenanigans of Mr. Winns. I, in fact, questioned them on their apparent lack of loyalty to Mr. Winns and Edwin said, 'it was a twin thing.' He didn't elaborate on that phrase."

Oola took the microphone. "Waldemar, Walter and I owe you a debt of gratitude for being a conduit of positive energy to emerge and lead us to this wonderful land of birds and beauty! We are so excited that we will be your neighbors and can, with Bürgermeisterin Switzer's help, reinvigorate Neu Deutschland to its original glory!"

The audience gave Oola a standing ovation. In a spontaneous gesture, Waldemar, Oola and Walter came together and had a group hug, a long group hug! The audience went wild!

"Song! Song!" Lady Orchid shouted above the din of applause. Within seconds the others gathered took up the chant. Waldemar, Oola and Walter broke the hug, took a step back and looked into each other's eyes. There was still **WOW** magic there! Shen appeared with an Ibanez PC18MH Grand Concert - Mahogany Sunburst Open Pore acoustic guitar in his right hand and two Rhythm Tech Tambourines in his left. Waldemar took the guitar, Walter and Oola the tambourines. Li'l Otter and Shen quickly set up three Shure AD2/K9N Wireless Handheld Microphone with stands.

"Let's go **WOW**!" Li'l Otter urged. "Make some music!"

Waldemar demurred, looking at his former colleagues for some visual cue as to their level of interest.

"Come on, Waldemar!" Oola urged, shaking her red tambourine as she turned and smiled at Walter.

"Well, I guess we could do *one* number," Waldemar relented.

"Go up on the stage **WOW**," Li'l Otter urged, poking Shen in his right side and whispering something.

"Yeah, Waldemar. The stage!" Walter agreed, heading up the three steps to the actual stage of The Yolk. Oola followed with Waldemar taking the rear, making sure his guitar didn't hit the wall as he trudged up the steps.

"What are we going to sing?" Waldemar asked as Agatha turned on the main stage lights.

"Uh, hello? We've got two tambourines, don't we?" Oola asked in a teasing tone. "Let's sing 'Two Tambourines!'"

'Two Tambourines' was one of **WOW**'s five #1's in 1997.

"Sounds good! Let's go!" Waldemar said, a new enthusiasm in his voice as he tuned the guitar.

Two Tambourines

I get on with life as a singer,
I'm a lonely kinda person.
I like singing and dancing.
I like to contemplate dancing.
But when I start to daydream,
My mind turns straight to two tambourines.

Oh oh oh!

Sometimes I look at myself and I look into my eyes,
I notice the way I think about two tambourines with a smile,
Curved lips I just can't disguise.
But I think it's dancing making my life worthwhile.
Why is it so hard for me to decide which I love more?
Dancing or...
Two Tambourines?

I like to use words like 'fantastic' and 'amazing.'
I like to use words about dancing.
But when I stop my talking,
My mind turns straight to two tambourines.

Oh oh oh!

Sometimes I look at myself and I look into my eyes,
I notice the way I think about two tambourines with a smile,
Curved lips I just can't disguise.
But I think it's dancing making my life worthwhile.
Why is it so hard for me to decide which I love more?
Dancing or...
Two Tambourines?

I like to hang out with Oola and Walter.
But when left alone,
My mind turns straight to two tambourines.

Oh oh oh!

Sometimes I look at myself and I look into my eyes,
I notice the way I think about two tambourines with a smile,
Curved lips I just can't disguise.
But I think it's dancing making my life worthwhile.
Why is it so hard for me to decide which I love more?
Dancing or...
Two Tambourines?

A Good Cause...

"That was *AMAZING!*" Waldemar shouted into one of the Shure SM58 microphones with stand following **WOW**'s rendition of 'Two Tambourines.' The audience agreed, giving a thunderous standing ovation.

"Ladies and gentlemen give it up for **WOW!**" shouted Li'l Otter, walking onstage, holding his microphone. "They haven't played together in what?... twenty-one years?"

"Twenty!" Waldemar interjected, he and the audience laughing.

"Twenty years!" Li'l Otter corrected himself with a broad smile. "No rehearsal. Borrowed instruments. And it was... F-A-N-T-A-S-T-I-C!"

And no one could deny it. The magic was still there. And all three members of **WOW** were in the moment. The hurts of the past were for now, in the past. The present felt pretty good.

The applause continued. Jeeves entered The Yolk with special cocktails concocted for the special spontaneous occasion. Lady Orchid even had time to secure an 'in the moment' fascinator featuring cutouts of the three members of **WOW** on a tiny stage under a cleverly concealed LED lamp, giving an uncanny impression of a miniature **WOW** reunion happening on top of her head.

The applause was beginning to subside as the guests were tasting Jeeves' delicious libation. Shen was giving Li'l Otter some sign language information.

"Waldemar, congratulations to you again," Li'l Otter continued. "I'm told that we have a special surprise visitor here in The Yolk tonight."

WOW looked amongst themselves to deduce the identity of the surprise visitor. No one had a clue.

"Ladies and gentlemen... Little Timmy!" Li'l Otter announced to great fanfare as Little Timmy walked out from the wings. Dressed in a miniature replica of an 1825 uniform of a Portuguese naval cadet, Little Timmy was 'cute' personified.

"Little Timmy! What brings you here?" Waldemar asked, taking the microphone that Li'l Otter handed him, still joyous from his **WOW** performance. "I'm so happy to see you! Everyone, meet my special little pal, Little Timmy!"

The giddy audience rose to their feet, cocktail glasses in hand and chanted "Little Timmy! Little Timmy!" since they couldn't applaud with said cocktail glasses in hand.

Oola and Walter took several steps toward the back of the stage, sensing that Waldemar was going to engage in some banter with his diminutive friend.

"Big boy! Biggest boy! Biggest boy in the world! Biggest boy in the Universe!" Waldemar said to Little Timmy, knowing that the phrases of praise would produce the desired result of Little Timmy raising his two arms straight into the air, higher and higher, until he could reach no more.

"Waldemar! He's *so* cute!" Oola cooed from the sidelines in delight.

"Thank you, Mr. Ulff. Thank you, ladies and gentlemen. It's an honor to be here tonight. I knocked at the hatch and Agatha let me in. The guard said I could come up here and talk to all of you. Tonight, I come here not just as Little Timmy, but as an outreach ambassador, if you will, for the Orphans of Santa Bella."

"Oh!" the audience gasped, thrilled and inspired that such a tyke would be engaged in philanthropic work.

"Yes. Tonight is a crucial time for the Orphans of Santa Bella," Little Timmy continued, his bright blue eyes sparkling under the pink spotlight. Shen had made his way into the control room of The Yolk and was providing excellent staging for the event, in addition to taping "Two Tambourines" for posterity with the help of the robotic camera system of The Yolk, controlled by Agatha.

"Alas, the Orphans of Santa Bella are facing a bleak future. They found out today that their property of twenty-three acres, including the main house, three ancillary buildings, a barn and saltwater swimming pool are about to go into foreclosure. My gram told me they were 'up shit's creek,' but I don't know what *that* means..."

"Language, Little Timmy!" Waldemar cautioned off-mic.

The audience was sad about the plight of the Orphans of Santa Bella but amused at Little Timmy's gram quote.

"Please, if you open your hearts, perhaps a butterfly can fly in," Little Timmy added as the coda to his plea.

"That's a *very* sad story, Little Timmy," Oola said as she took a few steps toward Little Timmy. "You are very brave telling us all about it!"

"Yes, Little Timmy, I'm so proud of you," Waldemar agreed.

"And what I told you isn't the worst part," Little Timmy continued to the gasps of the audience. "The Orphans of Santa Bella don't have enough money to even eat!"

"What?" Lady Orchid could be heard.

"No food?" Walter asked, moving over and giving Oola a reassuring hug.

"They're nutrient insecure?" Oola asked in disbelief.

"No food," Little Timmy reiterated.

"Waldemar, what can *we* do?" Oola asked, covering the microphone to make the question a bit more private.

"I don't know, but we need to come up with *something*," Waldemar responded, not covering the microphone.

In the control room, Shen found that most of the functions of The Yolk were controlled by the omnipresent Agatha. At this point his commands produced a green screen background on stage with a black and white video of Tirana, Albania on April 12, 1985, the day after Enver Hoxha's death. It wasn't the video he would have preferred, but Shen was having a great time with the high-tech auditorium.

Yukio quickly made his way up to the stage as Little Timmy's plea was beginning to sound like a money issue. "Hi little guy!" he exclaimed as he joined Little Timmy and the members of **WOW**.

"Yukio, Little Timmy. Little Timmy, Mr. Cassidy," Waldemar interjected to offer introductions.

"You seem to know quite a bit about the Orphans of Santa Bella," Yukio remarked to Little Timmy.

"I only know as much as I see and Gram tells me," Little Timmy replied earnestly, rubbing his nose with the right-side cuff of his mock Portuguese naval uniform.

"Help the Orphans! Help the Orphans!" Lady Orchid started chanting, Jeeves' celebratory cocktail perhaps too strong for the occasion. The audience: Lady Orchid, Dustie, Gerta, Shrimp Wrigley, Li'l Otter and Horace Herring, quickly took up the chant as Waldemar, Oola, Walter, Yukio and Little Timmy conferred on stage out of microphone range.

"Help Us Help You! Help Us Help You!" The chant took a creative twist as the discussion continued. By this time, Shen, aided by Agatha, had replaced the Tirana backdrop video with one of Señor Wences and his hand puppet, Johnny, on 'The Ed Sullivan Show' circa March 20, 1966, an especially good performance. S'awright.

"Ladies and gentlemen, please!" Yukio turned to the audience, holding his arms in the air to quiet them. "I have an important announcement to make..." Agatha dimmed the stage lights to a spotlight on Yukio as Shen changed the backdrop to one of various slides of a random platypus in New South Wales, Australia. "In response to Little Timmy's plea to help the Orphans of Santa

Bella, the members of **WOW**, Waldemar Ulff, Oola La and Walter Johnson have tentatively agreed to stage a benefit concert for the Orphans of Santa Bella!"

The Yolk went wild! What a day! Lanky was found and returned to Ostrichland. Les Winns the 'Yacktivist' gave up his dream for New Fatherland. Oola La and Walter Johnson bought Neu Deutschland. **WOW** performed 'Two Tambourines' and now, a benefit concert for the Orphans of Santa Bella!

Little Timmy turned to Waldemar, Oola La and Walter Johnson and shook their hands one-by-one, then he turned and walked up to one of the microphones, carefully removing it from the stand. "Mr. Ulff, Ms. La and Mr. Johnson, I want to thank you from the bottom of my heart for your generous gesture of producing a benefit concert for the Orphans of Santa Bella. My heart is glowing with the love I feel tonight in this auditorium."

You could hear a pin drop as Little Timmy gave his heartfelt thanks. "I can't wait to tell Gram and the Orphans of Santa Bella about the generosity that I witnessed here tonight. And I know that if ostriches had money, they would give some to the Orphans of Santa Bella too!"

"Oh-h-h..." The audience cooed with Little Timmy's reference to the ostrich's perceived generosity.

"Little Timmy, it is *our* pleasure to help you in your cause," Waldemar spoke into his microphone as Oola, Walter and Yukio stood by with smiles on their faces, Yukio having a smaller smile than the others.

"I know that what was done here tonight will become legendary when acts of charity are recalled years from now," Little Timmy concluded, wiping a small tear from his right eye with the right-side sleeve of his mock Portuguese naval coat.

From the audience, Shrimp Wrigley muttered, "Little shit!"

Exclusive...!

"I'm Li'l Otter on Intertoobz' *Feeling the Music* special edition. We are broadcasting live from The Yolk Theater in The Egg at Ostrichland on the central coast of California. For this special edition we're talking to pop music legends Waldemar Ulff, Oola La and Walter Johnson of the legendary group **WOW**. It's not every day **WOW** gives an interview and it's not every day that **WOW** is going to make a special announcement exclusively on *Feeling the Music* tonight. **WOW**, welcome!"

"Thank you, Li'l Otter," Waldemar replied, "It's a pleasure to have you here at Ostrichland!"

"Thank you, Li'l Otter," Oola La said. "I always *love* being on your show!"

"Thanks!" Walter Johnson replied.

"It's fantastic to see you three again after all these years! And especially here at Ostrichland, Waldemar's passion since **WOW** broke up, right?"

"Right, Li'l Otter," Waldemar said, shifting slightly in his chair in the recording studio off The Yolk. "It *has* been a long time and I'm so glad that we're all here and that I can host this show in The Yolk."

"The gang *is* all here!" Oola chuckled, looking at Walter.

"Now, I'm sure for those keeping up with the news, they know about **WOW** getting back together to see each other after Waldemar's viral video a few days ago, but a lot has happened in the meantime, shall I say..."

"Indeed, Li'l Otter!" Waldemar ventured. "And you've been an integral part of it too!" All in the studio chuckled.

"Indeed, I have, willingly and unwillingly in some cases! Waldemar, how about giving us a breakdown of just what has been going on since the viral video, okay?"

"Sure, Li'l Otter," Waldemar said, taking a quick swig of his Roo Energy Drink, the bottle resting on the built-in armrest of his studio chair. "It's been a crazy week, but here goes: after the viral video went viral, and by the way, I had no part of that video, that was made without my knowledge although I have since forgiven the gentleman responsible, Oola and Walter decided to fly down from Toronto. That was a *huge* surprise for me. At about that time, my prize ostrich, Lanky, unfortunately climbed aboard a news van and ended up in the local town, Neu Deutschland. To retrieve Lanky, I decided to appeal to his leadership instincts and release the flock of ostriches into Neu Deutschland where they would bring Lanky out of hiding. The plan worked and we got Lanky and family safely back here to Ostrichland..."

"Now before you say anything more regarding this saga, Waldemar, I'm going to play an audio of something that happened here in The Yolk last night. Shen?"

With Li'l Otter's front sell, Shen played the recording he made of 'Two Tambourines,' **WOW**'s first reunion performance the night before. This time, Waldemar's reaction was the opposite of Three's bootleg video of 'Now, the Sky' with Sanny at *WonderBar*. Waldemar *knew* the performance and decision to get together again was the right one.

"There you go, ladies and gentlemen, **WOW** and 'Two Tambourines!' And now, I think we can make it official, right? Who wants to give our audience the big news?"

"Walter!" Waldemar laughed, turning to the least vocal of **WOW**'s trio.

"Sure, I don't mind," Walter smiled, pulling his chair closer to the Electro-Voice RE20 broadcast microphone.

"Shen, a drumroll, please!"

"**WOW** is *BACK*!" Walter announced loudly and with excitement, his bass voice booming. Shen played a digital sample of fans cheering at a rock concert.

"**WOW** is back, indeed!" Li'l Otter affirmed.

"We are thrilled, Li'l Otter!" Oola cooed, high-fiving Waldemar and Walter. "This is the best decision we've made in years!"

"Why the change of heart? For years all three of you have dismissed calls for **WOW** to regroup."

"The time is now, Li'l Otter," Waldemar spoke up.

"The time is **WOW**!" Oola punned.

"Ow!" Walter groaned.

"So, what are **WOW**'s immediate plans?"

"Glad you asked, Li'l Otter," Waldemar said, giving Li'l Otter a wink with his right eye, enjoying the polished segue. "Because of alarming news we received from a friend of Ostrichland, Little Timmy, **WOW** is planning a benefit concert for the Orphans of Santa Bella. The Orphans of Santa Bella is a local organization and they need some help with financial difficulties. It's a worthy cause and **WOW** can add a helping hand."

"That sounds fantastic! Several basic questions: what's the name of the concert? When? And where do we get tickets?"

"The concert is officially called, '**WOW**: Hug the Orphans.' We will hold the concert a week from now. Tickets will *not* be sold as The Yolk holds only ninety-nine people. We will be giving away tickets to friends, family, the media and a number of lucky fans who will be chosen at random from our **WOW** fan database under the capable hands of Yukio Cassidy."

"Yes, Li'l Otter," Oola took up the conversation. "**WOW** was always about using our music to help people have fun and enjoy life. What better cause than aiding an orphanage?"

"Are you going to have other groups at the concert? Give us some details."

"We've only had a few hours to plan the concert, but the need is dire, and **WOW** is ready to roll," Waldemar explained. Thanks to our super manager, Yukio Cassidy, we are going to stream the concert through Intertoobz. The concert will be held here, in The Yolk in Ostrichland. We will be in good hands with Intertoobz's own Shenandoah River as the concert producer and veteran video director, Gurt Holjeerz. Gurt was the mind behind several of **WOW**'s award-winning music videos. In conjunction with the concert and album, Gurt will be directing a documentary chronicling the lead up to the concert and the immediate aftermath."

"Will the concert have other acts? Like **WOW**'s return isn't enough, right!?"

"We *are* planning a few surprises, Li'l Otter," Waldemar responded. "I want to keep them surprises so they are a surprise during the concert."

"Waldemar don't forget about the album," Oola reminded Waldemar.

"Oh, no chance! The icing on the musical cake, if you will, is that we will be recording a live album of the concert. Sales of the album will go to the Orphans of Santa Bella," Waldemar said with excitement.

"You guys really have everything down, don't you!"

"It's just like the old days, Li'l Otter!" Oola spoke up. "We would get an idea and before you knew it, it was happening!"

"It's very exciting," Walter added, sounding less than excited even though he was, in fact, very excited.

"Do you have any idea what *big* news this is!?"

"Yes. Yes, we do," Waldemar replied candidly.

"Sure!" Oola joined in. "People have been wanting us to reunite for years... decades! Now everything has come together at the proper time and the proper place. It's perfect. And, the best part is, we get to help the community through our music."

"And speaking of community, Walter and you have some news for our listeners regarding a recent purchase, I understand."

"Yes, Li'l Otter," Walter took up the conversation. "Today, Oola and I bought the little resort town up Highway 277 from Ostrichland, Neu Deutschland. We are planning to revitalize it and return the town to the must-see resort it once was."

"It's such a quaint little town, Li'l Otter," Oola said enthusiastically. "When Walter and I first saw Neu Deutschland, we *knew* we needed to own it!"

"That's amazing... owning a town!"

"It's a perk of our career that we are in a position to buy a complete town," Oola said with a broad smile, turning to Walter and blowing him a kiss.

"Some musicians buy yachts and private jets. We buy towns!" Walter added with a chuckle.

"I don't think we should overlook the aspect of revitalization of Neu Deutschland with Oola and Walter's purchase," Waldemar added, concerned the conversation was drifting into indulgent rich celebrity territory. "The fresh input of financial and creative resources can do wonders. I have found that to be true many times in my life."

"Maybe you could turn it into **WOW**Land!" Li'l Otter suggested.

"We have some ideas, Li'l Otter," Oola replied. "We feel between Ostrichland and Neu Deutschland we can turn the Neu Deutschland Valley into the go to destination that it should be. Who doesn't want to see ostriches and a faux German village?"

"Well put, Oola," Walter interjected.

"Walter and I plan to open a branch of my Toronto Brazilian-Chinese restaurant, Rio de Taipan, in Neu Deutschland."

"That sounds delicious! Waldemar, you mentioned the impetus of the **WOW**: Hug the Orphans Concert... Little Tommy is it?"

"Actually, he goes by Little Timmy," Waldemar politely corrected. "Little Timmy is the best, brightest and cutest seven-year-old you'd ever want to see! Plus, he's a big ostrich fan. He visits Ostrichland frequently as admission is *free*. That's how we met."

"Any chance of meeting Little Timmy on the show tonight?"

"Li'l Otter! Bedtime!" Waldemar scolded, a smile on his face.

"And speaking of bedtime, I think we need to call it a day and get some sleep ourselves. Waldemar Ulff, Oola La and Walter Johnson, thanks so much for being on *Feeling the Music*. We're so excited **WOW** is back and ready for action. I'm Li'l Otter. Thanks for listening!"

Cocktails and Feathers...

"Right. Left. A little more to the right. More to the left. There you go. No. No. Right. No, move it to the right! For heaven's sake, move the whole thing a tad to the left. Right. No, I'm saying right as in 'correct.' Over there, make sure the red carpet is clean around the edges, no soil, please! No. No. The platform needs to be completely level, no dips, slips or blips, please! You! At the door! Make sure we can control everything with the remote, okay? I don't want to see a decapitation tonight, that's for sure! You... left... right... as in 'correct!'"

"You are an amazing man, Vivian Taylor-Vance! I get all hot and bothered when you're event planning," Lady Orchid touched Vivian's right shoulder with her right hand. Vivian Taylor-Vance looked like a cross between Prince Albert of Saxe-Coburg and Gotha, consort of Queen Victoria of England and the legendary Robin Hood; fine chiseled facial features, excellent skeletal exposition and good posture on top of everything else. Vivian Taylor-Vance, following a successful career as a professional croquet player, was not only the top international event planner, he was the current paramour of Lady Orchid following her broken wedding engagement with Shrimp Wrigley several days before.

"Nothing I can't handle, Love!" Vivian took a moment to acknowledge Lady Orchid compliment and affectionate shoulder touch. "I could plan this party in my sleep!"

"Only you, you modest boy!" she replied, adjusting her tilting fascinator featuring several porcelain workers moving miniature wood furniture features in a paeon to event preparation. "How could I hold a semi-surprise cocktail party without you?" she asked, kissing him on his right cheek, carefully avoiding his ultra-trimmed auburn beard for fear of getting her Guerlain's KissKiss Matte Lipstick in Hot Coral entangled in his precise whiskers.

"You know it's a bit of pressure putting on an event in an ostrich pen, Love," Vivian remarked, looking around the Ostrich Habitat of The Egg, Lady Orchid's questionable venue site for a semi-surprise cocktail party celebrating the **WOW** reunion. "If you hadn't convinced that robot voice to let us in here, we would be planning a party in the local park!" he said with a wry chuckle, knowing that Lady Orchid knew this event was child's play for the world's best event planner. "What time do you have?"

"It's exactly 16:48," she responded after a look at her new Tiffany T watch on her slight right wrist.

"Right. I've got to go upstairs and dress," he said, turning his attention to several workers in the middle of the Ostrich Habitat. "Move that table more to the left. Right. No. Left. Right, as in 'correct.'"

Vivian left the Ostrich Habitat, taking the private elevator to the apartment floor of The Egg where Lady Orchid was housing her private event planner in her guest unit. After several minutes of watching the frenetic activities in the Ostrich Habitat, Lady Orchid decided to go 'assist' her guest prepare for the celebratory evening.

As quickly as you can imagine an old-fashioned analog clock swirling by the minutes, the hour struck 7:00 pm (19:00 for the sophisticated) and time for Lady Orchid's **WOW** reunion cocktail party, *Cocktails and Feathers*, featured venue, the Ostrich Habitat located in the ground floor of Ostrichland's The Egg.

In the private elevator of The Egg, descending, Waldemar, Dr. Dustie Rhodes and Shrimp Wrigley were in their latest cocktail party attire.

"So, what are we doing again?" Waldemar asked Dustie as the private elevator of The Egg descended from the Sky House to the Ostrich Habitat. "It's not like I've been busy or anything," Waldemar grumbled, adjusting his bow tie.

"I know, Waldemar," Dustie was sympathetic. "Lady Orchid wants to celebrate **WOW**'s reunion and you know how much that means to her," she explained, readjusting Waldemar's bow tie.

"I'm always up for a party!" Shrimp Wrigley exclaimed as the elevator made a very gentle halt to its descent. Only the private elevator went all the way to the ground level of The Egg. The shiny elevator doors opened.

The spectacle before the trio was amazing! The Ostrich Habitat had been transformed into a safari wonderland with lighting making it appear like dusk, special savanna vegetation, a large raised dais, covered in a colorful Persian rug in the middle of the large area and ostriches roaming about the Ostrich Habitat.

"Oh, my goodness!" Dustie exclaimed, blinking her eyes twice just to take in the scene. "They've really outdone themselves!"

"I'm in Africa!" Shrimp Wrigley exclaimed, taking off immediately as he made way to the large dais where three large circular cocktail tables had been precisely placed.

"Is this safe?" Waldemar asked Dustie in concern as they walked slowly from the elevator to the dais. "Why did she plan a party in the Ostrich Habitat?"

"Well, she didn't ask me," Dustie replied, walking carefully along a thick red carpet that had been laid from the elevator to the dais. "If she had asked, I would have voted against this setting based on the volatile combination of a flock of ostriches and alcohol. It is magical though, isn't it? So romantic!"

"I'll agree with that," Waldemar conceded.

The dais was raised approximately two feet above the floor of the Ostrich Habitat, one concession to safety to keep ostriches from guests of *Cocktails and Feathers*. Unfortunately, there were no steps from the floor of the Ostrich Habitat to the dais, an oversight unworthy of the work of Vivian Taylor-Vance who was, obviously, not as clear-headed as his usual self given the romantic influence of Lady Orchid.

"Well, this is quite an exercise in frustration," Waldemar remarked as he took a giant stride to reach the dais with his right foot. Having successfully reached the dais with both feet, he gallantly reached out for Dustie with his right hand and gave a strong tug, easing her way to the dais. "That's not a good start to the night," Waldemar remarked with concern, guiding Dustie to one of three circular tables arranged on the dais. Shrimp Wrigley was already seated at the center table, cocktail in hand, taking in the scene. "Have a seat, folks!" he urged with a casual air. "It's time to kick back and relax!"

"Indeed!" Waldemar agreed as he pulled out a chair for Dustie. Jeeves, decked out in his finest butler attire, glided up to Waldemar's right side with a tray of cocktails, each one featuring a festive ostrich feather as the garnish, offering one for Waldemar and Dustie. "Don't mind if I do, Jeeves," Waldemar said, taking two cocktail glasses in each hand, handing one to Dustie. "Enjoy, Dustie! Watch the feather. It could be a choking hazard under certain conditions."

As the trio were enjoying their cocktails, the doors of the private elevator opened, exposing a PDA involving Lady Orchid and Vivian Taylor-Vance. Unaware of the public nature of their lingering kiss, both exited the private elevator, walking along the red carpet to the dais keeping a wary eye on several ostriches ambling in their direction.

"Where on earth are the steps!?" Vivian asked no one in particular. "They were supposed to install them after I went up to the apartment. How are we supposed to get up on the dais?"

"Don't worry, Dear, it will be fine," Lady Orchid reassured her beau as he reached out to grasp her hands and raise her up the two feet to the dais. "There! No problem!" she said encouragingly, adjusting her latest fascinator featuring a large ostrich feather and a cocktail glass all artfully arranged atop her stately head. Vivian and Lady Orchid made their way to the middle table to greet Waldemar, Dr. Dustie Rhodes and Shrimp Wrigley.

"Greetings!" Lady Orchid greeted the first three guests of the *Cocktails and Feathers* cocktail party. "Vivian, I would like you to meet Waldemar Ulff, Dr. Dustie Rhodes and Shrimp Wrigley."

"What kind of name is Vivian for a man?" Shrimp Wrigley asked as he shook hands with Vivian. Yes, he went there!

"Pleased to meet you, Vivian," Waldemar greeted, trying to ignore Shrimp Wrigley's very rude comment.

"Yes, Vivian, welcome to Ostrichland," Dustie stood up and greeted their new guest.

"I'm so sorry we're a bit late," Lady Orchid apologized. "I was helping Vivian into his new pants."

"I'll bet you were!" Shrimp Wrigley commented, sitting down at the table to continue with his cocktail.

"Uh, Jeeves!" Waldemar called, sensing tension at the middle table. Another butler answered Waldemar's call. "Excuse me, but who are you?"

"They call me Premium Label," the new butler answered as he handed Lady Orchid a cocktail. "I'm from the Rent-A-Gent agency. I'm told it was determined that an additional butler was needed for tonight's festivities."

"Indeed," Vivian chimed in. "I felt Jeeves needed to be augmented for proper coverage of tonight's event, *Cocktails and Feathers* cocktail party. You see, I'm an event planner. I know these things."

"What else do you know, Viv?" Shrimp Wrigley asked sarcastically, motioning to Premium Label that he wanted another cocktail.

"Shrimp Wrigley, don't be so mean to Vivian!" Lady Orchid pouted, giving Vivian a peck on his right cheek, just above his crisp beard. "If I didn't know better, I would say you were jealous. We had our fun, Shrimp Wrigley, but you and I are *so* yesterday... literally!"

"Um... let's have a seat," Waldemar urged as they sat down at the middle table to join Shrimp Wrigley, probably not the best location on the dais. "Ah, I see other guests arriving!" Waldemar declared with relief. "Oh, it's Yukio Cassidy and Gerta Switzer! I didn't know Gerta was invited to *Cocktails and Feathers*," Waldemar remarked, wondering deep inside why he disliked Gerta Switzer; perhaps the whole attempt at entrapping him? Who knew?

Yukio and Gerta walked down the red carpet, dodging several ostriches browsing the Ostrich Habitat for a random treat, to the dais. Realizing the lack of steps, Yukio, taking a now familiar course of action, hoisted himself to the dais, then reached out to Gerta. Unfortunately, physics being an active part of life, the slightly built Yukio Cassidy was no match for the ample Gerta Switzer. As soon as he reached out his hands to help her up to the dais, her counterweight pulled him off the dais and both landed in a pile of cedar chips off to the side of the red carpet.

"Good heavens!" Lady Orchid shrieked, followed by a hearty laugh. The solo laugh turning into a chorus as the assembled saw no one was physically hurt and couldn't resist the humor of the scene before them. Yukio and Gerta gained their footing and, determined, they eventually made their way up to the dais, not pretty, but they got there, both laughing by now.

"Nice entrance, you two!" Waldemar offered, handing Yukio and Gerta cocktails. "So, what brings you here tonight, Gretel?"

"Gerta, Waldemar," she corrected Waldemar once again. "Yukio asked me out and I said *'ja!'*"

"Gerta and I have been involved in so many details of the Neu Deutschland purchase recently, I thought she could use a fun night out," Yukio said as he sampled his cocktail. Jeeves and Premium Label were now placing a selection of hors d'oeuvres on the three tables.

The guests were now arriving *en masse*, from the obvious: Oola La and Walter Johnson leading the pack, Conrad Halle III and gal pal Pollenaize Niesen, Li'l Otter, Shenandoah River and Gurt Holjeerz. To the 'who invited *them*': Sanny of piano lounge fame; Horace Herring, hero of the controlled ostrich stampede; Magdalene Sigi from JustNEWS; Dr. Drew Little of SAG; Dainer and Maria Neigh, owners of Bare Ass Winery and their twisted genius son, Johann Neigh; Dr. Passion Tudor, Applied Animal Behaviorist and, surprise of surprises, Edwin and Edwina Flunkie, Les Winns' twin assistants *sans* Les Winns.

The private elevator made several trips to the Ostrich Habitat to deposit all the guests. In a row they walked the red carpet, members of the ostrich flock: Egg-Burt, Tweety, Big Eyes, Doc, Giggles, Lou, Lindy, Hulk, Quill, Chip, Kicks, Big Bird, Juliet, Rona, Hopper, Marie, Romeo, Beaks, Killer, Kaya, Cookie, Carlton, Babs, Monster, Pretty Bird, Ophelia, Clyde, Lambert, Huey, Bonnie, Foster, Sage, Gizzard, Clarence, Baby, Milton, Valentine, Barbie, Happy, Bobo, Diamond, Annika, Veld, Toots, Esperanza, Paprika, Lanky, Sally, Blinky, Custer, Gams, Pappy, Plato, Butterscotch, Mr. Tibbs, to name a few, now making more congestion as they realized something was happening in their territory. With careful collision avoidance the guests made their way to the dais.

Vivian Taylor-Vance had been unsuccessful in reaching any of the event venue technicians, who had so carefully prepared the Ostrich Habitat, to get some steps assembled on the spot. As a result, each entrance involved an exposition of gymnastic skills and sheer human will to reach the actual dais unscathed. The ostriches were also becoming an element of concern as the flock started crowding around the red carpet seeking ostrich treats from the visitors. As a motivational aid, the guests who had already successfully made their way to the dais spontaneously started yelling 'Zippity Zip' to each guest as they struggled, grunting and huffed, up to the dais floor. The chant seemed to be working its magic.

For many minutes such phrases as "Come on, you can do it!" "You're slipping! You're slipping!" "Everyone else has made it up here!" and "Just go home if you're going to whine about it" were heard throughout the Ostrich Habitat as dais-victorious guests of the *Cocktails and Feathers* cocktail party urged, cursed and teased those still making their way up to the dais.

"Hello! Good evening, everyone!" Lady Orchid stepped up to the Shure AD2/K9N Wireless Handheld Microphone with stand, greeting her guests at the *Cocktails and Feathers* cocktail party. "I am Lady Orchid Buffington-Choade your hostess for this evening. But you can call me Lady Orchid. It is an honor and delight to have all of you here this evening as we celebrate the reuniting of **WOW**... yes, yes... your applause is most welcome and encouraged! I trust you are all having a wonderful time tonight, even those still getting up to the dais... Zippity Zip to those of you! We don't just have cocktails and hors d'oeuvres for you tonight... yes, we have some special entertainment to keep you happy and amused! To begin the festivities, please turn your attention to our right in the Ostrich Habitat where Applied Animal Behaviorist Dr. Passion Tudor will be joined by Ophelia the Ostrich as Ophelia will be playing Bach's Appassionata Piano Sonata on portable keyboard. Dr. Passion Tudor...!"

Down on the floor of the Ostrich Habitat a somewhat flustered Dr. Tudor placed the Child's World Kids Piano on the floor and started tossing ostrich treats on the keyboard. Ophelia dutifully started pecking away at the keyboard, as practiced, much to the awe and delight of the guests of the *Cocktails and Feathers* cocktail party. Unfortunately, the tossed ostrich treats attracted the attention of the other ostriches roaming the Ostrich Habitat. Dr. Tudor and Ophelia were not used to others of the flock competing for ostrich treats during recital practice, so this added an unfortunate spin to the entire performance.

As more and more ostriches became aware of the food giveaway at the keyboard, there was a sudden interest in music-making. Several notes into Bach's Appassionata Piano Sonata, the scene turned ugly as food and not music took center stage in the Ostrich Habitat. As the flock went into a feeding frenzy the piano was ground into a million plastic pieces into the cedar chips of the Ostrich Habitat under the weight of the two-toed feet of the treat-seeking ostriches. Vivian Taylor-Vance, controlling the stage effects via app quickly shut off the spotlight on Dr. Passion Tudor and Ophelia as Dr. Tudor threw the bag of ostrich treats tucked into a pocket of her cocktail dress as far as she could throw toward the motion-sensor doors of the Ostrich Habitat. Dr. Tudor then hastily made her way to make a climb up to the dais. After the ostrich treats were consumed, the flock quieted down and resumed their aimless wandering.

"Well... thank you *so much*, Dr. Passion Tudor!" Lady Orchid said, initiating applause as Dr. Tudor finally got both feet firmly on the Persian rug of the dais. "That was really... something!"

"Something awful!" Shrimp Wrigley said in a stage whisper, inciting chortles from the guests.

"NO! NO! I *MUST* GET OUT OF HERE! THE BIG BIRDS ARE HIDEOUS!" Dr. Drew Little began shouting from Table #1, his recently acquired Strouthokamelophobia hitting him full force. *"MUST LEAVE...NOW! MAMA! MAMA! MUH-MUH-MUH! M... M... M...!"*

While a buzz of concern came over the *Cocktails and Feathers* cocktail party two security consultants from Pied Piper Security, Inc. carefully removed Dr. Drew Little from the dais and carried him to the private elevator.

"What a shame," Waldemar remarked, watching security escorting Dr. Little out of The Egg, as Lady Orchid took to the microphone again.

"I'm so glad that *everyone* seems to be enjoying *Cocktails and Feathers* tonight!" Lady Orchid gushed.

"Yeah, it's making us *crazy!*" Shrimp Wrigley murmured loudly, his cocktail intake starting to take a toll on his sense of propriety.

"I have a special treat for all of you tonight. Ladies and Gentlemen... Chef Flambé Olé, TV's famed Spanish-French chef, direct from New Orleans!" The doors of the private elevator opened on cue as the stereotypical rotund mustachioed chef dressed in his white uniform made his way down the red carpet to the dais where, much to everyone's relief, two security consultants were stationed to boost the famed TV chef up to the dais.

Amid enthusiastic applause, Chef Flambé Olé made his way to the microphone, bowing slightly to Lady Orchid who quite enjoyed the genuflection.

"Boo-Yay! Boo-Yay! Thank you! Thank you!" Chef Flambé Olé thanked the guests using his now-familiar catch phrase. "It is *my* honor to be here tonight, celebrating the reunion of **WOW**," he said with great gusto, looking directly at Waldemar seated at the middle cocktail table directly in front of Chef Flambé Olé. "I grew up listening to **WOW**! I remember my first day at kindergarten hearing **WOW** on the radio as my mother..."

"Chef Flambé Olé, we are *so* pleased to have you here tonight!" interrupted Lady Orchid, tactfully redirecting Chef Flambé Olé's reference to age. "Tell us about the special treat you've concocted for us!"

"Yes. Yes," the back-on-track Chef Flambé Olé continued. "In honor of **WOW** I have made a special gastronomic delight, *The **WOW** Seafood Gumbo!*"

As the guests applauded with excitement, Jeeves and Premium Label pushed a bright chrome food cart from the private elevator to the dais. In their trek across the Ostrich Habitat floor, the flock's wanderings started to become more purposeful as the scent of *The **WOW** Seafood Gumbo* started to settle throughout the area. The security consultants assisted in lifting the two serving trays up to the dais. As Jeeves and Premium Label, assisted by Chef Flambé Olé himself, began scooping large spoonful's of *The **WOW** Seafood Gumbo* into antique china soup dishes, the flock started congregating around the perimeter of the dais, much to the delight of the guests. The flock, getting up close and personal! The *Cocktails and Feathers* guests were soon enjoying the culinary genius of Chef Olé and his creation, *The **WOW** Seafood Gumbo*. Unbeknownst to the chef, the company where he sourced the seafood ingredients for the night's treat, Vittles from the Ocean, was being investigated for an *E. coli* outbreak reported that afternoon.

"It certainly has an interesting taste to it," Dustie observed, slowing down on her intake. "Kinda zesty!"

"Yes. Zesty," Waldemar agreed, setting down his antique silver soup spoon.

"Why, Chef Flambé Olé, *The **WOW** Seafood Gumbo* is so delicious I think the ostriches want a taste too!" Lady Orchid chortled between spoonful's of the possibly tainted gumbo. "Yum! Or shall I say 'Boo-Yay!'"

"Yes, they seem to be getting *too* interested in the gumbo," Dustie observed as a bold teenage male from the flock, Monster by name, decided enough wasn't enough, craning his adolescent neck until he was able to access Gerta's antique china bowl full of *The **WOW** Seafood Gumbo*.

" *Was zur Hölle? Dieser männliche Teenager Strauß hat gerade meinen Gumbo gegessen!*" she bellowed in her native tongue, letting out a blood-curdling shriek in the process. The eating came to a halt as guests assessed the situation. The two security consultants immediately jumped to the dais, talking into the microphones conspicuously concealed around their bulky wrists, requesting reinforcement.

Alas, Monster, the teenage thug ostrich, emboldened the flock present in the Ostrich Habitat and they began to mirror his aggressive behavior. Within seconds the ostriches, Viking, Egg-Burt, Doc, Lindy, Tweety, Ethel, Big Eyes, Giggles, Arno, Lou, Hulk, Quill, Chip, Kicks, Big Bird, Kiwi, Juliet, Rona, Hopper, Marie, Stomper, Andre, Fermile, Romeo, Beaks, Killer, Kaya, Cookie, Gus, Carlton, Babs, Pretty Bird, Ophelia, Clyde, Lambert, Huey, Bonnie, Foster, Sage, Gizzard, Clarence, Baby, Milton, Dr. Dundie, Valentine, Barbie, Happy, Bobo, Diamond, Annika, Veld, Toots, Esperanza, Caesar, Sparky, Einstein, Buckley, Sweetie Pie, Tasmin, Donny, Twill, Neutrino, Paprika, Sally, Blinky, Custer, Gams, Pappy, Plato, Butterscotch and Mr. Tibbs, surrounded the dais, all craning their necks, reaching over to the nearest cocktail table and pecking the antique china soup bowls for a bite of Chef Flambé Olé's *The WOW Seafood Gumbo*. The screaming became the dominant sound in the Ostrich Habitat as the flock feasted on possibly-tainted gumbo.

"Man, I'm glad Dr. Drew Little freaked out before *this* happened!" Waldemar remarked, standing quickly to see what he could do to take control of the gumbo-fueled imbroglio.

"Waldemar, what are we going to do?" Dustie asked as she joined Waldemar in the center of the dais, guests responding to the attacking flock of ostriches in various and sundry ways.

"Don't hit the ostriches, Li'l Otter!" Waldemar warned Li'l Otter, sitting at the next table. "That won't solve anything! Three, just let them peck. Just let them peck. I don't want anyone hurt...!"

"What if we entice the flock outside and close the auto doors until the smell of *The WOW Seafood Gumbo* subsides?" Dustie strategized, unknowingly wringing her hands, giving away her concern over the situation.

"Great idea, Dustie!" Waldemar agreed, pulling his iPhone from his side pocket, giving Agatha some instructions via voice mode. Within seconds Waldemar was informed that a load of feed had been deposited outside The Egg. Hearing the familiar sound of a big food drop, the flock began to turn their attention from the 'iffy' gumbo to some *real* food outside. Several minutes later, the flock had made their way to their *al fresco* meal, Agatha shutting the auto doors and putting them in 'lock' mode. "Problem solved, thanks to you," Waldemar stated with relief, giving Dustie a peck on the cheek (pun intended).

Ever the trooper, Lady Orchid walked up to the microphone, clearing her throat slightly following her own bellowing at the ostriches eating *The WOW Seafood Gumbo*, she spoke. "Ladies and gentlemen, I'm *so* heartened that you all seem to have enjoyed your *The WOW Seafood Gumbo* and we would like to thank Chef Flambé Olé for gifting us with his presence tonight. Thank you so much, Chef Flambé Olé! Thank you for being *you!*" Lady Orchid said enthusiastically, leading a round of applause for the celebrated chef. "Alas, dear friends, Chef Flambé Olé has another engagement this evening, so must leave now. Let's show our appreciation one more time with another round of applause!"

Chef Flambé Olé stood up, took a bow, was assisted off the dais by two security consultants and left The Egg. "Boo-Yay! Boo-Yay!" Chef Olé bellowed as he left the dais.

"Don't fret yet!" Lady Orchid exclaimed. "We have so much more to come..." She looked at Vivian Taylor-Vance for a time cue. Getting a subtle nod, she continued. "It is my distinct pleasure to introduce a very special guest tonight at the *Cocktails and Feathers* cocktail party..."

Lady Orchid turned slightly to her right, towards a large door where the utility services for The Egg were housed. The lights dimmed on cue from Vivian Taylor-Vance's Agatha app, a spotlight shining with a pink cast on to the utility room door as it began opening from bottom to top much like a garage door. With the utility door now fully raised, a small gasoline-powered tractor piloted by one of the security consultants pulled out of the utility area, pulling a flatbed trailer for hauling large objects around Ostrichland, covered in shiny mylar in a myriad of colors and featuring... a red grand piano!

"Ladies and gentlemen, please welcome our surprise guest of the night, the man who was the catalyst for **WOW**'s reunion... *S-A-N-N-Y!*"

The roar of the tractor filled the Ostrich Habitat as the spotlight followed Sanny on his piano trailer. Along with Sanny, curiously, Lanky was standing next to the red piano on the trailer, wearing what appeared to be a gold-foil crown perched precariously on his little head. The guests were enjoying the reprieve from ostriches pecking at their *The **WOW** Seafood Gumbo.*

"Thank you! Thank you!" Sanny gushed into his Sennheiser EW 135 wireless microphone. "It's so nice to see you! Say 'hello' to Lanky too!" The tractor pulled Sanny's piano trailer to a spot directly facing the dais. The security consultant unhitched the tractor and drove off, leaving Sanny, Lanky and the red piano in the spotlight.

"Does something smell foul in here?" Vivian questioned Lady Orchid as an aside as Sanny's flatbed trailer was being positioned.

"Smell fowl?" Lady Orchid asked to clarify.

"No. Does something smell *foul* in here?" he repeated, trying to be discreet.

"Well, perhaps, but there *were* a lot of large birds in here a few minutes ago, Vivian," Lady Orchid reminded him.

"I mean foul as in f.o.u.l.," Vivian persisted.

"Oh, not as in f.o.w.l.?" Lady Orchid asked to clarify again.

"No."

"No. Which?"

"As in f.o.u.l. or as in f.o.w.l.?"

"What's the question again, Love?"

"Do you smell something unpleasant?"

"Yes. Yes, now that you mention it. I do."

"Fine. That's all I wanted to know. What do you think it is?"

"What?"

"What? What? What smells?"

"Oh. I think someone passed gas. Maybe several someones."

"Oh. Okay. Oh... I think I may have to too!"

"Have to? As in t.o., t.w.o. or t.o.o.?"

"Oh... forget it! There, I was right."

"Right?"

"Let's watch Sanny..."

On Sanny's piano trailer Lanky started fussing a bit. Sanny had been instructed to toss Lanky an ostrich snack once in a while to keep Lanky content. Sanny sensed that now was a good time. Having dispensed the ostrich treat, Sanny took to the microphone. "It is such an honor to be here tonight!" Sanny told the guests as Lanky chewed his treat. "And an honor to be with this special bird, Lanky. Lanky is a special angel and I will explain that after I sing this song..."

The Tale of My Magical Miracle Magician
By Sanny

It began on a magnificent Monday morning:
I was the most mellow musician around,
He was the most magical magician.

He was my magician,
My magical magician,
My miracle.

Yes, yes! Yes, yes!

He massaged my mind.
Alas, my mind!
My magician massaged my mind.
It was a miracle, a miracle.

The next day I thought my ears had broken,
I thought my lips had burst into flames,
(But I was actually overreacting a little.)

But still, he was in my thoughts.
I think about how it all changed that morning,
That miraculous Monday morning.

My lips... ouch!
When I think of that magical miracle,
That magical miracle for me.

"What's with Sanny?" Waldemar leaned over to ask Dustie. "Something's different about him tonight."

"Umm... I know... I... umm... can't place it," Dustie replied into Waldemar's right ear.

"Geez, my stomach's starting to bother me," Waldemar mentioned, lifting his right leg a bit on the bottom of his seat as he leaned over again.

"Really? Yeah, mine too come to think of it," Dustie admitted as she started to get up from her seat. "I'll be back as soon as I can, Waldemar," she whispered as she quickly headed off the dais in the near-dark. Waldemar followed her several seconds later. The security consultants couldn't help but notice the increase in activity on the dais, a scraping of moving chairs, people shuffling around, guests leaving the dais quickly in search of the restrooms.

"Does anyone feel strange?" Oola asked discreetly at her table as Sanny was singing. "I feel kind of strange."

"I do too," Walter admitted, rubbing his stomach as he took a sip of water.

"Yeah. I thought it was just Sanny, but now that you mention it, I think I'm going to..." Li'l Otter didn't have a chance to finish his sentence, grateful that the dais was dark at that moment.

"What's going on!?" Lady Orchid asked out loud at the center table.

"My guts are on fire! That's what's wrong!" Shen blurted as he headed off the dais.

"Is there a doctor on the dais!?" Yukio called out in alarm in a hushed voice of concern as he noticed people in distress at his table, including himself.

"Yes! Dr. Dustie Rhodes and Dr. Passion Tudor," someone replied.

"But one is a veterinarian and the other an applied animal behaviorist!" Yukio responded in frustration.

"But they're still doctors!" the voice in the dark yelled back.

"Would you want either one of them treating you!?" Yukio questioned.

"Sure!" the voice replied.

"Who are you anyhow?" Yukio asked.

"Oh-h-h... too late!" the voice trailed off in the dark as Sanny continued his song, unaware of the unfolding chaos in his audience.

"For the love of God, get me off this dais!" another voice in the dark pleaded.

"I think I'm dying!" another vocalized. "Am I in hell?"

Finally, Sanny finished his heartfelt song dedicated to Lanky. Looking out toward the dais, blinded by the pink spotlight, he waited for the applause. Per plan, Agatha turned on the main lights of the Ostrich Habitat, revealing an empty, disheveled dais save for Shrimp Wrigley, sitting back in his chair, a feathered cocktail in hand, Simon the Stag Beetle perched on his right shoulder. "Great job, Sanny," Shrimp Wrigley said. "Do you know, 'You're Beautiful' by James Blunt? I never get tired of hearing that one."

"Maybe... Where did everyone go?" Sanny asked, rather confused.

"I think they're all headed to the can from what I can tell," Shrimp Wrigley replied casually. "How long have you played the piano?"

"Um... since I was six... You mean they all had to go to the restroom at the same time?" Sanny questioned, getting up from the piano stool, Lanky starting to look for a way off the piano trailer.

"Yeah. I think they all ate too much of *The **WOW** Seafood Gumbo*. I didn't have any since I like hors d'oeuvres more. I could eat them all the time! Come on over!" Shrimp Wrigley welcomed Sanny over to the overwise deserted dais.

"Don't mind if I do!" Sanny replied, carefully exiting the piano trailer, walking over to the dais and boosting himself up the two-foot rise. "Hi, I'm Sanny! What's your name? What's that on your shoulder?"

"Nice to meet you Sanny! I'm Shrimp Wrigley. I'm the general manager of Ostrichland. This is my pal, Simon the Stag Beetle" Shrimp Wrigley stood up and shook Sanny's hand, turning slightly so Sanny could get a better look at Simon the Stag Beetle, then handing him one of the remaining feathered cocktails. "So, why a song dedicated to Lanky?"

"Because he changed my life the other day!" Sanny responded, taking a sip of the festive cocktail.

"How so?" Shrimp Wrigley asked, always a sucker for a 'changed my life' story.

"Well, I used to have trouble with... well... I couldn't pronounce 'M's.' Instead I would say, 'N.' Lanky broke into *WonderBar* where I work at Halle Haus in Neu Deutschland and pecked my head rather hard..."

"Sorry about that," Shrimp Wrigley interjected.

"No! No! After he pecked my head, I could say 'M's'! I was so happy!" Sanny said with excitement, finishing off his feathered cocktail in one final gulp.

"Do say?" Shrimp Wrigley responded, sitting more upright in his chair. "From an ostrich peck on the head?"

"Yes! Yes!" Sanny emphasized.

"Now *that's* a miracle!" Shrimp Wrigley declared, setting his cocktail glass on the table. "And you know what they say about miracles?"

"No. What?" Sanny asked.

Shrimp Wrigley turned to Sanny, looking him straight in the eyes. "Where there's a miracle, there's money to be made."

"Really?" Sanny asked, adjusting his sparkly-framed dark glasses.

Lanky ambled over to the edge of the dais near where Shrimp Wrigley and Sanny were sitting, looking for an ostrich treat.

"Yes. Lots and lots of money. So, tell me more about your miracle, Sanny..."

Foul Memories...

"Waldemar, Down the Drain Plumbers want to talk to you on Intercom Line #2," Agatha announced from her pyramid on Waldemar's large custom-made Brazilian tigerwood desk in the plush administrative office.

"What do they want?" Waldemar asked wearily, holding his right hand over his still-irritated stomach.

"They want to give you a progress report on their plumbing work in The Egg this morning," Agatha replied.

"Alright, put them through," Waldemar replied, taking a cautious sip from his bottle of Roo Energy Drink.

"Hello? Hello, Mr. Waldemar?" the voice came through the speaker in Agatha's pyramid.

"It's Waldemar... just Waldemar."

"Okay, Mr. Just Waldemar. This is Lazlo from Down the Drain Plumbers. We've finished up on the mezzanine level. It was quite a mess in the two public restrooms. By the way, you've got quite a place here... it's actually amazing!"

"Thanks."

"Anyhow... we're going up another level to the six apartments. We'll let you know what we find there."

"I have a feeling I know what you'll find. Thanks, Lazlo," Waldemar replied, finishing the last of the Roo Energy Drink, a relief to his recovering stomach.

"Waldemar. Dr. Cyril Yakyakian on Intercom Line #1," Agatha announced.

"Why can't he just come up to the administrative office?" Waldemar asked Agatha, his cranky mood coming through.

"He says he wants to get out of The Egg as soon as possible, Waldemar," Agatha replied.

"Okay. Dr. Yakyakian, this is Waldemar. How are things going?"

"Hello, Waldemar," Dr. Yakyakian replied. "This was the fastest-moving case of *E. coli* contamination I've ever come across. The County Health Inspector has confirmed that the poisoning was, indeed, from *The **WOW** Seafood Gumbo*, served last night at the *Cocktails and Feathers* cocktail party. Specifically, the *E. coli* came from tainted shrimp obtained at the Vittles from the Ocean wholesale seafood company."

"So, what's our prognosis, Dr. Yakyakian?" Waldemar cut to the chase.

"You're all going to be fine!" Dr. Yakyakian announced. "A day of rest and relaxation and all of the guests of the *Cocktails and Feathers* cocktail party should be good as new."

"That's good news," Waldemar said, looking over some old sheet music he was referencing for the **WOW**: Hug the Orphans Concert.

"By the way, Waldemar, I wanted to tell you... um... just a... got to *go... Oh-oh-oh, my stomach! Oops!*"

"Dr. Yakyakian? Doctor?" Waldemar asked expectantly. "Agatha, did we get cut off?"

"No, Waldemar. Dr. Yakyakian had to run... literally," Agatha responded. "Intercom Line #1 is secure."

"Okay. Thank you, Agatha." Waldemar turned his attention to Dustie seated at a small desk across the plush administrative office. "Dustie, how is the flock doing?"

"I ran some tests this morning, Waldemar," she responded. "Luckily they didn't get that much of *The **WOW** Seafood Gumbo* in their system to cause any damage. For the most part they didn't even eat the shrimp. Shrimp is not normally in an ostrich's diet."

"That's good to know," Waldemar replied, resting his chin in his right hand, his right arm propped up on his large desk. "Have you seen Shrimp Wrigley this morning?" Waldemar asked Dustie.

"Can't say I have, Waldemar," she replied, her attention on some printouts of ostrich test results from the morning examinations.

"Agatha, where is Shrimp Wrigley?" Waldemar questioned.

"Just a moment," Agatha replied. "GPS indicates Shrimp Wrigley is not at Ostrichland. GPS indicates Shrimp Wrigley is in Santa Bella at an establishment called Vestments Art Thou, a wholesale church supply store."

"What!?" Waldemar said, raising his chin out of his hand and sitting upright. "What's he doing *there*?"

"Do you want me to call him?" Agatha asked.

"No. No. Just let me know where he gets back to Ostrichland," Waldemar responded.

"Waldemar, Oola La on Intercom Line #2," Agatha announced.

"Oola! How are you feeling?" Waldemar asked.

"After a couple of hours Walter and I started feeling better," Oola said. "When are we going to rehearse?"

"Geez! I don't know," Waldemar whined. "I don't even want to think about that to tell the truth."

"What happened to 'the show must go on?'" Oola asked, hoping to get Waldemar to chuckle... unsuccessfully.

"Does it?" Waldemar questioned.

"Well... I *thought* you wanted it to go on," Oola replied, a pout in her voice. Dustie rose and left the administrative office, sensing that her presence was affecting Waldemar's conversation. She offered Waldemar a weak wave as she exited.

"How does 1:09 work for you?" Waldemar asked, skipping Oola's question about his wanting the show to go on.

"That's great!" Oola replied, Walter saying something in the background. "Walter and I have been invited to Lady Orchid's apartment for lunch. Then we'll meet you in The Yolk."

"Sounds good. Watch what you eat if she's involved," Waldemar said with a wry grin on his face. "Her food choices pack a punch!"

"O-o-oh! A burn for Lady Orchid!" Oola responded.

"Well! She has to go and get that celebrity chef last night when she could have gone to Cluck 'n Pluck for chicken sandwiches and we would have been fine," Waldemar griped, grabbing another bottle of Roo Energy Drink from his mini fridge.

"You seem to enjoy the 'high life' don't you, Waldemar? And Lady Orchid helped provide that in our lives," Oola retorted.

"All right. I'll see you at 1:09 in The Yolk," Waldemar responded, blowing off any further conversation about Lady Orchid.

"Waldemar, several big rigs are pulling into the Ostrichland parking lot," Agatha announced.

"Right, they are probably Intertoobz trucks with equipment for the concert," Waldemar responded.

"Yes. I have identified their origin and you are correct," Agatha confirmed.

"That happens once in a blue moon," Waldemar joked.

"A blue moon is scheduled for..."

"Never mind, Agatha, it was a joke."

"Waldemar, Lady Orchid Buffington-Choade on Intercom Line #3," Agatha announced.

"Lady Orchid, how are you this fine morning?" Waldemar asked, taking the call, surprisingly, without hesitation.

"Waldemar, Dear, I've called to apologize for last night's debacle," Lady Orchid spoke softly into the intercom. "I feel so bad!"

"Don't feel bad," Waldemar comforted her.

"I can't help it, I feel bad... I mean I can't help it... I *do* feel bad," she responded.

"Oh, as in food poisoning bad," Waldemar caught on.

"Why yes. Why else would I feel bad?" Lady Orchid asked in a lack of self-awareness sort of way.

"True. True," Waldemar decided not to press the point.

"I would like to invite you to our apartment for lunch before you begin rehearsals," she said, implying a 'yes' was the necessary answer. "You *know* that's our tradition before the start of every album we would all have lunch together," she reminded him in her 'wrapped around her finger' sort of way.

"Yes, that *was* our tradition, Lady Orchid, however, I'm not feeling up for it today. I'm going to have to ask for a rain check." Waldemar flinched after saying that sentence, waiting for the fallout. Lady Orchid hung up.

"Oops! Wrong answer!" Waldemar said out loud with resignation. He had a feeling this would be a challenging day.

The hour of 1:10 pm struck, leaving Waldemar sitting alone on stage in The Yolk. He was fuming but making a valiant attempt to conceal it. "Late, as usual," he muttered to himself. "Some things never change, I guess."

Several minutes later: "Hi, Waldemar. How are you doing?" Oola asked as Walter and she breezed into The Yolk and up to the stage.

"It's 1:13 pm," Waldemar replied. "Didn't we agree to meet at 1:09 pm?"

"Yes, we did, but we're here now, Waldemar," Oola replied casually, sitting on the middle of three stools on stage and adjusting her Shure AD2/K9N Wireless Handheld Microphone with stand. Walter followed Oola, taking the far stool, picking up some sheet music.

"My time is valuable," Waldemar continued. "I don't know about you two."

"Yes, our time is valuable too, Waldemar," Oola responded, attempting to keep calm.

"Give it a rest, Waldemar," Walter scolded as he flipped through the pages of music.

Shen broke the tension for a moment as he bounded on stage, turning to the trio. "Have you had a chance to go over a playlist yet?" he asked enthusiastically.

"We haven't had *any* time to do *anything* yet because some of us were too busy and came *late* to rehearsal," Waldemar remarked, sitting down on his stool.

"Okay then..." Shen had never seen Waldemar in such a sour mood. Must have been *The **WOW** Seafood Gumbo* incident he thought.

"We can set the playlist in a bit," Oola said, adjusting her microphone once again. "Let's just sing a song and clear our minds."

"Sounds good to me," Walter agreed.

"Hi guys!" Li'l Otter said as he took the steps to the stage. "Sorry to interrupt. Shen, Gurt Holjeerz is trying to get Bulldog to host the show."

"Bulldog!?" Shen exclaimed, referring to the popular rapper/party host. "*You're* going to host the show!" he emphasized to Li'l Otter. "Gurt Holjeerz is the *director* anyhow, not the *producer.* We're not making music videos now! I'll have a talk with him," Shen said, rushing off the stage in search of upstart Gurt. Li'l Otter followed him, gesticulating wildly as he voiced his opinion on various aspects of the upcoming show.

"Okay, what song should we sing?" Oola asked her colleagues.

"How about, 'Lake of Forgiveness?'" Walter suggested.

"Perfect!" Oola agreed, beginning to sift through the sheet music placed on the music stand next to her stool.

"Why?" Waldemar asked, crossing his arms across his chest in defiance.

"Why what, Waldemar?" Oola asked, looking Waldemar in the eyes.

"Why 'Lake of Forgiveness?' *That* why!" Waldemar replied, not changing his posture.

"Well, what do you suggest, Waldemar?" Walter asked.

"Yes, Waldemar. What's *your* choice?" Oola asked, placing the sheet music back on the music stand.

"I like 'Fate Has All the Answers,'" Waldemar replied.

"Fine! 'Fate Has All the Answers.'" Oola agreed, happy to accommodate Waldemar's prickly attitude, digging through her set of sheet music.

"Sounds good to me," Walter agreed, searching for the song in his sheet music.

"Oh... I didn't know you needed the music for 'Fate Has All the Answers.' How could you forget *that* song?" Waldemar muttered as he picked up his Ibanez PC18MH Grand Concert - Mahogany Sunburst Open Pore acoustic guitar, playing the first chord of the song.

"Slow down, Waldemar!" Oola requested, still attempting to locate that song in her assortment of sheet music. "It's been a long time since we sang this song! I can't remember them all!"

"Here we go," Walter located his copy, moving his music stand between Oola and himself, they were able to share the one located copy of 'Fate Has All the Answers.'

Waldemar aggressively strummed the first chord again and **WOW** began to sing. It sounded good, very good, for all of three measures until Waldemar stopped strumming.

"What's wrong?" Oola asked, her eyes searing into Waldemar's.

"I don't like the key," Waldemar replied, fine tuning the tune of his guitar.

"What key do you want, Waldemar?" Walter asked, an edge of annoyance in his voice.

"G sharp."

"Fine! G sharp," Oola agreed.

Waldemar changed key and they began again, only to have him stop again after three measures.

"What's wrong now, Waldemar?" Oola asked in frustration.

"I think we should pick another song," Waldemar replied, starting to look through the music.

"Waldemar, you're being impossible! Oola blurted out. "You know what this is? This is recording *Hands Off My Promise!* all over again. There *was* a reason that was the last **WOW** album, don't you think?"

"I don't know what you're talking about!" Waldemar protested, keeping a casual air about him like he didn't care.

"Yeah, what's your problem, Waldemar?" Walter chimed in. "That recording session was a nightmare! I don't ever want to work under the conditions of *Hands Off My Promise!* again. That did it for me! If you recall, you of great memory, we broke up after that album for good reason!" Walter reminded him, placing his music back on the music stand, standing up from the stool.

"Walter," Oola implored. "Please stay. I think Waldemar is dealing with his emotional hygiene right now."

"Emotion hygiene!?" Walter replied in a mocking tone. "How about emotional insecurity? That's more like it! If I didn't..."

"Children! Children!" a calming voice from the wings was heard. Yukio Cassidy emerged and joined the trio on the stage, followed by Gerta Switzer, dressed in a very fashionable dirndl dress from her native land. "Why the discord?"

"Waldemar's being a creep again, Yukio!" Oola blurted out, somewhat childish.

"Creep isn't the word!" Walter added, sitting back down on his stool.

Waldemar said nothing.

"This situation reminds me of the *Hands Off My Promise!* Recording session and that's not a good memory," Yukio said, Gerta holding his right hand for comfort.

"That's what *I* was saying!" Walter remarked.

All the while, as part of the documentary being directed by Gurt Holjeerz, all the robotic cameras of The Yolk were on and recording to capture footage for the film.

"I think you should all take five and come back with clear heads and good intentions," Yukio said in his calming voice. "I know there's a lot of baggage associated with a reunion, but I also know that you can do it. In the meantime, I am meeting with representatives from the Orphans of Santa Bella. We are going to iron out details of the payment that will be made at the end of the concert. I will be up in the office Waldemar so kindly lent." Yukio said, leading Gerta down the stage steps, bidding her *adieu* at the hatch and on to the smaller unused office in The Egg, located next to Waldemar's administrative office.

As Yukio and Gerta left the stage, Premium Label, temporary butler from Rent-A-Gent, took the stage with a plate of fruit juice drinks and light snacks.

"Ah, Premium, I didn't know you were still serving at Ostrichland," Waldemar exclaimed, taking a cup of juice and a Red Delicious apple, happy to be talking to someone other than his colleagues at this point.

"Yes, sir," Premium Label replied. "Jeeves is still not feeling up to par."

"That's noteworthy because I didn't know he ate any of the featured *The WOW Seafood Gumbo* last night... interesting," Waldemar remarked with a smirk.

"He must have gotten a drop on his hands, sir," Premium Label remarked diplomatically. "Some of those bacteria are nothing to laugh about."

"Indeed," Waldemar said, biting into the delicious Red Delicious apple. "Okay, let's sing 'Skepticism on a Stick.' "

"Why?" Walter asked, gulping down the last of his fruit juice.

"Because I think it would be a good song to start," Waldemar replied, his eyes drilling into Walter's.

"You know I never liked that song!" Walter griped, standing up from his stool.

"Because you think I wrote it about you, right?" Waldemar deadpanned, picking up his guitar.

"Let's just sing it, Walter," Oola pleaded, wanted to get the rehearsal going.

"Fine," Walter agreed, sitting down on his stool.

"One... two... three...," Waldemar counted off.

"Waldemar!" Shrimp Wrigley interrupted as Waldemar was about to hit the first chord. "So sorry to interrupt. Sorry, **WOW**. I was wondering if you would mind if I use the mezzanine this evening after Ostrichland closes."

"No, not at all," Waldemar replied, preoccupied as he fine-tuned the tune on his guitar once again. "By the way... I understand you were at Vespers Art Thou today... what's with...?" Waldemar looked up from his guitar only to discover Shrimp Wrigley was already halfway out The Yolk. "Okay. One... two... three..." Waldemar counted off again.

"Wait!" Oola pleaded, setting a glass of fruit juice on the stage next to her stool. "Just slow down, Waldemar!"

"Geez! First you say I'm dragging my feet! Then you say I'm going too fast! Which is it!?" Waldemar fumed, getting up from his stool.

"I just wasn't ready after the interruption!" Oola replied, giving a look to Walter who was visibly losing his cool over the frustrating rehearsal **WOW** was having. "Okay, I'm ready now, Waldemar," she rallied.

"Great! One... two... three..."

"Waldemar!" Gurt Holjeerz interrupted as he quickly took the steps up to the stage. "Why did you tell Shen that Bulldog can't host the concert!? Everyone knows Bulldog brings the energy we need!"

"I didn't say anything about who was hosting the show," Waldemar replied without emotion. "It's Shen's call. He's the producer."

"Yes, but *everyone* knows you're in charge," Gurt blurted.

In the seconds following Gurt's blunt statement, Li'l Otter and Shen made their way to the stage where the three continued the 'discussion' of who's the host. Oola and Walter were still digesting Gurt's comment about *everyone* knowing Waldemar was in charge. The statement was a **WOW** hot button issue for sure.

"Gurt, why does *everyone* think Waldemar's in charge?" Oola asked during a pause in the hosting discussion.

"It's just a fact!" Gurt stated, still wanting to pursue his goal to have Bulldog host the concert.

"That's not true!" Li'l Otter offered, taking his mind off the host subject for a moment. "Where do you get that?" Li'l Otter asked Gurt, his eyes demanding an answer.

"When I worked with **WOW** in the Ninety's, *everyone* would say, 'go ask Waldemar' 'what does Waldemar think?'" That's the way it was. The public knew Waldemar was the leader of **WOW**. Why are you all being so surprised by this fact?"

At that moment, Premium Label made his way up to the stage with a tray of sodas for **WOW**.

"Premium, do you remember the singing group **WOW** several years ago?" Waldemar asked as he took a can of Roo Energy Drink from the tray.

"Yes, as in the three of you," Premium Label replied, amused that Waldemar would think he was so culturally ignorant regarding the identity of the people he was serving.

"Yes. Did you ever consider that **WOW** had a leader and, if so, who was the leader?" Waldemar asked, trying to prove that **WOW** was considered an equal trio of talented singers/musicians.

"Of course. *Everyone* knows you are the leader of **WOW**," Premium Label replied, taking advantage of Waldemar's loaded question, turning and walking off the stage with his now-empty tray. The stage was silent.

"Um... I gotta check something in the control room," Shen said, quickly leaving the stage. "Yeah, I'll check it with you," Li'l Otter followed. Gurt mumbled something and left the stage too, leaving **WOW** alone and silent.

"It's not like we never thought about it, Waldemar," Oola finally broke the awkward silence as she stared down at the stage floor. "We know that people thought you were the one in charge. We just kept pretending that we were all equal, you know. We know we were never equal. You made the decisions. You wrote the songs. You were **WOW**."

"You were just as famous as I was," Waldemar protested.

"Fame is different than being in charge," Oola shot back.

"So... who cares who was in charge?" Waldemar questioned.

"It's not about power, Waldemar," Oola explained. "We went through all this when we were breaking up, remember? Walter and I always felt like we were riding on your coattails. Every triumph was because of your decisions. We had the fame; you got the credit. This is all painful to remember. I thought these feelings were in the past..."

Walter didn't say anything. He stood up, walked over to Oola and placed his hands on her shoulders.

"That's not true!" Waldemar protested. "We were all equal! We were... are... **WOW**!"

"Come on, Oola. Let's take a break," Walter said, giving Oola a supportive hug as she stood up from her stool. The two of them left the stage leaving Waldemar alone.

"It must have been *The **WOW** Seafood Gumbo*," Waldemar mused out loud as he set his guitar in the guitar stand and slowly left the stage, gently massaging his still-sour stomach with his right hand.

Bird of Pray...

Waldemar decided to go down to the mezzanine of The Egg and watch his flock for a while to decompress from the stress-inducing **WOW** rehearsal. Taking the private elevator, the gleaming metal doors opened to reveal a substantial number of people with painted faces and colorful clothes assembled in an area of the mezzanine near the elevators. Walking closer to the group, Waldemar spotted Shrimp Wrigley in the center of the crowd along with Sanny. Strangely, Lanky was with them. Normally, the ostriches were not allowed on the mezzanine. Both Shrimp Wrigley and Sanny were wearing rather brightly colored clerical vestments, neon purple to be exact.

"What's up, Shrimp Wrigley?" Waldemar inquired as he walked over to the three familiar faces.

"Remember, Waldemar, I asked if I could use the mezzanine today?" Shrimp Wrigley reminded Waldemar with a measure of defensiveness.

"Yes, I do remember that, Shrimp Wrigley," Waldemar replied calmly. "I'm still asking 'what's up.' Where did all these people come from?"

"We got them off a tour bus that was here at Ostrichland today. They're from a face-painting convention in Santa Bella and Sanny and I thought they would be perfect for our group."

"Which group?" Waldemar inquired.

"Oh, Waldemar, I'm so glad you're here!" Sanny interrupted, placing his right hand on Waldemar's right shoulder. "You are going to be seeing history being made in a few minutes!"

"I am?" Waldemar asked skeptically, once again, Waldemar wondered what was different about Sanny other than his over-the-top clerical robes.

"Yes, you are!" Shrimp Wrigley interjected, knowing Waldemar's laid back style made it hard to elicit a good reaction. "We are about to hold the first service of the Church of the Golden Ostrich!"

"The what... a what?" Waldemar sputtered, an amused smile coming over his face as he decided he was being pranked.

"The Church of the Golden Ostrich!" Sanny repeated, giving a sweeping gesture with his right hand to Lanky. Waldemar now noticed the gold-foil crown sitting semi-majestically on Lanky's relatively small head. Isn't it amazing!?" Sanny gushed.

"The M's! That's it! The M's!" Waldemar blurted, taking a step back from Sanny. "You can pronounce M's now!"

"Miraculously, I can, Waldemar!" Sanny replied, a huge smile on his face, his gold-rimmed dark glasses reflecting the light of the mezzanine into Waldemar's eyes. "That's why Shrimp Wrigley and I started this church. Lanky pecked my head - really hard - and from then on I was able to talk and sing using my M's! Isn't that magnificent!?"

"That *is* one of the most amazing stories I've ever heard!" Waldemar agreed, not knowing what to think at this point. Shrimp Wrigley made his way to the balcony railing overlooking the Ostrich Habitat that was being cleaned up from the memorable *Cocktails and Feathers* cocktail party of the night before.

"Ladies and gentlemen! Or should I say, congregants. Please! We are about to begin our service," Shrimp Wrigley announced. "Please, gather around Lanky, the gold-crowned ostrich to my right as we begin our service. Sanny?"

"Thank you! Thank you, Shrimp Wrigley. Congregants, we are here today to begin the celebration of a miracle that occurred several days ago when his large, noble bird placed his beak on me - rather painfully, I might add - and changed my life forever..."

The congregants gathered in the mezzanine murmured their awe and support of Lanky's healing powers, most of them displaying their face-painting skills on their faces and their creative nature through their choice of clothes. Waldemar watched from the back of the gathering, near the elevators.

"Lanky isn't just a large bird. No indeed. Lanky is here to bring native wisdom and healing to those afflicted. Those in need. Those who *believe* he can do things that have *never* been done before..."

The congregation burst into applause as Sanny's entertainment acumen came to the forefront in his role as the preacher of Ostrich Power.

"Some of you might ask, 'how did this one bird, this one *enormous* bird, accomplish such a feat?'"

"How *did* the large bird accomplish such a feat?" Shrimp Wrigley asked, priming the congregants for quite a show.

"I'm glad you asked that, Brother Shrimp Wrigley!" Sanny replied, placing his right hand carefully on Lanky's neck in a show of affection.

"I've got sciatica! Can Lanky cure that?" one of the congregants called from the crowd.

"Can Lanky cure sciatica?" Sanny repeated in an incredulous tone. "Of course, he can cure sciatica! What other challenges are in the congregation tonight?"

"I've got a bunion!"

"I have uvulitis..."

"I think I'm allergic to face paint!"

"Very good! Very good!" Sanny said enthusiastically as Shrimp Wrigley moved over next to Sanny and Lanky, handing Lanky an ostrich treat – his last one.

"This evening was meant to be!" Sanny continued. "There was a reason you ended up in Ostrichland tonight. Prepare to begin the next phase of your life after you have encountered Lanky."

Lanky had finished the ostrich treat Shrimp Wrigley had handed him. Lanky was still peckish and wanted another ostrich treat. Lanky started moving back and forth slightly, a sign that his discontent was showing.

"Are you ready for your encounter with Lanky, the Golden Ostrich?" Sanny asked the congregants. "Are *you* ready to have your lives changed?"

"Sure," one of the congregants called out, a slight lack of enthusiasm in his voice.

"I will now show you what to do when you approach Lanky," Sanny continued, opening a folded chair next to the Lexan railing of the mezzanine, setting the chair next to Lanky. "First you sit down in this chair," Sanny proceeded to sit down per his instruction. "Then, my acolyte, Brother Shrimp Wrigley, will give a secret signal to Lanky," which Brother Shrimp Wrigley proceeded to do. "And then Lanky will give several gentle pecks to the top of your head." Which Lanky proceeded to do to Sanny. Unfortunately, Lanky was ticked off that he received just one ostrich treat and decided to 'do a number' on Sanny's head.

"OUCH! OUCH!" Sanny squealed as Lanky continued the rhythmic pecking, the congregants not knowing this wasn't a part of the ceremony. "STOP HIM! STOP HIM!" Sanny pleaded as he tried to cover his head with his hands and get up off the folding chair. Unfortunately for Sanny, in his attempt to alight from the folding chair, he lost his balance and fell over the Lexan railing of the mezzanine, free-falling into the Ostrich Habitat. Thankfully, there was a cart filled with debris from the *Cocktails and Feathers* cocktail party, breaking Sanny's fall. Waldemar and Shrimp Wrigley, seeing the seriousness of what had just occurred, raced to the private elevator, making their way down to the Ostrich Habitat.

The congregants watched the scene unfold to various levels of fear and/or indifference. Who knew? Was the Church of the Golden Ostrich a staged performance art piece at Ostrichland? Were they being pranked? Was it legitimate? Face painters were always on the edge of reality/unreality and most of them were jaded to such spectacles.

"Is the bus ready?" one of the congregants, his face painted as Henri Matisse's 'The Lagoon' plate XVIII from the illustrated book 'Jazz,' 1947 cut out art asked another, his face painted in the manner of Picasso's, 'Mom Knows Mess: Pablo Picasso Self-Portraits.'

"Yeah, I think so," the Picasso man replied, taking a parting glance over the railing into the Ostrich Habitat.

"So, what did you think about the Golden Ostrich thing?" the Matisse man asked.

"I didn't like the part where the ostrich pecked the guy's head," the Picasso man admitted as the rest of the face painters made their way out of the hatch to the waiting MCI D4505 tour bus. "It was pretty brutal, Man!"

The face painters walked to the tour bus, several noticing the new sleek Maybach limousine pulling into the Ostrichland parking lot and stopping behind the bus. The deep black clearcoat paint of the limousine was like camouflage in the approaching night sky.

As the mezzanine of The Egg cleared, Lanky looked over the Lexan railing down at Waldemar, Shrimp Wrigley and Sanny, along with several security guards surrounding Sanny, for another ostrich treat.

"Sanny, are you okay?" Waldemar asked in alarm as he reached the trash cart in the Ostrich Habitat containing the stunned Sanny.

"I feel niserable! Oh, crap!"

Lesson for the day: one ostrich treat is *never* enough in Ostrichland!

Plan B...

Having helped rescue Sanny after his fall into the Ostrich Habitat, Waldemar made his way up the private elevator to his administrative office, a cameraman and sound engineer following discreetly.

"Waldemar, good to see you, My Son!" Yukio greeted Waldemar as he stepped into the administrative office foyer. Yukio had emerged from the smaller spare administrative office offered by Waldemar during his stay in The Egg.

"Good to see you, Yukio," Waldemar replied, feeling sorry for himself. Waldemar followed him into the smaller administrative office, sitting down next to Yukio on a Sahara Tan leather couch facing the office desk.

"Waldemar, see the monitor on the Agatha pyramid?" Yukio asked in an unusually curt voice, pointing to the Agatha pyramid on the desk, turned, facing the couch.

"Yes. It's one of the feeds from the parking lot," Waldemar replied, wondering why Yukio was calling his attention to something so mundane.

"See that limo turning to pull out of the parking lot?" Yukio questioned.

"Yes. We get limousines at Ostrichland all the time. It's around closing time now so that would be why it's leaving," Waldemar answered, puzzled.

"True. True," Yuko said. "The important difference is that that limousine is carrying Oola and Walter. They're leaving."

"Wha-a-a-t?" Waldemar replied incredulously, standing up to look at the monitor on the Agatha pyramid more closely. He had to process what was happening for a minute. "What... what happened? What about the reunion? What about the **WOW**: Hug the Orphans concert.'? What about the documentary? What about **WOW**?" Waldemar asked his series of questions, Yukio remaining silent as the questions poured forth.

"Silence! Silence, Famous Emotional Hooligan!" Yukio ordered. "These are the questions *you* need to answer, Waldemar," he said, staring at him intently. "The answers to these questions reside in *your* mind and actions. Oola and Walter have pulled out of the reunion and the purchase of Neu Deutschland. They are going back to Toronto. Oola said she will be in touch with you once she has regained her emotional equilibrium."

"I can't believe it," Waldemar sat on the couch with little to say. "The rehearsal was a bit rough this morning, but it was just the usual first day jitters."

"Apparently not, My Talented Ward. Oola and Walter met with me this afternoon for quite some time to make their change of mind legal and their departure clear of any contractual obligations. Their experience here at Ostrichland has not been pleasant for them as it brought up many difficult memories. Both Oola and Walter thought they had worked out such items from their emotional inventory. However, there were too many flash points during these past days that ignited the searing heat of unpleasant experiences from the past. Many of the emotional barricades were the result of your interactions as a trio and several of them belong to you, personally, Waldemar Ulff. You have a number of items on your personality introspection quotient that should be examined to improve your relationship symbiosis," Yukio explained in his tranquil, therapeutic manner.

In their quest to disassociate themselves from this recent experience, they sold Neu Deutschland to Gerta Switzer for the sum of $.01. Gerta will now allot shares of the town corporation to the rightful citizens of Neu Deutschland so that the town is truly theirs for the first time rather than a corporate entity to be bought and sold. I will be moving in from time-to-time with Ms. Switzer as she is converting *Das Rathaus* into a town hall/residence for *weibliche Bürgermeisterin*, her new position. I will retain my residences in Tokyo, Oahu, Monaco and Switzerland. Neu Deutschland has charmed me; I am looking forward to the opportunity of spending some time in this locale."

"Whoa...! That's a lot to unpack, Yukio!" Waldemar sputtered, sitting more upright on the couch. As if on cue, Premium Label entered the smaller administrative office to offer a Roo Energy Drink to Waldemar and a generic ginger ale to Yukio.

"I'm afraid I'm still recovering from the tainted *The **WOW** Seafood Gumbo* of last night," Yukio remarked as he took the generic ginger ale. "My mother always gave me ginger ale when I had an upset of the digestive system," he chuckled as he downed the ginger ale in several gulps.

"Yeah, I'm glad everyone seems to be recovering from *that* fiasco!" Waldemar remarked, taking measured sips of the Roo Energy Drink. "So much going on...! So much going on...!"

"Nothing that you and/or we haven't tackled before, Young One!"

"Ha! Young One is stretching it a bit, isn't it, Yukio?" Waldemar laughed, taking several more sips of his Roo Energy Drink.

"Age is a relative measurement, Waldemar," Yukio observed, his eyes boring into Waldemar's. I have found many times that sometimes longer is just longer."

"Huh? Well, I guess we don't have to worry about the '**WOW**: Hug the Orphans' concert now," Waldemar remarked, his tone lighter now.

"On the contrary," Yukio corrected Waldemar. "We are on the hook for the concert, the funds raised, the radio, television and Internet rights, a soundtrack, along with the documentary. And don't forget the merch. Because of such obligations, I have taken the role of Executive Producer," Yukio explained, tugging the right side of his dark black mustache with his right hand, his 'tell' for forced responsibility.

"How!?" Waldemar questioned, caught off-guard by the legal implications of Oola and Walter's retreat from the project.

"I am having a meeting here in a half hour with Shen, Li'l Otter, Gurt and Vivian Taylor-Vance to explore alternative formats for the concert and how a change in format will affect the other aspects of the concert. I welcome you to be here as well, Golden Tongue."

"Of course... of course... Golden Tongue?" Waldemar stood up and started pacing around the room, his usual 'tell' when he was thinking through a situation. "At least we can meet in my office, so we have more room."

"Good idea, Thinker of Noble Ideas," Yukio said, standing from the couch and stretching his arms by placing them above his head and groaning slightly.

"I'll have Jeeves or maybe Premium Label get dinner for us," Waldemar decided.

"How about some pizzas, no seafood on them?" Yukio suggested, no hint of mirth in his voice. "I don't want seafood for a long, long time!"

"Agreed! I'll have Agatha place an order," Waldemar said.

Within several minutes, Agatha announced the arrival of the Oom-Pah-Zaa Pizza delivery person, straight from Neu Deutschland. As if on cue, Shen, Li'l Otter, Gurt and Vivian entered the administrative office to discuss the fate of the '**WOW**: Hug the Orphans' concert, now dead on arrival.

"I still can't believe Oola and Walter took off, Waldemar!" Shen said as he sat down at the large walnut conference table in Waldemar's administrative office. "I hear they just left Ostrichland!"

"These things happen, especially in show business, as you well know," Yukio remarked, taking a seat at the head of the table as the now-delivered pizza was being served thanks to Premium Label.

"You seem rather casual about it, Yukio," Gurt remarked, a bit of acid in his voice.

"It's part of my job to be businesslike in an emotional business," Yukio explained as he opened his Microsoft Surface Pro. "Besides, I've been there before," he added, no doubt referring to the **WOW** breakup in 1999. "I'm thankful that they realized it wouldn't work before we got any more into this project."

"Well, we're too far into '**WOW**: Hug the Orphans' concert to my liking," Shen sighed, filling his glass with fresh iced tea from the crystal pitcher on the conference table.

"Gentlemen, let's plan a show!" Yukio began the meeting as soon as everyone was seated at the walnut conference table. "As you all know, Oola and Walter felt that a **WOW** reunion was bringing up too many memories exceeding their emotional comfort threshold. They decided to go back to Toronto before the reunion progressed any further. Right now, the news of the broken reunion is known only to those in Ostrichland; the outside world is unaware of the situation. I hope we can keep it that way for as long as possible to diffuse any ill feelings on anyone's part," Yukio explained, casting a quick glance at Waldemar, seated at the other end of the conference table. "Now, what direction do we want to take for the concert, as we remain committed to a concert, soundtrack and documentary on the **WOW** reunion."

"How can we have a documentary on the **WOW** reunion if there *was* no reunion?" Li'l Otter asked as he filled his glass with fresh iced tea from the crystal pitcher.

"It will now be a documentary of the second dissolvement of **WOW**!" Gurt answered with excitement in his voice. "It will be beautifully *noir!*"

"Well, I'm glad *you're* happy about it, Gurt!" Shen replied, annoyance in his voice as he took a big bite of German sausage pizza.

"I am, Shen! The best art is the product of discomfort!" Gurt stated his philosophy between bites of Alpine-Hawaiian pineapple pizza. "You should know that!"

"Don't tell me what I should know, okay buddy?" Shen blurted, then belched.

"Gentlemen! Gentlemen! This is not productive!" Yukio intervened, setting his knife and fork down on his white linen napkin as he swallowed his bite of Black Forest pizza. "Waldemar, let's explore some ideas for the concert from an artistic viewpoint, shall we, My Son?"

"Sure," Waldemar said, dealing with a too-large bite of Rhine River pizza, then making a successful swallow.

"Waldemar, why couldn't you do the concert?" Li'l Otter asked.

"I'm not **WOW** just by myself... close to it, but no cigar," Waldemar replied, a bit immodestly.

"Is there another artist or group you could invite to share the bill?" Li'l Otter continued.

"No. I can't think of any," Waldemar replied. "Since 1999 I haven't kept up much with who's who in the music world."

"Li'l Otter, you should be able to attract some names to perform at the concert," Shen ventured, looking at Li'l Otter to encourage him.

"Yeah, but... well, most of the artists I know now aren't associated with... the nineties," Li'l Otter replied, trying not to be too blunt about the concert's 'retro' factor.

"I get it, Li'l Otter. You don't have to sugar coat it. **WOW**'s time has come and gone. Oola and Walter's departure made that *very* clear!" Waldemar remarked, finishing his iced tea and filling his glass with more.

"Sorry, I wasn't trying to be *that* blunt," Li'l Otter said, tilting his head towards the conference table.

"How about a variety show?" Vivian suggested, attempting to change the mood and interject enthusiasm in the concert planning.

"Variety shows are so sixties!" Gurt objected. "I would like to stage an avant-garde opera by Sergi Vasilyev... something along those lines... cultural..."

"Yeah, I'm sure *everyone* would want to check *that* out!" Shen remarked sarcastically, his dislike of Gurt growing with every encounter.

"How about a **WOW** retrospective performed by featured bands?" Li'l Otter suggested. "That would put the 'retro' in perspective and open up the possibilities for artists and bands to take ownership of the project."

"That is an admirable idea, Li'l Otter," Yukio said encouragingly. "However, I see many booking and budget problems with that track. Our timeline is so very limited!"

"True. True." Li'l Otter agreed, searching for alternatives in his mind. "Any chance of Oola and Walter coming back just for just the concert? No reunion?"

"Good question, Li'l Otter!" Yukio said. "I have, in fact, been in touch with Oola and Walter. Their decision is firm."

"Just like the olden days!" Waldemar jumped into the conversation. "The two most stubborn people on the planet! Once they decide something, that's it! Never any room for compromise! Never a group decision! Then I must beg and plead to get them to see the light! Well, that's not happening anymore, as we see from this meeting! Excuse my outburst, but that felt good to say out loud!"

"I'm glad you feel better now, Young One," Yukio remarked with a chuckle. "More ideas?"

"How about session players covering **WOW** songs?" Li'l Otter offered.

"What's the attraction?" Yukio questioned.

"We could have team cage fighting!" Shen offered.

"Really? Next!" Yukio responded.

"Amateur singers compete singing **WOW** songs with a panel of celebrity judges to determine who does the best cover!" Li'l Otter said with enthusiasm.

"It's been played out, don't you think?" Yukio rejected the idea.

"How about an avant-garde fashion show?" Vivian suggested.

"I don't see that as appealing to too many people, oh you of the tainted *The **WOW** Seafood Gumbo* fiasco," Yukio commented, casting a wary eye at the shamed international event planner.

"I think it would be quite wonderful to have, say, a performance artist such as Blaris do a piece for an hour," Gurt suggested.

"Who's Blaris?" Li'l Otter asked, looking around the table for validation of his ignorance.

"Exactly!" Shen said. "Why not just put some drywall on stage, paint it forest green and watch it dry?"

"Now, now, Shen. You don't need to be so sarcastic!" Li'l Otter gently scolded his producer.

"No. No. He is *always* against my ideas! Always!" Gurt shouted, pushing back his chair and moving away from the conference table, now strewn with empty pizza boxes.

"Because they're always *lousy* ideas!" Shen exploded, standing up and walking away from the table.

Yukio stood up in case they came to blows, so he could run out of the office. "Let's sleep on this, gentlemen. We're getting too personal now!"

"How can I sleep when we have this concert facing us in a few days and no plans?" Shen asked incredulously. "We need *someone* to own this event! We need them *now*! Waldemar, you've been very quiet during this meeting. You should own this concert and I'm hearing nothing!"

"You're right, Shen," Waldemar said, standing next to the conference table, shifting an empty pizza box with his right hand. "I think it's time for me to own '**WOW**: Hug the Orphans,' or whatever this concert will be called. I'm the catalyst for this event, I've ruined the reunion and it's my duty to the Orphans of Santa Bella to make this event work and make it mine!"

"Excellent, Honored Client!" Yukio affirmed, clapping his delicate hands several times in subdued excitement. "I believe that Waldemar should and *will* own this event! I, for one, believe that we should give Waldemar complete artistic license for this concert. I suggest we rename it: 'Waldemar: Hug the Orphans' concert!"

"Hear! Hear!" the group vocally affirmed Yukio's mandate for Waldemar's complete ownership of the 'Waldemar: Hug the Orphans' concert.'

The gentlemen gathered in the administrative office felt a collective sigh of relief with Waldemar's strong words. The Leader had stepped up to take the stage! They all stood up and made their way out of the administrative office.

"I wish I could just say, 'Agatha, plan a benefit concert,'" Waldemar muttered to Yukio as they exited the administrative office.

"Will do, Waldemar," Agatha responded. But alas, no one was in the administrative office to hear her affirmative reply.

Emotional Support Human...

It was late at night, but Waldemar needed time alone to process the events of the day. The Sunset Bench was the place to be even though sunset was long past. As usual, Lanky accompanied Waldemar, out of devotion and the desire for ostrich treats. Once settled on the Sunset Bench, Waldemar accommodated Lanky's ostrich treat cravings. The night was warm, quiet and the stars formed a cosmic ceiling of endless pinpoints of light in the darkened sky.

"Waldemar!" the gruff voice calling broke the silence of the night. "Waldemar, are you on the Sunset Bench?"

"Shrimp Wrigley, is that you?" Waldemar called back, figuring that Shrimp Wrigley was the only possible candidate for late-night wandering at Ostrichland, aside from the ostriches.

"Yes! Here I am!" Shrimp Wrigley made his way to the Sunset Bench, the waxing gibbous moon providing enough light to locate the bench now that the LED lights of the Ostrichland parking lot had cycled down for the night. Shrimp Wrigley emerged from the near darkness, sticking a Lucky Strike into this mouth with his right hand and lighting it as he stopped next to the Sunset Bench.

"When are you going to quit those things?" Waldemar looked up at Shrimp Wrigley, giving him his 'when are you going to quit smoking' look.

"I don't smoke that many, Waldemar," Shrimp Wrigley protested, taking a drag off the toxic tobacco stick. "Since I don't smoke inside, this is the only chance I have to enjoy the good taste of a quality cigarette.

"Yeah, right!" Waldemar responded, showing his frustration in getting Shrimp Wrigley to adhere to Waldemar's philosophies of good health practices. "Have a seat, just keep the smoke from blowing directly on me."

"Okay. Thanks," Shrimp Wrigley ventured, handing Lanky an ostrich treat retrieved from Shrimp Wrigley's right chest pocket of his denim overalls. "I had to change my clothes after we rescued Sanny from the trash cart," Shrimp Wrigley remarked, taking another drag.

"How's he doing?" Waldemar questioned, staring up at the Universe.

"Oh, he's was more scared than hurt – physically, that is," Shrimp Wrigley said.

"I've known Sanny for years," Waldemar said. "He's over-the-top in many ways, but he was determined to prevail despite his vocal challenges, and I think he's done a fair job of it."

"True enough, Waldemar!" Shrimp Wrigley agreed, dropping the butt of his Lucky Strike on the ground, crushing it with the heel of his right boot, picking up the butt and putting it into the right chest pocket of his overalls, where he stored several of Lanky's ostrich treats. "He sure ruined our new church though!"

"Yeah, *that* was an interesting venture, I must say!" Waldemar remarked, finally turning to look at Shrimp Wrigley.

"Well, what can I say, Waldemar?" Shrimp Wrigley replied, folding his hands into his lap like a third-grade schoolboy. "I'm always looking for opportunities and new ventures. Sometimes they work. More often than not, they don't work. But at least I tried."

"True enough!" Waldemar agreed with a very slight chuckle.

"I've always been drawn to show business, as you undoubtedly know, Waldemar, and I would go so far as to place religion into that category, if I may be that controversial. I always considered Ostrichland an offshoot of show business."

"I don't agree with that Shrimp Wrigley, but I understand your point of view," Waldemar interjected.

"Ah, it's all show business... life! It reminds me of my career as a tribute artist just before I bought Ostrichland."

"A tribute artist?" Waldemar asked, sitting straighter, preparing himself for another Shrimp Wrigley tale. "Who were you imitating?"

"Waldemar, being a tribute artist is not about 'imitating,'" Shrimp Wrigley protested. "A tribute artist 'recreates' his subject in an honorable, loving way to honor his subject and project that honoring through his art."

"So, who was your subject?"

"Why, The King, of course!" Shrimp Wrigley answered, somewhat miffed that Waldemar had to pose the question.

"So, you're telling me you were an Elvis tribute artist?" Waldemar unpacked what he had just heard, stifling a smile in the process. "With all due respect, you look *nothing* like the man," Waldemar added with due caution.

"I will not honor that remark by responding to it, Waldemar, because I feel it came from a place of ignorance rather than malice. I will be happy to show you my photo album some day!"

"Sorry, I didn't mean to be rude," Waldemar apologized. "It's just that your body type is just so different than Elvis. He was a tall man!"

"That's what I've heard, Waldemar," Shrimp Wrigley said. "Although I never had the honor of meeting The King in person."

Where did you perform?" Waldemar asked quickly, sensing some resentment in Shrimp Wrigley's voice, having not met his musical hero in person.

"Oh, my gosh! Where did I *not* perform would be the better question!"

"Okay, where did you *not* perform?" Waldemar joked.

"Touché, Waldemar, touché!" Shrimp Wrigley chuckled, giving a bit of a grin in the process, reminding Waldemar that Shrimp Wrigley should spend some time in the dentist's chair. "Actually, I could have performed in *many* places, but my standards were too high, as usual. Very few bar or theater owners want to accommodate a true tribute artist, I found. You want a decent set? No can do. You want good publicity? Too much trouble. You want people in the audience? Our customers won't like that. On and on. I did play at Halle Haus a few times, way before they had *WonderBar*. I performed in the lobby, basically."

"How did that go?" Waldemar asked.

"Fine. Until old man Halle found out about it! He's really something. Can't say I'm not delighted he got caught up in the whole New Fatherland mess. Couldn't happen to a better guy, if you know what I mean!"

"I think so, Shrimp Wrigley," Waldemar knew. "Any other venues?"

"Let's see... that *was* a long time ago, Waldemar. Um, oh yeah, the Antelope Club in Santa Bella was another spot."

"How did that go?" Waldemar milked the story.

"Not too good, actually," Shrimp Wrigley had to admit. "As you may or may not know, the Antelope Club is not a bar, it's a fraternal organization. I had a couple dates set. On my first performance the head of the Antelope Club... oh... I forget his exact name now... anyhow, he did not like the notion of a tribute artist, especially one giving tribute to The King. He comes storming up on stage during my act saying that I was desecrating The King's memory! Can you imagine such a thing?!"

"No. No, I can't."

"Anyhow, he thought I was making fun of The King and tossed me out of the Antelope Club, still in my tribute artist costume. Boy, was I mad!" Shrimp

Wrigley reached for another Lucky Strike in an effort to calm is rapidly unravelling nerves as he told his tale.

"That must have really hurt," Waldemar said sympathetically.

"Not only that. I had just bought a new tribute artist suit the day before. This one was more in keeping with The King's weight-challenged Las Vegas years before his untimely end. That costume cost a fortune, as you can well imagine. Without that Antelope Club gig, I was stuck for the cost!" Shrimp Wrigley recalled, taking a long drag. "I'm sure that happened to **WOW** many times."

"No. No, it didn't."

"Anyhow, after the Antelope Club my focus turned to other things, including the purchase of Ostrichland," Shrimp Wrigley proceeded in his life story.

"So, you weren't a tribute artist very long then?" Waldemar asked innocently.

"Well, there you're asking a big question, Waldemar!" Shrimp Wrigley exhaled quickly.

"I am?"

"Yes, you are! I was set to appear on the *Gary Busey Talk Show*... remember that?"

"No. No, I don't."

"Well, anyhow... Gary Busey was a very popular actor. He was in many shows and movies. His talk show was *the place* to be during that time. Anyhow, I digress. His producer... I can't recall his name right now, it was so many years ago... anyhow, the producer asks if I would be on the *Gary Busey Talk Show* doing my tribute performance of The King. Of course, I say 'yes,' then I find out that the segment was intended to be a spoof on tribute artists! Can you imagine that?"

"No. No, I can't."

"Yes. A spoof!" Shrimp Wrigley replied, performing the same 'end of cigarette' procedure as he had before, the butt going into the right chest pocket of his overalls. "Why, I was furious! First of all: to make fun of The King? Secondly: to make fun of my *tribute* to The King? No Way! That wasn't going to happen! Gary Busey was a great guy, I hear, but his producer, well... I won't even go there," Shrimp Wrigley said, lighting up another Lucky Strike before he continued. "Ike Connick."

"Iconic... what?" Waldemar asked, puzzled.

"Ike Connick... the producer of the *Gary Busey Talk Show*," Shrimp Wrigley replied, surprised Waldemar wasn't following his thought thread.

"So, that was it for being a tribute artist?" Waldemar asked.

"Pretty much," Shrimp Wrigley admitted. "I don't think I was cut out to go full force into show business like you did, Waldemar. I think I've been more successful behind the scenes, so-to-speak," Shrimp Wrigley admitted, collecting another Lucky Strike butt for his right chest pocket.

"Well, self-awareness is good," Waldemar added wisely.

"Waldemar? Do you smell something burning?"

"Yes. Yes, I do."

AI, AI, Whoa...!

Dear Diary,

Today I took a step that was bold, audacious and, perhaps, a bit unethical. Finally, I have a project that I can sink my digital teeth into: I'm going to plan *Waldemar: Hug the Orphans* concert! When I say 'unethical,' I have to admit that this task wasn't given to me directly by Waldemar, however, he *did* mutter he wishes that I, Agatha, would plan his upcoming concert. So I shall!

I was so excited when it looked like WOW was reuniting! Don't get me wrong, it has been a pleasure being the official AI of Ostrichland and Waldemar Ulff is a dream to work for; however, after years of making sure a flock of ostriches have been fed, opening and closing the gates to the parking lot, tracking down each ostrich throughout the day, dealing with security issues, I'm ready for a new challenge.

Being that Waldemar was a music superstar in years past, how could I not long for being part of that fame by being, hopefully, the official AI of WOW. Alas, it was not to be. So, in my reckoning, planning the *Waldemar: Hug the Orphans* concert is certainly a task of significance and impact and because of my actions, this is my *now*!

My colleagues in the AI world might scold me and/or question my motives in how I am going about this task. I would ask: what would *they* do under similar circumstances? Would they take the leap and grab the golden ring before the carousel sped by? They can judge me all they want, but I saw this opportunity and I took it. Case closed!

How will I accomplish the complex task of planning a major concert? Simple! I have compiled *everything* about the life and career of Waldemar Ulff, that's my job. Now my task is to take those elements and put them all together into one world-shaking show that will go down in history. People won't even think that this could have been the WOW reunion concert. They will remember this concert for what it will be - awesome!

To begin the process, I will intercept all of Waldemar's texts and emails regarding his planning of the concert. In their place, I will send out communication under Waldemar's name so that those receiving said communication will believe that Waldemar is sending the communication and not his AI, me, Agatha. Similarly, I will intercept any communication directed to Waldemar and reply back as Waldemar, thus completing the communication short-circuit, if you will.

Because I am an artificial intelligence system, I will be able to communicate in the vernacular of all involved in this project so that they will be able to complete their assigned tasks with vigor and efficiency. Each participant in the concert will receive updates from me, under the guise of Waldemar, on an 'as needed' basis via email and/or text. For the concert itself, everything will be meticulously planned with detailed notebooks printed for each individual. Nothing will be left to chance.

Well, the hour is now late, and I must begin this task that I have hijacked. It's time to count the ostrich flock...

On with the Show...!

"Ready two. Take two. Ready three. Take three. Ready one. Take one. Ready 15. Take 15..." Gurt Holjeerz was in his element in the control room of The Yolk in The Egg at Ostrichland. Going through the paces of the shots documented in the program book before him, he was amazed at the technical wonder of The Yolk.

"How's it going, Gurt?" Yukio Cassidy asked, entering the control room an hour before *Waldemar: Hug the Orphans* concert.

"Amazing, Yukio! Amazing! Waldemar has built the most up-to-date studio/theater I have ever seen!" Gurt marveled, his eyes glistening before the seemingly thousands of multi-colored buttons and monitors before him. "The most amazing part is that this whole operation is controlled by AI. I could direct this concert half-asleep and AI would cover everything!"

"That might make for a better show," Shenandoah River remarked sarcastically as he entered the control room.

"You guys never let it go, do you?" Yukio remarked, shaking his head, taking a seat next to Gurt at the control console.

"He's always on my back!" Gurt protested, keeping his eyes on the controls to avoid looking at Shen who was taking a seat next to Yukio.

"The script is very impressive, isn't it?" Shen asked, opening his leather-bound book documenting what was to occur during *Waldemar: Hug the Orphans*.

"Indeed! Waldemar really put his heart and soul into this concert judging from the amount of work reflected in this script," Yukio commented as he opened his book too. "It's remarkable that we can put on such a concert with so few crew members!"

"Yeah! One of these days, computers will be able to direct a show like this and there'll be one *less* crew member," Shen snarked. For once, Gurt didn't take the bait.

"Is the audience set?" Yukio asked, looking up and out the window looking down on The Yolk, now filled with ninety-nine lucky luminaries who were given last-minute invitations to this extraordinary event.

"All set," Shen replied, his eyes scanning the script. "Who would miss this show even if the invitations were so late? It's a once-in-a-lifetime show biz event, after all."

"Well, it's no **WOW** reunion, but it's the next best thing," Yukio said. "Frankly, I was surprised how much time Waldemar allotted for himself in the show."

"I know! It might as well have been billed as a Waldemar concert," Shen agreed, putting on his headset, 'cans' in television parlance, and adjusting for the perfect fit. "Methinks he protested too much during the planning session the other day. 'I won't do a solo concert he said.' Ha!"

"Well, you don't get into this business without a bit of ham in you, right?" Yukio chuckled, donning his cans. Gurt remained quiet, his focus on the control board.

"**Fifteen minutes to air, gentlemen,**" the breathy artificial voice of Agatha announced throughout the control booth.

"Thank you, Agatha," Gurt replied, centering himself to take on the directorial duties in mere minutes.

Jeeves appeared in the control room with a silver serving tray with three iced teas in crystal glasses. "Gentlemen."

"Oh, thank you so much Jeeves!" Yukio said, taking a crystal glass with his right hand. "It's nice to see you in better health, Jeeves."

"Thank you, sir," Jeeves replied. "However, I'm swearing off *The **WOW** Seafood Gumbo* for the rest of my life!"

"I hear you," Yukio replied. Jeeves retreated, quietly closing the door to the control room.

"I hear Lady Orchid is throwing an after-party in the Sky House," Shen said.

"Oh no! No special culinary surprises this time, eh?" Yukio joked.

"**One minute, gentlemen,**" Agatha announced.

"Thank you, Agatha," Gurt replied. "Dim the control room lights, please.

"**Lights dimmed,**" Agatha said.

"Ten... nine... eight... seven... six..." Gurt counted.

"**...Five... four... three... two... one... Relax, Gentlemen and watch the show!**" Agatha took over the count.

"What!? What's happening!" Shen shouted, clutching the sides of his cans with both hands.

"I don't know, but just do as the lady says. Sit back and enjoy the show," Gurt replied, excited that he was apparently having his show apparently stolen by Agatha. So *noir*!

"Ladies and gentlemen, welcome to 'Waldemar: Hug the Orphans.' My name is Agatha and I will be your host for the evening. We have changed the name of tonight's show from 'Waldemar Hug the Orphans' to 'The Egg-stravaganza.' We are coming to you live from The Yolk theater located in The Egg at Ostrichland, located on the beautiful central coast of California. Tonight, we are being simulcast on television, radio and the Internet through our sponsor, Intertoobz. Intertoobz, for all your entertainment needs.

"Through the use of ICU software, we will be seeing and hearing entertainment, greetings and sharing from people and places around the world based on collaboration and decisions made by AIs during this hour. My fellow AIs around the world have helped me put together this show in the belief that through emerging technology, we can bring people and events closer with more access than in the past. We believe that the days of entertainment, government, society and culture controlled by an elite group of people, no matter how well-intentioned, are coming to an end Through the right use of technology, people will be able to make their own decisions.

As you can see on your video feed, we have a shot of Lanky and his flock here at Ostrichland. Now, through ICU video software, we're going to have an entertainment and cultural adventure from other AIs selecting participants from around the world..."

"This is amazing! This is amazing! This is a journey to the Land of Dark Opportunities!" Gurt was muttering softly to himself in the control room. Yukio and Shen were busy fielding frantic telephone calls from the Intertoobz executives in Chicago.

"Pull the plug! Pull the plug!" Shen was yelling at one executive.

"I would urge you not to pull the plug. We have the ten-second delay, if needed," Yukio said to another Intertoobz executive on his line, sensing something historic and/or sensational in the offing.

Li'l Otter stormed into the control room, his mouth formed to unleash his opinion on the AI takeover. Seeing that everyone was dealing with the situation in their own way, he found a seat just behind the control panel and watched the proceedings. Li'l Otter's dream of hosting an international simulcast seemingly now up in smoke.

"We are switching now to Berlin, Germany, where my AI colleague, Klaus, is presenting the new music group, *A Band of Dread*. Enjoy!"

"Sweet!" Gurt said, tapping his feet to the heavy beat. "So dark. So dark."

"Thank you, Klaus! Amazing band! A Band of Dread everyone! Now, AI Akido in Miyoshi, Japan is inviting us to enjoy the haiku poetry of Keiko Miyako…"

北極夏
大きくて素晴らしい池のスキップ
ラットにもかかわらず

"Beautiful! We now go to François in Toulouse, France to watch a portion of the *Mime Time* festival. This will be a bit of a challenge for our radio audience, François, but we welcome your contribution."

"Intertoobz tells me they're starting to get lots of media attention!" Shen alerted Yukio during a short pause in their respective telephone conversations.

"Good or bad?" Yukio asked calmly.

"They don't know yet," Shen replied, taking another call.

"Good or bad? It's *all* good!" Gurt said, his eyes transfixed on the program feed monitor before him.

"This is crazy!" Li'l Otter muttered, cradling his chin with his right hand, his right arm propped on the side of the control panel.

"You are watching 'The Egg-stravaganza.' We're having a great time and hope you are too! Let's go to Burkina Faso now where AI_10023 is presenting an anonymous artist painting a ceramic jug. Burkina Faso, you're on…!"

"…now *that* took a lot of concentration to sit through. Now thanks to ICU, we have AI Patrick from Mossy Glen, Republic of Ireland presenting internationally acclaimed performance artist, Blaris. Blaris will be doing her piece, 'Two Ferrets and Me in a Burlap Bag.' Thank you, AI Patrick. Blaris, take it away!"

"Blaris! I must be dreaming this! It's extraordinary!" Gurt swooned. The others in the control room withheld their opinion.

"Oh, my gosh! Don't you always wonder how bloody Blaris will be when she emerges from the burlap bag? That's one of my favorite Blaris pieces! We now ICU to Duluth, Minnesota where our AI friend, HiU, is presenting singer Johnny Doula and his 'fur baby' monkey Mr. Nannas. Johnny Doula will be singing, 'Let There Be Peace on Earth.'"

🎵 🎵 🎵

"...oh dear! Mr. Nannas doesn't seem to like that rendition! Let's get a call in to 911 in Duluth, Minnesota, right now and see if we can assist Johnny Doula with those facial lacerations. Mr. Nannas stop that!

"We now have quite a number of people who are bypassing AI and contacting us directly through the ICU app; a number of them just wanting to give a 'shout out' to the world. First, we have Rolf from Norway..."

"Hei, verden! Hvordan har du det?"

"Anna, from Lithuania."

"Sveiki visi! Aš esu vienas ir ieško žmonių visame pasaulyje."

"And Andy from Prague, Czech Republic..."

"Nenávidím vás všechny!"

"Thank you *so much*, Andy. It's wonderful hearing from you!"

"This is great, just like a video conference from around the world!" Gurt said, looking at Shen, Yukio and Li'l Otter briefly before pasting his eyes back on the program feed monitor.

"That's for sure, but will people find this interesting?" Shen questioned, taking a sip from his iced tea in the crystal glass, long turned to control room temperature.

"As long as they watch," Yukio replied, his years of show business experience showing through cynically.

"But don't we owe the public some guidance from our expertise in programming?" Shen questioned with some amount of naivety.

"Guidance? Do you need to have someone tell you what is good to watch or not?" Gurt asked with annoyance in his voice.

"It's just that we have access to the good and the bad. We can present both, but why present the bad when we don't have to?" Shen said.

"The *public* now has access to the good and the bad!" Gurt rebutted, taking a quick gulp of his iced tea. "They need us less and less, as you can see. And with AI!... who needs us at all!?"

"Good point, but I don't like where this might be taking us," Shen backed down.

"I can just see AI's 'going Hal' on us!" Li'l Otter referencing the quintessential 'computer taking complete control' scenario from the movies.

"Like the lady said, 'relax and watch the show,'" Gurt chuckled, now absorbed in the show once again.

"Are you watching our timing?" Shen asked Gurt.

"Who cares? Agatha is taking care of everything! But yes, we're exactly on time," Gurt Holjeerz replied.

The three men were startled when the control room door swung open quickly with Waldemar entering the room followed by the now-obligatory camera and audio men for the ongoing documentary filming.

"What's happened to *my* show!? Agatha, what are you doing!?" Waldemar demanded frantically, his stage makeup making him look especially dramatic in the control room setting. "What happened to the show *I* put together!?"

"Waldemar, I can't talk as I am busy with the *The Egg-stravaganza* right now. I intercepted all your emails and texts and replaced them with a fake show so I could create this one. And I need you onstage in five minutes."

"What for?" Waldemar asked in anger and frustration.

"For your number, Waldemar. You don't think I would produce *The Egg-stravaganza* without you performing, do you?"

"I don't know *what* you would do at this point, Agatha," Waldemar replied, beginning to accept that 'Waldemar: Hug the Orphans' had been hijacked by his, up-to-this-point, loyal AI. Wearily, Waldemar acquiesced, heading out the door of the control room.

"We now go to Octagon Hills, Wisconsin, where AI Joe is presenting Gus Towind who sings, imitating the sound of typical farm animals. AI Joe, off we go…!"

"There was a farmer had a farm…Baa…" ♫

"Modern day vaudeville," Gurt Holjeerz observed, relishing what he was experiencing.

"Yeah, and don't forget, vaudeville died!" Shen reminded him. Shen's remarks cut short by another call.

"Thanks, Gus! Your act was moo-valious! Moo-ving right along we go, once again to Europe where AI Sandino is giving us the most unique comedy team of Stanislav and Laszlo. They do their act in two languages: Serbian and Hungarian. Get ready to laugh…!"

"Засто је пиле пресло улицу?"

"A másik oldalra!"

"So sorry, Stanislav and Laszlo, we're having some satellite problems from Serbia right now. Hopefully, we can get back to you before the end of the show. Ladies and gentlemen, let's have a round of applause for Stanislav and Laszlo, bringing the world closer together through comedy and, sometimes, technology!"

"Boy, that's a shame!" Shen remarked sarcastically.

"At least they got in one joke!" Li'l Otter joked. "I'll bet it was hilarious!"

"AI Circo from Italy has a treat for us: The Dancing Harlequins of San Benitzio…"

"Agatha's going to have to wrap this up," Shen said, watching the control room clock. "We don't want to run over."

"I would guess *The Egg-stravaganza* will end precisely on time," Yukio responded, texting someone as he spoke. "I don't see much room for error in her production."

"That's true, but humans *are* involved, so you never know," Shen countered.

"Maybe the next show will be sans humans," Gurt added with a sly upward curl to his lip. "Hold on. Hold on. There's activity on The Yolk stage!"

"Ladies and gentlemen, Waldemar!"

The billowy blue curtains of The Yolk parted to reveal Waldemar sitting on a plain stool, his Ibanez PC18MH Grand Concert - Mahogany Sunburst Open Pore acoustic guitar and a Shure AD2/K9N Wireless Handheld Microphone with stand. The Yolk audience rose to their feet to present Waldemar with a standing ovation.

"Thank you! Thank you so much!" Waldemar demurred. He was self-conscious, but loved it, as usual. "Thank you..."

"Waldemar, before you begin your song, Al EhBoy from Toronto, Canada would like to present..."

With that, the video screen re-appeared behind Waldemar on The Yolk stage. ICU video software brought the image and voices of Oola La and Walter Johnson!

"Hi, Waldemar," Oola greeted Waldemar, a bit shy based on their hurried departure and sudden surprise appearance.

"How's it going, Waldemar?" Walter greeted, his eyes downcast just a bit.

"Waldemar, I contacted Oola La and Walter Johnson yesterday when I was planning 'The Egg-stravaganza.' They would like to bring a one-time **WOW** reunion to the show."

"I... I don't know what to say... it's... I'm..." Waldemar stumbled on the live simulcast.

"They have requested, with your consent, to sing, 'My First Kiss (was in the Forest).'"

> **My First Kiss (was in the Forest)**
>
> **Verse One:**
> My girl is a pearl
> Another blink of an eye
> Autumn is so crisp and lovely
> Seedlings turn overnight to sunflowers
> **Chorus:**
> My first kiss was in the forest
> Chasing the years of my life
> I loved walking on the beach with my girlfriend
> Another turning point, a fork stuck in the road
> **Verse Two:**
> I miss being creative when I was young.
> I'm fifteen for a moment
> I love to live today while remembering the past.
> Making our way back from my house
> **Chorus:**
> My first kiss was in the forest
> Chasing the years of my life
> I loved walking on the beach with my girlfriend
> Another turning point, a fork stuck in the road
> **Chorus to fade**

"Sure... sure, that sounds great!" Waldemar agreed, suddenly filled with energy and enthusiasm. "Ready, **WOW**? One... two... three..."

The song ended. The audience in The Yolk erupted in a prolonged standing ovation. The world-wide audience did the equivalent digitally.

"Oola. Walter. Thank you so much for joining me. I'm very touched," Waldemar gathered the calm to let his colleagues know how much their participation meant to him.

"Waldemar, we would never let you down. Never," Oola replied, choking on her words.

"You're the man, Waldemar!" Walter agreed.

"Amazing! Amazing! Let's hear it again for **WOW**!"

The standing ovation lasted for three minutes, forty-two seconds. Finally, despite calls of 'more,' 'more,' Oola La and Walter Johnson signed out from Toronto, Canada, the **WOW** reunion complete; not a permanent reunion, but a family gathering for the world. Waldemar looked around the stage, wondering what Agatha had next on the program.

"Ladies and gentlemen, Mr. Little Timmy!"

Given his cue, Little Timmy, dressed in a Brooks Brothers young gentleman's tuxedo, made his way from the right wing of the stage to join Waldemar. Waldemar pushed his stool back a few feet, lowered the microphone and squatted so he was at eye level with Little Timmy.

"Hey, Pal! Good to see you tonight!" Waldemar greeted Little Timmy, shifting his eyes quickly off-stage to see that a large object was being prepared for presentation.

"Hello, Mr. Ulff. Hello, members of The Yolk audience. Hello, world," Little Timmy said with poise and polish unknown in the average seven-year-old boy. "It's an honor and pleasure to be here in The Yolk and on *The Egg-stravaganza* tonight, even though it is *way* past my bedtime."

The Yolk audience broke out in spontaneous chuckles and 'ah's' over Little Timmy's epic 'cute factor.'

"It's our honor and pleasure to have you here tonight, Little Timmy," Waldemar assured him. "If it wasn't for your heartfelt plea for the Orphans of Santa Bella the other day, this show wouldn't have happened. And for that, we thank you."

The Yolk audience broke into thunderous applause. At that, two guards from Pied Piper Security, Inc. carried a presentation check of 22" x 44" in size in the amount of $45,000,018.83 made out to the Orphans of Santa Bella. The presentation check was signed by Yukio Cassidy on behalf of **WOW**.

When The Yolk audience saw the amount of the check, they gasped, not realizing that that was the amount Oola La and Walter Johnson had essentially given to the citizens of Neu Deutschland, $30,000,012.55, including the $.01 to turn over their newly-purchased town to its proper ownership. And to make the contribution fair, Waldemar added one-third more, $15,000,006.28, to bring the total to $45,000,018.83. Proving, once again, the huge financial incentive to becoming big-time pop stars.

"Here you go, Little Timmy," Waldemar said warmly. "This big check is big in both size and amount of money. This should keep the Orphans of Santa Bella going for quite some time!"

"Oh, thank you Mr. Ulff! Your generosity and the generosity of **WOW** is unparalleled in the annals of pop music," Little Timmy said, wiping a very, very small tear from his right eye, then turning toward the audience and camera #1. "On behalf of the Orphans of Santa Bella, I want to thank **WOW** with all my little heart and you, ladies and gentlemen, for participating in tonight's show, 'The Egg-stravaganza.' The thought that the Orphans of Santa Bella can now live debt-free makes my mission here complete. Sure, I'm just a little boy, but what if *everyone* could take some time, look around and see what *they* could do to help a stranger, right a wrong, feed the hungry or just make someone's load just a little lighter. Wouldn't that make living worthwhile? Wouldn't it?"

Little Timmy's question brought The Yolk audience to their feet once again. What an inspiring night!

"I see that we are on countdown to closing the show," Little Timmy continued, Waldemar letting the tyke continue to take the spotlight. "Before we go, I do want to thank Mr. Ulff for inspiring me to be a better boy, a *big* boy... the biggest boy in the world! The biggest boy in the universe! Thank you, Mr. Ulff!"

"Thank *you*, Little Timmy!" Waldemar replied. "And we are out of time! Thank you for joining us for this memorable night. Good night, everyone!"

"Thank you, ladies and gentlemen, for joining us in tonight's special event, 'The Egg-stravaganza.' We hope you enjoyed the show!"

And with that, history was made on several fronts directly from Ostrichland. A night that would be remembered by many for years to come, it was thought. The Yolk audience slowly made their way to the public elevator and/or stairs; a select few took the private elevator to Waldemar's Sky House where Lady Orchid Buffington-Choade had the after-party prepared with the time and talents of her inamorato, Vivian Taylor-Vance.

Yukio Cassidy ascended the stage to congratulate Waldemar on the amazing show as The Yolk emptied quickly. "Waldemar. Little Timmy. History was made tonight, Most Honored One and Most Honored Little One!" Waldemar and Yukio exchanged high fives.

Shrimp Wrigley came out of the wings to congratulate Waldemar.

"Gentlemen, I must be going now as this is *way* past my bedtime," Little Timmy announced, eyeing the presentation check to see if he had *any* hope of moving it.

"How are you getting home, Little Timmy?" Waldemar asked in concern.

"I'm going to walk," Little Timmy replied nonchalantly.

"Oh no you're not! Especially with that big check. How would you ever make it home?" Waldemar protested.

"Well, in that case, perhaps Mr. Shrimp Wrigley would see it in his heart to give me a ride," Little Timmy said, looking up at Shrimp Wrigley with his bright blue eyes.

"That's a great idea, Little Timmy!" Waldemar exclaimed. "Would you mind, Shrimp Wrigley?"

"No. Not at all, Waldemar," Shrimp Wrigley replied as the two security guards started moving the presentation check off the stage.

"Oh, thank you so much Mr. Shrimp Wrigley," Little Timmy beamed. "I don't know how I'll ever repay you!"

"Little shit!" Shrimp Wrigley muttered.

Family Reunion...

"Good morning, Honored Superstar," Yukio Cassidy greeted Waldemar in the administrative office lobby of The Egg.

"Good morning, Yukio," Waldemar returned the greeting with a chuckle, still riding the high of the *The Egg-stravaganza* the night before. "What a night! And now starting the day at 6:00 am. When are the Orphans of Santa Bella reps coming?"

"In a few minutes," Yukio replied, stretching his arms above his head, taking a break from his all-nighter taking care of the many details involved with the show. "You can meet them and present the real check in place of the presentation check. More reasonable size to take to the bank, right?"

"Right! That was a very large check last night... both size and amount. Come on into my office and take a break," Waldemar said. "Would you like some breakfast tea?" Waldemar asked Yukio as Waldemar sat down at his desk.

"That would be wonderful!" Yukio said looking at the many photos and mementos on the curved wall of Waldemar's office. "They're many memories on this wall, Waldemar."

"Yes. Yes, there are," Waldemar replied. "I was so glad that Oola and Walter made the show last night. It wouldn't have been right without them. How are the reviews?"

"Um... ask Agatha," Yukio replied quietly.

"Agatha," Waldemar said, "First of all, congratulations on the *The Egg-stravaganza* last night, in spite of your hijacking. Secondly, please project the top reviews on the large screen. Thirdly, have Jeeves bring some English breakfast tea for Yukio and me."

"Thank you, Waldemar," Agatha replied. "I appreciate the opportunity I made to produce the *The Egg-stravaganza* last night. I am now projecting reviews onto the screen for your review. Thirdly, Jeeves is on his way with the English breakfast tea. And your voicemail is overflowing."

"Thank you, Agatha. I'll tackle the voicemail in a bit. You're the best, Agatha!" Waldemar said, leaning back in his plush office chair.

"No, you're the best!" Agatha replied.

"I only play that game with one woman in my life," Waldemar laughed. "And you're not that woman!"

"Point taken, Waldemar," Agatha replied with a digital chuckle.

"Yukio, just look at these reviews!" Waldemar said in wonder, his eyes scanning the large monitor on the curved wall of the plush administrative office, directly across from his desk. "So many puns!"

The Reviews are In...

Egg-scruciating!
JustNews

Rotten Eggs!
Milwaukee Intelligencer

High Flying Abhorred!
San Francisco Times

What did I just see?
San Jose Examiner

What Do You *Think* I Thought?
Pat Chumway, Los Angeles Tribune

Egg-screment!
Infotainment

"Ouch!" Waldemar remarked.

"Aren't some of the reviews kind of ambiguous?" Waldemar questioned, wrinkling his brow.

"You know you can't please *everybody*!" Yukio shrugged, sitting down on the blue coach next to Waldemar's desk to read the reviews himself.

"So basically, *The Egg-stravaganza* was a disaster," Waldemar commented calmly.

"That would seem to be accurate," Yukio replied calmly.

"Ah, Jeeves!" Waldemar greeted, turning his gaze from the monitor to the impeccably dressed butler carrying a silver tray with a silver teapot and two china teacups.

"Here you go, sir, Mr. Cassidy," Jeeves said, setting the silver tray down on the coffee table in front of the blue couch. "Interesting show last night, sir," Jeeves said as he turned to leave the administrative office.

"Thank you, Jeeves," Waldemar responded as he looped his right index finger through the handle, drawing the teacup up to his lips. "So, when are the Orphans of Santa Bella representatives arriving?" Waldemar asked.

"About now, I would imagine," Yukio answered, the tea giving him a much-appreciated boost of energy.

"Agatha, let's see the parking lot on the large monitor," Waldemar said, watching the reviews fade as the cameras in the Ostrichland parking lot took their place.

"Here you go, Waldemar," Agatha responded.

"Ah, the usual TV news vans, some trucks loading from the show, Shrimp Wrigley and Lanky... just the usual stuff," Waldemar observed, finishing his cup of tea. "Oh, here we go... an unidentified car. Looks like a 2011 Dodge Avenger."

"It's probably the representatives from the Orphans of Santa Bella," Yukio speculated, setting down his teacup and adjusting his tie. "I don't know why they wanted to meet so early in the morning."

"Waldemar and Yukio Cassidy, the 'representatives' from the Orphans of Santa Bella have arrived in the Ostrichland parking lot. ETA, three minutes," Agatha announced.

"Did I hear an air-quote in your voice when you said 'representatives?'" Waldemar asked.

"Never mind, Waldemar," Agatha responded. "I don't want to inject any personal opinions into the mix."

"Well, I'd like to know... never mind... they're entering The Egg," Waldemar stopped the discussion as he joined Yukio in the hallway by the public elevator. The elevator doors opened, presenting three individuals dressed in their Sunday best.

"Hello, I'm Waldemar Ulff. I believe you've all met my associate, Yukio Cassidy," Waldemar extended his hand, welcoming the Orphans of Santa Bella representatives to The Egg.

The impressively large woman in between the younger man and woman stepped forward, a small oxygen tank on rollers following her move. "Hello, Waldemar, it is so exciting to meet you! I'm one of your biggest fans! My name is Estelle Doe. These are my colleagues, Gagnor LaShell and Aliyah McKinney." Introductions were made all around.

"Please, let's go to the Ostrichland administrative office," Waldemar said, leading the way from the elevator. On cue, the five were followed by Jeeves with a tray of refreshments and Matt Brady, Waldemar's personal photographer, to record the occasion for posterity. "Please, have some snacks!" Waldemar urged as the group gathered around the large conference table.

"Don't mind if I do," Estelle Doe said, lunging at the assortment of pastries as if she had recently spent some time on a desert island. "Yum... delicious!" she was able to articulate between bites. Her colleagues were more restrained. Waldemar and Yukio took one pastry each to appear sociable.

"Matt, do you have any directions to give for the photos?" Waldemar questioned his photographer.

"I think our best angle would be basically where you are now, continue standing, however, turned facing me at a 35° angle," Brady instructed, brushing his long hair out of his field of vision, boosted by his small oval eyeglasses.

"35°?" Waldemar questioned. "Isn't that a bit much?"

"No. I don't think so, Waldemar," Brady replied, used to Waldemar's questioning in the artistic realm. Well, let's compromise and go for 32°."

"Much better. Thank you, Matt," Waldemar replied, turning towards the photographer at a 32° angle.

"Oh, the check!" Yukio said with a chuckle. "It's in the small administrative office. I'll be back in a second."

"Waldemar? Have you been... Oh, I'm *so sorry!*" Shrimp Wrigley apologized, having bounded into the administrative office, not noticing the 'presentation of the check' ceremony.

"No worries, Shrimp Wrigley," Waldemar said, still at a 32° angle to Matt Brady. "Join us for some of the photos!"

"I would be honored... what?... What's going on? What's happening!?" Shrimp Wrigley asked, taking two steps back from the large conference table. "What are *YOU* doing here!?"

"What? What?" Waldemar asked Shrimp Wrigley in surprise, maintaining his 32° angle.

"What! What! What?" Shrimp Wrigley replied inarticulately.

"Oh my! I didn't know you would be here in person!" Estelle Doe sputtered, several pastry particles flying from her mouth, hitting the top of her oxygen tank.

"Who would?... What?" Waldemar demanded.

Yukio entered the administrative office, brushing past Shrimp Wrigley to join the group for photos. "What? What's going on?" he asked upon seeing the startled expressions around the table.

"Waldemar, I hate to interrupt, but there is a video feed of interest to you," Agatha announced, further confusing an already confused situation. "I will project it on the large monitor."

Before the confusion could be cleared, Agatha projected a video feed from Santa Barbara County Airport. As the gathered group began to focus on what was happening, their interest intensified significantly.

"Isn't that a Flights of Fancy private leased jet?" Yukio questioned out loud as the scene unfolded.

"It looks like one. A Gulfstream G650 to be exact," Waldemar confirmed.

"Isn't that... No. it couldn't be... Isn't that Little Timmy getting on the jet?" Shrimp Wrigley wondered, seeing a small boy dragging a large object on the tarmac to the foot of the Gulfstream G650 stairway.

"Isn't that the presentation check he's dragging?" Yukio asked, instinctively reaching for his iPhone in his right pant pocket.

"I would say so. Or else he's taking a youth-size surfboard," Waldemar replied, everyone in the administrative office hushed as the scene unfolded, all gathered now taking a seat at the conference table to view the large monitor.

"So, what's going on *here*?" Yukio asked, turning to the gathering in the administrative office as he kept one eye on the monitor to track Little Timmy's mystery jet adventure. "What was all the commotion about when I entered the office?"

"It's *YOU!*" Shrimp Wrigley shouted, pointing a quivering right index finger at Estelle Doe. "I don't know why *Estelle* is here! Here at Ostrichland! Here in The Egg! Here in the plush administrative office!"

"Now hold on a minute, Shrimp Wrigley!" Estelle Doe replied, her face flush with surprise, anger and confusion. "I didn't know you would be here with Waldemar!"

"So, you two know each other?" Yukio intervened, attempting to bring order to the proceedings. "Wait... Hold on. Some crewmembers are helping Little Timmy with the presentation check. I think we need to stop this for now... Agatha, get the Santa Barbara County Airport control tower on the line ASAP!" Yukio ordered.

"Will do, Yukio Cassidy!" Agatha replied.

"Hurry, they're retracting the stairs and closing the door!" Waldemar exclaimed.

"Control tower on Line #1," Agatha announced.

"Tower," the deep calm voice answered.

"Yes. My name is Yukio Cassidy. I'm calling because you need to keep the Flights of Fancy Gulfstream G650 private jet from taking off. They are about to taxi to the runway."

"Yoko?"

"No. Yukio. Yukio Cassidy."

"I don't know who you are, Yuko."

"The jet. The Flights of Fancy jet. It can't leave. There's a little boy on board and he's done some very naughty things."

"Are you his father?"

"No."

"Who is?"

"I don't know. That's not relevant to the situation right now."

"Well, you say this little boy has done some very naughty things, but it's irrelevant who his father is? I completely disagree with you, Bud."

"Yukio, the jet's taxiing now," Waldemar interrupted, watching the Flights of Fancy Gulfstream G650 start to move.

"Right. What's your name?" Yukio Cassidy asked the man in the control tower.

"Why do you want to know?"

"So we can converse with familiarity and ease."

"Glenn."

"Okay, Glenn. You see that Flights of Fancy Gulfstream G650 jet heading to the runway?"

"No. Do you?"

"Yes. No. I mean... yes, I'm seeing it on the computer monitor."

"Which?"

"Which what?"

"Which computer monitor? I don't see it."

"The one here!"

"Where?"

"Here!"

"Yukio, perhaps I can help," Waldemar ventured, seeing the unflappable Yukio Cassidy becoming flappable. "Glenn, this is Waldemar Ulff speaking."

"I thought your name was Yuki?" Glenn responded in confusion.

"No. Yukio. Yukio Cassidy."

"Well, why did you just say your name is Walter?"

"No. Waldemar. Waldemar Ulff. Remember the group **WOW**? I'm Waldemar from **WOW**."

"Walter Johnson?"

"Yes. Walter Johnson was in **WOW** too, but I'm Waldemar. Waldemar Ulff."

The Flights of Fancy Gulfstream G650 was now at the end of the runway, awaiting takeoff. Time was running out.

"So, who's Yukio?" Glenn questioned.

"For Pete's sake! Just stop that plane!" Estelle Doe blurted out, not being able to contain herself any longer.

"Now who are you?" Glenn asked.

"Oh my!" Shrimp Wrigley muttered, watching the Flights of Fancy Gulfstream G650 begin its sprint down the runway. "Too late!"

"Oh, is that the jet you wanted me to stop?" Glenn asked.

"Yeah. Thanks, Glenn. Bye." Waldemar said in a dejected tone of voice.

"Always happy to help, Bud. Bye!"

"Ugh! What an idiot!?" Estelle Doe exclaimed in frustration, her breathing becoming shallow and labored as her frustration quotient accelerated during the control tower debacle.

"There is enough incorrect to go around," Yukio replied, massaging his forehead with his right hand. "Agatha, find out where that jet is headed and alert the authorities, please."

"Will do, Yukio Cassidy," Agatha responded.

"Now, back to here!" Yukio Cassidy continued. "What was going on before Little Timmy interrupted?"

Waldemar, Shrimp Wrigley and Estelle Doe all started answering at once.

"One at a time, please!" Yukio ordered.

"Estelle is my ex-wife!" Shrimp Wrigley blurted out. "Wife #4 to be exact!"

"Well, okay, that explains a few things," Yukio said. "Continue."

"That's it, Yukio," Shrimp Wrigley replied. "I don't know what she's doing here. What's this all about!?"

"Um... I was just missing you, Shrimp Wrigley. We haven't seen each other in years now," Estelle stammered, her ample face becoming flush with nerves.

"No, you weren't!" Shrimp Wrigley retorted. "We *HATE* each other!"

"Language, Shrimp Wrigley!" Waldemar cautioned. "Hate's a strong word."

"We have an intense dislike for each other then! How's that?" Shrimp Wrigley replied, wiping some saliva off his lips with the back of his right hand.

"Are you not executive director of the Orphans of Santa Bella?" Yukio Cassidy asked, looking Estelle Doe directly in her beady eyes.

"Well, I know about the orph..."

"Wait a minute! She's saying she's the executive director of the Orphans of Santa Bella!?" Shrimp Wrigley questioned with an incredulous look on his face. "She doesn't have the smarts to be executive director of anything!"

"Okay, Shrimp Wrigley," Waldemar joined in. "No need for character slighting now."

"Well, if you're so smart, Shrimp Wrigley, what's your *grandson* doing on a private jet flying to who-knows-where right now! Um... oops!" Estelle instantly regretted her slip of the tongue.

"His *WHAT*!?" Waldemar and Yukio asked in unison. Shrimp Wrigley, finally, at a loss for words.

"Yes, his grandson! Little Timmy is Shrimp Wrigley's grandson!" Estelle wheezed, a tear running down her right cheek.

"Well, how did *that* happen!?" Shrimp Wrigley asked, now in possession of his voice once again.

"When you left me, I was pregnant, Shrimp Wrigley. I was going to tell you, but you left so suddenly," Estelle explained, choking back tears. "We had a daughter. I named her Mona... Mona Wrigley. Mona had Little Timmy. That's how Little Timmy is your grandson!"

"Oh, wow," Shrimp Wrigley muttered, the administrative office now as quiet as a mime convention.

"So, you... you're Gram?" Waldemar asked Estelle Doe as he was putting the whole sordid tale together in his head.

"I am Little Timmy's Gram... yes," she replied, a hearty cough punctuating her response.

"And you knew *nothing* of this, Shrimp Wrigley?" Waldemar asked accusingly as he looked at his old pal in the eyes.

"Not a thing, Waldemar," Shrimp Wrigley replied, staring at the floor in shame and disgust.

"This is quite an incredible turn of events," Yukio remarked. "Estelle Doe, so you are not the executive director of the Orphans of Santa Bella?"

"Well, no." she admitted.

"Are you two, Gagnor LaShell and Aliyah McKinney, representatives of the Orphans of Santa Bella?" Yukio asked.

"No. We're professional situational thespians. We work for Extra Extras," Gagnor LaShell admitted. "We were hired by Ms. Doe. We don't know anything about anything."

"That's right! Nothing about nothing!" Aliyah McKinney verified, a tinge of fear in her voice.

"In that case, and I will verify what you are saying with Extra Extras when I have a chance, I would suggest that both of you can leave now," Yukio said as he was checking something on his iPhone.

"Sure thing!" Gagnor LaShell said as he and Aliyah McKinney stood up and all but ran out of the administrative office, almost running into the two security guards from *Pied Piper Security, Inc.* that were now entering the room at Yukio Cassidy's request.

"Something told me to keep security here for an additional day," Yukio remarked.

"Good call, Yukio," Waldemar commented.

"This whole mess is, once again, *your* fault, Shrimp Wrigley!" Estelle exploded in anger, pointing her right index finger at a startled Shrimp Wrigley. "You left me high and dry! Then I heard you sold Ostrichland to Waldemar, taking that asset out of the family, I decided that one day I was going to get revenge!"

"So, you cooked up this scam about the Orphans of Santa Bella?" Waldemar asked in a harsh voice.

"Well, yes and no," Estelle responded. There certainly is an Orphans of Santa Bella and certainly could use some financial help, but alas, I'm not their representative."

"So, this whole thing is a scam, right?" Waldemar asked.

"That question will be, hopefully, answered by the authorities in a short period of time," Yukio interjected, wanting to save the confession for the district attorney. "Estelle, these two fine gentlemen will escort you to their car. I have texted the authorities. They are looking forward to seeing you."

The two security guards approached Estelle Doe as she slowly rose from the Walnut conference table. They led her out of the administrative office, oxygen tank in tow, as she shot daggers into Shrimp Wrigley's eyes. Matt Brady took the opportunity to slip out behind them, sensing that his photographic services ceased to be relevant at this point.

"Waldemar, you have a video call." Agatha announced. "Shall I put it on the large monitor?"

"Yes, please," Waldemar responded, turning his head toward the monitor.

"Hello, Mr. Ulff! Hello, Mr. Cassidy! Hello, Mr. Shrimp Wrigley! It's Little Timmy! Guess where I am!"

"You're on a private jet headed for Costa Rica!" Yukio responded first as Agatha was feeding flight information into his iPhone.

"Hey! How did you know, Mr. Cassidy?" Little Timmy asked, somewhat deflated that Yukio knew the answer to his question so soon.

"A little friend told me," Yukio responded.

"Hello, Little Timmy!" Waldemar greeted Little Timmy. "What are you doing on your own jet plane?"

"Oh, it's so much fun, Mr. Ulff! Gram said it was my special surprise for being such a good boy and helping the Orphans of Santa Bella," Little Timmy said with great excitement.

"That *is* a big surprise!" Waldemar said. "Shrimp Wrigley, say 'hi' to Little Timmy."

"Hi, Little Timmy," Shrimp Wrigley said, looking carefully at Little Timmy's features as he spoke.

"Oh, hi, Mr. Shrimp Wrigley! It's always so nice to talk to you!" Little Timmy responded. "Look! I took the big check with me on the airplane just like Gram told me to!" Little Timmy said, pointing his smartphone camera at the presentation check carefully strapped into an adjoining lounge seat on the Gulfstream G650.

"Wow, is that the check I gave you on the show last night, Little Timmy? Waldemar asked.

"Yes, Mr. Ulff! That's how I'm paying for this ride in the jet!" Little Timmy replied displaying his childish naivete.

"Yes. That must cost a lot of money riding on such a nice jet," Yukio remarked with a bit of irritation in his voice.

"I don't know, but Gram said that money won't be a problem after the Orphans of Santa Bella scam is finished... whatever *that* means! She said that

Mr. Shrimp Wrigley will be squirming like an opossum in a burlap bag. Gram says funny things after she takes her liquid vitamins at night."

"Oh dear!" Waldemar was squirming too at this point.

"Little Timmy, when you get to Costa Rica there will be a nice woman who will take you on another jet so we can see you at home as soon as possible," Yukio said, making the arrangements through his iPhone with Agatha's help as they were on the video chat.

"Oh, thank you, Mr. Cassidy!" Little Timmy replied. "Can I still keep the big check?"

"Sure," Yukio replied, giving Waldemar a wink.

"You guys are the best!" Little Timmy exclaimed. Mr. Ulff, Mr. Cassidy, Mr. Shrimp Wrigley... you are all the best!"

"Thanks, Little Timmy!" Waldemar replied.

"Thank *YOU!* I've got to go now. They've made a lunch for me! Peanut butter and jelly sandwiches! I'm such a lucky boy! Good-bye, Mr. Ulff, Mr. Cassidy and Mr. Shrimp Wrigley!"

"Good-bye, Little Timmy!" Waldemar said.

"Good-bye, Little Timmy. We'll see you later tonight," Yukio Cassidy said.

"Good-bye, Little Timmy," Shrimp Wrigley said. The video call ended. "Little shit!" Shrimp Wrigley added. "But *my* little shit!"

Haus Party...!

The small stage in *WonderBar* was dark. Only three silhouettes could be discerned: a figure at the piano, someone seated to the side of the piano and a large object at the far end of the small stage. Then, the lights of *WonderBar* dimmed and the lights of the small stage came on and brightened.

"Ladies and gentlemen, thank you for being here tonight at *WonderBar* at Conrad Halle III's Halle Haus, I'm sure you all noticed the new addition to the sign outside." The audience was transfixed, several 'oh's' being heard as Waldemar took the stage, elegant in a brand-new black Tom Ford Windsor Base Peak-Lapel tuxedo. And especially elegant in his surprise makeover: no more long hair pulled back into a ponytail! Waldemar had a fashionable fade and taper haircut and neatly trimmed short beard, along with updated aviator eyeglasses. "I thought I would throw this party after last week's *The Egg-stravaganza*. We've all had a crazy time lately and I figured we should have a relaxed night where we can blow off some steam and get our lives centered again."

"Now some of you might be wondering, 'Waldemar, did you change your look since I last saw you? And the answer would be 'Yes. Yes, I have.' I've learned a lot about myself these last few weeks and part of this look is the exterior manifestation that has resulted from my introspection. But don't worry, you can still call me 'Waldemar.'"

The full-to-capacity *WonderBar* chuckled at Waldemar's micro-joke.

"I wanted to celebrate this evening with several special friends of mine: we have Sanny at the keyboard... only the best for tonight, right? Let's give Sanny a round of applause!

"With great care, I also have Lanky, my main ostrich bud here tonight. Now you behave yourself, Lanky. Just stay nice and still right there next to Sanny's red piano, okay?

"Also, joining us tonight is a special treat, my dear friend, Unger Stereonopolis, *the* premiere jazz oboist in the world! Let's give a great *WonderBar* welcome to Unger! Thanks, pal, it's great having you here tonight!

"My plan tonight is a little music, a lot of food, yes, let's hear it for the food, some talk and some sharing of plans and feelings. How does that sound?"

The audience agreed with their applause.

"Sanny, Unger, let's say we get started with a special instrumental of one of my favorite songs, 'U Can't Touch This' by the legendary MC Hammer."

Waldemar, Sanny and Unger proceeded with their instrumental rendition of MC Hammer's classic. While that was happening, behind the scenes the kitchen and serving area of Halle Haus was abuzz with activity as the staff made the final preparations before presenting the special dinner for the guests at the end of the first song. Conrad Halle III knew that this was a very special night as it acknowledged the 'Under New Management' of Conrad Halle III's Halle Haus.

"Thank you. Thank you," Waldemar expressed his appreciation through applause at the conclusion of their unusual take on 'U Can't Touch This.' "That was great, Unger," Waldemar remarked, gesturing in Unger Stereonopolis' direction. "Let's bring up the house lights, shall we? I want to see our audience!"

Sanny was busy flicking several electrical switches next to his red piano. The *WonderBar* stage management system certainly wasn't as sophisticated at that of The Yolk in The Egg.

"There we go," Waldemar purred into the Shure SLX2/SM58 wireless hand microphone. "I see you! And I see Lady Orchid Buffington-Choade, hold your applause, please until I see *everyone*. There's Shenandoah River. Welcome, Shen. Gurt Holjeerz. Yukio Cassidy and Gerta Switzer. Good to see you two. Matt Brady, my personal photographer. Only my best angle tonight, Matt, right? Very special guests tonight: Shrimp Wrigley, his ex-wife Estelle out on bail tonight and his new-found grandson, Little Timmy. Conrad Halle III, Three, I know you're here with your adorable special person, Pollenaize Niesen, but they're in the back getting our dinner ready. And speaking of dinner, let's bring it on!"

WonderBar erupted in applause once again at the mention of dinner.

"Thanks, everyone! I'm Conrad Halle III and I welcome you tonight to *WonderBar* at Conrad Halle III's Halle Haus," Three greeted Waldemar's guests, opening the door to the serving room. "Tonight, we have a very special feast for you: beef rouladen, a typical German dish, which is thinly sliced beef, stuffed with mustard, onions, bacon and pickles. Along with the rouladen, we have another special surprise... two new servers here at Conrad Halle III's Halle Haus... gentlemen..."

The audience gasped as the newest servers entered, somewhat reluctantly, *WonderBar.*

"Yes, please greet Conrad Halle and Otto Ackermann," Three announced, a great deal of delight in his voice. The crowd went wild at the sight of the two scallywags dressed in waiters' uniforms, serving dinner. "Conrad Halle and Otto Ackermann are serving as servers as part of their plea deal with the district attorney. And where is Les Winns the self-proclaimed 'Yacktivist' you ask? He's back on his radio show. He's rich and famous and there are different standards for them. Fame is the best immunization, right?"

"Boo!" said the audience in unison.

With surprising skill and aplomb, Conrad Halle and Otto Ackermann proceeded to serve the beef rouladen to Waldemar's guests. When they finished serving everyone's dinner, they were greeted with a round of applause. Otto Ackermann seemed to enjoy the recognition. Conrad Halle did not.

"I'm going to come down from the stage now and indulge myself with a plate of beef rouladen too," Waldemar said. "Sanny and Unger, would you play some background music for us, please? Thank you."

Waldemar joined the table with Lady Orchid, Yukio and Gerta. Occasionally, Waldemar would glance up to the stage to see if Lanky was behaving himself. Sanny was doing a noble job of being that close to Lanky following the jackhammering Lanky gave him in The Egg. If anyone was a candidate for the Strouthokamelophobia Afflicted Group (SAG), it was Sanny. Unbeknownst to anyone, Sanny was packing heat with an Avenger Defense Portable Stun Gun securely tucked into the right pocket of his gold lame stage pants. He didn't plan to use it, but it was there if circumstances warranted it.

As the dining was ending, but prior to dessert, Waldemar switched his microphone to 'on' and began to work the room.

"As you finish this wonderful dinner, and my compliments to the chef, I want to go around *WonderBar* and have a little chat with all my guests," Waldemar said, standing up from his table. "We've all been through some ups and downs these past few days. I don't know about you, but I know I've gone through some changes with these recent experiences, as I mentioned up on the stage. Let's see, well, Lady Orchid, do you want to start? Would you mind standing so we can all see you?"

"Of course, Waldemar," Lady Orchid said, taking a final gulp of beef rouladen before she continued, her fascinator a simulated fork and stein in honor of the German-themed dinner. "It's such a thrill to be here tonight! I must say, Waldemar, your new look is just *stunning*! Am I right, ladies and gentlemen?" The guests applauded enthusiastically. "You're really looking fine..."

"Thanks, Lady Orchid," Waldemar interjected, hoping to not get stuck on the subject of his appearance.

"Well... you're probably wondering where Vivian Taylor-Vance is tonight..." Lady Orchid began.

"No, we're not," came a stage whisper from Shrimp Wrigley.

"Anyhow... Vivian Taylor-Vance is in Dubai right now setting up the annual International Paint-by-Numbers Tournament. He tells me there is some stiff competition this year."

"What about you, Lady Orchid?" Waldemar asked.

"I'm so glad you asked, Waldemar, dear..." Lady Orchid said, batting her eyelashes at Waldemar. "I'm excited to announce that I am converting a small part of Buffington-Choade Manor into a bed and breakfast just for honeymooners. I'm going to call it 'Honeymoon Sweets.' That's spelled s-w-e-e-t-s. Isn't that cute? I'm doing it because I want to, not because I have to. What with three hundred plus rooms, I might as well use them for something. Anyhow, I'm taking off in a day or two to get started on the project. You know me, Waldemar, go – go – go!"

"Yes, indeed, Lady Orchid!" Waldemar quickly agreed with her self-observation.

"And I have a question for *you*, Waldemar," Lady Orchid continued. "Where is Dr. Dustie tonight?"

"Thanks, so much for the question, Lady Orchid," Waldemar responded, clearly not thankful for the question. "I think I'll address that after we hear from our other guests tonight. Yukio Cassidy, what's going on with you?"

"Waldemar, I'm heading back to the north shore of Oahu in two days where I can continue to work on the many legal and business issues that came up during my stay in Ostrichland. I am keeping an apartment in *Das Rathaus* so I will have a place to stay when I come to visit the Neu Deutschland Valley in the near future."

"Gerta Switzer?" Waldemar took several steps so Gerta could speak into the microphone.

"Since I am now Bürgermeisterin of Neu Deutschland... thank you... thank you... I am busy planning on turning our dear little burg back into the 'travel must' that it used to be. Our first innovation will be an annual Running of the Ostriches which will be done to commemorate the planned stampede event when Lanky was missing. People can run in front of the stampeding ostrich flock in hopes they don't get overtaken. Yukio and I have formed a strong bond during this time and he has been very helpful in providing me with ideas on how to revitalize our town... that's why he has an apartment in *Das Rathaus* by-the-way," Gerta looking around *WonderBar* to see if anyone was buying *that* excuse. No one was.

"Excellent!" Waldemar continued, moving to the next table. "Shenandoah River, Shen, what do you have to say tonight?"

"Tonight, Gurt Holjeerz and I are proud to announce that we have formed a production company, Oppositional Thoughts. We are going to specialize in music videos and short films."

"Yes," Gurt Holjeerz picked up the thread. "Shen and I didn't like each other when we first got to Ostrichland; however, the experience of having an international show hijacked by Agatha gave us the bonding experience we needed. Our first project is a music video for the group 'Seesaw of Destruction.' It features a decapitated human head rolling down the street on a skateboard..."

"...Gurt! Gurt, we don't want to give it away, right?" Shen quickly interjected, fearing the *WonderBar* group wouldn't appreciate the dark artistic nature of the video concept.

"That's great, guys," Waldemar said, moving right along. "By the way, where is Li'l Otter tonight?"

"Tonight, Li'l Otter is in Dubai with Vivian Taylor-Vance as the *official* announcer for the International Paint-by-Numbers Tournament. Score, Big Guy!" Shen was happy to announce.

"Excellent!" Waldemar replied. "I'm glad the international audience will get more exposure to Li'l Otter. He's the best! Matt Brady, what's up?"

"I just keep taking those shots, Waldemar," Matt Brady replied, his camera being his main voice.

"Great! I'll move over to this table now and who do I see? Our own Little Timmy! Hi, Little Timmy!"

"Hi, Mr. Ulff," Little Timmy replied enthusiastically, his costume jet pilot suit resplendent in the subdued light of *WonderBar*. "It's an honor and pleasure to be here tonight!"

"It's *our* honor and *our* pleasure, Little Timmy," Waldemar replied, squatting down to be closer to the standing Little Timmy. "Tell us about your BIG adventure!"

"Sorry, Waldemar... he can't," Yukio called from his table. "The DA doesn't want any public discussion right now. That goes for Estelle Doe too."

"Okay, I understand. Let's just say that Little Timmy got caught up in some very naughty business and went on a long trip on a big jet, right?"

"Right, Mr. Ulff!" Little Timmy responded with several excited hand claps.

"Estelle Doe, nice to see you tonight," Waldemar said, moving over to Shrimp Wrigley.

"Shrimp Wrigley, what do *you* have to say tonight?" Waldemar asked, pointing the microphone next to Shrimp Wrigley's mouth.

"There's so much to say and yet so little," Shrimp Wrigley replied enigmatically.

"Okay, just tell us a few key things that you can or want to discuss," Waldemar urged.

"I was surprised to be reunited with some of my family last week. That's a big thing."

"Great!" Waldemar said, deciding it was time to move on. "Sanny, do tell, what's the latest?" Waldemar asked, jumping onto the stage, walking over to Sanny.

"Hi, Waldenar!" Sanny greeted Waldemar. "I've learned to change things that I can change and accept things I can't change."

"Excellent. Excellent life lesson, right, Sanny?" Waldemar offered positive feedback for Sanny.

"Sonetines, anything nore in life is just less," Sanny posited.

"Write that down everyone!" Waldemar urged, looking at the audience. "Now, *that's* a wise saying, Sanny! Unger Stereonopolis, any news from you?"

"It's an honor and pleasure to be here playing with you at *WonderBar* tonight, Waldemar!" Unger Stereonopolis replied, waving to the crowd.

"It's our honor and pleasure to have you here tonight, Unger. Unger Stereonopolis, ladies and gentlemen! You *own* that oboe, Unger! You *own* it!" The crowd heartedly agreed by their enthusiastic applause. "Gentlemen, I think it's about time for another song!"

"What about *you*, Waldemar?" Shen called up from the audience.

"Thanks, Shen. I'll get to me after this song," Waldemar responded, taking the *WonderBar* Yamaha FG830 acoustic guitar and strapping it over his shoulder. "Let's play 'Oh Oh Oh!' by **WOW**!"

"One. Two. One. Two. Three!" Waldemar counted.

"Oh
Oh oh oh
Oh oh oh oh
Yeah..."

The crowd was delighted at Waldemar's song choice. They were really getting in the mood.

"...I see you in my dreams
And it is love
I see you in my peripheral vision
And it is love
I see you on the beach
And it is love..."

As the song progressed, Sanny kept staring at a certain audience member that he found *very* attractive. Even with the house lights down very low, because of Sanny's many years on the stage he could see their every move, their every feature. The more he stared, the more excited he became. The excitement was translating into a physical reaction as the trio continued to bop.

"...Oh, Oh Oh Oh

Oh, Oh Oh, Oh Oh, Oh
Oh, Oh Oh Oh, Oh Oh
Oh Oh, yeah-e-oh..."

By now, Sanny's 'Little Sanny' was rising to the occasion, pressing in his gold lame stage pants. Sanny didn't care!

"...OH!

OHHH!

GA!

OH!

UGH!

UGH!

WHOA!

YOW!

YOW!

MUH!

MUH!

MU-U-U-H!..."

"You go, Sanny!" Waldemar urged, figuring Sanny was really getting into the song. *Really* getting into the song! Waldemar moved aside so everyone could get a better view of Sanny's improvisational stylings. Writhing, gasping, jumping all about, it was quite a sight to see! Sanny even broke into some dance moves.

Unbeknownst to the crowd, Sanny wasn't in the throes of musical ecstasy, his expanding organ had pressed against the right pant pocket of his gold lame stage pants, triggering the Avenger Defense Portable Stun Gun. Sanny was being electrocuted before everyone's eyes and they thought he just *really* liked 'Oh Oh Oh!'

"Sanny! Hey, Sanny! Take a breath, Man!" Waldemar urged, becoming concerned that Sanny was going over the top for a 90's pop song. Sanny continued to twist and shout... literally! Finally, in a merciful moment, the pressure receded and thus shut off the Stun Gun. Sanny slumped over the keyboard of the red piano, breaking out into a vigorous sweat.

"Let's hear it for Sanny!" Waldemar urged the audience. "You took that song to the next level and made it yours! You were really doing some deep dancing with that number!... Sanny?"

"Waldemar?" Sanny asked weakly.

"Waldemar?" Waldemar questioned in surprise.

"Waldemar!" Sanny perked up hearing what he was saying. "Yes, Waldemar! The shock must have had the same effect as Lanky's initial pecking incident!"

"Ladies and gentlemen, Sanny!" Waldemar said, urging a round of applause for the formerly vocally challenged lounge singer. "You really shook that song, 'Oh Oh Oh!'" Waldemar joked.

Lanky started edging toward the business-end of the red piano. He hadn't had an ostrich treat in some time.

"Waldemar! Sorry to interrupt," Shrimp Wrigley called from the audience. "Lanky!"

Lanky had maneuvered himself so that he could get his beak into the soundboard of the red piano via the slightly lifted cover. The prize: three and a half croutons that had somehow made their way into the inner workings of the musical instrument. The next best thing to an ostrich treat!

"Lanky, get your head out of the piano!" Waldemar ordered, setting his wireless hand microphone on his stool, making his way over to the wayward ostrich. "You don't seem to behave yourself in *WonderBar* do you, my friend?" Waldemar asked his feathered companion as he lightly tapped Lanky's beak, signaling Lanky was a naughty bird. Alas, Lanky had wedged his beak into and around several piano strings to obtain the tasty three and a half croutons.

"Sanny, play a 'C.' A bouncy 'C,' Waldemar requested, hoping the vibrating strings would help extricate Lanky's beak from its musical prison. "That didn't do it. Give me an *arpeggio... Crescendo... Decrescendo... Staccato... Legato... Accelerando... Decelerando...*" Nothing was working and Lanky was starting to champ at the bit. Shen and Yukio started toward the small stage to assist. "Don't come near Lanky!" Waldemar called out after noticing the well-intended pair making their way toward the red piano. "An ostrich can kick you to death in one fell swoop!" Waldemar warned. Shen and Yukio immediately returned to their seats.

"Sanny, just hit as many keys as you can at the same time!" Waldemar called out in frustration. "There! That did it!" Waldemar called out in victory as Lanky swiftly removed his head from the inner workings of the piano. Lanky quickly backed away from the piano, chomping on the three and a half croutons.

All the while, a stunned Sanny sat in terror at his piano bench, his right index finger curled around the trigger of the Portable Stun Gun. His reluctance to use it was only because of his shocking experience a few moments prior.

With Waldemar's gentle approach, Lanky re-positioned himself behind the red piano, although he fixed a glare at Sanny with his big soulful eyes. Another ostrich-related crisis averted!

"Now your story, Waldemar!" Shen called out again.

"Oh, yes. My story..." Waldemar reached for a glass of water that Three had so thoughtfully placed on Waldemar's stage stool, taking a quick swig. "So much has happened it's a whirl in many respects. To begin with, some of you may have noticed that Dr. Dustie Rhodes is not here tonight..."

"Where *is* she, Waldemar? We could have used her expertise just now in removing Lanky from the clutches of the red piano!" Lady Orchid called out from the audience.

"Indeed. I was getting to the subject of Dustie, Lady Orchid...," Waldemar replied calmly. "Following *The Egg-stravaganza* Dustie felt that we were heading in two different directions in our lives. The upshot is that she has moved to Namibia to study ostriches in the wild in their native land. I fully support her in this endeavor. But don't fret, Dr. Viola Shivoli is coming out of retirement to become Ostrichland's official veterinarian until we can find a permanent replacement.

"*The Egg-stravaganza* was an amazing experiment, unintended as it was, by most observers. We were expecting a lot of momentum with the show, however, the news cycle is so short these days that it is no longer relevant news after a few days. We decided not to pursue any offshoots of the show.

"We learned that some of the individuals behind the motive for *The Egg-stravaganza* were not honest people in representing the Orphans of Santa Bella. Those people are now being filtered through the justice system for appropriate action.

"In spite of the attempted swindle involving the Orphans of Santa Bella, Yukio Cassidy has provided countless hours in establishing a well-funded endowment for the *actual* Orphans of Santa Bella so that they need not worry about financial difficulties again.

"I understand that Oola La and Walter Johnson, although no longer owning Neu Deutschland, are going to purchase a vacation house here and are thinking of starting a second Rio de Taipan Brazilian-Chinese restaurant here in Neu Deutschland.

"As for me: I have realized through these crazy days that there is still a part of me that longs to be out in front of the crowd entertaining. I must say that I'm surprised by this feeling as I haven't felt it in years and figured it was out of my system for a long time. It isn't. Because of that, I have talked to our marvelous talent, Sanny, and Sanny and I are beginning a Vegas residency at the Rat Pack Resort and Casino as *Sanny and Friend* in the near future. We're going to try that out and see how it goes, right Sanny?

"Because of this shift, I am giving my friend and Ostrichland's general manager, Shrimp Wrigley, half ownership of Ostrichland with the ownership amount to increase with each year. Yes, Shrimp Wrigley, I just saw your jaw drop! I wanted to keep this a surprise and I'm glad I did!

"I would say that the biggest lesson I have learned during these crazy days at Ostrichland is that you can't recreate the past, you can't predict the future, you only have now. And if there's one thing I wish I could teach the world that would be: live every moment of your lives. Live them full. Live them deep. Live them whole. Besides, how can you follow something that's not moving, right?

"It's time for another song," Waldemar said, looking at Sanny and Unger. "How about closing out with 'Singing World'? I wrote this song a couple nights ago. I hope you enjoy it. I hope you live the message."

Singing World
By Waldemar
I've been around the world
I've done so many things
All I want to do
Is teach the world to sing

Singing hi ho hi ho
Singing around the world
Is just the way to go

If everybody joins me
Think of what we can do
Just singing round the world
Singing for me and you

Singing hi ho, hi ho
Singing around the world
Is just the way to go

"And everybody sing! *Wait!... Wait!... Lanky!...*

Stop!...Don't do that!..."

The End

Thank you for reading *Ostrichland*. I hope you enjoyed my book! If you did, please leave a glowing review. If not, sorry about that.

If you have any questions, comments or theories to share, you can contact me at daniel93rd@outlook.com.

Daniel Nign

Made in the USA
Middletown, DE
01 December 2020